A FLORIST CALLED DAISY

A FLORIST CALLED DAISY

ELSIE G. BEYA

atmosphere press

Published by Atmosphere Press

Cover design by Beste Miray

atmospherepress.com

Mourn for the dead and fight like hell for the living.
-Salena Godden.

My family became one person smaller in 2021,
and he is missed every day.
Derek – always in our hearts, minds and memories.
This one is for you, Darling.

To my Hubs; The Hayden to my Lexi. The Han to my Leia.
The (quite literally) Stewart to my Daisy.
This one is also for you.
I love you to the moon and back, my love.

1

"Ooh, he's much better looking in real life, actually," I muse, flicking the too-long fringe out of my eyes. Like my thoughts have to be said out loud as official confirmation. Never in a million years did I expect to be at the Cardinal afterparty. Nor did I expect to be faced with their lead singer, Stewart Burns.

With a wave of my hand, I try and fail to get the attention of the barman for a glass for my bottle of Prosecco.

Following on from the high of the live concert, with adrenaline still fizzing in my veins, I am in no way ready to collapse into my crisp hotel bed. Especially not as my best friend, Izzie, is already snoring her head off. A badly timed migraine clouding her vision, ruining all plans of drinking the night away to her favourite band, and then out clubbing until sunrise.

Rob, my other best friend, was already drunk at the gig, spilling most of his double vodkas down my tights; hence I've got my short legs on full display. All or nothing, that's Rob's motto for a night out. And life. On the way to the bar, he was already heading up to his hotel room with a curly-haired guy. Good for him. Though that does mean I won't see him for the next forty minutes to several hours.

As inconspicuously as possible, I observe the figure a few steps away. Izzie was right; he's gorgeous. Just an hour ago, I saw him on stage, eyes closed, sweat dripping from every tendril of his dark brown hair. His voice filling the auditorium with words and lyrics as smooth as pressed silk. He might be in a boyband, but they were much more talented than I expected.

"Stewart Burns," I mumble in disbelief, glancing at Cardinal's frontman again. Izzie would kill to be in my place right now, her celebrity crush within touching distance.

He's good looking in person, there's no denying that. I will, of course, deny it outwardly and loudly if anyone were to ask. He needs no additional flattery to his already inflated ego, supported by countless selfies online. But dammit, he is gorgeous. Further away from the pretty, clean-cut boyband type I assumed. I know his name, of course, everyone does. Everyone also knows the public sex scandal that trails behind him like the strong scent of honeysuckle on summer evenings.

I half regret not paying attention to the photos Izzie swoons over online. Though with the perfect background framing his face, the ring light reflecting in his eyes, and the inevitable filtering; he always looked like every other man with an editing app. A standard pretty boy on the internet, using his face to sell his songs.

Yet, now that Stewart's here as a person, not a filtered image on a screen, I can appreciate him. I chuckle quietly to myself, 'appreciate,' as if he's an oil painting from the 1700s and not in a boyband. He's kind of scruffy looking, but who wants polished perfection? After all, a dirty bad boy pirate is much more my type than a suave, suited and booted polished man.

Stewart's coffee-coloured hair is too long to be neat, just kissing his shirt collar. Messy, tangled, and the length of his fringe, which he keeps pushing out of his eyes, is clearly for fashion, not practicality. His beard is heavier than I realised, expecting a light dusting of designer stubble, like specks left in the bottom of the teabag box. The shape of his mouth is simply perfectly kissable. Surely mouths like that only exist in drawings of perfect Disney princes? I commit the lines of his gerbera petal pink lips to memory. And fuck, his eyes; almost as mesmerising as the shape of his lips. Sea blue with a hint of deeper, darker waves, lined with the longest eyelashes I've ever seen. They put my false ones to shame.

Despite the rainbow lights bouncing around the function room, the overlapping chatter and loud laughter merging with the booming music, my focus is entirely on Stewart. I'm usually an avid observer, wandering around and revelling in watching others and noticing details and ticks about people. I've even let the silver plates of miniature pizzas and portions of chips that wouldn't fill my mouth, let alone my stomach, pass me by.

Stewart positions himself in front of the industrial-style bar. I bite back a smile; good-looking he may be, but such a poser. All about the image.

He carefully moves the large vase of flowers to his left, framing his shoulders. The rainbow bottles of tempting spirits lining the shelves provide his backdrop. The lights dance off his eyes, mirroring the blue delphiniums nestled in the floral display. He asks, no he doesn't; he *instructs* the barman to stay out of the shot. Thanks, mate. Now I'll have to wait even longer for my Prosecco to be opened and poured. Eye roll. I watch with bemused amusement as Stewart pouts slightly, raising then lowering his heavy brows; looking seductively, presumably to best appeal to his fans and online presence, at the phone lens held aloft in his large hand.

"Such a poser," I scoff. What is it with me not being able to keep my thoughts inside my head tonight?

His eyes slide in my direction. I half snort at nearly being caught in full swooning mode, then ask the barman, again, for a glass. Stewart turns back to the phone, and I hear the click of the phone's camera. The moment is perfectly captured before he posts online to share with his adoring fans and the world. Risking another glance for purely educational purposes, of course, I notice Stewart is editing and layering the photo with filters and colours that best suit the aesthetic. Will he finish it off with a witty caption or just a champagne bottle emoji?

He leans both arms on the bar. Legs stretched out behind him, poured into skinny jeans the colour of soot.

"He really does have beautiful thighs. Delicious. I'd quite like to—"

"Sorry? Were you talking to me or about me?" Stewart asks, in a soft Scottish accent, amusement and arrogance on his features in a wicked smirk.

Shit. Did I say that out loud?

"I'm more well known for my thighs than my musical prowess, actually."

Fuck the Force, obviously I did compliment his thighs loud enough for him to hear. I shake my head and scoff a little. Typical arrogant male, assuming every compliment is about him. My comment was, but how can he be certain? It's not like he's the only person here. Realising he's still smirking at me, my hazel eyes widen and heart rate stutters. My blushing cheeks reveal that I was indeed talking about him. And his delicious thighs.

Great first impression there. Though why do I care?

If Izzie finds out I've managed to both offend and flatter Cardinal's frontman, she will never let me hear the end of it. I could ignore him, look the other way and feign complete ignorance, yet I can't quite stop myself from looking at him. Has he got some magnetic Jedi power on all single women? Nan did teach me the importance of good manners, best not to blank him completely, especially after inappropriately complimenting his thighs. How embarrassing. Should I say sorry? Is that what he's angling for?

A quick quip clings to the tip of my tongue. 'Actually, are you not more well known for shagging a married A-List celebrity outside a party in London three years ago than for your songs?' Yet it doesn't make it out into the open, like a clematis, steadily sticking to the trellis and growing upwards. Usually, my remarks are less considered and blurted out like sprawling, choking bindweed; hard to control.

"Who might you be? The official thigh inspector?" Stewart asks before I can apologise, snipe at him or at least attempt to form a believable excuse.

With the bottle of chilled Prosecco in my hand providing a barrier, I look into Stewart's blue eyes as he raises his brows in question. For once, I am at a total loss for words. Maybe it's being starstruck, faced with an apparent celebrity, or perhaps that I've been caught blatantly commenting on his appearance. Or is it simply because he's much more attractive than I ever realised? Whatever the reason, any and all answers to his questions lodge themselves in my throat like the bitter taste of coffee.

"Are you a member of the lighting team? Production company? Press? The new PA intern? Crazy stalker? Although I don't recognise you as one of the usuals."

That can only be a good thing. I wonder if he'd know Izzie as being an almost stalker, or just for being her long-legged, glamorous gothic chic vision?

"Who *are* you here with? Fuck, you're not a fan, are you? Shall I call security?" he continues, clearly not perturbed by my silence. I presume he's used to people being rendered speechless in his presence. His eyes, the colour of the sea on a cold winter's morning, stare back into my own, waiting.

Brazenly, he reaches out and lifts the stolen, no, borrowed, lanyard from my chest. He grins, his eyes sparkling.

"You're Des, huh? You've changed a wee bit since I last saw you."

Shit. I look to the access all areas pass resting against Stewart's palm, which I found in the quiet bar just off the hotel foyer. I am definitely not Des, who, according to the photo, is a middle-aged man with little hair but an impressive moustache.

Come on, Daisy, blag your way out of this. With a false smile, I loop the lanyard from around my neck, hating how it gets tangled in my wavy hair that's always knotted, and place it on the bar.

"That is clearly a clerical error. I'm flying solo. I'm here from—" Come on, brain, engage. Stewart notices as my eyes flip over anything and everything. Searching for a company name to latch on to and claim I'm a part of. My brown eyes snag over a bottle of vodka behind the bar, which is better stocked than the off-license back home, might be a bit much if I claim I'm from Absolut but then proceed to drink Prosecco...

A slow smile spreads over Stewart's face. He knows I'm blagging this. The flashing disco lights shine in his eyes, like his amusement.

I sigh out and offer him a handshake. Might as well be honest.

"I'm Daisy. Officially abandoned by my best mates due to either a migraine or a better offer. I decided to gatecrash this party to fill my night."

He shakes my hand, his palm warm against my skin. I want to lick it a little bit. The thought makes a bubble of laughter creep up inside of me; how ridiculous.

"Stewart." He nods and smiles, those blue eyes twinkling with humour. Like I wouldn't know his name.

"Nice to meet you." Nan would be proud of my politeness.

"And yourself." He beams, his teeth, as expected, perfectly straight and whitened. "So what do you do, Daisy?"

"I'm a florist."

"A florist called Daisy?"

I roll my dull-as-ditch-water eyes. He thinks I'm joking, I'm used to this response. Quite often people ask if I changed my name to match the job, or felt my name forced me into my career. No, to both.

"Yes."

"Did you florist these flowers?" He points to the large display on the bar.

His accent is surprisingly sexy. Though that may also be partly down to his mouth, which looks nothing short of tempting. He clears his throat and I jolt, tearing my eyes from his lips.

"I think you mean 'arrange' and no. Although I wish I had. Those ranunculi are gorgeous. The lilies are overpowering, though. Traditionally, of course, they are a symbol of sympathy and death. Plus they can stain, and can be lethal to cats, so I tend not to use them in displays unless specifically requested."

I'm rambling, nervous. Becoming flustered. I shouldn't care about boys in bands. It's not like he's Ronan Keating, the ultimate and best thing, only good thing, to come from a group of singing boys in suits. Stewart probably hasn't ever stepped foot on a rugby pitch by choice.

"Right," a small smile plays on his features. "A florist called Daisy."

"You make it sound like a sequel to *A Streetcar Named Desire* when you say it like that."

My eyes lock on to his. Holding one another's gaze for a moment too long. An extra beat passes by, weighted with both silence and, what is that? Lust? Not like with Brett, my ex, who I met back in college. That was a very steady, slightly tedious friends to lovers over canteen lunches and £1 pints at the union. And actually, he fancied Izzie at first. Standard. I was the second-rate stand-in.

This instant attraction to someone is new, exciting, invigorating almost. Or it would be exciting if Stewart was a bloke I actually had a chance with, someone I could see again. Maybe. And not some boyband member who would clearly cause more trouble to my quiet life than they're worth.

2

"You're going to kick me out, aren't you, Stewart?"

And all before I've had a drink, too. I'll have to sit in my hotel bed and sup on the overpriced Prosecco alone, if I can get it open. There's always bibles in hotel rooms, but never a corkscrew.

Stewart laughs loudly, head thrown back and broad neck exposed. I can almost taste the salty sweat drying against his pale skin. Why am I finding him so compelling? He's not my type at all.

His laughter attracts the attention of other guests, yeah, like it's just his laughter they're taking note of. The women seem to send daggers in my direction from beneath their false and perfectly lined lashes. To be fair, I'm at a loss as to why I'm holding the attention of Stewart too. Yet I can't find it in myself to complain. If Izzie were here with her flowing locks and confidence to give Darth Vader a run for his money, I'd be as forgettable as Farrah next to Beyonce in the Destiny's Child lineup.

"Do you promise me, a florist called Daisy, that you're not some stalker who's either going to kill my band and me or write an exposé?"

"And what have you got to hide from the world?" I ask

with a very out-of-character flirty flick of my hair. I've never flirted with someone I've literally just met without several WKDs in my bloodstream, and that was heading towards ten years ago. I have higher standards than a poser who sings to teenagers for a living, surely?

"Wouldn't you like to know?"

Yes, please, indeed I would. What? I scream at myself and hope I haven't said any of those alien thoughts out loud.

Fuck the Force. Where is that barman with the glass for this Prosecco?

To break the mounting sexual tension that has come at me unexpectedly, I hold up my handbag towards Stewart.

"I have no plans for murder, I promise. I couldn't fit a knitting needle in here, and selling secrets of boybands to the world isn't my kind of fun."

"Cardinal are *not* a boyband, and a knitting needle?"

"Straight down the ear canal. You would drop dead in an instant," I tell him, matter-of-factly. My arm raises to be level with his pierced ear, making a swift stabbing motion as if I actually have a long pointed needle in my fist. He looks terrified. Really, I can't blame him. What is the matter with me, talking about murder weapons, for goodness sake?

"I saw it on *Midsomer Murders* once and thought it was brilliant." I grimace.

Murder weapons and an admission of watching murder shows, and not even cool ones, the ones that elderly couples watch on a Sunday night. What is my brain doing to me? Intentionally embarrassing me in front of a random singer, who could use this as a funny snippet in an interview; *'I once met this weirdo who said she'd kill me with a knitting needle.'*

I need a drink desperately. Could I attempt to pop the cork of the Prosecco without making even more of a fool of myself? Best not to even try. I'd probably end up firing the cork into Stewart's nose or something.

The bartender, clearly going for the world record of slowest bar service in the land, sets down two flutes. I know the barman must be run off his tortoise speed feet, but how can he mess up the request for one single glass?

I'm not like the skeletal girls at the other end of the bar whooping over cocktail choices and requesting an extra shot of peach schnapps, while also sending flirty looks to Stewart. He surprisingly largely ignores them. Must be part of his game plan. Treat 'em mean and all that shit. I've fallen for that once or twice. Though maybe I have to be both married and famous for him to take a keen interest.

"I actually only asked for one glass," I state.

"Apologies, madam, I thought you two were–" The barman's fingers dance between the space separating me and Stewart, who has scooted himself so our arms are practically touching. I imagine it's very unlike a boyband member to be alone and not sharing drinks with any woman he meets. Though judging from the stares he's attracting, he won't be alone for the rest of the evening. I almost hold up my bare left hand to prove I'm not married and watch him retreat instantly.

"We're not."

"Gatecrashing my party and not even offering me a drink. You're bold as fucking brass, a florist called Daisy. I like it."

"I learnt everything I know from Beyonce."

"Ah, the whole independent woman shit." He scratches at his beard.

I'm sure I can smell lavender emanating from his clothes with the movement and closeness. Not very typical for a poser boy. Nan and the whole care home reek of the stuff. I must be mistaken, unless, in fact, fame and fortune is fragranced with floral lavender notes and not metallic money like we're led to believe.

"Shit?" I ask. He is not about to diss Beyonce, is he? It's practically blasphemy. If he declares he doesn't like Star Wars I may have to sacrifice him to the Dark Side.

"You know Beyonce has a whole team behind her, telling her what to say, what to do, what to wear. She'll be micro-managed to the hilt."

"Like you?" I fire out.

Stewart smirks. It's painted across his face like a work of art. Probably a semi-permanent feature. They must teach all musician types how to flirt and smirk. *'Lesson one: how to make a woman weak at the knees using only a smile.'*

"I don't tend to follow the rules."

"Madam? One glass or two?" The barman asks in a frazzled tone. His hand hovers over the empty glass. He's clearly intending to take more notice of a "Famous Person" than myself, a lowly florist from Cumbria.

I sigh, shrug and roll my eyes, ensuring that Stewart notices my indifference. "Fine, pour him a drink. There's clearly not enough free alcohol to go around to quench his insatiable thirst."

I pass the Prosecco bottle across the bar, then don't know what to do with my hands. Especially after the whole

'I could murder you with a knitting needle' debacle. Awkward. I push my nails into the flesh of my palms and hope I look both normal and mildly attractive.

Even after he's slagged off Queen Bey herself, I hand Stewart a glass of cool, crisp alcohol. My skin fizzes like the bubbles as my fingers make contact with his. Like a still in a film studies class, we both pause for a second or two at the touch. What is this? Some instant connection shit that only exists in the movies come to life? No, that's unlikely. Impossible even. We clink glasses, and I ignore my heart-rate speeding up. The two of us watching the other drain the alcohol in one fluid gulp. It's more sexy than I could ever have imagined.

His legs are outstretched, and the kaleidoscope disco lights slide over his face. Every few seconds he raises a hand in acknowledgement of other party goers, and fiddles with his fringe. A group of pretty women in heels and black dresses of various styles sidle up next to him. Without flinching, he orders them all elaborate ombre cocktails, accompanied by a wink of his ocean blue eyes and a promise to join their giggling gaggle later.

"Great gig, by the way," I say.

Stewart's dark curved eyebrows, probably shaped and plucked each week, jump towards his hairline underneath his long fringe. "You were at the gig?" He places the empty flute back onto the bar.

I absolutely do not watch the muscles flex in his arms.

"Yeah," I shrug, nonchalant, noncommittal, bypassing the fluttering of my heart, the beatings of the misplaced winged butterflies. I am not allowed to find Stewart from Cardinal this attractive. Izzie will kill me. Kill me with a fucking knitting needle.

"So, you are a Cardinal fan, Daisy?"

"Not really." I shake my head and hope he's not too offended. I don't know why I care. It shouldn't matter to either of us. "My best mate is a fan. I'm just here for the ride."

My eyes close and my teeth grit at the phrase as he chuckles. Excellent choice, brain.

"Just here for the ride," he repeats, a smile evident on his face.

Truth be told, Izzie had been banging on about this Cardinal gig in Edinburgh for ages. She'd already been to several other shows this tour, yet had convinced Rob and me to join her on the final night. It was nice to see her so enthusiastic about something, especially after her having such a tough couple of years. But at pushing thirty, shouldn't Izzie be over the boyband phase by now? Whatever her reasons.

"This mysterious friend you keep mentioning." Stewart nods again.

He thinks I'm making her up. I consider showing him a photo of Izzie in all her gothic glamour, but I don't quite want to be rejected by him. I'm always at least second best to Izzie. She's beautiful, a Zantedeschia Odessa to my common, well, Daisy. But there's no striking black bloom to cast a shadow right now. I'm at a party, so why not allow myself a few minutes being the centre of attention? It happens so infrequently, no one is here to witness it and rake over microscopic details, or pass the gossip around my hometown like rainwater flooding the rivers. I can just float along with the night like the tides.

"Not mysterious, very real." I counter, my fingers twiddling my hair. More flirting? What is the matter with me tonight? There's a difference between enjoying the fleeting attention and asking for it. "She's sleeping off a migraine."

"And your other friend?"

Damn, he's a good listener. Attentive. I'd forgotten I even mentioned Rob.

"Last I saw of him, he was shoving his tongue down someone's throat."

Stewart smiles then rubs his hand over his bearded chin again. "So, Daisy, did you have a plan after stealing Des' pass?"

"I always have a plan. I wanted to sneak into the party, have a few drinks, throw a few shapes on the dance floor, chat to some people, and then collapse onto my laundered hotel bed which I don't have to worry about making in the morning." I pour myself another drink—that first one didn't last long—and smile. Trying to ignore the shaking of my hand. It's the alcohol, just the alcohol.

"Sounds like you've got it all sussed out, then."

"Of course." My eyelashes fluttering as I reply. Stop flirting; this is ridiculous. "I am an expert at following plans and gatecrashing."

"Beyonce teach you that too?"

The laugh explodes from my lips like confetti. Nice. Similar quick wit to my own. I wonder if he uses it as a defence mechanism too.

"You've stolen a drink; you can leave if you want. I paid for this bottle. I plan on drinking the rest myself."

"Maybe I don't want to leave," his gaze lingers on my eyes, not for long, as they are the colour of the river after rainfall; dredged by mud and not at all mesmerising. His eyes jump to my mouth. Slightly more appealing than my murky eyes, with coral lipstick and a clear gloss. My heart pounds under the intensity of his blue eyes. Do they teach them the art of seduction at boyband school too?

Stewart startles as someone places their hands on his broad shoulders.

"Stew come on, we've got shots ready to go," the man says swaying, looking like he's already had one or two.

Stewart looks from me to his friend.

"You don't have to babysit me," I assure him.

He's probably desperate to get on with his party; no doubt working his way through all female guests. He's got a reputation to uphold; pretty boys are always players. He's had an almost endless lineup of girlfriend changes in the papers over the years. They were only interrupted by the sex scandal outside of a wild celebrity party in London, which every single news outlet seemed to report about for weeks, if not months, and is still mentioned now. Actually, I don't recall him being 'spotted' with anyone for a while. He must have found a way to be a serial shagger in secret.

"Come on, Stew! Bring your wee friend," the man laughs, pulling him by the arm before staggering away into the middle of the party.

"You can join me? Us?" Stewart asks.

"I've got my own drink, thanks." I lift up the Prosecco bottle.

"Ok, sure. I'll—" He points a finger towards a throng of people, invited people, milling around beneath the lights, between the tables of pocket-sized fast food piled high. He takes a few steps away backwards. Annoyingly, it's hard to look away from him.

"Thanks for, you know, not kicking me out. I won't cause any trouble."

"Shame." He winks, a smile dancing on his face.

Stewart turns and is welcomed with a screech into the crowd. He's offered drinks, hugs, and smiles into phones held high.

I finish the drink in my shaking hand, the bubbles tickling my nose and tongue. I exhale loudly, both relieved he's gone so I can relax, yet also kind of missing the attention. There's definitely something about him.

I fill my glass to the brim; time to drown this whole memory in alcohol, try to forget about Stewart Burns. If only these Prosecco bubbles would silence the fizzing of my heart...

3

I ignore the wobble in my legs as I weave through the guests dancing enthusiastically and chatting loudly. Stewart's sat alone in a booth, slap bang in the middle. Both arms are thrown across the back, legs spread. Taking up as much room as possible, I try to ignore him. Will myself to keep my gaze steady and focused on the door, not turning towards him.

"A florist called Daisy! Come have a drink!"

My head whips around before I can act nonchalant. Dammit. Still, just because I've looked at him doesn't mean I have to engage in conversation. I come to a halt in front of the booth.

Stewart pours red wine into a glass, assuming I will indeed join him.

He slides the drink towards me. His wrists are adorned with bracelets. Wooden beads that jar with silver charms in the shape of, no. Is he wearing Star Wars jewellery? The Rebel Alliance symbol hidden beneath my dress seems to bounce in delight against the pounding of my heart.

"Every time I look over, you're staring at me. I can't decide if you're trying to eye-fuck me or are sizing up how best to kill me?" Great. My mouth has decided to take control before my brain has chance to behave with reason, standard.

Someone squeezes past me and places a tray of colourful drinks on the table.

"Obviously, Daisy, I'd kill you with a knitting needle," he says smoothly. That Scottish accent jolts my heart. And other places.

Well played. A smile tries to pull at my lips, but I frown to control it. I push my nails into my palms, attempting to stop my mind from ticking off boxes on my 'ideal boyfriend list' against Stewart. I mentally strike a thick red line through his name.

"Join me for a wee drink. What's the worst that could happen?"

My mouth opens to fire a sassy comment but doesn't find one. I can't stop my brain running through that ideal tick list, despite the warning tape alerting me to tread with severe caution.

Though my brain, heart and all regions south of them thud loudly in protest. Fancying a pretty boy from a band; what a cliche. Those eyes of his are as beautiful as swimming in the sea, but for so many reasons, I will not be jumping into bed with a man who probably keeps the sexual health clinic in good business.

His eyelid flickers as he meets my eyes. "Will you join me for a drink, a florist called Daisy, please? I'll drop the highly exaggerated flirting act and everything."

The act. Of course, Stewart Burns wasn't flirting with me for real. He probably thought I was an easy target. The lone, limping warthog. Hobbling on three legs with only half its tusks, brains trailing out of its already concave skull. A weakling amongst the scores of prime, delectable zebras. I'm disappointed and pissed off to discover I'm disheartened by this dismissal from him, even if he is a poser who obsessive teenage girls would catfight over. And my best friend.

But I might as well sit down. Who am I to turn down free alcohol?

"Where are your fellow bandmates then?" I ask after taking a small sip of wine.

Another member of Cardinal, with trademark ginger hair and a figure akin to a golf club, is grinding against a blonde woman on the dance floor, not a slither of air between them. Not unexpected; they're probably all slags.

"One's got a migraine and the other had a better offer." Stewart shrugs, a smile appearing on his lips, which I mirror instinctively, then swallow it down with a large mouthful of wine. "You don't like me much, do you, Daisy?"

"I don't know you."

"Aye you do. You've been to see my band. You recognised me, thighs first, but still."

"I know you're Stewart Something Burns from Cardinal, but that's it."

Several well-dressed attendees throw him a wave or smile, a raucous hoot or place a drink down in front of us on the already full table. The drinks are for him, of course, not me. Why does anyone else matter when there's a pop star in dire need of free alcohol?

"Christopher."

"What?" I ask, leaning a little closer to him.

"It's my middle name. What's yours?"

"I don't have one." My mother didn't even choose my first name, let alone a second. I pick at the cuticles around my nails, replacing the hurt my mother caused me with physical pain. Why break the habit of a lifetime? I shrug and rub at my forehead before taking a large slug of wine.

"What don't you like about me? What's my most repulsive feature?" Stewart says after returning from the bar, which seemed to take him an age. He barely took two steps before someone stopped him for a handshake, hug or selfie. A packet of fruit pastilles and another bottle of wine in his hands. I already prepare myself for the hangover tomorrow; it may hurt more than Izzie's migraine.

"It's maybe not you, just the whole social media rabbit hole I dislike. Things only seem to count if they're documented in posed pictures online and inspirational quotes from people paid to share them. Life has become a vanity competition; it's destructive. We should be focusing on ourselves, instead social media forces us to look sideways..."

Oh great, now I've started, I'll never shut up. Damn that Prosecco, it makes my mouth run away with me. "I thrive off a plan, don't like to veer from it. But you end up getting sucked into social media. Hours and hours of pointless scrolling. You start to find things, stupid things that just cause issues..."

Stewart's head tilts, he seems to be really listening, not distracted by scrolling on his phone or changing the subject like Izzie always seems to do. "Give me an example."

I drain my wine and wonder how I can explain yet keep myself removed. For reasons unknown, I feel comfortable with him, safe almost. Yet I still don't want to blurt out all my hidden secrets. "I have a friend from college who self-harms. She has for years. I started, I mean, she started looking for support online, but it ended up being vicious encouragement. She avoids social media now, as best she can."

"That's tough on your friend," he soothes, topping up my glass. "Seems quite an extreme reaction for you to despise social media because of a friends' experience."

"If you have a bad day, not you and your superstar lifestyle, I'm sure your life is perfect, but for us normal, average people, sometimes you want to follow one bad thought and wallow momentarily before picking yourself back up. The computer or whatever seems to remember it. Like it's all programmed to bring you down, to remember that one bad moment. Then it purposefully prays on your vulnerability until you get lost in an endless scroll of negativity." I sigh, rubbing my forehead before chuckling awkwardly. "Sorry, I got too high up on my soapbox. Prosecco makes me a right chatterbox. I should've stuck to vodka."

He pouts and regards me with a thoughtful look. "You're a complex yet interesting woman, Daisy. There's more to you than that harsh outer shell. I know you're talking about your own bad experiences, yet I can't figure out just what that relates to."

There's a silence between us, waiting for me to step in and fill it. I don't. I remain silent. I watch as my fingers thread through his hair before I can stop myself. The disco lights flash like a kaleidoscope over my outstretched arm, Stewart's face and open-necked oversized shirt.

"So, tell me something about you, Stewart Christopher Burns, that I won't find via a search engine."

It turns out we have a ridiculous amount in common with each other. We both have the same top three drinks;

vodka, red wine, not merlot, then coffee. *Wuthering Heights* is our favourite book. Stewart even claims it turned him into a romantic. Our thoughts as we dissect the themes and characters are identical. We feel the same affinity for the sea and beaches. Particularly our shared favourite place in the world, the Isle of Cumbrae. He goes on holiday with his family there each year. I usually take a solo trip in summer, and it's where I long to live and open my own florists. Stewart and I spend what feels like hours talking about the Scottish island. I trace patterns on his bare arm without me noticing for fuck knows how long.

Various people approach him with drinks and offers of drugs, and I think sex, but he's quick to dismiss them and move the conversation along.

He places a hand on my thigh, over my dress, thank the Force, or I believe my leg might burst into flames. I know I should bat his hand away. Give him a speech about how his touch is non-consensual. But reason and rationality, sensibility even has been silenced by my heart.

"We've established that I'm a romantic, yep?" Stewart asks.

"Pathetically so." I nod and smile playfully, unsure what he's going to say next. I look at my phone. There's no sign or word from Rob, so he must be extremely invested in his latest choice of sexual partner. At least one out of the three of us will be getting some tonight.

"So tell me, a florist called Daisy, what is this between us? A twist of fate bringing us together? Are we soulmates, like Heathcliff and Catherine?"

I gulp, will my heart to keep a steady rhythm and not deviate, skipping beats as if walking home drunk on a Saturday night, stumbling and leaving the well-trodden path.

"It's a conversation," I reply, but don't believe my words.

"Is it?"

"It is." I raise my palm from his hand, putting a stop to lovey-dovey, lyrical words that I know are dancing on the tip of his tongue. Longing to escape, to float around my mind like summer butterflies on heliotrope blooms.

Stewart's hand grasps around my wrist, pulling it towards his mouth, kissing my pulse point while looking at me with those lustful eyes. He pulls me closer; I should resist. But I don't. His mouth, stained with red wine, leaves kisses like footprints up my bare arm, neck, jaw, then pauses for a fraction before forcefully smashing his lips to mine. It's at this point that I should definitely push him off, of course. At the very least not respond, keep my lips clamped together and refuse to fall prey to this physicality of him.

Predictably, I don't. I was never going to, was I?

No preamble, no tentative kisses; just straight into tongues duelling and dancing, mouths wide and moaning. Dammit. He's a good kisser. Well, figures doesn't it? He's had tons of experience, usually reported about online.

His hands go to my waist and slide lower to my hips. Stewart pushes his fingers into the flesh there, making me shiver and loop my arms around his neck instinctively to tug at his hair. It feels so silky soft. Why do men always have such luscious hair? Truly unfair. Why am I thinking of hair right now? How am I able to be thinking of anything other than getting utterly lost in this moment? Stewart kisses at my neck, teeth grazing the skin. I exhale his name as he pulls me towards him. My legs irritatingly, yet wonderfully naturally, slot either side of his thighs. My feet kick into the table and nearly send the abandoned drinks skittering. My body tingles. The air around us seems to fizz with electricity. So much so that my handbag vibrates against my ribcage.

Oh, fuck the Force, no, just my phone. Obviously.

Jolted by the ringtone, I pull away from Stewart. His eyes have deepened to a darker blue like stormy seas, dangerously enticing. He runs his fingers through his enviable silken hair, leaving it sticking up at odd angles like he's just woken from a restless slumber.

I extract my buzzing phone from my handbag. It's Rob. Figured karma would have manifested as Izzie asking specifically what I was doing with my tongue in Stewart from Cardinal's mouth.

"Rob?"

"I need you, Daisy! Come up to the room! It's fucking urgent!" Rob screams hysterically into my ear before hanging up.

Odd. But still, a cry for help is a cry for help.

I hitch the handbag up on my shoulder, extract myself from Stewart's lap and stand up. Smoothing down my floral dress and flicking my hair in a dismissive manner, ignoring how a strand of the waves gets stuck in my earring.

A group of women catch my eye, staring from their high-heeled flock of poker straight hair and bright red lipstick. Practically seething at me for holding the attention of the illusive Cardinal frontman.

"Alright, fun's over, Stewart Christopher Burns. I'm needed elsewhere."

"Shame, the night was just getting interesting." He throws me a slightly cheesy wink.

"Feel free to think about me at any given time in your future." What the actual hell was that? Inviting myself into his wank bank? Just when I thought I couldn't get any further into the depth of embarrassment after the knitting needle conversation. Stewart laughs loudly.

"Maybe I'll see you around, a florist called Daisy, if the fates align once more," he says distractedly, fingers on his phone screen. Bored of my presence and already moving on before I've even left the room.

Well, what did I expect?

4

"What the hell happened, Rob?" I ask after helping one of my best mates and only housemate into sweatpants and then a taxi. Between him on the way to hospital and Izzie struck down with a migraine, this weekend has been a washout, and more than just the constant rain.

Rob fiddles with his silver eyebrow ring with chunky fingers and nails painted a pale pink like sweet Williams. Currently, his hair is bleached and tipped in a hot pink to contrast with his nails and coordinating t-shirt that's way too tight for him, yet he has the confidence to pull it off. Were I to wear it, I'd resemble a blancmange.

He wriggles on the seats. "The lube must have had additives in it."

"Did you not check?"

Rob stares his pale blue eyes at me and blinks several times. "I had other things on my mind, Babe. If I got him to read out a list of ingredients, it might have ruined the moment."

Like he ruined my moment; a phone call when I'm in the midst of essentially the best kiss of my life with, gulp, Stewart Burns. Stewart must have Jedi powers. It's so not like me to flirt outrageously or indeed climb on the lap and into the mouth of men I've only just met.

I just want to forget about the whole afterparty thing. My cheeks push up. Shit. I'm smiling. Grinning almost manically. Ok, so maybe I don't want to forget it all. Stewart was such a good kisser, with great thighs and eyes that made me almost weak at the knees. But still, I'll keep those details to myself. No one else needs to know. Rob would never let me hear the end of it, probably playing Cardinal each time I walked into a room for years to come. And Izzie; she'd be insanely jealous, and it's not worth an argument or the distress it would cause. She'd throw the girl code at me and probably refuse to acknowledge my existence ever again.

"Might have saved you from coming out in hives, though, Babe."

"Did I ruin your night?" Rob asks as he looks away from the cars zooming past, their lights flashing in the night like fairy lights on a Christmas tree.

"I've been to see a boyband in concert. It was hardly my perfect night to begin with."

Rob flicks at his fringe. "Cardinal are not a boyband. They were pretty good."

"There's maybe more to them than I first thought," I agree, sort of. Once I got past the screaming teens...

"Fit, yeah?" Rob asks as the taxi stops at red lights. I look out towards the lit-up old buildings of Edinburgh now restored into hotels and shops.

"What? Who? Is he?" The questions fire out of me before I can think. How does Rob know how attracted I am to Stewart? Rob and I have been best friends and housemates since the day we met at uni. He appeared in my student life in Cornwall surrounded by bottles of vodka, more clothes than one man needs, VHS copies of Friends and a terrible sense of direction. He stumbled into the digs and announced I was, in fact, in his newly assigned room, and he would not be moving again after lugging his belongings halfway across the country for a fresh start away from his homophobic parents. I shrugged and offered to have the top bunk. We've been firm friends since and live together in my Nan's house after she moved into the local care home a few years ago in Cockermouth.

"Who are you on about?" Rob looks puzzled.

"Who do *you* mean? The band?" I ask.

"The drummer, fit as fuck," Rob sighs wistfully and blows me a kiss. "Dreamy eyes,"

Typical Rob. His one-night stand got cut short due to an allergy, and yet he's already drooling over another man. There's literally no stopping him. I should call ahead to the hospital and ensure there are no cute male doctors on duty.

"They're alright if you like that pretty boy type,"

"You don't," Rob snickers, then winces.

Well, actually... My cheeks flame.

"Dare I ask about the state of the other guy?" I ask, changing the subject.

"Patrick. Fit as fuck. Deep mysterious eyes, curls that—"

I sigh and fiddle with my earrings. "No, I mean, how is he? You know?"

Rob sighs and closes his eyes. "Deliciously thick and—"

"No! I don't want details of his cock!" I shout, making the taxi driver startle a little. "I mean is he ok? No allergies, reactions?"

"He said he was getting a tad uncomfy on his arse, but to be honest, Daisy, I left pretty quick. No one needs to see a cock affected by hives."

"Yet you called me."

"Who else would I call? Izzie? She's been throwing up since lunch, and if it was anything less than Stewart from Cardinal offering her a shag outside against a wall in full view of the passing world, I doubt she'd move."

He's right, really. I try to mostly ignore Izzie's fangirl attitude. Once, she cried herself to sleep outside of Stewart's hotel room after she felt a song Cardinal had just released 'spoke to her on endless levels.' In her defence, she was extremely drunk, and it was a poignant anniversary for her. But she's not in the same league as some of her fellow Cardinal friends. One of them writes fan-fiction. I've read it. It's the single most disturbing thing in the world. Christian Grey has nothing on Eddie from Cardinal in that woman's mind.

I get why Izzie latched on to her sister's favourite band after her death. I encouraged her to find a reason, a light to pull her through the darkness of grief. I mock Izzie for it, for liking a sort of boyband when she dresses like a goth and is pushing twenty-six, but she knows it's all in jest. She would never go to the flower markets at stupid o'clock in the morning or travel the length of the country to the RHS Flower Show each year. Everyone's different.

The cars and buildings whizz by in shades of black and grey, like storm clouds drifting over the sea. The windows reflect back the yellow lights from the cars. The inside of the buildings locked up for the night, like forgotten secrets or hidden memories. I can't see the stars due to the light from the city burning upwards, stretching towards the moon, not like back home in Cumbria.

"Where were you, anyway?" Rob asks.

"In the bar."

"Liar." He laughs. My brown eyes widen. The fuck? "You wouldn't pay hotel bar prices."

"I bought a full bottle of Prosecco, actually," I reply smugly.

"And wine?"

"How do you—"

"Your lips are practically purple and a bit swollen. You down it straight from the bottle? Not like you to splash the cash, Babe. You're usually squirrelling away all your money into savings accounts."

I wipe at my lips. I imagine Stewart's to be stained the same colour, yet with an added tint of my lipstick.

"Nan gave me a few quid. I'd have bought you a drink if you weren't being such a slag."

Rob shrugs. "I like sex. It doesn't make me a slag."

"You don't like relationships either."

"Says the woman who has dated Brett on and off for years."

"It's easy with Brett. I don't have to think," I counter. Perhaps not the best basis for a relationship, but I never wanted a long-term commitment. My career comes first.

"Easy but boring. You need to live, Daisy! Have more fun!"

"Come on, you know I—"

"Yeah, yeah, you've got the whole life plan laid out. Fair enough, you want your own florists, but there's no room in this magical plan for anything fun."

Neither he or Izzie share my drive to be my own boss. Rob likes to be told what to do at work and in the bedroom, as I am well aware—we share a wall back at home.

"Flowers are fun!" I exclaim, but my tone feels forced.

"Not as fun as sex."

"Tell that to your cock."

My eyes seem to blink in time with the taunting second hand on the clock above the reception desk of the hospital. Rob and I have been here for what feels like hours. The squeak of shoes on the highly polished floor is constant, with nurses, doctors and patients rushing past in blurs of green scrubs and ever-present scent of antiseptic. Rob keeps dozing off against my shoulder before wincing and sitting bolt upright, complaining that he feels his cock may fall off.

I watch an elderly couple shuffle by hand-in-hand. Their papery thin skin and bluish veins showing like aged cheese which I only buy at Christmas.

"Hey, Babe?" I say to Rob as my hands tear slithers of last year's celebrity gossip from glossy magazine pages.

"Yeah?" he asks, rubbing his eyes.

"Do you believe in fate? Soulmates and that? The universe pushing people together?"

"Why the fuck are you asking me that now?" Rob laughs. The nurses behind the desk glare at him.

Playing it down with a shrug, I focus on trying to rip neat, straight lines from the pages of the battered magazine and ignore the blush staining my cheeks like the red poppies inked on my leg. Stewart's face, his sparkling eyes dance through my brain, whether I want him there or not. It's like he's a lighthouse against the midnight skies and dangerous waves. I should be viewing him as the hidden sharp rocks, ready to destroy me. He'd definitely sink my friendship with Izzie if she ever found out I'd kissed him. But actually, I feel he's the bright beam against the darkness.

I'm like a spiky stemmed rose, wrapped in tough outer guard petals to protect myself. Never wanting to let anyone get too close, despite enticing them with my fra-granced bloom. If people can inch past the sarcasm and deflection, they're doing well. But as soon as they grasp the long stem, nope. I push them away with skin-splitting thorns. Yet with Stewart, I dropped my guard almost instantly. And felt an immediate connection with him. I don't know if he's like that with everyone. I suspected not seeing the faint blush like peony petals on his cheeks as he shared his secrets. (He can't sleep without copious amounts of lavender spray, he spends a fortune on books that he never finds time to read before buying more, his anxiety seems to come to life in the darkness, he's a romantic—that one I guessed from Cardinal's lyrics.)

I scrunch the strips of coloured paper into balls and then throw them into the empty plastic coffee cup.

"I'm about to have a doctor examine my swollen cock and you're asking me about soulmates?" Rob half laughs.

"Sorry, yeah. Too much wine, maybe," I reply dismissively, rubbing at my forehead.

"Why? Did you meet the other half to your incomplete, career-focused, yet pessimistic soul at the hotel bar?"

"No, no. Of course not. That would be—"

Accurate. Right? Fuck, maybe Cardinal are actually masters of hypnotism and Stewart's brainwashed me into believing I'm destined to be with him. I shudder from the cold whooshing through the doors and nothing else, like the tingle of something I can't place jumping up my spine.

Rob stands up and shuffles himself before sitting tentatively back down on the squeaky plastic chair. He mumbles about the waiting time, but quietly so as not to draw attention to himself.

"Any other of life's big questions to be answered?"

"The girl code. Is it acceptable to break it for a soulmate, do you think?" I feel my cheeks burn again like Darcey roses. My words sprinting ahead to the finishing ribbon while my brain barely crosses the start line.

"The girl code?" He flicks at his fringe before picking up his coffee. "I don't know. It's all unwritten feminist shite that no one understands. Not even women, if you're asking me. Babe, you're not about to jump into bed with Izzie's ex, are you?"

I cringe and shake my head. A man who looks akin to a vampire but with more piercings, black lipstick and platform boots is so not my type.

"Her dad?"

"What? No!"

"Then I think you're safe. You and Izzie have distinctly different tastes. You like rugby lads; she likes goths."

My lips twitch like the last leaf on an autumn tree shaking in the breeze, deciding whether to cling on for longer or be free. "She likes Stewart from Cardinal."

Rob snorts, coffee spurting from his nose and back into the cup. "She does. She's like a fangirl. Obsessive. Whatever her reasons, it's pathetic."

"I guess," I mumble. "But it helps her; she loves that band."

"Stewart Burns from Cardinal isn't a rugby player or Jack Sparrow, so he's clearly not your soulmate."

"Is kissing a celebrity crush breaking the girl code? Or

does it not count? Soulmates win out against friendship, right?"

"How much did you drink at the bar, Babe? You're making no sense. I know everything about you. You would not let Stewart or anyone who didn't spend at least half of his life on a rugby pitch anywhere near your mouth or bed."

I stretch my arms towards the ceiling, ignoring the guilt I feel at never telling Rob all my secrets, despite us being as close as double flowering carnations. Another thing to add to the self-harm; kissing Cardinal's frontman.

"He's quite attractive," I admit.

Rob places a hand on my forehead. "Maybe you need a doctor. This doesn't sound like you at all. I suggest you go back to the hotel and down a fuck ton of water and sleep it off."

I smile and pat his leg. "I'll wait here with you."

"Head back to the hotel, Daisy. I'll be here all night. City living, huh?" He looks around the busy waiting room. Quite a difference from the small town life we're used to. Our nearest A&E is thirty-five minutes away if the roads are clear, and there's usually more staff than patients.

"Are you sure?"

"Yeah. Go to bed. Or deviate from your plan and find some fun. Or a soulmate, or celebrity crush, whichever appears first." Rob grins then laughs loudly. "Break away from your plan for a night."

"I stick to plans for a reason." I cross my arms across my chest.

Rob winks a pale blue eye at me as I stand up. "Go against it. I dare you, Babe. But, do try to resist the temptation of Cardinal's Stewart Burns, and don't shag him in full view of the passing public," he cackles.

I raise my middle finger and shake my head, ignoring images of fantasy dancing in my brain. Maybe I will go and find some fun. Blue delphinium eyes and shining silver rings kind of fun.

5

The cold air dances across my bare shoulders and legs as I step out of the taxi from the hospital. Goosebumps raise from the night on my colourful inks depicting poppies, agrimony, betony and foxgloves adorning my thigh and calf.

Looking up to the night sky, exhaling smoke in a failed circle. I never could get the hang of smoke rings. When I took up smoking, I imagined looking sophisticated and cool. A transformation from a sooty duckling to a graceful swan as beautiful as Audrey Hepburn in *Breakfast At Tiffany's*. In reality, it's expensive; easy to get the hang of, but damn hard to stop, yet a great excuse at parties to sneak away and have a few minutes of peace. At nineteen, I had a phase, wholeheartedly encouraged by Rob, to use a cigarette holder like the illusive Holly Golightly. But I looked more akin to Disney's monochromatic Cruella de Vil.

A shadow stretches beneath the orange light as I lean against the hotel wall.

"A florist called Daisy." That now familiar Scottish accent creeps into my ears, nestling itself tauntingly on my earrings.

I look in the vague direction of the man who I kissed then dismissed before racing to Rob's rescue. Listen to me, trying to play it down, when minutes ago I was convincing myself Stewart was my soulmate.

"Stewart Christopher Burns." I rearrange my mouth in a flat line. Definitely not attempting to quirk up into a smile. Nope.

"Where did you run off to?"

"The hospital," I respond while lighting another cigarette. It will provide a barrier between the two of us, if nothing else.

"Don't tell me I've got you pregnant from just one kiss?"

I roll my eyes, concentrate on counting the cars going past, the number of tattoos on the huge gym type men who surely must be bouncers, anything to stop me from laughing. We clearly share the same sense of humour.

Is it more than a coincidence that I've run into Stewart again? It can't be a twist of fate; that's for romantic cliches, right? This is real life, not the pages of a book or stills in a film. I am not the William Thacker to his Anna Scott. I will not be swayed by all the glitz and glamour that follows Stewart round like remnants of glitter from sparkly Christmas cards.

"Seriously, you ok? Is this fate bringing us together once more?"

I watch in both surprise and wonder as his fingers thread through the bleached blonde locks dancing over my shoulders. I shiver again. Is it the cold or something more? I swallow down that romantic notion as if it's a shot of vodka. It's freezing and I forgot my coat; of course it's the temperature.

"Can I have a smoke, by the way? I'm all out."

"Don't you need to look after that precious voice of yours? The teenagers will be heartbroken if they can't hear your sultry tones," I retort.

He laughs. My lips quirk in a smile. Sirens and cars echo in the distance, both increasing and disappearing into the night. People in various states of drunkenness stumble and chatter loudly after escaping from the party and not decreasing their volume to make up for the lack of booming bass.

I look at him and he tilts his head. Dammit, he's like a puppy. Everyone loves a puppy. Yes, that's the point, isn't it? I'm neither the first nor the last to find him attractive. Images and videos of Stewart and the disgraced actress pummelling into one another outside of a celebrity-filled party dance a salsa around my head. I will not be following in her footsteps. I ignore the fact I distinctly glance down the darkened side of the hotel.

Stewart plucks the smouldering cigarette from my fingers. Inhales slowly, then hands it back. He exhales perfect smoke rings. Of course he fucking does.

"My friend has got himself into a bit of a sticky situation after an allergic reaction to some lube. I took him to A&E and left him there. His cock has swollen up to mammoth proportions. Not in a good way," I explain.

Stewart blinks at me before setting himself down on a low wall edging the hotel. "*My* best friend was just with someone who had an allergic reaction to some lube too. I mean, his arse isn't in the best of states either. Must be a dodgy batch."

"Are you just repeating me? I know boybands are known for cover versions, but come on, have a little originality. You're not a parrot."

"Honestly! He's just had the doctor round. I can show you the photo if you like?" He offers me his phone. Stupidly I look at it before my head turns away. Rob is the world's biggest over-sharer. I know all the ins and outs of his sex life to be shocked by anything.

"Seeing Rob was scarring enough." I shudder and raise my palm to dismiss the phone from my vision. But it's too late; the image has already imbedded itself into my retinas.

A string of drunk and happy people climb into the line of waiting black taxis. Laughing and singing, high-pitched phrases being slurred as if it's the funniest thing in the world. A few of them see Stewart and ask for photos. He obliges, smiling tightly as they start singing Cardinal songs before driving off into the night. Usually it's me as designated driver back at home with Rob and Izzie. Izzie always volunteers me to stay sober and drive her home. Even tonight I've had to look after Rob, though luckily I haven't had to pay the taxi driver to clean up the vomit, or indeed start scrubbing the interior of my own car after midnight.

"Rob?" Stewart asks, returning from doing the whole superstar act, as if our conversation wasn't interrupted by selfies and shouts.

"Yes, Rob, my best friend." I fire Rob a quick text to check he's doing ok.

"What was the name of the guy he was with?"

"Patrick, I think," I reply as Rob sends a string of aubergine, flame and crying face emojis.

"Hi, a florist called Daisy; I'm Stewart, Patrick's best friend."

I frown, then roll my eyes in stupid realisation. Of course he is. Eddie, Patrick and Stewart make up Cardinal.

I knew this, Izzie witters on about them enough. I should've made the link sooner. Damn that Prosecco for slowing my thoughts. I hand Stewart a fresh cigarette and light it for him.

"Then you do indeed deserve a smoke if you've seen what I've seen."

"Speaking of the devil," Stewart says, exhaling more perfect smoke rings. He raises a hand to a slightly hobbling man with deep green eyes and hair that curls around his ears. Legs also poured into skinny jeans and an oversized jumper the colour of pine needles drown his frame. Heavy but delicious thighs; must be crucial for any and all boys in bands.

"Am I glad to see you, pal? Eddie's pissing me the fuck off," Patrick says dramatically in an accent similar to Stewart's.

"Why? What have you done now?"

"Fucks sake. I haven't done anything! He's winding me up about, you know, how my night went. Or didn't go as the case may be." He glances towards me, then waggles his eyebrows and sends Stewart a very obvious wink. "And who is this?"

"Pat, meet a florist called Daisy. Daisy, meet Patrick," Stewart says before handing Patrick his cigarette.

Patrick looks at me, giving me a once over before facing Stewart. "I thought you weren't doing this any–"

"I'm not. Daisy's different."

"Aye? She not–"

"No, she's not."

"What the?–" I ask, tempted to put my hands on my hips and demand to know the truth of their mysterious chat.

"Hold up. A florist. Called Daisy? That's the line you're going with?" Patrick addresses me.

I nod. "I am."

"It sounds like a cover to me. Are you sure she's not a hooker, pal?" Patrick scoffs.

Stewart blushes, and instead of calling him out for thinking I'm a prostitute, I hand Patrick a business card from my handbag.

"See?"

Patrick raises his eyebrows. They get lost beneath his curls. "A florist called Daisy. From a place called Cockermouth?" He laughs, and places a palm on Stewart's shoulder. "Seriously, pal, where do you find these girls?"

"Yes, Cockermouth. Though we called it Knob-a-gob as kids."

They both snigger like they're in the classroom. I roll my eyes. Schoolboy humour, why do men never grow out of it?

Patrick passes the card to Stewart after scanning it. "I have no need for flowers, Hen. Or prostitutes, certainly not female ones."

"Daisy isn't a prostitute, pal. The fates have brought us together," Stewart says with a smile, sliding my business card into his wallet.

"In that case, hello, Daisy. I'm the one and only Patrick Wallace. Top rate drummer with Cardinal. We've just finished a tour—" he holds out a palm which I shake limply, more distracted by the flash of pink showing high on Stewart's cheeks.

Patrick smiles and throws me a wink. It would be charming were I not all too aware of the state of his various body parts hidden beneath his jeans. Egocentric; definitely another requirement when pursuing a music career.

"I didn't recognise you at first, but unfortunately I could probably identify you by your arsehole in a photographic line-up," I quip.

"Well, clearly your internet search history is interesting, Daisy." He winces as he sits down on the low wall and exhales, not smoke rings I'm pleased to find, into the night air highlighted by the bright lights of the hotel.

"This from a man whose one-night stand failed due to an allergic reaction on both ends. Yes, pun very much intended."

Patrick's mouth drops. Stewart laughs loudly, and people turn to look at him, yet he pays them no attention. Patrick blushes. Cute. They're stupidly compelling these men. I wonder what the other one, Eddie, is like.

"You told her?"

"Daisy's best pal is the man you attempted to spend the night with, Pat," Stewart explains.

"I was sick of Eddie winding me up about it, hence coming here—"

"Intending to come here, are you? Might be more successful than your earlier attempt, pal. Though you're not really my type."

"Ugh, you're as bad as him. I'm going to bed." Patrick frowns, yet has a playful glint in his dark eyes. "At least I'm not the one who gets caught shagging against a wall." He winks and stubs the cigarette out beneath his boots before sauntering off with a wide-legged stance.

"Fuck off, Pat. I'll call you the morn for breakfast."

Patrick turns as he gets to the hotel, stroking a palm down the wall. "Lovely wall this. Is it up to your standards, pal?"

Stewart smiles, yet his eyes have hardened to a deeper,

colder blue. His eyes flit towards me and away. Three times.

"Pat's my best pal. In and out of the band. Grew up together, all that. We wind each other up y'know. Harmless banter."

I nod. Though it sounds like he's trying to convince himself more than me.

Stewart rubs at the back of his neck and licks his lips. "I'm not as much of a slag as the papers report. In case you wondered."

"I didn't."

There's something about Stewart that is magnetising. He taps his shoes together rhythmically, his ankles on show. Momentarily, like a flare of fireworks in the pitch black sky; I wonder if his skin feels as smooth and delicate as it looks. The word 'soulmate' dances around my head.

"Fancy a drink in my room, Daisy?"

"Just a drink?"

"We could see what happens?"

I shrug. Know that I shouldn't. Izzie would, at best, disown me, never speak to me again. At worst, skin me alive and torture me to death to the melody of Cardinal songs. Probably.

"I tell you what. I'm going to finish another smoke and then walk–"

"Walk? Not strut? Swagger?"

Stewart ignores my interruption with a roll of his sky blue eyes. "Walk across the foyer to the lift. Invitation lasts for as long as the doors remain open."

"Smooth."

"Smooth as butter." He winks.

I laugh quietly, walking towards the welcoming hotel doors surrounded by an impressive arch and lit up in purple lights. They remind me of Anemone petals.

I'm not the type to jump into bed with a practical stranger. It's not like I'm at college anymore. It's against my whole belief system, and the whole unwritten girl code; Izzie fancies Stewart.

Well, technically, she has a slight obsession with an image of a man in a band who sings. A man in a band who she holds close to her heart, who helped her deal with grief and loss.

I shouldn't act on any feelings, however fleetingly yet weighted they may be.

But Rob did encourage me to have fun, live a little. And what Izzie doesn't know won't hurt her.

My heart thuds as the hotel door swings closed behind me, and I look across the spotless white tiles, past the wooden desks in front of black walls, lit up by purple lights the same as outside. My cheeks push up into a smile as I look towards the lift and think of Stewart's eyes, blue like larkspur blooms.

I'm totally going to act on it, aren't I?

6

There's two options; a chair or sofa, both reminding me of desert marigolds. The sofa matching the silver stems, and a chair in a mustard yellow, the same as the blooms. I could wait on the sofa right by the door. Essentially the first thing to see. Desperate and eager like Ackbar, my overfed cat, waiting for tuna. Mewling until I cave and drop flakes onto the kitchen floor. I dismiss that option as soon as my arse graces the sofa. Far too keen. Glaringly obvious. I might as well be sitting naked.

The chair it is then, tucked into the corner by the lifts. Perhaps the location makes it more obvious overall, nonetheless I sit in the velvet seat. Try a few poses, then just sit. I wring my fingers together and try not to think of anything.

Stewart, a hand running through his dark hair, scans the open plan foyer, yet I'm hidden from view by a kentia palm in front of the chair. He saunters, definitely not a walk, towards the lifts. He's stopped en route by a group of women wanting a selfie, then is offered a bottle of Champagne by the staff. He refuses both claiming he's tired.

I watch him behind a smile, track the changes in his

features as he sees me, waiting expectantly in the marigold-coloured chair. His eyes run up my bare legs.

"Ah, there you are, Sweetheart."

"Ok, the *'Sweetheart'* thing. Is that a term of endearment you use on all women so you don't have to remember their names, or are you hoping to pull off Han Solo vibes?"

"Don't tell me you love Star Wars too?"

I reach below the collar of my floral printed black dress and place the Rebel Alliance charm against my palm. If it's fate, I might as well embrace it. Just for a night. A few hours of romance, what harm can it do?

I flick my fringe from my eyes and hope it removes the image of Izzie holding the illusive girl code rule book from my head. A celebrity crush doesn't count. Soulmates or not. Right?

"Favourite Star Wars film?" He bends down, his hand cupping around my wrist, leaving feather-light touches on my skin.

"*Revenge of the Sith,*" I reply seriously, knowing he'll laugh, which he does. Dammit, when did I start wanting to make him laugh?

"What is it really?"

"*A New Hope.*"

"Had you said *Return of the Jedi*, I'd claim you were perfection personified."

"So, the Sweetheart thing?" I ask, ignoring the blatant lie dressed as a compliment, watching members of staff wheel luggage and room service towards the lifts.

"I'm not half as cool as Han Solo." Stewart shrugs with a lick of his lips.

"Although you may be a bit scruffy—"

"Who's scruffy looking?"

A smile dances on my face, but I carry on regardless. Stewart won't sway me from my train of thought with quick-witted Star Wars quotes and a wink. Though honestly, he probably will.

"You may have the swagger of Han, yet you fall short due to your admission of being a hopeless romantic, Stewart. Han Solo is far too practical for romance."

"I know." Stewart shrugs, does an adorable head tilt that totally should not work but does.

I smile slowly. Very, very clever response; using Han Solo's words to Princess Leia.

He sits down with me, and I blink at him in surprise. I expected him to whisk me straight into the lift, sprint down the corridor to his hotel room and land in a naked heap in his bed.

Instead, Stewart and I talk easily. He slips into a flirtatious mode more than me; maybe he's used to it. The conversation flows with ease, not that it was stilted at the party earlier.

He asks for a close inspection of my thigh tattoo, which I refuse. No one should see the reasons behind the full colouring of inks on my upper leg. That is a secret I shall never intentionally reveal.

Stewart's intuitive too, intelligent and observant. He throws jokes back at me as easy as Rob and I do. Referring a lot to my whole killing him with a knitting needle disaster, asking me about flowers. And even trying to pull out of me the truth behind my hatred for social media. Clearly, he picked up on my attempts at skimming over my self-harm issues. I bluff my way out of it by showing him my uncut arms. A common misconception about self-harm is that people only slice at their wrists. Stewart seems to fall for it.

Stewart stands up and steps away, tripping over the pattern on the carpet. He pushes the button for the lift, and I stand next to him. My eyes flit to his face, then away. He's hard to resist. Surely Izzie can't blame me for being attracted to him?

The doors slide open and he steps inside. I wait a beat—a fraction of a beat—before following him inside the lift.

"Just because I'm in this enclosed space with you—"

His hands caress my jaw in an action that feels far too intimate for a one-night stand. "Are you going to stop fighting this soulmate connection between us, or are you going to drag it out for longer?"

I stare at his eyes, reminding me again of delphiniums, and my mouth opens a fraction. Fuck it. I lean towards him and kiss him. My hands go to his neck, the ends of his hair touching at his shirt collar, then scratch through his beard. Stewart pulls back and licks his lips. I feel a sting of dismissal, like jellyfish tentacles grazing my bare legs in the sea.

How had I read this so wrong?

Stewart scratches at his neck and runs a hand through his hair. "I'm not rejecting you, Daisy."

I scoff and wish I had a bottle of vodka to drown my embarrassment in.

"I'm all too aware of the CCTV in this lift. And trust me, neither of us wants this to be headline news tomorrow."

"Headline news? Surely that only applies if you're with a married actress in a public place?"

Stewart chuckles a little; it sounds brittle. His shoulders square, tension creeping into his posture like it did outside with Patrick. I almost apologise.

"Maybe only on a slow news day; it may be headline news. For your sake as much as mine—"

The lift doors slide open and a man in a grey business suit steps in, phone held to his ear, talking loudly about exchange rates and time zones. He nods in acknowledgement after hanging up at Stewart and says his daughter is a big fan. Stewart nods and smiles tightly before the man makes another phone call, almost identical to the last, and ignores us both once more.

Stewart traces his fingertips down my arm. Goosebumps follow his touch.

He leans towards my ear. "Two minutes, and we'll be behind a locked door, no cameras."

"I might have changed my mind by then," I reply in a bored tone, ignoring the swoop of my stomach from his accent.

"Let's see, shall we?" he says with an eyebrow raise.

The silence in the room is almost overwhelming.

Stewart stands in front of me, he rests his forehead against mine. The feel of his breath against my face, my nose, is warm and delicious like freshly baked bread. The silver chain around his neck attracts me like a magpie searching for treasure. My fingers dance along the edge of the cool metal. I trail my nails into the hairs poking out from the collar of his shirt, drawing the eyes to the hollow of his neck.

One of my hands tangles in the longer hair down the back of Stewart's neck, just dancing on the collar of his shirt. He pulls me closer, chest to chest, the space between us filled with lust and craving. The two of us joined from clavicle to hip.

Stewart's thumb presses into my hips, which makes me gasp out. My mouth remains open as I lock on to his blue eyes.

He bends his head to kiss my neck again. I feel his tongue, his teeth, his lips on my skin there. He scrapes his teeth on my earlobe. I kiss and lick at his neck in return, fingers scratching, pulling on his hair and scalp.

With one hand and thumb still pushing that insane pressure down on my hip, his other hand trails up my back and tangles in my long hair. I raise myself onto tiptoes and kiss his neck, all the way up to his ears. I moan at the pressure from him against my hips and everywhere else, straight into his ear before licking at the shell of it. Stewart moans into my neck, his hand at the back of my head reacting by furling around my hair, tugging it slightly.

"Daisy," he murmurs quietly.

Already I love the way he says my name. What? I do?

I pull away from him a fraction and stare into those sea blue eyes. Both of us tilt our heads and push our lips closer. My heartbeat pulses out kiss, kiss, kiss, like a chant at a party.

He licks his bottom lip. I can almost taste the red wine. Predictably my eyelids flutter closed. I inhale his woody, spicy, lavender-tinged scent. A linger of a sweat.

He spins me around; my back is now pushed next to his chest. It reminds me of the great expanse of the ocean, all-encompassing and imposing, safe and welcoming. Something I wouldn't mind waking up to every morning. Hearing the swish of the waves against the rocks as steady as his heartbeat. Shit. Has being this close to Stewart and his romantic heart overtaken my own thoughts? Usually I can silence any fanciful daydreams, leave them in the pages of books. Never allowing them to follow me out into the real world.

His warm breath on my ear lobe makes me shudder. Those fingers, years of piano playing evident in the strength behind them, push into the flesh of my hips. His teeth graze against my neck. The muscles in my stomach flutter as his fingers push into the skin. Paired with his lips mouthing at my neck and jaw; I feel my knees might give way at any second. That wouldn't kill the mood at all... The breath catches in my throat and he smiles against my neck.

I turn to face him, noticing how the rest of the room has blurred into muted colours and shapes, him as my only clear image. My only thought.

He lifts and pushes me against the wall, my ankles cross behind his back, my hands in his hair. "Bed, or?"

"You're well known for shagging against walls; do you not take every opportunity to do so?" I ask, my shaking fingers undoing the buttons on his shirt, throwing it off his arms, then unfastening his jeans.

"You, a florist called Daisy, are such a wee menace."

I scramble through my brain for another witty comment. Well, it's either that or an alien romantic notion that creeps into my head whenever I look at Stewart with too much thought. But I can't make the synapses join quick enough.

Stewart pulls me towards him, his mouth on mine, and we kiss again before I can even attempt to resist. Though really, I'm way past that now.

***

I jolt awake, a weight across my stomach. Memories start to return slowly, as if drenched in treacle. Just enough so I can't remain in denial for long, no matter how easy that would be. Fragments of memories dart across my mind like a camouflaged leopard. Showing more and more spots of truth peeking through the long foggy grass of stale alcohol, until it all becomes clear and vivid. Basking in the glorious sun of the morning after the night before.

Shit.

It would be simple to forget about everything else, to just focus on the physical attraction with Stewart. But I know it ran deeper than that. As the vodka bottles emptied, our honesty increased, nestled naked beneath sheets as soft as petals. Topics became deeper, darker. Dreams and hopes, fears and phobias, worries and regrets. I can try to lie to myself, say it was the alcohol. But it wasn't. It was the company. Never in my life have I felt so at ease with someone. I didn't want to sleep, didn't want the sun to rise, so I could stay wrapped in his arms, talking and kissing lazily. The darkness from outside the windows swallowed us both up, making us feel safe, cocooned. Until we fell asleep, bodies intertwined like our souls.

Stewart shuffles in his sleep. I rub my forehead, hoping it brings some clarity. Nothing more can happen; this is nonsense. I'm not a swooning fangirl nor a model he usually dates, and Stewart is certainly not my type. Despite the compatibility. I don't want a relationship or even a string of dates with anyone, let alone a pop star.

I slide out of the bed, dress in haste, then tiptoe from his room without even a backward glance. But I have no other option. What else can I do? Declare that Stewart makes me believe soulmates do exist? Put a man I've only just met above my lifelong friendship with Izzie and her celebrity crush and misplaced feelings, which got her through the worst time of her life? Allow myself to be vulnerable; build up my belief and faith in someone other than myself, then wait for it to all go wrong? See how long it takes for Stewart to up and leave me, just like everyone always seem to in my life?

It's not worth it. My heart constricts in my chest as if being entwined by coconut-smelling gorse bushes. Prickles and thorns deflating my heart and feelings, while the scent of the little yellow flowers lingers on my skin as the door clicks closed behind me.

7

I'm sat up, fully dressed yet wrapped in crisp white sheets of the generic hotel bed, nursing a cold cup of coffee, trying not to think of anything. Of Stewart.

I've never met anyone who shared the same sense of humour, the same views on pretty much everything. Even when we both argued, punctuated with kisses and tickles, about the best Star Wars film. Stewart and I spent all night laughing, talking, kissing and touching. I never wanted to wake up. It pained me to leave him only hours later.

"Was he beautiful?" Izzie asks from the chair by the window. She's now migraine free and full of regret for missing Cardinal. She admits she even put sunglasses on and got a taxi to the venue last night. However, she threw up en route and had to retire to her bed again. I watch her eating crisps like a delicacy between her fake polished black nails. Izzie is beautiful, perfect purple lips paired with her cat-like lined eyes. She's a gothic version of a Bratz doll. And she knows it.

Rob lies moaning in a heap, complaining about his banging head and aching thighs. But actually, I know it's his cock as well as his pride that is feeling battered.

"Who?" I ask, despite knowing. Giving myself time to

paint on a face of distance. Lies, fucking lies.

"Stewart," Izzie rolls her eyes. Obviously she means him. When does she not?

"Yeah, he was fine," I mumble before taking a gulp of coffee. Dark, like his hair.

"'Fine?' Daisy, you must have incredibly high standards. Strange really, as Brett is distinctly average. Admit it, Stewart is fit as fuck."

I nod to appease her. What else can I say? 'He has eyes I want to dive into, a mouth I can't stop thinking about, the most delicious of thighs, and a cock which I think might have been made just for me?'

"Daisy said she thought he was fit," Rob says with a twiddle of his eyebrow piercing.

"What?" Izzie spins to me.

"No, I don't think I did. He's not my type," I rush out and try to keep my breathing steady and the colour away from my cheeks.

"She was drunk. Got on about soulmates and shit."

"You don't believe in soulmates. Or romance. You're an independent woman, having no need for a man, and all that Beyonce shit you spout off at us," she laughs.

"I believe in—"

Izzie cuts me off, as usual. "I mean, I can't blame you. Stewart is beautiful. But he's mine, ok?"

I raise the coffee cup again to my lips. Look into the liquid, a film on the top and nod. Izzie sounds unhinged, immature. It reminds me of playground chat when we were seven, planning our weddings to Boyzone members. We're adults. She has no claim over a man she doesn't know. She is a fan of his music, the image he shares online. She doesn't know Stewart. I gulp the cold coffee. Like I do.

I know him, the real him, more than she does. This is ridiculous. I must have been swayed by too much alcohol and lyrical, romantic prose that fell from his lips. Still, a stubborn streak strikes a match in my brain.

"Do you think you and Stewart would be a good match? Seriously?"

Rob's lip curls as his eyes widen in my direction. He's looking at me like I've announced I don't like flowers anymore. Something that will never happen.

"Of course."

"Why? Do you have a lot in common?" I ask.

Izzie blinks at me. "I'm like a massive fan of him and his band."

"You'd be a walking ego boost for him. What man doesn't want that?" Rob comments as he zips up his suitcase.

"Exactly."

"What about outside of the band? What's his favourite book? Film? Food? Place?"

Fuck. What is the matter with me? Maybe I'm still drunk. Maybe I'm trying to ease my guilt by proving to myself I'm a better match for Stewart than she is. Surely then the breaking of the girl code I did is justified.

Rob laughs. "What is this, training for Izzie going on Mastermind? Specialist subject; the extracurricular activities of Stewart from Cardinal. Question one, how many women has he fucked against a wall in full view of the public?"

Izzie narrows her eyes at me. "He doesn't read. His favourite film is Star Wars—"

"Which one?"

"The one in space."

I scoff. Realise I'm becoming as petty and immature as

she is and hate myself for it. I count the stripes on the curtains.

"His favourite food is vegan cheese pizza, and his favourite place is the beach. He finds the waves inspiring."

"Which beach?" Knowing myself that the answer would be a tough choice for him. Kames Bay or Bell Bay on the Isle of Cumbrae. I'd choose Kames every time, yet I can see why Stewart might pick the idyllic pink quartz sands of Bell Bay.

"Is there a point to this, Daisy, or do we need to make you another coffee?" Rob asks, already flicking on the kettle.

"You say he's yours, Iz, but what if he's destined to be with someone else?"

"He's not. That band means everything to me, and no one will take that from me. I feel a connection between us. What did they sing first? Did they open with 'Without You Here'? It's actually a cover of a song by The Halcyon," Izzie says firmly before changing the subject. I shake my head as subtly as I can. I've never understood the fangirl mindset. Well, aside from when I was seven and thought Ronan Keating was cute. He still is, of course, but I no longer fantasise about living in an Irish castle with him.

"Not a clue, Babe," Rob answers, stemming Izzie's chart history of Cardinal. "I was downing shots before they swaggered onto stage."

"I can't believe I missed the whole night," she grumbles before reapplying her lipstick. "What did you do after the gig?" Izzie asks as she watches the world go by from the window.

Rob and I exchange quick glances before she notices. I swallow. The coffee threatening to reappear.

"We just hung out in the bar," Rob replies for us both quickly. "Nothing too special, right, Daisy?" He's protecting his secrets. Rob doesn't know I've got my own.

I look up to the ceiling. I wonder if Stewart is still asleep in the hotel suite? Will he care that I'm not there? There was something between us right from the first look. The word soulmate flashes across my eyes like a beam from a lighthouse in a storm. My head spins with these instant feelings I have for Stewart.

"Nothing to tell, apart from me getting drunk and talking shit, apparently. Sorry, clearly I'm still under the influence. We missed you." I smile and hope it looks more sincere than I feel.

"Did you pull anyone?"

"No!" I shout out, far too loud to be normal.

Izzie flicks at her hair, glistening like spilled oil catching the light. "I meant Rob."

Of course she did. My cheeks burn, and I busy myself with looping my earrings in, taking far too much concentration than needed.

"Nah, slim pickings, really."

"Did you think of me when you two were, no doubt drinking Prosecco and dancing into the small hours?"

"All the time, Babe." Rob smiles as he places a kiss on her head.

"Of course," I reply. Liar.

I tear a piece of paper from a notebook. I rip it into shreds until the urge to cut at my skin fades.

All I have to do is make it until the train at lunchtime without interacting with Stewart, and all this can be forgotten. My cheeks blush a little and my stomach swoops. Well, maybe I'll replay the night over internally. Once or twice. Izzie won't ever know. The girl code will still be intact.

***

I exhale shakily as I reach the street outside. The cold Scottish air sticks to my lungs. The biting wind whips my bare legs.

"Your best pal is a stalker, that's the issue, right? Or do you make a habit of doing the whole cut and run before six am, Sweetheart?"

I spin. Recognising his voice instantly, like the tides to the moon, my eyes are pulled towards him. He's even more handsome in daylight. Stewart is leaning against the side wall of the hotel, cigarette in his fingers.

"She's not a stalker." I cross my arms, hating how his voice is enough to make me smile.

"She's pretty intense. Mind, who can blame her?" The arrogance he plays up to colouring his tone now he's not behind closed doors. I frown, walking slowly towards him. A huge security guard in sunglasses, despite it being January, steps closer to Stewart.

"It's cool, B. She's a pal." Stewart nods as the mysteriously named B slinks into the shadows. "Izzie, isn't it? Your wee pal?"

"Yes."

"You failed to mention she was a stalker. You just kept harping on about the girl code."

"I'm not apologising for having morals."

"Stalkers don't have a moral compass."

"She's not a stalker," I repeat.

"Tori, Izzie, Livia, they're all stalkers. Eddie has a restraining order on Tori, and usually where there's Tori, there's Izzie."

The difference is, Izzie has her reasons for being so into Cardinal and the man I spent the night with. A reminder of her sister, of memories, Sophia, singing along in her bedroom. Everyone has a passion, an interest. But then, not everyone's best friend ends up in bed with theirs. Though if Izzie woke up on a bed of lily of the valley flowers it wouldn't exactly be the same.

I wonder what Tori's reasons for being a fully grown adult who loves boybands are. Maybe she doesn't need one. If I'm honest, they're not exactly a suited boyband perched on stools and standing up on the key change. Cardinal are, in fact, an indie band, not the next Westlife I paint them to be. They don't even wear suits. But for all intents and purposes, they're a boyband; and I will never refer to them as anything else.

"Aye, you can't go against the girl code Beyonce has drilled into you, can you?" Stewart chuckles. He has no idea.

The silence lingers between us. I'm desperate for a smoke, yet don't trust my fingers to stop shaking enough to light one successfully.

"Izzie's pretty, isn't she?" I ask, hating how I hold my breath and wait for a response. Part of me, the stupid, selfish part Beyonce would berate me for even having, wonders if Stewart finds her attractive. Why wouldn't he? Compared to Iz, I'm the trampled dandelion to her orchid.

He stretches out a hand and lightly touches my wrist. "I think I'll stick to her flower arranging best friend."

I smile, flick my fringe from my eyes and try not to

appear too flattered. I recall skimming over the details of her last night, telling Stewart how she has a bit of a celebrity crush on him. Playing it down, so he didn't instantly drop me for my gorgeous gothy best friend who would stroke his ego way more than me.

"I thought there was something special between us, Daisy?" His eyelid flickers nervously. The arrogance dropping, replacing his tone with a softness I recall from last night.

My heart stutters, like a skimming stone merrily skipping along the top of the water, before hitting a Stewart-shaped rock and plummeting to the river bed. It doesn't matter what we said or how we felt; I must forget about him. I have a careful plan to follow. I cannot dive into a relationship, or anything, certainly not with a man whom my oldest friend has a misplaced celebrity crush on. I shrug. Keep him at a distance.

Stewart sighs, rubs a palm over his beard. "I'm a romantic; that's a given. But this wasn't all one-sided. It's more than my poet's heart running away with me,"

"Perhaps I only wanted a night of decent sex..."

"Maybe you're scared, Sweetheart,"

"Scared? Of what?"

He exhales perfect smoke rings into the morning air. I feel my lips pouting a little as I watch his. "The soulmate thing. Falling in love."

Dammit. How does he see right through me? Perhaps because I've never been so open and unapologetically me for as long as I can remember around anyone. I even keep parts of me hidden in front of Nan, Rob and Izzie.

Stewart touches my shoulders. I feel myself being pulled beneath the waves, swayed by his words and this weird connection between us. He steps closer, his fingers threading through my hair.

"What do you want, Stewart? Do you need compliments before you move on to the next woman? Fine, you were excellent in bed. Gold star standard. Do you have a website where I have to leave a review or something?" I snap to push him away because that's what I do best; build a wall around me. Keep myself protected from hurt.

"Don't dismiss it, me, like that, Sweetheart. It was great sex, gold star for you too. But it runs so much deeper," Stewart implores straight into my ear as if I'm a coquettish teenager who is going to fall headfirst into his heart with the bare minimum of words. I shiver, but still, beside the point.

I hate how I preen under his compliment. Feeling my cheeks pushing up into a smile while my lips twitch into an almost smirk. I'll file that away for a bad day. A boyband rock star rates my performance in bed. One for the CV. 'As well as completing a degree in botany followed by a BTec in floristry, I also have three years experience working in a florists. And an extremely handsome yet arrogant member of a band rates me very highly in bed. Shall I ask him to pass on a reference?'

I lean away from him and fiddle with my earrings.

Stewart's confession of being a huge advocate of Emily Bronte's work snakes into my head, like Cathy's ice-cold ghost hand through the broken window pane of *The Heights*. Maybe he is being genuine. Still, I create distance; the alternative doesn't bear thinking about.

"I got caught up in it last night. This cannot go any further. It ends here. It should have ended when I left this morning."

"I don't know why you're insistent on rejecting me." He looks pretty adorable, all pleading eyes, turned-down lips and ruffled hair. Maybe that's all it takes to sway his usual choice of woman. It might just be working on me too. "Why the sudden three sixty?"

I exhale loudly. If I explain to him about Izzie, maybe he'll understand. Yet the words don't make it from my throat. I look away from him and concentrate on counting the bricks in the wall. I try to resist him, stand tall, like a sunflower; neither needing nor wanting to lean towards Stewart like he's the sun. But all flowers need sunlight.

"I can't do this to Izzie."

"You're throwing the girl code shit at me?"

"She's my best friend."

"And I'm my own person. You're your own person. You, we, don't need validation from—"

"You've got my card. If I mean that much, come and find me when your terribly busy boyband schedule allows. If not, give me a ring when you need a bouquet of flowers for the next in a long line of dates for you. I might even give you a discount." I bluff. Fully expecting him to suddenly run in the opposite direction. I expect it's all about the chase, the back and forth. As soon as the mouse rolls over and plays dead, the cat saunters away, losing interest.

"If Heathcliff can dig up Cathy, then I can certainly make a trip to see you."

"You're such a dick." I laugh dismissively, rolling my eyes, despite the *Wuthering Heights* reference making my heart skip a beat.

"Wait—are you really leaving it like this?" Stewart asks, eyes widened in shock that he's being rejected.

"Looks like it."

"Daisy, don't go—" Stewart's fingertips graze along my arm. I extract my arm from him and sigh. Allow myself to get lost in his eyes one last time, for a second or two.

"If you ever tell Izzie or any of the stalkers about this, I will indeed kill you with a knitting needle, Stewart Christopher Burns."

He laughs. The sound follows me, making me smile as I walk away from him. "There's something about you, a florist called Daisy."

I ignore him as I push open the hotel door and head back inside to pack. Back to reality.

8

I flop back on the faded sofa with a sigh, the scent of talc, tea and general old age mustiness clinging to my floral dress.

"Girl, you look exhausted."

Trust Nan to always be direct. No wonder I'm branded as brash and cold upon first meetings. And sarcastic, which I wear as a mask to keep people distanced. Learnt from the best and all.

"The shop has been crazy busy, and I had exams last week for college too." I exhale, flicking my too-long fringe out of my eyes.

"Lot of deaths? Funeral flowers?" Nan enquires as she sips her milky tea from a bone china cup and matching saucer, her ever-present crossword book cast aside for now. "It's the cold, you see, kills us off in the winter months, and what with Christmas, there's always a backlog of funerals into January and February. Dorothy from the room next to me has had three this week."

"Dorothy had three funerals? Nan, I can only afford to give you the one," I reply, helping myself to a slice of cake.

She shakes her head and smiles with a roll of her dark brown eyes behind her glasses.

"It seems bouquets are a popular choice for January birthdays, actually," I explain.

It's a valid point. What do you buy someone who has a birthday straight after Christmas? Inconsiderate bastards. And with Valentine's Day rapidly approaching, there's been orders to plan for and all those extra cliched red roses to clear the shelves for.

"You are well named, Daisy." Nan looks proud.

Seeing as she was the one to name me, Nan takes full responsibility for me becoming a florist. '*I paved the way by gracing her with that name,*' she always tells people. My mother wasn't so kind, pointing out that I'm named after a weed and not a flower.

"Jane's going to look into me running my own flower stall at the market this Spring. Once all those lovesick fools have spent their wages on Darcey roses." From a business point of view, Valentine's Day is a huge profit margin, but personally, despite being a florist and loving cut flowers, I just find it predictable, unimaginative and mass marketed. There's no real romance to it anymore, not that I have or indeed want anyone to share it with.

"So proud of you," Nan says, the gold of her rings glinting under the bright lights. They always make me smile. I've never seen her without them.

She pats at her fudge-coloured curls, which the home cuts and perms for her each month. No wonder the fees are extortionate. I wish mine was naturally that colour. Unfortunately, I inherited mum's darker locks, which from the age of thirteen I've dyed blonde, after Nan's friend commented that I was the spit of my mother. I carve as much distance as possible between myself and the woman who did nothing but grow and give birth to me.

Nan is and always will be my parent and favourite person in the world.

Frank, a man with a beige cardigan stretched over his rotund stomach, inch-thick glasses and still a head of jet black hair, approaches Nan slowly, shuffling on his slippers, pushing his metal walker. I recognise him from the home, of course, and being one of Nan's admirers. Apparently he was impressed at the speed at which she beat him at chess once, three years ago, and keeps asking her for a rematch. And a date.

"How was your weekend in Scotland?" Nan asks. She dismisses Frank with a flitter of her hand. He shakes his head and turns painfully slowly on his camel-coloured slippers.

"It was—"

I had a very out of character one night stand with a member of a band who my best mate fantasises about to an unhealthy level. Actually, part of me feels he may be my soulmate. We have so much in common and share the same thoughts on a variety of subjects. Weirdly, even now, I keep thinking of things I want to talk to him about, or tell him. It was also the best sex of my life, and he had the most delicious thighs. Excellent mouth. Wicked sense of humour too, made me laugh when his tongue wasn't in my—

"Why are you blushing?" Nan frowns, her coral-painted lips pushed together in amusement.

Shit.

"Interesting. It was interesting, Nan." I fan at my face with my hand and avoid her eyes, and annoyingly think of that Scottish accent saying my name as he lay beneath me in his hotel bed, my thighs either side of his. "Hot in here today, isn't it?"

Nan raises a sparse brow at me before she slices a scone and puts half on my plate. My waistline won't thank me for it, but Nan likes to feed me.

"Did you go to the castle in Edinburgh?"

"Nope. I made it to the National Museum, though. I didn't have time to go to the library." I knew it was a big ask for Rob and Izzie to join me, so I didn't even mention it. We always seem to do what Izzie wants anyway. I've stopped suggesting ideas. Instead go along with hers. It causes less fuss.

"Such a little book worm, you, Daisy."

"Books and Star Wars, and flowers. That's my thing."

"And that singer you idolise," Nan adds on after a noisy slurp of her tea.

"Beyonce. Obviously, but everyone should love Beyonce," I say with a definite nod.

"I can't imagine museums are Rob's thing. Did Izzie keep you company?"

I wave at the carers walking past the resident's lounge.

"Fuck no—" I cover my mouth, Nan's never liked me swearing. "Sorry. No way. She had a whole weekend itinerary planned." Trailing from one expensive hotel to the next on the hunt for Cardinal, and then a full wardrobe change complete with heels and full makeup, before hanging round the venue early to get a glimpse of Stewart.

Luckily, though not for her, the migraine ruined all those plans. Izzie gave a good fight against the migraine, insisting she was fine and downing a combination of painkillers and a shot of vodka. But the way her eyes scrunched closed in the dull January sun, closely followed by her throwing up in the first bar we got to, it was a losing battle. I walked her back to our hotel, drew the curtains in her room, even smoothed tiger balm on her temples and tucked her up in bed. She insisted she'd only need an hour to sleep it off, but we both knew she was being hopeful and blatantly lying.

"What did you do up there then? See a show?"

"Izzie's favourite band were playing a concert that got cancelled last year. She was hoping the frontman would fall in love with her and propose on the spot." I roll my eyes as my scone-stuffed cheeks burn red.

"Bless her cottons." Nan smiles and pulls that face that we all try not to around Izzie. The whole 'oh the poor love for losing her sister' sympathy smile.

"I know. They're a nice distraction for her, really. Just—"

"Just what?"

"I think she gets tangled in it. They're a replacement for Sophia that is teetering on unhealthy."

Izzie is partaking in bereavement counselling, but usually returns from sessions claiming it was 'a crock of shite.' And if anything, her 'interest' in Cardinal is intensifying, especially with her friendship with Tori, who was her big sister's best friend.

I rub at my forehead, I might as well tell Nan. "I bumped into one of them from the band in a bar. He was—" my lips twitch and pout trying to form the appropriate word for Stewart, eyes that mirror the sea and quick-witted humour matching mine—"nice. Not what I thought, I guess."

"I'm sorry, Daisy, did you just say a man was nice?"

"Yeah, I know. He's not even a rugby player!" I should not have even looked twice at a man in skin-tight jeans who I imagine couldn't catch a rugby ball without first watching an online tutorial. I scoff. I doubt Stewart watches the rugby, probably never even been to Murrayfield despite residing in Edinburgh himself. What was I thinking? That pesky phrase 'soulmate' clangs loudly in my head. Again.

"Good grief, this is a surprise. Nice chap then, this musician?"

"Nice but flirty with it." I laugh and wave my hand dismissively. Ignoring the shaking of my hand and jumping of my heart, the smile on my lips making my eyes scrunch closed. "But I can't mention it to Izzie because it would become a whole thing." And she'd be devastated if she knew I slept with him, or indeed still think of him whenever I use blue flowers in bouquets at work. Or occasionally recall that accent and his fingers at night. And she'd definitely start a long-running argument with me, if not hate me forever and refuse to acknowledge my existence.

"Come on now, Star Wars and flowers are your things. This band is Izzie's."

"Yeah, you're right. Hers, not mine." The guilt thuds in my head, my heart. Pretending I haven't spent a night with the man Izzie has a poster of in her house and several framed selfies; it seems both hilarious and heartbreaking. She would kill me. Probably. Definitely hate me for it. "This guy, there was maybe something about him, Nan."

About us. I recall Stewart's selfie taken when I was still in the hotel suite with the caption, *'I think there's something about you.'*

I pull a completed crossword page from Nan's book and fold it before tearing it into squares. The now irregular edges feeling fluffy as the pulp is exposed.

"Maybe this nice man can bring a bit of light relief to

your life, Poppet?"

"No, it was a fleeting, chance meeting."

Imagine the levels of control and lack of routine the arrival of a pop star would bring to my life? The scars hidden beneath my wildflower tattoos thrum with the thought. I stack the ripped paper squares on the table, pushing down the springy tower until they fall like melting snowmen. I sprinkle them into my empty mug, the remnants of tea soaks in, resembling muted browns of the angel amber kiss pansy.

It wouldn't be worth it, soulmate or not; I'd lose my best friend over it, over him. And friendship should always come first. Apparently. I've already broken the girl code, but as long as I keep Stewart Burns locked up in my head, all damage will remain hidden. Izzie will never know my betrayal, and I can live my life in the peace of her shadow. It's easier this way.

Izzie will, in time, deal with her grief twisted round Cardinal lyrics and shows, and I'll forget about my crazy one-night stand. I blink away images of silver Star Wars bracelets, the scent of lavender, and the feel of Stewart's beard against my palm. And thighs. I pray to a god I don't believe in that my flaming cheeks fade quickly.

"You're awfully distracted today, Daisy. What are you thinking about?"

"Flowers," I reply on instinct, picking at invisible fluff in my hair. "Delphiniums. Siberian Bugloss. Flax. Hydrangea."

All blue like his mesmerising eyes.

"Fine, I believe you. Thousands wouldn't. Were they good then, Izzie's favourite band?"

The frontman was nothing short of excellent in bed.

Gold star standard.

"Better than I thought. Not typically my thing." I raise a scone to my mouth to try and hide the smile playing on my lips.

"You know what they say, Daisy? A change is as good as a rest. And you work far too hard."

Everyone says this. Rob often claims I don't have enough fun, that I never let my hair down. But I need to stick to the many plans I have pinned to my brain and desk. Otherwise I feel I'm drowning, like I have no control over anything. I have to be in charge of something, feeling like it's all going to work out. Without a plan, the bitter sting of hidden memories of self-harming bubble to the surface. And I try my hardest to silence them with rules, plans and routine. It doesn't always work. My thighs throb. I squeeze my nails into the flesh and momentarily feel I have control over the thoughts.

"Nan, if I want to own my own florists within five years, I need to work hard," I say, but she's distracted by her approaching friend Moira, with lips and matching blusher the colour of hot lips gerbera daisies, far too bright for a woman probably pushing eighty, yet I admire the boldness.

Moira rolls over in her wheelchair, hair as white as snow, plate full of cake slices on her knees. I see her eyeing up my scone. I take a bite before she guilt trips me into passing it over.

"I bet even that Beyonce has weekends off," Nan comments as she and Moira do a bit of cake trading. Nan gains a Bakewell tart in exchange for a lemon slice.

On a boat in St Tropez, Beyonce relaxes, not in Edinburgh, where it was freezing and pissed it down nearly the entire time.

My phone buzzes in my dress pocket.

"Who's that? Not the nice chap from the band?"

"Ha!" I laugh out loud and then slap a palm across my mouth. As if I'll ever hear from or see him again.

The other residents, the ones who can hear well enough, turn their heads in my direction. Moira places a hand protectively over her newly acquired lemon cake. My cheeks flush again, yet Nan looks, as expected, completely unabashed.

"It's Izzie."

'Look at this bitch who stole my man! See you later for pizza and wine, Babe!'

My fingers scroll over the link she's sent.

'Stewart from Cardinal and supermodel Ella Egan; The hottest new celebrity couple in town.'

Stewart's bright blue eyes twinkle in the photo, his arm slung around a skinny taller than average blonde woman.

Fuck the Force, she might be the most beautiful woman in the world, aside from Beyonce. Endless legs, long straight blonde hair and the biggest sparkling emerald eyes to ever exist. Of course she's tanned to perfection, not orange fakeness from a bottle, but sun-kissed, almost shimmering, despite it being February.

Ella Egan sparkles like a star fallen from the sky, like the Shenzhen Nongke Orchid. She's so beautiful it's like she's been created by scientists to depict the perfect woman, like the orchid, which is worth £160,000 per bloom.

In floral terms I am well named in comparison; being so common and ordinary that people dismiss or ignore my existence. Perhaps my mum was right about being named after a weed.

I sit back against the sofa again, inspecting the photos with more interest than I ever expected.

A weight settles in my lungs, maybe in my heart too. I'm from a small town in Cumbria. Stewart is in a band living his best life on the Edinburgh and London party scene. He's dating a model with cheekbones that could cut slate. I, a florist called Daisy, would never be enough for a man like Cardinal's Stewart Burns.

"You ok, my girl?"

"Yeah. Just Izzie telling me something about that guy."

"The nice one?"

I chuckle; it sounds and feels hollow. "He's dating a model apparently,"

I despise myself for falling for Stewart's endless streams of bedside chatter. Clearly he's said it all before. I slap my palms on my thighs and shake him from my head. Must try harder to leave that one night locked up tight in my brain, hidden in the past where it belongs. It clearly means nothing to him. And should mean nothing to me.

"Are you jealous?"

"No!" I bark out, but the colour blooming on my cheeks says otherwise. I delete the message from Izzie, looking for a moment at the black screen and my dejected face reflecting back at me.

"I didn't want to see him again, or anything, anyway,"

"Sure, Poppet, whatever you say," Nan replies with a small smile.

9

I'm emptying the silver buckets of their water down the large Belfast sink in the back of *Bunches and Baskets*. The scent of stagnant water, with floating slimy green grey leaves jumps to my nostrils. It's one of the worst things about being a florist; the death and decay of the blooms. Each stem has a lifespan. That and the early mornings.

I jump in shock at seeing a black furry caterpillar crawling down my dress. Shit, where did that—Oh great. My fingers pick up the offending item; not a bug but the left strip of false eyelashes. I almost rip my right eyelid in two as I peel the other, now defunct lash off. The glue left behind feels as tacky as wet play-dough. I use the coconut-scented soap to scrub at my eyes. My eyes water like I've just watched a programme on rescue puppies. I pat my face dry with the scratchy blue paper towels.

The bell above the door jingles, cutting through the classical music drifting overhead. The whoosh of cars increases and then fades as the door shuts with a click.

"Just a moment, love," Jane, my boss, says, followed by a louder, "Daisy! Visitor!"

My spine tingles and I just know it's him. Even before I see those delphinium blue eyes. I've got foliage in my still damp hair, a smear of orange pollen trailing up my arm, puffy eyes streaming like a leaking tap, and a dress splashed in the stagnant water from the buckets. But what can I do about that now?

It takes the breath from me seeing Stewart standing in the middle of the florists, lingering like lilies that never seems to fade. A smile pulls at my lips, and I try to rein it in, to bite it back. But it's pointless. I know my cheeks are flushed like magnolia petals.

"A florist called Daisy," he says, in the exact same tone I remember. His eyes sparkling, crinkled at the edges, heavy brows raising as a smile covers his face.

Long checked open buttoned coat that skims his knees, dark blue shirt with the top few buttons undone, ever so inviting, black jeans and those ever-present DM shoes. He looks divine.

The rainbow shades of petals in buckets and the greens of the hanging ferns make his eyes seem even more blue. The neutral colours of his outfit make him stand out against the backdrop of bright petals.

"I'm going to take this cake topper down to the hotel. I won't be long," Jane says, wandering past in a blur of pink and the scent of mint. "Make sure that bouquet gets done for when I'm back."

"Sure," I reply automatically. My eyes still trained on Stewart's smiling face. I rub my forehead, expecting the motion to jolt me from my daydream.

As the bell above the door jangles and it clicks closed, the silence is overwhelming. Even the radio signal picks up on the atmosphere and crackles with static. My hands go to my hair, roots in dire need of being done. I look like a school girl with two matching plaits either side of my head. At least I'll fit into the teenage fangirl narrative Stewart's used to seeing from the stage.

"What are you—Why are you here?" I blurt out, then feel my cheeks burn.

"Hello to you too, Daisy. I'm fine, thanks for asking. Good journey down across the border and everything, yep, I found this place relatively easily..." Stewart chuckles as he rubs at the back of his neck.

"Hey you." I smile at him fondly, like he's a lamb leaping in the spring meadows. "What are you doing here? Why are you here? I don't understand. I thought you?—"

Despite fondness rounding my cheeks, I know I'm directing the questions a little too harshly.

"You thought what?"

"I thought you had a girlfriend."

Shit. Maybe he does. Maybe he has several. Maybe he doesn't care. Maybe he expects me not to care, either.

"Do you not?" I ask, trying to prepare myself for the answer.

"Nope."

"Are you sure?"

"Yep. Pretty sure I'd know if I was dating anyone. I wouldn't be here if I wasn't single, Daisy. I'm not that much of a slag. Or a cheat. Anymore." His face grimaces momentarily and he blushes a little.

"So, why are you here?" I repeat.

He rakes his eyes up and down the height of me and smirks. Then trails his fingers up my bare arm. "I thought that was obvious?"

"Yeah, that's not creepy at all."

"A single and wholly available man comes to visit you, takes time out of his overwhelming work schedule and gets called 'creepy.' What a catch you are, Daisy."

I laugh a little, not missing the emphasis on his relationship status.

"Would you rather I tell you my murder weapon of choice?"

Damn that first conversation. Stewart's never going to let me live that down.

Stewart steps towards me, his toes pointed together. He holds a hand out and my fingers lace with his instantly, like palm fronds woven together. The weight of his hand, his fingers with the rings, pressing against mine.

The outside noises of cars and people chattering, the squealing of brakes and the beep from the pedestrian crossing all fade into nothingness.

"You didn't think I'd turn up here. In Cockermouth, did you?"

"No, shocking that."

"Isn't it just." He tilts his head and places a gentle kiss on my cheek. "Good to see you, Sweetheart."

"'*Sweetheart*' again. Are you expecting me to be like Princess Leia? Because if you are, you will be terribly disappointed."

"You know Han and Leia end up together, despite their bickering and apparent dislike for one another. They're destined to be, aren't they? Everyone can see it from the start."

"Han also says he'll either end up liking or killing Leia. So, what does that tell you?"

"Unless you've got knitting needles to hand, I think we might be safe." He rubs the back of his neck. "A question for you. What do you buy a florist? Flowers clearly aren't going to cut it."

"Vodka, obviously," I answer flatly, yet feel my cheeks being pushed up in a smile.

"Funny you should say that," he muses, that slow smile spreading across his features. He holds out a matte black gift bag tied in silver ribbons. I bite back another smile. He remembered vodka is my favourite drink. Already I know that the contents are going to be more expensive than probably my entire daily wages. Even the gift bag screams pound signs.

With shaking hands, and after removing a slimy green leaf from my wrist, *attractive*; I pull the bottle from the bag. A metallic silver bottle of mammoth proportions sits in my palms. The name Belvedere shines up at me, even more tantalising than a diamond ring.

Shit, why did I think of a ring?

"Just for you." He rotates the bottle, the same colour as the rings on his fingers. It's etched with my name (well, with the words 'a florist called Daisy.')

"You idiot." I protest weakly, flattered yet overwhelmed.

The personalisation on this gift probably cost more than my usual Lidl's own vodka that I can drink without tasting.

"I can't accept this, Stewart. It must have cost—"

He cuts me off and taps at the etched words. "I can't give it to anyone else, can I?"

"Thank you."

"You're welcome. Now, can I kiss you, or would you rather insult me or comment on my thighs first? I wore my best jeans especially."

I purposefully rake my eyes across his thighs, poured into tight denim the colour of coal. They are delicious-looking thighs, no doubt about that.

"I mean, you do have damn good thighs. Shame about the rest of you." I try to keep a straight face but end up laughing. He joins in.

"Yep, that'll do it, Sweetheart."

His hands cup my jaw, I want to touch him, long to, but I'm holding the bottle. I'm terrified of dropping it, so I grip on to it tighter. The pad of his thumbs smooth against my cheeks. My heart is beating out a rhythm too quick for me to keep up with.

Slowly, painfully slowly, Stewart lowers his face towards mine. I know before he does it, that he's going to lick his bottom lip. The gentle brush of his lips on mine, the weighted pressure as we both tilt our heads and open our mouths. It makes any cocooned caterpillars in my stomach burst out and flutter their colourful wings. Hands still caressing my face, he stands up straight, a smile reaching his blue eyes.

"Come on, Daisy. I'm taking you out."

In a way I admire the arrogance of him, how he expects things to just work out in his favour.

"I can't leave work." I frown.

He nods his head and shrugs. "Sure, we'll wait for your boss to get back."

"I can't leave."

"But ..." He scratches at his neck, looking at me in puzzlement. "But I've got a car waiting outside."

"This is my job! I can't just waltz out,"

"Can you take an early lunch?"

To be fair, I am quite hungry, having been in the shop since eight. And I did only shovel a yoghurt claiming to be full of antioxidants or whatever the latest healthiest vitamins are, in my mouth followed by a coffee. But that's totally beside the point.

"Stewart, it's half ten. My lunch is for half an hour, at—"

"Only thirty minutes?"

"Yes, welcome to the real world full of proper jobs. We have actual schedules and routines. What a novelty for you." I pat at his cheeks patronisingly.

"Can you not skive off?"

"No, Jane will sack me. And I need the money."

Probably not a concept Stewart has to contend with but still, surely he knows not everyone makes their wages through putting rhyming couplets to music, and extracting money from teenagers eager to hear his voice.

"If I walked up to you on stage mid gig, would you leave?"

"I'd want to leave stage if you turned up,"

"Maybe I want to leave work, but I can't. I won't, and you wouldn't either. Stop over romanticising it."

I start to scan my eyes over the colourful flowers. They linger over the delphiniums and globe thistles a fraction too long. I look at him, eyes mirroring the blue blooms depending on the reflections of the lights, and on which persona he's presenting.

"I'll go and explore this wonderfully named town then, Sweetheart. I'll come get you later. What time do you finish?"

"Fuck, I've got work tonight," I gasp out in sudden realisation.

Not only has Stewart chosen the day where I resemble Jabba the Hutt with schoolgirl plaits, but he's also chosen one of the two nights in a week where I'm at my second job until after eleven at night.

"What is this? A twenty-four-hour florists?"

"No, at the pub just up the road."

"You work two jobs, Daisy?"

"Yes." My cheeks pink, but I shouldn't feel ashamed. Right now, Stewart is the one who's come into my small town world. He's the one that is more out of place, standing there in his designer coat. Suddenly I'm embarrassed at the chasm of difference between our bank accounts, as if the vodka didn't make it glaringly obvious enough.

"I remember working two jobs, in fact, I think the most I had at once was four."

"You?"

"Yep, I didn't come out of the womb clutching a microphone, you know?"

While I'm desperate to find out more about Stewart, the person not the facade, these blooms won't arrange themselves. I pull out a stool from behind the counter and nod towards it.

"Have a seat. I need to get on."

"I'm allowed to stay am I?" he asks with a cheeky grin.

"The first instance of distraction and you're out. You can go and spend your millions in the local independent shops, help the economy."

"I pay for everything in diamonds, is that legal tender down here?"

I laugh. Stewart's hands find mine and he pulls me towards him. I stand in between his jeaned legs, for once taller than him. He pulls me closer. My hand rests on his shoulder. He turns his head and kisses my neck. My knees threaten to buckle.

Oh shit. I know that my underwear doesn't match today. Today, when does it ever?

I hear the click of his phone camera and frown but soften it with a small smile.

"Do not post that online. Come on, tell me about rising through the ranks to get to pop stardom."

"A beautiful woman hanging off my every word, now that's something I can do."

"And drop that act, or I will make you go and sit in the car. And I'll tell the world about your lavender spray." I push my lips into a flat line. I'm absolutely not entertaining him when he's playing up to the rock star persona.

Stewart sighs. "My family owns a bakery. It's been a family business for hundreds of years. My brother and I are supposed to carry on the family name and such. It's expected. The done thing. You know, following the tradition, how dare I want to step out of line when our lives are mapped out for us and any future generations." He exhales loudly, a scowl on his face. I want to smooth the frown away with my fingertips.

"And you don't want to be a baker?"

He shakes his head, fingers dancing along the rainbow rolls of ribbon as if they're his usual black and white piano keys. "Baking the family bread is literally not my bag. I was always far too musical, lyrical. Nose always buried in a poetry book since I could read. I started writing poems first. Then songs. I bought a guitar, begged for piano lessons. My parents indulged me. They thought it was a hobby. But it was—sorry, a pretentious artiste moment approaching here, Daisy—it became everything. My whole reason for living was music. Music made my life complete. I get utterly lost in it."

"I do feel like a different person when I'm flower arranging. It always makes me happy. Brings me joy. Lifts my mood."

"That's it, like that thing that makes you the best version of yourself. So I joined bands, like you do at school, with Pat, then we met Eddie."

"And the rest is history?"

He nods, his eyelid twitches again before he sighs out. Stewart avoids my eyes, looking down again to his hands, which are laying palms up on his denim-clad legs. I start to see him under an honest, bare bulbed light. Shining into all corners of the room, nowhere left to hide, even cobwebs and dust are on show. He looks vulnerable, hunched over a stool surrounded by flowers, not a screaming fan or instrument in sight.

"My parents kicked me out when I was seventeen. I moved in with Pat and his family. I worked I don't know how many jobs for us to afford a flat. Eddie was working at an accountants. Pat was in other bands, so we could save up for all the shit that goes with recording and producing."

"You produce your own music too?"

"Yep, always have." He smiles proudly. "You're really not a Cardinal fan are you, Daisy? It's why the band will never make it on a global scale. We want to just do this independently."

I imagined Cardinal to strut out on stage and follow orders from a management type person. Like controlled puppets, manipulated in the most cost-effective yet money making way.

He flexes his fingers before balling them into fists. "My parents and family, brother especially, still don't support the band, my career. They don't come to my shows. They don't congratulate me. They don't believe I've achieved anything."

"That's tough on you, Stewart."

My hands squeeze his. Like it's the most natural thing to hold his hands in mine. He shrugs. It's a carefree gesture; he carries it as a weight. Letting out a long sigh, his posture straightens momentarily, before he leans forward a little and looks to his feet.

"As long as we don't talk about the band, then the relationship is manageable. At best. When they let me in the house."

I open my mouth to ask more when he slaps his hands on his thighs to change the subject.

"Anyway, so I get the working two jobs thing. I still had a paper round at twenty-two because it fitted around everything else."

I smile a little, cutting the ends off the rose stems, apologising when one hits him in the chest.

"I was saving for my music dream. Is that what you're doing, following the floristry dream?"

"Yes. I've got a five-year plan to follow. I started a college course last September in business. From next month I'm doing my own flowers for the market, to see how that goes, and build up a portfolio of my work. I like a plan."

"Good for you, Sweetheart."

"But also, my Nan's in a care home. It's always been just Nan and I since I was—" I gulp a little, step away from him and the counter, choose a spool of ribbon, pretending it's much more of a quandary than it is, to avoid his eyes. "Younger."

"What happened to your parents? Sorry Daisy, that

was a tad direct. You don't have to answer."

"I won't actually, but that's a reflection on me, not you."

I rub at my forehead, fiddling with my fringe, feeling a dull ache of tension, and pang of emptiness within me. Ignore the glinting of my floral knife, that had I owned one at fifteen, would have been much easier than snapping the plastic casing on disposable razors to fish out the blade. I snip the hessian ribbon a little too aggressively. Then continue to cut off smaller sections, revelling in the satisfying slicing sound the blades make. Realising Stewart is watching, I raise my scissors and shrug, hoping the blush on my cheeks isn't too prominent.

"Just checking the blades. It's my turn to look out for Nan now. I was a pretty wild teen, kicked off and shit, and she always did her best by me. She's well enough still, just needed more support than I could give her. The fees are extortionate, and she won't let me sell the house to cover them, even though it's hers, and Rob and I don't need all that space. I need to plan for the future. She's like a pack-horse, my Nan; it will take another world war to kill her off."

"Can I meet her?"

"No." I almost laugh at his directness. I place the eucalyptus and stocks on the counter, lining them up to check for the length against the white roses.

"Does she like Bronte? I could sway her with my quotations; '*I have just returned from a visit to my landlord—the solitary neighbour that I shall be troubled with.*'"

"That opening line is just so romantic. I'm weak at the knees instantly," I deadpan.

"I'm saving the '*whatever our souls are made of*' quote

for bed tonight," Stewart winks at me and I laugh.

"I am expecting gold star standard performances later; you've been warned."

"I like a challenge." He shrugs then licks his lips. "Can I meet your Nan then?"

"No. What will I say? *'Hi, Nan. Meet Stewart, a singer I slept with last month, who's here to, what? Attempt to sweep me off my feet?'*"

"Once you and I are official, and you're thoroughly swept off your wee feet, can I meet her?"

"Your confidence is to be admired."

He tilts his head, overemphasises batting his enviously long eyelashes. "No one can resist these rugged good looks."

"I'm only interested in your thighs," I say, wrapping the ribbon around the completed bouquet.

10

Following a shift at the pub, in which Stewart sat diligently at the end of the bar and charmed Mark, the landlord, into letting me finish early, I successfully snuck Stewart into mine and Rob's shared house while Rob snored loudly upstairs.

Stewart requested a coffee, insisting he wouldn't sleep, even after silent, rushed sex on the kitchen table. I pushed open my creaking bedroom door, coffee in hand, and felt my eyes turning to hearts like I had transformed into an emoji. A contented warm feeling and a reluctant sense of adoration flowed from my pores for him.

"Maybe soulmates do exist," I whispered quietly.

Ackbar, my fat cat, blinked at my words, his goblin green eyes the only distinguishing feature showing in the black fur curled up atop Stewart's bare chest. Stewart supine on the bed on top of the duvet, one hand over Ackbar's fluffy black back, the other thrown across his eyes. One foot on the floor, head nestled into the pillow, dark brown hair splayed out around his head. His suitcase, phone, coat, shirt and Star Wars-themed socks lay heaped on the floor, as messy as his hair. Fast asleep and breathing deeply as if he were expelling all negative thoughts on each exhale. Lucky him.

After spraying leave in conditioner in my tangled hair, which smelled like I poured a banana smoothie on my head, I clambered over Stewart's sleeping form. He hadn't moved. Even Ackbar seemed set for the night. I pulled the purple knitted blanket from beneath Stewart's legs. Fuck only knows how he can attempt to sleep in jeans, the most uncomfortable items of clothing ever invented. Closely followed by bras. Clearly invented by men to torture women.

I placed the soft blanket over his legs and stomach and couldn't deny myself from placing a gentle kiss on his cheek, just to convince me that this was reality and not a dream. My eyes widened.

I kissed his cheek? What the fuck is wrong with me?

***

I've been watching Stewart with a secret smile for far too long to be normal, like I'm in a REM song, about to silently count his eyelashes.

After he fell asleep last night, I lay awake for ages, images of Izzie thrusting a gold-edged book titled 'the girl code' playing on a loop in my head. I hadn't thought of her all day. Not once. I felt awful that I hadn't. I should have pushed Stewart out of the florists and sent him to Izzie's instead. Yet, for the first time since I can remember, I'm following my heart. Putting myself first, and realise I haven't stopped smiling since I saw Stewart. It's a nice, welcome change.

Stewart snuffles, starts to awaken, stretches his long legs and jolts as his feet hit my bedroom wall. His phone beeps. He sits up and reaches for it blindly before saying good morning and kissing my forehead. "Sorry, Daisy, I forgot to turn my phone off."

"Who's texting you at seven am?"

"Just Pat, he says—"

"He says what?" I ask when Stewart doesn't complete his sentence.

Stewart rubs the back of his neck. "Pat likes to wind me up."

"Is this some lads banter between you two? 'Have you fucked the florist yet and shit?'"

"No! No!" He says, voice raised, eyes wide.

"Very quick protest there."

He runs a hand through his hair and licks his lips yet definitely avoids my eyes. "I swear, nothing like that. We send each other stupid video messages instead of texting sometimes," he says, his eyelid twitching, not looking at me, the flush still high on his cheeks. His fingers scroll through his phone then he holds the screen up to me. Patrick, with his dark curls, eyes sparkling cheekily, and a cigarette between his fingers starts talking as I tap on the screen. "Hi Pal, just checking in. Eddie and I pulled an all nighter and finished that mix, will email you the now. More importantly, though, have you wooed the florist with lyrics to the song you've written about her?"

A smile pushes up my cheeks as I hand Stewart back his phone. "Written me a song, have you?"

"It's about you, not for you."

A knock on my bedroom door startles us both.

"Babe?" Rob calls from the landing.

Dammit, I haven't fixed the lock on the door, so there's nothing to stop him from barrelling in and discovering

Stewart in my bed. I have never been more relieved to not live with Izzie before in my life.

"Give me a sec." I rush out and not so gracefully climb over Stewart. He finds this amusing and snorts ridiculously before burying his head in the pillow. Sneaking out of the smallest possible crack of the door, I see Rob leaning against the bannister in his work suit.

"You didn't have to get up, Daisy."

It was that or risk you barging into my room and finding a minor celebrity tangled in my sheets.

He quirks an eyebrow at me. It gets lost beneath his newly dyed bright blue fringe. His colleagues at the estate agents like to bet which rainbow colour Rob will be sporting each week.

"I'm not interrupting anything, am I?"

I shake my head, my eyes widen, and cheeks blush. "Of course not!"

"Coffee?" Rob tries and fails to peer into my room, where Ackbar has snuck out. I pull the door closed with a slam and hope Stewart remains in bed. If I refuse caffeine, especially upon waking, Rob will certainly know something is going on. I have no choice but to follow him down the stairs.

"Sure."

"One cup or two?" Rob asks as he's halfway down the stairs.

Fuck. My cheeks blush as red as Darth Vader's lightsaber.

"One, of course." I chuckle nervously.

I pour the liquid the colour of Stewart's hair into my favourite Star Wars mugs, then catch myself and hide one full cup in the microwave. This is exactly why I am not a morning person; I'd forget Beyonce's name before nine am. Rob appears in the kitchen looking puzzled but fighting back a smile.

"Just a question before I go to work." He grins, his eyebrow ring dancing in the morning light, reflecting his, what—amusement?

"Yeah?" I ask, more of a squeak than a word.

Instantly imagining Stewart sauntering down the stairs as if it's an everyday occurrence to be here. I bet he's the type to strut around naked. Then, of course, Izzie would turn up, and the whole thing would develop into a blazing row full of high-pitched screams and naked selfies before eight o'clock.

"Good night?"

"That's your question?" I sound like a high-pitched bird as opposed to a functioning human. He's so going to know there's something strange going on under our shared roof.

"Come here a minute."

I take a slurp of the coffee, so hot it burns my taste buds, and follow Rob into the hallway.

"Whose shoes are these?" He points to Stewart's shoes, abandoned at the bottom of the stairs. Rookie mistake.

My eyes widen and I breathe out slowly to stop my cheeks from blushing and completely showing my embarrassment.

"Where?" I question.

The clock ticks loudly from the kitchen. If I stall for long enough Rob will have to abort his mission of inquiry and leave for work.

"Those shoes."

If Rob did not live solely in Chelsea boots, I could attempt to turn it on him. But he would not be seen in scuffed Burgundy DM shoes. He lives in Chelsea boots and Chelsea boots alone. Black. Always black. He even wore them on the beach for two days on holiday in Ibiza years ago, until he succumbed and invested in a pair of flip flops. But no one was allowed to mention them ever again.

"Mine," I respond with a hopefully casual shrug. He's not going to believe that for a second.

His eyebrows furrow. "For real?"

"Yes."

"They're obviously way too big for you, with your little pixie feet. Those men's Doc Marten shoes, you're telling me they are yours?"

"Yes," I say. Ackbar's arrival down the stairs brings a distraction to escape the situation and let him outside.

Rob follows me to the back door in the kitchen. He weaves around the bar stools just like the cat. I sigh quietly and look out at the back yard where Ackbar stretches in the morning sun.

"I'm actually going to use the shoes as plant pots," I say in what I hope is a convincing and nonchalant manner.

"Plant pots?" Rob snorts. He's always been in charge of the garden. I may be a florist, but green fingers and soil under my nails, I have not. Unless they're cut flowers, I'm at a loss with them. Jane won't even let me deal with the ferns in the shop.

I nod at him, swallow a laugh down and replace it with coffee and the most straight of faces. "It's the right time of year to start titivating the garden."

"Titivating," he repeats, folding his arms across his suited chest, the buttons pulling, purple tie appearing psychedelic as the sun catches the silken threads.

"I thought it would make an unusual change, using

shoes as plant pots."

I'm aware he isn't falling for this, but the lie has begun. I need to follow the road of it. I pull a sheet of paper from the notepad and start ripping it into strips. Lining them up on the counter before rolling them into tiny uneven spheres. Scooping them into my palms, I squeeze as hard as possible without grimacing.

"I read it in a magazine."

"What magazine?"

"One when I was, was at the—" Where would I read a magazine with enough time to decide to revamp the garden like I'm on GroundForce? "I read it when I was waiting for my smear test," I blurt out with more volume than necessary. That'll shut him up.

"Ok, Ok. Please, no talking about your cervix." He shudders. "I figured you just had a man in your bed and were being coy."

"That would make far more sense, wouldn't it?" I nod, my fringe dangling across my face. I hold Rob's gaze and try not to grit my teeth so obviously.

"So there's a man in your bed, right?"

I should admit it, otherwise he might go and look for himself. Seeing Stewart would provoke more questions than answers.

"Yeah."

"It can't be Brett."

"Really?" It's nearly always Brett. I wonder why Rob is adamant it isn't this time.

"For one, he only wears Adidas shell toes, and two, I saw him yesterday with his new bird."

"Oh?"

"Not a patch on you, not that either of them looked especially invested. But that's beside the point." He raises his eyebrows and a knowing smile dances on his lips as he fastens his coat. “So why the secrecy?”

I shrug. I am nowhere near awake enough to create a convincing lie.

“Daisy, we tell each other everything.”

“It’s complicated.” That’s so cliched, a pathetic attempt at a get-out clause.

Rob looks both annoyed and amused as he pulls open the front door. “Enjoy your day off, Babe. Titivating the garden or whatever. I want all the gossip later. None of this plant pot shit, the truth.” He winks and cackles as the door closes behind him.

11

"How's Izzie?" Stewart asks as he takes a few selfies. I berate him playfully for being such a poser as he steals the cigarette from my fingers after putting his phone down.

I know Rob will go apeshit at me for smoking in the house. But Stewart is my excuse; I'm in dire need of a calming smoke after fantastic sex. I feel sweat drying on my skin, my racing heart slowing down, the smile pushing up my cheeks. I lean over and hold a mug stained with dried-up coffee granules colouring the insides towards him as a makeshift ashtray.

"Might need to work on your bedside manner, Stewart, if you ask how my friend, more specifically, your fan, is doing straight after sex."

"Better than during." He shrugs with a smirk.

"If you're thinking of my best mate during sex I think this has run its course."

Though I wouldn't be hugely surprised if he admitted to as much.

"Fuck, no, Sweetheart. You hold my full attention." He places a kiss on my bare shoulder. "I only think of you."

"I guess that's a compliment. Probably not appreciated by any of the other women you've been with, though, best to keep that to yourself in future."

"Yep, they didn't like it when I called them Daisy." He winks. "Kidding, I told you I don't sleep around anymore."

"Sometimes I can't tell when you're being serious or sarcastic."

"That's how I feel with you."

"Sarcasm?" I ask, just to be difficult.

He shakes his head and blows out perfect smoke rings towards the ceiling. I'm only a tad envious. I run my fingers through his hair, the colour of Black Jack—

"Hibiscus rosa-Sinensis."

His blue eyes pull towards me with a frown on his features. "Sorry?"

My eyes widen. Shit. "I didn't mean to say it out loud," I blurt, my cheeks blushing.

"What does it mean?"

"It's a flower—" I blush. I'll be spouting off actual feelings soon.

"Naming flowers post-coital is your go to, is it? What is it again? I'm going to google it."

"You'd never spell it. You don't write lyrics in Latin, do you?" I cover my eyes and sigh out, but smile. "It matches the colour of your hair."

"You're quite adorable, a florist called Daisy."

"Izzie's fine." I loop back to Stewart's original question, ignoring the burning of my cheeks as best I can.

"Does she still see me as the man of her dreams?"

"What can I say? She has zero taste in men."

"So, you think she might be ok with this? Us?" He holds my gaze. Blue eyes meeting brown. My lips struggle to form words under his scrutiny. I give up and lie back to watch the sunlight dancing on the ceiling. A lorry going past outside rattles the windows loudly. It gives me time to form a response.

"I mean, is there anything to tell?"

"You can be so cold, Daisy."

I wince. Pushing people away, that's always my first tactic. Don't let anyone get close. No one can hurt me if they can't get through my highly defensive walls.

"What is this, Stewart? What label are you going to romantically tie to us?" I ask, try not to snap, not that I'm angry at him. More at myself for allowing him to start sneaking through my usual impenetrable defences, already preparing myself to be let down and then cast aside.

"I want you, Daisy. For more than a night here and there. I want to date you, but—"

There'll always be a but, won't there? Sometimes it's dressed up in top hat and tails as a however, yet it's always there lurking.

"You're hung up on this girl code. This is real life, not some American chick flick." Stewart laughs a little, tucks his arm under my shoulders and pulls me towards him. My head rests on his heart, fingers instantly dancing shapes through his chest hair.

Izzie is a good excuse, girl code or not. I can keep myself protected from falling for Stewart by shoving my best friend in the way like a roadblock.

"I don't really understand the issue. Loads of people fancy me."

"Modest, much?"

"Excuse me, Daisy. I was once voted *Heat* magazine's sexiest man—"

"The sexiest man of a specific fortnight? What an accolade."

He clutches his chest, pretends to be mortally insulted. "Brutal."

"Honest."

The whipped cream clouds drift past the window. The sky behind them a murky grey, lined with soft sunlight shining in yellow stripes like lighter shades of green on peacock plant leaves.

Maybe now I should explain Izzie's reasons, how her interest with Cardinal is tied up with grief, but the words don't make it from my head. Perhaps I'm scared it will chase him away.

"I can't date you. I mean, I won't ever be a Cardinal fan. I won't be swooning over you from the front row."

"Good. That's not who you are."

"I can't date you." There's so many reasons. My heart constricts, deflates like a grounded hot air balloon. I take the almost finished cigarette from his fingers and inhale deeply. No, it doesn't calm me.

"Have we reached a stalemate?" he asks. I avoid his oceanic blue eyes.

"I can't date you," I repeat, like one of Cardinal's annoyingly repetitive yet catchy songs.

"Can't or don't want to?" Stewart asks, propping another floral patterned pillow behind his head.

I love him at moments like this. Did I think *'love?'* I correct my thoughts. Shit, Daisy, don't go down that risky road of love. Yet. Nope, not even yet. Don't even get started on that journey. Unpack the suitcase and remain where you are. Alone. Oh, great, yes, let's venture on the anxiety-laden road of loneliness instead, shall we?

I *like* Stewart at moments like this. *Prefer* him at moments like this. When it's just him, being a totally normal, everyday person; no airs and graces. No arrogance or assumptions of how he nor anyone else should act or be around him. All pretence lost, his ridiculous job and all those expectations that come from within himself and surrounding people melting away like golden ice cream on a hot summer's day. He could literally be anyone. It reminds me of the first night when we spent hours together, bodies intertwined and voices hushed, honest and overlapping. The fluffy grey blanket pulled up to cover our naked chests, even though we were both emotionally laid bare and exposed. We watched the sky dilute from blackest midnight to the white clouds of daylight, frost kissing the windows.

"Do want to. I think." I stub the cigarette out and place the mug on the desk.

I'm going to have to douse the whole house in Febreeze to try and eradicate the smell of smoke from Rob. I pull a sheet of paper from the printer, start tearing strips off it and watching them curl like Japanese Arisaema blooms as they fall into the bin.

"Hey, what happened to your leg, Sweetheart?"

"Caught it with my nail in the shower," I shrug. It's almost the truth. I did scratch at my thigh with my nail. Repeated the action until the skin showed blood blooming beneath the surface. It eased some guilt about lying to Rob.

Stewart seems satisfied with my response. "Is this just sex, just a physical thing?"

I lie down next to him, one hand in his hair.

"What if it is?" That's all I've been expecting, on one level. What I assumed Stewart was looking for.

"I want more than that, Daisy." He blushes slightly and rubs at his eyes. "Dating with my choice of career is complicated, to say the least."

"You've dated loads of women, though? I thought you were seeing that model? Ella?"

"Ella's just a pal. The press like to report I'm dating any female within arm's length of me. I don't get a huge amount of privacy or time away from the band. But I do want to try, with you, Daisy. I really believe we're soulmates, Sweetheart."

Being written about in the papers, I can't think of much worse. I focus on that and not how my heart jumps over his romantic words.

"I'm ridiculously private. I do not want to be pulled apart in the papers for dating someone who writes songs for pre-teens."

Stewart laughs, mumbles that I'm so brutally honest, and how he finds it refreshing yet equally frustrating.

"Unless you want to sneak around, keeping you hidden from my friend and the press nonsense that goes with you and your band, I don't see what else we can do." I shrug.

"That could be quite fun, actually." He kisses my neck, cheeks and lips before he pulls back and strokes his fingertips along my jaw.

"What am I going to do—hide you in the shed if Izzie arrives while you're here?"

"If that's what we have to do until that girl code deems it the right time for you to tell Izzie we're dating, then yep."

Life was not meant to get this complicated. Especially not my love life. Am I stupid for wanting to follow an unwritten girl code when I just might have found my soulmate? Is it, should it be a one or the other situation? Girlfriend over soulmate? In this case, would Izzie ever forgive me for dating her celebrity crush? More importantly, the man who she fully believes helped her come to terms with the death of her sister? Fuck, I'm a terrible person. The worst of friends.

"I mean, can you even date? Have you not always got teens or press trailing you?"

"Things can be kept a relative secret; sneaking round, last-minute meet-ups and stuff."

"Lots of travelling, no routine or schedule." My head starts to spiral with it already.

"It'll be fun!"

"Sticking to a plan is fun," I counter, yet neither of us believe it.

"We're like Anakin and Padme, keeping our relationship quiet from anyone who would judge us," Stewart chuckles.

"Yes, because that ended so well for them both."

"I admit, things would be easier if I were a baker and you a florist, just starting out in a new relationship. But my career is too crazy for that level of normality. No one wants or needs pressure from screaming fans or newspaper reports when they first start dating. This, honestly, could be good for us, for lots of reasons. I was gutted when I woke up and you'd gone. It shouldn't have felt like that if it was just sex."

"You didn't seem overly bothered when I saw you outside," I comment, feeling puzzled.

Stewart's cheeks flush pink as he avoids my eyes, staring instead at the lampshade. A cobweb in the corner hangs like a forgotten Halloween decoration. "As soon as I woke up, I got dressed and went after you. Obviously, I had no idea where your room was, and you weren't roaming the corridors like you would've been in a romcom film—"

I laugh a little, unbelieving this in a way, yet the blush creeping up his neck from his chest, and the way he's staring at the ceiling tells me he's not lying.

"I pieced together that you knew Izzie, once Pat pointed out Rob at breakfast. Outside you just strutted off. I didn't know what you wanted, what you felt. I phoned your florists a million times that week."

"No, you didn't."

"I kept hanging up, couldn't think of what to say."

My heart skips a beat, which I can't ignore. "Wait, you were our hoax caller?"

"Yep. There's something about you. Let's give this a try. Indulge my romantic nature."

"So, what are we talking about here? Snatched moments of—"

"Bliss."

"I was going to say hot sex." I laugh. He smiles, but it doesn't reach his eyes. "No, it's more than that, I know. But I'm not great with emotions, dating and shit. I'm a pretty closed book."

Ackbar jumps on the bed but ignores me and heads straight for Stewart. Traitor. Stewart tickles Ackbar's fluffy ears.

"I'm scared. This isn't part of my plan," I say honestly, eyes scrunched closed, attempting to erase some of the embarrassment. Pushing my fingertips into my tattooed thigh lessens the fear in me slightly. It's nowhere near a slice from a blade, the release isn't the same, but it's something.

I don't add on I'm scared life won't catch me. Like cherry blossom petals, I'll be swept along on the gentlest of breezes. Then I'll land, hitting the ground, unforgiving, and be left, torn and ruined. Stamped on and squashed. Izzie would land on her feet like a sleek black cat. She'd probably stomp on me even if I landed daintily.

"You don't have to be scared. It's a wee bit of a turn-on being kept a secret." Stewart leans down to kiss my smile, but falters, pulls back and a fleeting vision of worry colours his eyes. His eyelid twitches. He bites his lip before exhaling deeply. "My romantic heart needs reassurance. Do you want this, Daisy? Me? And all the madness my life involves? Me and you as a couple?"

"Does that ego of yours need constant inflation?"

"I don't show this side of me on stage. Or outwardly anywhere really."

"Don't give me that. I've heard your songs."

"Lyrics are open to interpretation. My emotions are still hidden, in a sense. I'm not exactly poetic and lyrical to Pat at home. He's definitely not my type. It must be you."

"It's my irresistible Northern English charm." My lips pout for a kiss, but he stays distanced.

"Please, Daisy," Stewart almost begs, his cheeks flushing pink like tuberosa flowers. "I need to know this. There's been too many mistakes for me to put my all into this and for you not to be on an equal level to me."

"Did someone break your heart?"

"I break my own by being too..." he sighs. "By being me and not the image of me that people tend to have."

"So why is this different?"

"Because you don't give a fuck about my band." He laughs. "And therefore, you know me. You don't see me as that guy from Cardinal. That first night we were together, you said we could be soulmates. Do you still believe it?"

I struggle to answer. I've never found it easy to be honest with feelings and even more difficult to vocalise them.

My phone rings, saved by the tone from deciding anything right now. I smile at Stewart apologetically but feel relieved to be given a little more time to get my thoughts and feelings in order.

"Hold on. Hello?"

"Hi Daisy, it's Sally from the care home." The smile slides off my face instantly. I feel my heart and stomach drop towards my toes, hands shaking violently as I scramble from the bed and grab my crumpled clothes.

I almost drop the phone, then push it to my ear with my shoulder as I get dressed in haste. The words from the other end of the phone circle round my head. Swirling faster, matching up with the tears springing to my eyes.

"I'll meet you there." I throw the phone on the bed. It hits Stewart's bare chest. I blink at his presence, forgotten he was there momentarily.

"Daisy?"

I pull the dress over my head and grab at my phone again. "It's my Nan. She's been taken to hospital."

His eyes widen as he stands up and pulls me into a hug. I want to collapse into it, but I push him away as I step into my underwear.

"Shit! Rob's got my car."

Fucking typical. I bite my lip and feel it wobbling as worst-case scenarios rush through my head. My hands swipe the tears from my cheeks. Trying to remember the name of the taxi firm we always use.

Stewart picks up his phone. "I'll get Des to drive us."

"What?"

"My driver. Give me a wee tick to get dressed."

12

I can't stop my brain from imagining the worst possible outcomes awaiting as we drive to the hospital. Ordinarily I'd make a comment about how Stewart has a driver. But right now I can't think of anything but Nan.

It's a broken hip, she's not at death's door, but what if something goes wrong? What if Nan never wakes up after the operation? What if she's banged her head and wiped her whole memory?

Ok, time to try and keep my spiralling thoughts in check. The breath stutters out of me, switching from shallow panic to gulping silent sobs.

"She's all I've got," I say out loud.

Stewart places his palm on my thigh. The pressure replaces the building itch of the buried scars beneath my dress. Exhaling, I wrap my fingers around his wrist.

"Nope. You've got me too. Do we need to collect anyone en route? Call anyone? Your mum or dad?"

"She lives in Spain," I blurt, then stop myself from saying anything else.

"Did you live there at any point too, or just have free holidays in the sun every summer?" Bless him, trying to lighten the mood by distracting me. But he doesn't know the mere mention of my mother does the exact opposite of bringing a smile to my face.

"When did your parents move to Spain?"

I find an old receipt in my pocket and fold it into small pieces before tearing along the lines, the falling shapes laying on my knees like snowflakes or really bad dandruff.

"I—can't, can you just—"

"I'll shut up," he says with a soothing caress to my thigh.

I forget my manners as Des, the driver, stops the car outside the hospital, climbing out without a backward glance or acknowledgement. Nan would not be happy with that. I almost run across the tiled foyer, weaving amongst patients and visiting families. The tang of antiseptic invades my senses, the squeaking of the floor beneath people's shoes. The overlapping chatter and sense of urgency hang in the air like the everlasting lingering of phlox in warmer months.

"What are you doing?" I question as Stewart appears by my side. He pulls a hat low over his ears.

"Coming with you."

"What? Why?" I lean over the desk before he can answer. "I'm looking for Enid Gordon. She came in with a broken hip from the care home in—"

A high-pitched squeal resounds around the atrium, and my head is pulled towards it. A girl, surely no more than twelve is pointing and squealing at Stewart.

"Sorry, this sometimes happens." He squeezes my shoulder gently. "I'll meet you there."

"Where?"

"In your Nan's room or ward." He steps away and holds his arms out for the hysterical girl.

"Hey! Don't cry! It's great to meet you! I'm Stewart. What's your name?"

After endless corridors, I finally track down Nan. She's propped up in bed, her skin pale and washed out aside from the bruising already colouring her skin with deep purples and yellows. Her light brown curls wispy, glasses sitting low, avoiding touching a cut on the bridge of her nose.

"Nan!" I exclaim, running towards her.

She frowns, her sparse brows pulled low over her eyes a shade darker than my own. "What are you doing here, Poppet?"

"Sally said you had a bad fall. Are you still in pain? What did you hurt? Nan, look at your face!" I hug her. The ever-present scent of talc sparking off memories from my childhood.

Nan raises a hand and waves it dismissively. "Fuss about nothing, girl."

"You've broken your hip!"

"Fractured. Besides, I've got another."

"What happened?" I perch on the edge of the mattress.

The words from the manager at the care home echo back into my head. Nan will have to be moved to a ground-floor room, at least while she recovers. And she'll need additional care. I know what that means; more money. I'll find a way to pay for it; I'll have to. Taking the floristry market stall as my own sideline will have to be put on the back burner. I won't have the money to cover both more fees for Nan and the stall as my first independent venture. Fuck. I push my nails into the bones of my knees to relieve some stress.

There's a tap on the door as Stewart, his hat twisting in his hands, shuffles on his feet. I smile before I can rein it in.

"Hey. Do you want me to wait out here?" he asks.

Nan looks beyond me. She sizes up Stewart. "Who's this? Taxi driver? Pass my handbag, I'll pay him now. You're always short of cash, Daisy."

Stewart chuckles a little. Compared to him everyone is short of cash. He's not the one scrimping and saving for a shop, business course, stall, van, stock, rent, Nan's fees, a mortgage. All of the above and more.

Nan leans around me and looks Stewart up and down again, despite one side of her face swollen in purples like spilled ink from eyebrow to her cheek.

"How much was the taxi then, Petal?"

Colour stains my cheeks. "No, Nan. He's with me."

"Well, this is a surprise." She stretches an arm out. Her milky skin looks alien exposed in the flimsy hospital gown, not cocooned in her standard hand knits or silken blouses. My shoulders relax a little as I usher him in.

"Nan, this is Stewart. Stewart, my Nan, Enid."

"Hello, Poppet. Nice to meet you. Excuse the state of me," Nan says with a pat to her curls.

"Hello, Enid. Lovely to meet you, though terrible circumstances." Stewart places the gentlest of kisses on Nan's papery skin of her cheek. My heart soars.

"The pleasure is all mine, I'm sure."

"Nonsense." He sends her a charming smile. His phone silently rings with a glare of flashes in his hand, which he largely ignores. "I'm spending the evening with two gorgeous ladies. I am the lucky one here."

"Now where's that accent from? Edinburgh?"

"Correct."

Nan glances at me with a mischievous mirth on her lips. I try desperately to shake my head subtly. "Are you the same nice chap she met after that show a month or so back?"

My cheeks flame. Surely they'd be visible from space. Stewart looks at me and smirks.

"I don't know, am I?"

"Not sure about nice, but you may have cropped up in conversation," I admit, not looking at either of them and ignoring my embarrassed cheeks. "How are you feeling, Nan?"

She ignores my question. "Are you actually in a relationship, Daisy?"

"I maybe wouldn't go that far." 'Yet,' my heart thuds.

"She struggles to let her guard down, Stewart," Nan explains with a slow shake of her head, as if I've vanished from the room and she's known him forever.

"I've realised. Though between us, I'm ridiculously romantic, Enid, so perhaps it balances out," he replies, pulling a chair towards the bed, setting himself down like it's the most natural thing in the world to pay attention to an elderly woman that's of no relation to him.

"You just need to take it slow. Give her time to come round to the idea. It's her mother's fault, I'm afraid to say." Nan twists her fingers together like she's plotting to take over the world. Shove a cat on her lap and she'd resemble a battered super-villain.

Stewart looks at me with a slight frown.

"Nan!" I hiss, embarrassment and a hint of rage colouring my cheeks and creeping down my chest.

"It is. We could blame your father, but seeing as no one knows who he is..."

My eyes dart towards Stewart, who raises his brows in shock, then clears his throat and rearranges his features.

"I'm guessing you haven't told Stewart anything."

"It's not his issue," I grit out.

Stewart's phone buzzes again. He glances at it then watches the exchange between Nan and me.

"Go on, then. We're here now." She crosses her arms. "You can't be in a relationship if he doesn't know your history. You have to be honest and open about the past, about what made you who you are. Childhood experiences are a huge part of shaping lives."

"Nan! This is ridiculous! I—"

"You're an honest soul, Stewart love, I can tell. I bet you've told Daisy your background and such."

His eyes slide to mine, and he pushes his lips together to hide a smile. "I have, actually."

She pats his cheek. "I knew it. Go on then, girl."

"No."

"Daisy always believes she's at least second choice. Usually the last choice, if I'm honest. She's a pessimist. She doesn't get that from me, I assure you. In a field of dandelions, you can see wishes or weeds."

"As a florist I'm obviously going to see the weeds," I mumble.

"Is there a specific reason for the pessimism?" Stewart directs his question at me, his face showing a picture of concern and puzzlement.

I rub at my forehead, then squeeze my hand around

my Star Wars necklace charm.

"She thinks everyone she loves will leave her," Nan answers for me.

I sigh, pushing my teeth together. They do. Eventually. My eyes fill with tears. I can't bear to think of a life without Nan in it.

"Her mum left when she was six and moved to Spain with the boyfriend. For various reasons, Daisy didn't go."

"Nan, that's enough," I state. Lying in a hospital bed or not, I am not ready for Stewart to know the full extent of me and my fucked up life. "I'm going to speak to a doctor." I turn and stalk out of the room.

***

Three cigarettes and a shared attempt at coffee from the machine later, Stewart and I are in the waiting room. The TV is precariously balanced in the top corner of the dull grey room. I've been to speak to the doctors, chase the nurses and generally annoy everyone with questions until they instructed me to remain in the waiting room until Nan comes out from theatre. Stewart was on his phone when I returned and has ignored the persistent buzzing of it since, claiming he'll deal with it 'the morn.'

I've flicked through colourful pages of magazines, noticing neither pictures nor words.

I try and fail to do sums in my head. How long will Nan be in the ground floor room? Or will that price increase be permanent? I'll of course pay the difference. I will always put Nan first. But it will mean the dream of owning and running my own florists is now a few steps further away than it was. No amount of careful planning can be prepared for life's curveballs sometimes. I know this, but it doesn't make me feel any better. Stewart is on his phone, tapping away at a game I can't begin to understand. I slide a palm beneath my thigh and press my nails into the flesh; imagine I've pierced through the skin to calm my racing mind.

Paramedics pushing a stretcher rush past the windows. I grab Stewart's hand instinctively as my heart thuds against my chest. I'll never admit to it, yet I feel soothed by Stewart's thumb tracing across my wrist.

"You look like your Nan, same eyes. Not the perm, though," he comments.

A smile tugs at my mouth. Better than looking like my mother. All I got from her was naturally dark hair, the shape of my eyebrows and a nicotine addiction.

"The thing with your mum, Daisy?" Stewart asks almost tentatively.

I guessed he'd ask about it. Actually, I'm surprised Nan didn't force it out of me or tell him herself.

"I was six when she moved to Spain. I stayed in Cockermouth with Nan," I state, like I'm recounting a recipe, not abandonment issues.

He eyes me warily, knowing I'm not being entirely honest. "I'm guessing that wasn't your choice then?"

I shred the cover of a magazine into small strips. Line them up on my lap, the wibbly edges looking like snakes, eels, shorelines. Veins. Cuts.

"No. She left me behind."

"You expect everyone to leave like she did?"

I nod. "She took my big brother David. But said it was too much hassle to take two kids with her." I exhale shakily and rip the paper into tiny frayed-edged squares.

Twenty years later and the rejection still stings. I scrunch my eyes and expel a sigh, despising how she's made me another statistic of childhood trauma.

"Mum told me I wasn't good enough," I croak, hating how my voice splinters with emotion.

"Daisy—" Stewart soothes.

I haven't told him everything, just enough. And I haven't said a word about the scars on my thigh. They've started throbbing as if I'm back to being fifteen and the cuts are fresh and weeping; yet on some weird soulmate shit level, I feel he knows. His hand caresses my leg gently, exactly where the ghost pain radiates from. I ball my fists, feeling the paper in my palms, the dig of nails into my flesh. I empty the scrunched-up torn paper onto the table.

I rest my feet on his legs. Watch him twisting his rings, want to reach out for his hands, but don't.

"Thank you for telling me, Daisy. I get your whole independent woman shit now. Relying on friends, not a man, it makes sense; your obsession with this fucking girl code."

I roll my eyes and I open my mouth to give him a lecture when he suddenly springs up.

My head jolts to his face, then to the still closed door.

"What's the matter?" I ask in confusion, realising no one has arrived, bringing the worst possible news. "Are there more pre-teens wanting selfies?"

"No. Nothing, Sweetheart." He shakes his head, tugs on his hair, places the hat on then pulls it off again.

A late-night talk show plays on the TV screen behind him. The guests on the bright red sofa seem to scream for my attention. A tall skinny redhead, hair the most vivid of oranges, and a shorter dark curly-haired bearded man in double denim throw their heads back in muted laughter. I gasp, noticing two members of Cardinal are on TV, with the third directly in front of me.

"Shit! Stewart! You had to leave for work. An interview. That interview!" I point to Eddie and Patrick in front of a live audience accompanied by a suited suave presenter.

Stewart dances his fingertips along my jaw. He looks totally relaxed.

"It's fine, really."

I shake my head and hold his wrists, the bracelets jangling with the movement. "It's not fine! I didn't even ask, didn't even realise!"

"This is more important."

I ignore the tears springing to my eyes. "This is your job, your career. I'm just some girl—" Guilt thuds in my head, swirls with the worry and dread already nestled there. I knew he had to leave, that his schedule demanded he travel to Manchester earlier. Yet, as soon as the care home called, I clean forgot. He didn't even think twice about coming with me or staying at the hospital either.

The spiralling thoughts of having zero control over anything build up, and I feel a little faint. I push my nails into my thighs and squeeze as much as I can stand. That familiar urge to cut at my skin increases. I rip another page from the magazine, ball it tightly and squeeze it as if it were a stress ball. There's not enough sheets of paper in the room, hospital, town, to quell the anxiety and self-harm pressure from within me right now. Instead, I scratch frantically at my legs, ignoring the pain, willing for the pale colour to change into patchy reds and purples before pinpricks of blood appear.

Stewart pulls my wrists sharply. “Daisy, you’ll hurt yourself.”

Yes, that was the point. Not that I can tell him. I grip onto his arms and will myself to breathe through it. Closing my eyes, I rest my forehead against him as he hushes me to breathe, that I’m ok.

“Ever since you gatecrashed my party, you’ve been wonderfully lodged in my heart. This, you, Enid—is more important than discussing my views on late-night TV with my pals.”

Ugh, he’s so romantic. Usually I would have a sarcastic quip ready, but the threat of losing Nan, worries about finances as a result, and my loss of control over my carefully planned life, has wiped all witty comebacks from my mind.

“You mean that, don’t you?” I ask instead.

“I might be a lot of things, but I’m not a liar, Sweetheart.”

I hold Stewart’s hands, love yet hate how my fingers slot together perfectly with his.

13

I jump and gasp as a wooden chair full of jam jars clatters, then skitters across the worn floorboards of the church hall in a spiral of oranges and reds. A familiar voice apologises profusely as I cover a smile with a hand, then rub frustratedly at my forehead as Stewart knocks over a silver pail of roses on my stall. He then accidentally crushes a few trying to retrieve the now empty vessel, the water splashing on his shoes. All of the roses squash beneath his feet. Ruined. Typical that it would be the most expensive flower on the stall.

"Your apparent disguise is futile if you insist on destroying the place and thus drawing attention to yourself." I put the book down and pull out the dustpan and brush from beneath the table.

Stewart shrugs and removes his sunglasses, probably a key factor in the clumsiness, but leaves on the knitted hat in grey and black stripes. The pale blue denim jacket he favours sits atop a deep blue fastened shirt, oversized, of course, so he doesn't look too formal, and jeans that are more holes than denim. His favourite burgundy shoes complete his outfit. He may not be glaringly obvious, but he stands out against the yummy mummies in leggings and waterproof coats pushing sticky-handed toddlers in buggies and the old dears in ankle-grazing pleated beige skirts.

"Hi, a florist called Daisy!" He places a kiss on my forehead and traces his fingers down the side of my face. I lean into his touch slightly before righting myself and squeezing past to clear up the shattered vase and crushed blooms. I frown and thrust the dustpan out towards him.

"Why should I clean up your mess?"

Stewart looks blankly at the brush as if I've handed him a pair of miniature secateurs and asked him to prune a bonsai tree into a sphere while blindfolded. Clearly he's used to having everything done for him. I bet he has a cleaner for his and Patrick's shared flat.

"Sorry, I'll—" He blushes a little and steps back, kicking over an empty vase that smashes on the floor.

"Forget it. You'll just make more mess."

Stewart scratches at the back of his neck before righting the buckets. He puts them in the wrong place and mixes the lisianthus with the freesias. But at least he tried. Sort of.

"Sorry, Sweetheart. I like to make an entrance."

"You also don't do subtle. Please take that hat off. You look ridiculous."

"This is Fendi, Daisy. Do you know how much this cost?"

"Designer or not, you don't suit it."

"Good job, everyone will just be looking at my thighs." He winks playfully, making me smile, despite trying to keep a straight face.

"I doubt the clientele in this church hall are going to be bothered by your presence, delicious thighs or not."

I sweep up the shards of glass and look forlorn at the bruised and battered roses. They might be my least favourite, but they are a hugely popular flower and costly. "You're paying for these," I state.

He fishes his wallet from his pocket and throws his credit card on the stool I just vacated. "Do your worst, Sweetheart."

I empty the broken glass into the bin and put the roses in a bucket for compost. "I am actually going to charge you for that damage, you know? I haven't got hoards of teenagers funding my bank account with their pocket money."

He shrugs and fiddles with his rings.

Fine, at least I warned him. He doesn't even glance at the screen to check the amount before tapping his PIN. I pass back the card and receipt.

"Fucking extortionate this florist!" he says incredulous, then smiles at me. I sit back on the stool and turn round a few ready-made baskets.

"Those roses are ruined. I should have charged you for loss of earnings. Just shy of a hundred pounds is chump change for you anyway."

He sits on the other stool, back facing into the hall, after moving the textbook, and flicking through it. He rubs a hand over his dark brown beard lining his face.

"You haven't even said hello to me, Daisy,"

"I was thrown off by the destruction of my stall."

He leans towards me and we kiss briefly after checking no one is looking our way.

"Hey you." My face breaks out into a full smile that would rival a circus clown. I loop my arms around his neck as his hands slide up my thighs. Inhaling the scent of him and feeling I may prefer it to my all-time favourite sweet yet strong fragrance of lily of the valley.

"Now we've said hello, I'm going to have to tell you how fucking gorgeous you look today—"

"Just today? What a charmer."

"Today and every day, I imagine, and I do imagine quite a lot about you." His hands run across my waist and hips. My breath catches in my throat but I get away with it. Just.

"You look gorgeous as fuck. What time do you finish here so I can have my wicked way with you? Also," he places a kiss on the tip of my nose. "I've really missed you."

"If you promise not to repeat it, I will confess that I missed you too. A little bit. I'm done at three and will happily let you do whatever you wish to me afterwards, behind closed doors, not in public. But first, how did you find me here?"

"Enid told me." He stands up, helping himself to the flask of coffee, the scent momentarily covering floral notes and the tang of cheese drifting from the stall next door.

"Nan?"

"Yep. Popped in for a wee chat. She's looking well. Nice room, looking out across the gardens."

I'd hope it at least had a nice view of the sprawling landscaped gardens surrounded by buddleia and trees full of twittering birds and the odd squirrel. The jump in fees each month for the ground floor room and walk, or rather shuffle-in shower, combined with the additional care needed while she recovers from her operation, is extortionate. And the recovery is slow. Very slow, thus costly.

Wait, what?

"You went to see Nan? *My* Nan?"

"Of course." He nods sincerely as if there would be any other response.

My heart aches in the best way. I bite down on my tongue then fiddle with stems of stocks in myriads of purple to distract my misted eyes.

"How's the stall going?" Stewart asks, coffee in his hand. He glances around before taking off the hat at last.

"Excellent. I've made £100 from one sale. How's life in your high-flying boyband?"

"Completely ignoring the boyband insult. Interviews in between recording and producing. The usual madness, but at least we're mainly in Edinburgh for a few weeks. We've got a wee cottage by the coast to record and produce in. It's a beautiful wee place, hidden by woodland, so we can actually relax. Hard to leave it, really."

"Yet here you are."

"Wanted to see my favourite florist."

"And my Nan," I add, stealing back my own coffee from his hands.

"You should come stay over."

"Should I?"

I smile at a few passing customers who largely ignore me and the stall as I pretend not be bothered by Stewart's invitation.

"Don't make it into an independent woman thing. You could come up. Stay over for the weekend."

I'm being difficult through my reluctance to accept instantly. Maybe I'm testing him, seeing if he really wants me there.

"I'm inviting you, Daisy. Will you come up next weekend? Please? I'd love for the guys to meet you, and Ash, Eddie's better half. Do you need me to convince you?"

"I know you have a thing about sex in public, Stewart, but I'm at work, and there are children bobbing around."

He stretches his leg out to kick at me gently while rolling his eyes. "That was one time."

"One time you got caught."

"First and only time, thanks." His teeth are gritted, yet eyes still sparkling.

"Only time you've got caught?"

"Wee menace." He licks his lips, fingers tapping out a rhythm on his thighs. "It's a really pretty wee cottage; you'll like it. Five minutes from the beach, it's not Cumbrae, but there's a wee castle nearby. There's also a projector screen and Star Wars DVDs."

As if the offer wasn't enough already.

"Add in red wine or vodka and it sounds perfect."

"There's always alcohol close by with us. I could quote from *Wuthering Heights* as we stroll on the beach as the sun sets behind the castle, hands intertwined like our souls."

I click my tongue, then sigh. "You went too far with the romance, Stewart."

"Fuck, I've scared you off, haven't I?"

I shrug and plant a kiss on his cheek so he knows I'm joking. "I spook easily. What can I say?"

The smile slides from my face as I recognise the bounce of blonde curls and broad shoulders from years of rugby playing on the other side of the hall. Shit.

"You ok?" Stewart asks, a frown on his heavy brows.

"Someone I know has just walked in." My hand fiddles with the necklace charm against my chest.

"The stalker?"

"Brett," I comment, then shake my head and frown at Stewart. "Don't call Izzie a stalker. He will definitely know who you are, though."

My ex Brett's little sister is a huge Cardinal fan. I'm pleased it's a school day and she's not trailing behind him.

"You'll have to make an understated hasty exit or, I don't know, hide?"

Stewart looks behind him, completely nonplussed. He points to the stall table draped in black fabric that touches the floor.

"I'll fit under there, right?"

Before I can make a comment about folding his legs underneath himself in skin-tight denim that hugs his thighs deliciously, he crouches down and shuffles under the table.

"Fuck!" he exclaims, hitting his head. My hands reach out to steady the vases of purple stocks.

14

Brett approaches with his usual boy-next-door cheeky grin. His curls dance round his head like a cherub. I wish my limp waves would spiral like that. I was always jealous of his hair.

"Hiya, Daisy."

"Hi, Brett." I paste on a smile for my on/off ex-boyfriend. "How's things?"

"Grand. You?"

"Good. Can I help, or?"

Brett pushes his lips together, his eyes skimming over the flowers. "Aye, I'll take this for Mam, thanks. Also, what are you doing tonight?"

"I've got plans. I think."

I will myself to look directly at him and his green eyes, not to glance even for a split second towards the table, where I can just see the toes of Stewart's shoes poking out.

"You think?" Brett chuckles.

"I mean, I'm busy tonight," I correct, and it would have been casual had Stewart not traced a finger across my ankle, making me squeal like a mouse.

"I could bob in after work on Monday instead? Or you can come round to mine. Whatever works."

Brett's not being brazen or assuming. This is how it always goes for us. There's constant break-ups and make-ups. Nothing ever changes; it's how we seem to roll. It's easy, nice and safe almost, to fall back into that predictable routine. Part of me always screams that Brett is waiting it out, just hanging round until Izzie notices him as anything other than my ex. I know he likes her, probably more than he should. More than I should let him get away with.

Brett stretches a curl out, a habit he has and does often. "You're annoying as hell, Daisy."

"You're no walk in the park either," I fire out before I can stop myself.

"You pick a fight about anything and are possibly the most sarcastic woman on the planet. But you know," he shrugs his wide shoulders as he scoops up the basket of flowers. "It's me and you. We always end up back together."

I pick up my notebook and tear out a sheet without thinking about it.

It wouldn't be any different, it never is. But stepping back into the familiar pattern does sound easily appealing, at least there would never be any curveballs with dating Brett. Unlike with the man hiding beneath the table. I rip the paper in half, lining up the straight edges.

"We could move in together. Sell your share of the house to Rob, and buy our own place. Call me, Daisy," Brett finishes as he saunters away, as casual as can be. Like he hasn't just suggested we live together.

I pull at the neckline of my floral dress and feel myself sweating. I rub at my forehead, brushing away my fringe from my clammy skin. I track Brett and his ash curls across the hall. He turns to wave and I smile tightly.

I exhale loudly as the door swings closed behind him. I'm grateful for the stool, almost collapsing onto it, yet surprised it doesn't splinter under my weight. My fingers keep my mind distracted from this unexpected twist by ripping the paper into strips. They curl as they land on my knees and the floor, looking like shrivelled lily petals.

Stewart pokes his head out from beneath the table cloth.

"So, are you going to call your ex or just move straight in with him?"

"It was always very on and off. It never worked out."

"Then why keep trying?"

"He was always there."

The sinking realisation brings an image of my mother to my mind. Brett, for as much as we didn't work, being friends more than anything, he was always present and consistent.

Stewart shuffles out from under the table and stretches his arms towards the vaulted ceiling but remains on the floor. He almost appears innocent and far younger than his twenty-seven years as he glances up at me from beneath his dark hair and long lashes. With a ringed finger, he traces the shape of the wildflower tattoo on my calf.

"You can call Brett. Even move in with him, if that's what you want."

Right. I swallow. Wonder if Stewart is using the reappearance of Brett as a get-out clause. Anxiety thuds in my chest. Swirls in my stomach like a whirlpool. Maybe I'm not what he wants. Well, why would I be enough? Images I keep seeing printed on gossip sites or magazines of Stewart hand-in-hand with the model Ella Egan circle my head.

"Do you want me to call him?"

Stewart licks his lips then picks up various strips of paper from the floor, rolling them into tight spirals. "If you want."

"What do you want me to do?"

"You're the one being asked out." He holds my gaze. His features are serious, a hint of a frown. He lifts his head to look around. Satisfied that no one is taking the least bit of notice, he stands up, his eyelid twitching. "What's with the paper?" He unfurls a few spirals he made, reminding me of seashells.

I blush a little then stand up and pretend to be improving a few bouquets. "I do it when I'm—" feeling out of control? To replace the urge to self-harm? "Overwhelmed. Anyway, I'm sure you get daily sexual requests from numerous sources. Does it matter anyway?"

"Does what matter? If you want to get back with your ex?" He frowns, drains the coffee, then knocks the empty flask over with his foot.

I smile a little; he's so clumsy at times, a juxtaposition to his smooth onstage persona. I pick up the paper scraps and place them in the bin so I don't have to look at him.

"If you're seeing Ella Egan..."

Just this morning there was a report of the two of them planning a holiday to somewhere exotic. Ella's got huge doll-like green doe eyes, like ferns, similar to Izzie's. Luscious blonde locks the colour of zinnia elegans blooms which Rapunzel would be jealous of. Dainty, almost innocent, cherub features. Not an ounce of fat on her anywhere. Except her tits which are, of course, in exact proportion to her hips and tiny waist that's probably the size of my wrist. She's skinny, enviously so for the average woman. Nan would say she needs a few pies, but she is beautiful. No wonder Stewart is trying to palm me off with Brett.

"Your low opinion of me never fails to astound. You know me better than that, Sweetheart. I am not the type to date two women at once. It goes against my fanciful romantic heart. It's a press thing. Good publicity. Ella's a pal. Nothing more."

The man on the stall next to me starts packing away thick wedges of cheese into a cool box. I don't look at Stewart. I busy my hands with picking at stems.

"What am I?" I ask.

"A florist called Daisy." Stewart smiles. "I don't want to hold you back if you want to be with your ex." He rubs at the back of his neck. The silver Star Wars bracelet catching the light.

An image of Han Solo appears in my head as I start to empty the water from the pails into a large bucket. How he expects Leia to say she's in love with Luke and leave him. Brett's definitely not my brother, though.

"I don't want to be with Brett."

"So, what do you want?" Stewart asks. His eyelid flickers; he's trying to go for a casual enquiry as he takes a few photos of various flowers and very obviously does not look at me.

I sigh out and outwardly list the reasons why things between us shouldn't, wouldn't work. "One of my best mates thinks she's in love with you, and the other had a failed attempt at shagging your best mate. The press and pretty much the entire teenage population trail behind you like a shadow. You're in a boyband—"

"I'm not in a boyband, you wee menace."

I smile but ignore his interruption. "I should be focusing on my career. I've got a plan to follow. You can do better than me in all categories; desirable and essential." Stewart shakes his head, yet I scoff, thinking of Ella Egan. How can I, at barely five foot three, ever match up to a model of skyscraper height and beauty usually only found in work produced by Jean-Michel Bihonel? The digital sculptures in marble and dried flowers are some of the most beautiful sights I've ever seen.

"Daisy, you can do better than me." His thumbs draw shapes on my palms, like a secret.

"You clearly don't know Brett." I wrap up my scissors and knife in my bag, fingertips smoothing down the flat side of the blade slowly. The cool metal against my skin makes me feel calm.

I turn to the stall next to me and pass over a spare bunch of hydrangeas. The lady smiles at me in thanks, and I exchange polite chatter for a few moments. Stewart takes a few photos of the remaining flowers, making an ombre of colours and uploads it to his square photoed profile.

'No rain, no flowers.'

***

I press up closer to the car as a hoard of chattering school children and their harassed teachers in fluorescent jackets come round the corner.

Stewart doesn't notice them, too caught up in himself? Or me? Huh, wishful thinking.

He ends up tangled amongst the uniformed children who reach his hips; he twirls in circles, being taken along with them. He hovers his hands above their bobbing nit-infested heads, trying to keep his balance. The teachers apologise in passing, then as they recognise his face, swap their sorries for excited squeals. Stewart smiles, clearly trying to keep his cool and feet planted on the floor. Maybe he should have kept the hat on after all? One of the ankle biters walks straight into him and he grips onto the lamp-post for support. I bite my lip to swallow down a laugh. He swerves and spins to escape the children.

He may be a celebrity with prose to rival Bronte, but as he struggles to keep upright amongst the squealing children, I realise he's still a person with faults. Not perfect after all.

He eventually joins me at the side of the pavement, cigarette in my fingers, a smirk that would be usually found on his face covering my own.

Stewart sighs, looking all dishevelled and knocked off balance, quite literally. Cute, very cute.

"Disgusting wee things," he comments as he watches the children retreat.

"Smooth as butter," I hand him a cigarette.

He pulls a string of bright pink bubblegum from his jeans. It stretches against his fingers. His face contorts in a look of horror as he tries to flick it off.

"You, in a delayed response to your question, Stewart. You."

"What question was that?" he asks, exhaling smoke rings.

"I want you. I want to date you."

A smile erupts on his face, and my heart rate increases at the sight of it. "Anything else? A castle? Diamonds?"

"Let me decide when and how to tell Izzie."

He frowns a little but nods. “Ok?”

“I mean it. She’s my friend. I’m the one—”

“If you say breaking the girl code, I might scream. Daisy, it’s a pile of shite. You can’t choose who to fall for. That’s the whole point of love and soulmates,”

“But—”

Stewart places his hands on my shoulders. “Izzie is your best pal. She should be happy that you’re happy.”

I sigh. Maybe he’s right. Izzie’s apparent love for Stewart and even Cardinal is misplaced, filling the void of losing her sister, but I can’t be the one to break that bond. Her bereavement counselling should ease things, and once she starts taking steps forward in her own life, living for herself and not Sophia, then she’ll be more accepting of me dating Stewart. I hope.

“So, anything else? Bars of gold? Designer hats? Signed Cardinal merchandise? I could write you a song.”

“Exclusivity,” my mouth blurts out, not listening to reason over my heart. Shit, I’m going to ask him to marry me next if I don’t take control of my emotions.

“What?”

“That’s what I want. Just you. And just me. Shag, kiss, fuck anyone against a wall outside at a party, and that’s it.”

The words burst from me quickly, yet I mean them. It makes me cross, disappointed with myself to admit that I want him. It goes against my entire nature to be so reliant on a man. On anyone else but myself.

“Ok.”

“Ok?” I mirror his response as a question, expecting more of a kickback.

“It will be crazy, exciting and probably frustrating, but

fuck. I want this, want you, Daisy. More than just for sex, by the way."

"Dammit. I only wanted you for your body. Those thighs especially."

We both laugh. Stewart licks his lips, glances towards me, then away before settling on my eyes.

"Do I need to inform anyone that you're going against your life plan? You do like a highly detailed plan if the ones on your desk are the norm."

He's right. Ticking things off a list makes me feel accomplished. I need to have some form of control, manipulation, over at least one thing in my life. Otherwise my thoughts spiral, and I self-harm. It evolved from cutting slices in my skin to manipulating flowers, and tearing pieces of paper to shreds, lists, monthly, yearly and five-year plans. Sometimes I spend too long looking at the shiny blade of my floristry knife. Or pushing my nails into my skin, fighting the need to transform an internal thought into something physical. It will always be a battle. I don't always defeat the blade.

"There's no way I would have planned to date a member of a boyband, but there's something about you, Stewart Christopher Burns."

Stewart cups my face, and the tip of his thumb pushes gently into my lower lip, pulling it down in a super unpredictably erotic move. I feel the back of his nail jolt over the scar usually hidden in my mouth. My breath catches and sticks to my lungs like frost to bare branches on early winter mornings. The blood in my veins sears, melting the breath caught. I'm warmed by the juxtaposition of being so exposed yet readily accepted for being entirely me. It's akin to him seeing my soul, the whole of me, just as I am.

15

It's dark by the time the wheels of my battered red Yaris crunch over the gravel driveway leading to what has only been referred to as 'the wee cottage.' Stewart and the rest of Cardinal are locked away recording the next batch of three-minute songs that will have teenagers the country over, and Izzie, screaming in elation.

Rob is under the impression that I'm at a conference on using natural flora and fauna in bouquets. Izzie didn't even question where I was going. I'll pluck a few sprigs of marsh arrowgrass, coltsfoot and sea aster and quickly shove them into a hand-tied posy with a few silk flowers from the back of the car to show Rob. It's all about covering the tracks.

I smooth down my dress as I climb out of the car. It's way too tight to drive in really, but I felt an effort is required when spending a full weekend with Stewart, his bandmates and Eddie's fiancee. First impressions count and all that. The pale grey dress with yellow and orange hibiscus printed flowers stretches, probably more than is intended, across my figure and down to my knees. Were I in a more loose-fitting outfit, I'd have snatched up an almond croissant or two from the service station. But sometimes sex comes before snacks. Only sometimes.

Laughter and the clinking of glasses increases in volume as the front door slides open, casting a yellow light over the path. Stewart fills the doorframe, the soft light surrounding him, as his shadow stretches out to touch at my toes. A smile breaks out on my face, like sun behind the clouds. The stones beneath my heeled boots grind, and the suitcase clatters, jarring against the music from the cottage. A small wooden outdoor table dotted with stumps of candles, overflowing ashtrays and empty wine bottles filling the surface ruins the picturesque, quaint image.

"A florist called Daisy!"

I stretch my arms up to his neck as his go to my waist. He scoops me up and spins me round like I'm the ballerina from my childhood jewellery box. I squeal happily before I can stop myself, then kiss him. My heart feels warm and gooey; that feeling of comfort on cold days, slurping soup from heavy mugs in front of the fire.

He pulls me into a hug. I lean into him and loop my arms around his ribs. My cheek against his heart. *Where I always want to be.* The thought scares me, but I just go with it for now. I'm feeling too giddy to psycho-analyse everything. I can bury my feelings beneath sarcasm and wit later.

"Hey, you. Just Daisy is fine, really. You don't have to include my job description."

"Nah, I like the full title."

I kiss him again, all tongues and biting at lips, before a glass smashing from inside jolts us apart.

Stewart picks up the suitcase and ushers me inside the long hallway. 'The wee cottage' conjured thoughts of thatched roof and exposed brickwork, heavy beams and dark wood panelling. The hallway is bigger than my living room at Cockermouth, and there's not a cramped tiny room or Aga in sight.

"Fuck, I like this dress," he comments as he looks me up and down. Twice. Maybe worth missing out on baked goods for.

Patrick appears from a doorway, two glasses of wine in his hands. His hair curls round his ears, green eyes avoiding mine despite a smile on his face. He nods, handing me a glass.

"At last, you're here. Now Stew can actually relax and have a fucking drink." He nudges Stewart before handing him the other glass.

"Hi, Patrick." I smile.

"He thought you'd stand him up," Patrick adds on by way of explanation. "He hasn't shut up about you all fucking week."

"Alright Pat, that's enough," Stewart replies, attempting to be subtle, shaking his head at his bandmate.

Another head pokes around the door, Eddie, the final member of Cardinal with his gingery hair, long limbs, pen behind one ear, cigarette behind the other. I have a vague memory of seeing him at the afterparty, dancing closely with a blonde woman. The rainbow lights hid just how bright orange his hair is in reality.

"Never mind all week. He hasn't shut about you since January."

"Oh really?" I ask, finding Stewart's hand and squeezing it. He shuffles on his feet, his toes pushed together in, of course, Star Wars socks.

"He's suddenly taken a keen interest in writing about various flowers too. And keeps trying to book us gigs to play in Cumbria," Eddie continues, raising his eyebrows at Stewart.

"You two are fucking nightmares," Stewart mutters quietly.

"Come in, Daisy. I'm Eddie. I could describe you in terms of flowers and lyrical rhymes, but nice to meet you at last."

Stewart looks at me then away, blushing like sweet meadow flowers.

Eddie disappears back into the room, where the volume has decreased a little, then pokes his head out again. "Sorry in advance. Ash, my better half, is beside herself about having a fellow woman in close proximity," he says with a slight grimace. He's taller than Stewart, skinny, all angles and limbs, even his skinny jeans appear baggy, his t-shirt in muted greys and black stripes. That hair, though, it's so vivid I can't stop glancing at it, reminding me of the orange blooms of crocosmia scorchio.

"Is she here?" comes a high-pitched squeal, followed by a tall, slender woman in an oversized hoodie and leggings. I look at her heels, which are clearly the reason behind her height; they must have her kissing six feet. She claps her dainty hands and a huge engagement ring glints beneath the lights. I'm relieved I recognise her as being the blonde dancing with Eddie a few months ago, despite her hair now being darker.

"Daisy! I'm Ash! Finally, another girl!" Ash pulls me into a hug. She smells of jasmine, citrus, and wine. "You're beautiful! Good work, Stew!"

"Ash has been a wee bit excited," Stewart says, shaking his head as he strolls past holding the suitcase. "Our room's through here, Sweetheart."

"Who can blame me, Stewart? When was the last time I had female company with you lot? He's gay and you don't date."

Stewart flicks her forehead. “I date now, thanks, Ash.”

“At last! Boys are disgusting. At least now I have an ally. Welcome to the madness, Hen. Come sit down. You’re so pretty! Stew says you’re a florist? Love your boots! Finish that wine; we’ve got shots lined up after this bottle!”

Ash reminds me of a bird. High pitched but tuneful twittering, flittering from one subject, one place to another. I smile at her and feel we could be firm friends as she tops up the wine, having only drank a few mouthfuls. I sit back on the large pale pink velvet sofa and look around the room while instantly feeling relaxed and comfortable with her.

Once the band are finished in the studio, Eddie hands everyone decaf coffees as the grandfather clock in the hall strikes one and he yawns loudly. He claims that they need to be more sober than not come nine the next morning, and coffee might help chase away the liquor.

My eyes are scratchy with tiredness, yet it’s hard to stop watching and listening to Cardinal in their element; as a band and the tight-knit unit they are. I spend a lot of time laughing and watching the others, their little Cardinal family, especially Stewart. How relaxed he is, laughing almost constantly when he’s not singing; how they’re all so comfortable with one another, yet so welcoming to me, invading their close-knit unit. I don’t feel like an outsider at all. They include me in any and all conversations, stopping a flow of dialogue so I can be filled in on background information. My Star Wars references are understood instantly. I’m not living in Izzie’s shadow, nor am I the one responsible for getting her home safely after most of a bottle of vodka.

“Pals, I need to go do some more work,” Stewart announces with a pat on my shins.

"You don't," Patrick counters from the armchair in the corner, beneath the empty bookshelves.

"He always does this, Daisy. He never stops," Ash tells me. "Pissing annoying that he can work even when drunk."

"Leave it 'til the morn, Stew. We've got all week," Eddie says slowly, his eyes closing, amber-coloured eyelashes catching the light.

Stewart shakes his head, moving my legs from his. He places a hand on my thigh and kisses me before pushing himself up to standing. "I'll just check this mix. I won't be long."

"You're such a perfectionist," Eddie comments, another burst of energy in his veins, picking up his guitar and tuning it across his knees.

"You're just a lazy sod. It should be perfect, Eddie. You get it, right, Sweetheart?"

"Are you a perfectionist too, Daisy?" Eddie asks yet doesn't wait for an answer. "Trust you, pal, to find someone as sarcastic yet precise as you."

"No amount of perfection is going to make your mum and dad love it, Stew," Patrick says with a shrug.

I manage not to cough as I inhale on my cigarette. My slightly widened eyes go to Stewart, who, despite the alcohol and ridiculous amount of fruit pastilles in his system, falters as his spine goes rigid, as if Patrick's words have chased the alcohol from his veins.

"I'll go over this mix, then I'll come back," Stewart replies flatly yet doesn't move.

"Patrick!" Ash snaps, throwing a cushion at his curls. "Fucker! What did you say that for?" she hisses, looks at me, then away; almost weighing up what to say, she twirls a lock of dark hair around her fingers. Stewart opens the door, then turns to face me. Licks his lips and smiles, but it doesn't quite reach his eyes.

"Sorry, pal." Patrick winces before lighting a smoke.

"You're right, though," Stewart replies, looking at the floor as he scratches at his beard.

"Sorry both of you, I've put you in an awkward position," Patrick continues his apology.

I lean over and put the mug down. Eddie's strumming of the guitar starts again, then stops. Patrick picks up his guitar, placing it on his knees. His eyes dancing along the three of us on the sofa. I swallow under their stares and will my heart rate to slow down for fear they may hear it.

"It's not that awkward. I already know. We've talked about Stewart's parents," I say quietly. Stewart shuffles on his feet and sends me a smile.

Ash blinks. "When did you tell her?"

"The first time I went to Cumbria."

I'm not sure why they're struggling to believe us. Stewart can talk as much as Ash when he gets started.

"Fuck me. He's usually such a closed book about it." Eddie half laughs, looking at me.

"Stewart? A closed book? I can't shut him up." I laugh as Stewart flicks Eddie on the ear.

"He's blacklisted all questions about his family in interviews. He doesn't talk about them."

"I am still here, you know?" Stewart chuckles.

Ash agrees with a nod. "How did you do it, Daisy? Have you got Jedi powers? Use the Force?"

"He just told me." I shrug, smiling at Stewart. Realising that he's not as open and honest with everyone as standard. It makes my heart feel fuzzy.

"Fuck me," Eddie repeats, smiling. He and Ash share a look which leads to Ash pulling me into a hug. "She's good for you, Stew."

"I know." Stewart smiles before winking at me and closing the door behind him.

I look out of the large bedroom windows into the woodland surrounding the garden. The whispering rush of the leaves creates a calm soundtrack, especially after the entire night of chatter and music. The walls of the bedroom are a hushed green, low lights dusting over like silver ragwort plants. It's a sanctuary; shelves lined with thick candles and Stewart's scent of lavender filling the space. He loops his arms around me as his chin rests on my shoulder.

"I guess you're not tired?" I ask, closing the curtains.

"You know me, Daisy. I don't sleep." He shrugs then counteracts his words with a yawn.

I smile and lay down on the bed, stretching and yawning. My eyes will not be open for much longer, my lashes becoming weighted with each blink.

"You creative types keep strange hours."

He shrugs and joins me on the bed. "Yep, we do."

"You, Stewart Burns, are going to completely ruin my sleep schedule."

Usually, on a Friday night, me and Rob would order pizza, watch endless reruns of Friends or Naked Bodies and polish off a bottle of wine while Rob shares exacting details of his sex life. Sometimes Iz joins us if she hasn't got a better offer. I'm usually the punchline of Izzie's jokes, but I'm used to it. It's a familiar routine. Wonderfully normal and understated.

Yet after slotting seamlessly into a world I never thought about, with Stewart next to me, I'm exhausted, but my cheeks are aching with laughing and smiling so much. I've never felt so accepted or loved for being just me before.

My heart seems to be filled with warm contentment that almost cancels out the tiredness. Though I'd better get a lie in tomorrow.

Maybe Nan was right. Do I need a change in my life? But still, the walls of defence are stacked high.

"I don't know if I believe in the whole soulmate thing," I say, always ready to keep people at a distance.

"You do," Stewart states with utter confidence. "If you didn't, you wouldn't have greeted me at the wee florists with such a beaming smile, nor would you have let me stay at yours, meet your Nan, or let me stay after destroying vases full of roses, or indeed; be here with me now."

I blush a little. Dammit. He knows me already, like he can see through me, despite skulking in the shadows. Still, I don't want to be transparent to him or anyone.

"Maybe I'm just always pleased to see those thighs of yours,"

"Maybe you shouldn't be too scared to fall, Sweetheart."

"I'm not scared," I snap, then laugh a little as he raises his brows at me. "But I didn't plan this."

How pathetic does that sound? Whoever plans to date or even fall in love with careful consideration? It shouldn't be something one can plan for; that's the whole point.

"Even the best laid plans take detours. Enjoy it."

He blinks slowly, those sparkling blue eyes almost too bright to be real. My hands go to his face, smooth over his beard as he leans in and kisses me. He moans deliciously, which in turn makes me shiver. Tiredness replaced with lust.

"Can it wait, your need for sleep? I really like this dress, Baby."

"'Baby.' That's new. I kind of like it."

"Mixing things up. Keeping you on your toes."

"Dress on or dress off?" I ask, tugging at the hem of his t-shirt and pulling it over his head. His hands run up my thighs, pushing the material higher. I falter and watch his face as his hand creeps up my skin. If anyone is going to notice the scars on my leg, it would be Stewart.

He tilts his head and smiles before a frown passes over his features. Both hands on my thighs, seemingly not as observant as expected.

"You ok?"

I smile and nod, blinking away thoughts that could ruin the moment.

The door bursts open and Patrick barrels in, piece of paper in his hand, a pen tucked between his teeth. I jolt; at least Rob always knocks.

Stewart looks to the ceiling and groans. I blush, mortified that minutes, even seconds later and Patrick could have witnessed a much more explicit, nudity-filled sight.

"Thank fuck. I was worried I might walk in on you in a compromising position."

"What do you think this is?" I ask with a laugh, hitching down my dress and standing up. Replacing embarrassment with sarcasm; always a good tactic.

"I sit like that on Stew all the time," Patrick replies instantly.

"You wish I'd let you." Stewart shakes his head, reaching for his t-shirt after fastening his jeans. "What do you want?"

"I've got the bridge for that track. Listen—"

"I'm not recording it now, Pat. We're going to bed. Daisy's been at work all day before coming up here, and it's now inching towards two."

"But—"

"No, Pat. It'll keep."

"But you never usually refuse—"

Stewart stands up and pushes Patrick towards the door. "You want to work, and I want to do extremely filthy things to my girlfriend. I wonder who's going to win that battle?"

"Ugh, young love," Patrick groans before spinning dramatically, his curls twirling as he slams the door closed.

"Do not bother us until the morn, Pat! Or I'll slash your drum skins!" Stewart shouts. He turns to me with a grimace. "I'm sorry, Sweetheart. That man has no boundaries."

"Have you always been closer to Patrick rather than Eddie?"

"Yep. We've literally been in one another's pockets since we were seventeen, so we're ridiculously close. I'm used to him wandering in at all hours, but I appreciate you're not. I'm just going to—"

"It's ok," I shrug. If I'm dating Stewart, I have to get used to band life in all manner of ways.

"Who are you closest to—Rob or Izzie?" He props a chair beneath the door handle, to keep Patrick out, I assume, then returns to the bed.

"Izzie and I have shared history. We've been friends

since playgroup. Small town life, you know? I spent a lot of time at hers when my mum left."

"And you met Rob at uni?"

I exhale. I love so much how he bypassed the issues regarding my mum without even considering it.

"Yeah. First day. We got on really well, and he didn't want to go home to the South Lakes. But after graduation I wanted to move back for Nan, and do my BTec locally, so he came with me. Izzie was at the local college too, she and we sort of became this little trio."

But actually, I think Izzie was jealous I'd made a new friend without her being instrumental in it. She invited herself along to events and meals Rob and I were having until we always asked her first to save an argument about her feeling left out.

"Where did you go to uni, Sweetheart?" Resting his forehead against my neck, fingers tracing across my collarbones and the Rebel Alliance charm necklace.

"Cornwall."

"Could you get further away from home?" He laughs.

"That was kind of the point," I mumble and pull a sheet of lined paper from a notepad on the floor. I tear it into strips as always and drop them off the edge of the bed.

"I thought you liked it in Cumbria?" He sits up and watches me shred the paper.

"I do now. It's not very exciting when you're a teenager. I couldn't move to Spain like I thought I wanted—" I glance at him, ignore the flushing of my cheeks and stinging of hidden scars. He frowns questioningly. I grab another piece of paper and scrunch it into a ball, passing it from one palm to the other before throwing it towards the bin.

"I wanted to live with mum when I was a teen; she wasn't so keen. But then I found my love for flowers. They've got the Eden Project linked to the uni in Cornwall, so I had to go there."

I don't know what it is about him, their Cardinal clan, that makes me lower my guard a little and open my mouth to release more than sarcasm.

"Was it a laugh, uni, being a student and shit?"

I chuckle a little. Although he's had a life I can't imagine, Stewart has missed out on the things I've experienced.

"I was quite wild in a sense; partying, drinking, generally living it up, spending my student loan in Topshop, the usual."

Stewart smiles, then picks up the scraps of paper from the floor before he lays back down on the bed. "Why calm down? You spend a lot of time being serious and sensible, Sweetheart."

"And you mean that in the best way?" I ask with a pout, then play with his hair as he blushes.

"Obviously. I wouldn't change a thing about you, Daisy."

"Nan. Real life, responsibilities. My career. Being a student was a break from reality, an escape."

Maybe that's why I didn't self-harm at university. I was allowed to be carefree and do whatever I wanted; it's expected of students. We were all exploring the unknown in a relatively safe and secure environment of lecture halls, student digs and nightclubs. The final hurrah before the rest of our lives began.

"I'll push you away. It's what I do," I admit quietly with a sudden, unusual burst of honesty.

The lamp dusts his features in soft yellow light, and

Stewart smiles at me fondly. "You push me every single fucking day, you wee menace."

"Just know that I don't mean it when I try to back out of it, of us. Just don't let me go."

"I'm impressed, Sweetheart. You're directly quoting my songs." He smirks, placing his hand dramatically across his heart.

"That was purely accidental. If I wasn't so tired, I'd quote Beyonce instead."

"I am not going anywhere, Daisy. I promise."

Stewart holds my jaw, his thumbs stroking at my cheeks, and implores into my brown eyes that are nowhere as captivating as his. He's trying to counteract my mum leaving, convincing me he's different; from her and everyone else who always leaves. He looks at me with such intensity. I run my hands through his hair, down his face. I smile at him but can't find any words.

I click the light off then lace my fingers with his, shuffling close to him.

"I'm scared you'll leave," I confess into the darkness, my words as delicate as a thread of spider silk blowing in a storm.

"Daisy, I'm not going to leave you. I wish you'd believe me."

"Me too."

16

Having sent Stewart a photo of the church spire against the fading sunset, then berating him for replying with several pouting selfies, I return to the pub, Rob and Izzie leaning across the table. She looks fed up, rolling her eyes, while Rob appears to be telling her off in hushed hissed tones and pointing of fingers. I left in a huff for a smoke after we got talking about the future.

"Daisy had a man over," Rob announces as I shuffle myself into the chair around the wobbly dark wood table.

Oh, for the love of the Force. How and why is this topic of conversation better?

I roll my eyes at Rob, who is smirking. He never did ask me about the mysterious man I had staying over. I assumed he'd forgotten, as the same day his casual fuck buddy Zach declared his feelings for him, and they started dating. Clearly, he's been waiting to quiz me about it; the back room of one of the many pubs in Cockermouth is apparently the ideal location. It's full of underage drinkers and students propping up the always sticky bar. Not even the new owners and reupholstered seats can chase away the pub's reputation of being the creche.

"Brett?" Izzie sighs, her interest already waning as she

scrolls through her phone.

"Nope. A different one."

Izzie's glass full of wine en route to her mouth pauses in mid-air as her lips drop open. "No!" She extends the word as if it's the most shocking news she's ever heard. "Are you sure it wasn't Brett?" she asks Rob, not me.

"Positive. Brett wears trainers. This one left his Doc Marten shoes on the stairs."

"What colour?"

I wonder if I stood up and left now, would they even notice? Rob would. Izzie, probably not until she needed a lift home. I think of Stewart, with Eddie and Ash and Patrick. How they would fall over each other to help one of their Cardinal family out and do so without a moment's hesitation.

"Burgundy, scuffed to high hell and back. I almost had a heart attack over the state of them."

"Oh my god! Stewart from Cardinal has those shoes."

Fuck. I fiddle with my large hooped earrings.

"Yes, Iz, Stewart Christopher Burns must be the only person in the world to wear burgundy DMs..." I reply sarcastically, also pushing her away from the truth.

"How do you know his middle name?"

"Because you never stop wittering about them," I say, cheeks burning.

Izzie blinks at me before rolling her eyes. "So, who was he?"

"Someone who can't polish shoes," Rob comments as he opens a packet of peanuts.

"Just a guy I met at work." I start ripping the cardboard coaster, damp with condensation from my soda and lime. Guess whose been volunteered to be designated driver again? Even though Izzie could easily walk the ten minutes up the road to her house.

They both turn to me, wide-eyed.

"Please tell me he wasn't buying flowers for his girlfriend?"

"No, some of us have morals, Rob. I meant the pub."

"You mixing business and pleasure?" Izzie asks. "What the hell is the matter with you recently? You're like a new woman."

"A better woman?" I ask cautiously. She shrugs in response.

Rob nods his head and fiddles with his eyebrow piercing. "I think so. You seem more relaxed, Babe."

"So are you dating the guy who owns the same shoes as Stewart from Cardinal?"

My cheeks flame, and I avoid her eyes. Instead, I focus on the wine bottle shimmering beneath the lights in green and almost purple where the liquid fills it.

"Who says I'm dating any guy?" I ask, separating the coaster into various layers of cardboard.

"The trips away, laundry when you return, including your skimpiest underwear, and the smile on your face is a giveaway, Babe," Rob snorts. "Plus, I've heard you having phone sex."

The fuck? My skin blares red from my toes to my forehead.

"Daisy, you minx. Though I guess anything has got to be more exciting than Brett."

I sigh loudly. Brett isn't boring. I mean, he didn't set me alight in bed, but we always had decent sex and conversation, and he was good company. Yes, we spent a lot of time talking about rugby, but that doesn't make him boring.

"Just because you don't like rugby, doesn't mean it's dull," I counter, my nails pressing into my thighs beneath the table.

"It's not fun."

Neither is the occult, screaming that sounds like a violent throat infection over heavy guitars and drums, or skulls tattooed onto arms, but there we go. Everyone is different.

"So, who is he?" Izzie prompts again, reapplying her deep purple lipstick.

"Like I say, a guy I saw at the pub." Clever, not technically a lie.

"Is he local?"

"No, hence the phone calls," I admit. "And no, I'm not discussing my sex life with either of you."

Rob sends me a wink. I dread to think just how much he's overheard. "Iz, she's always on her phone. Honestly, it's forever glued to her hand or ear these days. She's constantly at his beck and call."

I shake my head, mouth full of fizzy liquid, which sizzles in my throat as I gulp it down. "So not true. He works unusual hours, that's all."

"Can we see a photo?" Izzie asks, her eyes flittering toward my phone on the table. I snatch it up and shove it in the bottom of my bag.

Rob winks at me. "Not got any of his face, huh?"

"Fuck off, Robert," I reply with a smile. "Izzie, how's things going with Alex?"

"Really good. I mean, he's no Stewart from Cardinal, but..."

Rob raises his palm; salt from the peanuts sticks to his fingers. "Don't let her distract you, Babe. Daisy, we want and need all the details of this man. There's something that doesn't add up."

"I agree. Is he married?"

"No, Daisy's not the type."

Izzie pouts her purple lips and nods slowly. "It would explain things. The last-minute trips away, the secrecy, reluctance to tell us."

The two of them pout and nod their heads. Clearly deciding they're on the right track. I exhale loudly.

"He's not married." I avoid their eyes and look around the pub. The pale yellow walls, dotted with prints and historical photos of Cockermouth giving the impression of being a sophisticated place. I've been coming here since I was fifteen. Hidden behind the photos are scrawls of graffiti and fixtures from long gone dartboards. In places, the old green paint shows through, reminding customers it used to be an Irish bar welcoming any and all underage drinkers bold enough to swagger up to the bar and ask for half a pint of snakebite.

The clatter of pool from the adjoining room, the clinking of glasses and empty bottles drift into my ears. Happy chatter drowns out the jukebox playing The Killers.

"Can you prove he's not married?" Izzie asks and nudges at her empty wine glass, meaning I should drink up and buy another round. Even though she definitely hasn't paid for anything tonight.

"Is my word not enough?" My hands sliding beneath my thighs. Nails pushing upwards.

"What's his name? I'm going to stalk him on social media and find out the truth."

You already do, Iz, I say internally.

"Can you not just respect my privacy at the minute?

It's complicated–"

"Because of his wife?"

"Shit, has he got kids?" Rob asks. His stunned face momentarily being replaced by a dashing smile to a passing man in tartan trousers and high polished black boots.

"No," I snap.

"Is he an escort that you've fallen in love with? Were you his escort?"

"What the fuck, Rob?"

He shrugs and flicks his bright yellow fringe. "It's a good earner, and you're always saving your money, counting pence as well as pounds."

"Babe, you need to stop watching trashy American dramas," I say. Ignoring the fact that Stewart had a few years of using prostitutes. That was a conversation I never thought I'd have. Especially not with my boyfriend. The memory plays out in my mind as Rob gives Izzie the latest update on some trashy reality lifestyle show he's been avidly watching.

"Daisy, Sweetheart, I don't want to be a dick, but please don't smoke in the car. Des will kill me."

I clicked the lighter and slowly turned to face him. Stewart placed a brief touch against my thigh. I pulled the unlit smoke from my mouth and held it between my fingers. I crossed my arms and stared out of the window. I placed the cigarette back in my mouth, just to be difficult; clicked the lighter three separate times, noting how he inhaled sharply with each flicker of the flame.

I caught Des' eyes in the rear view mirror, and I returned the lighter and cigarette back to my handbag. I kicked at my handbag in frustration. Neither of us had been bold enough to mention the story in the papers that day about Stewart's alleged liaisons with sex workers. But the way he avoided my eyes told me it was true. "You didn't think you should tell me that you have a preference for using prostitutes?"

"Don't—" he started, then stretched a hand to soothe my thigh. "Hear me out before you—"

"You failed to tell me that you use hookers for your own sexual gratification," I hissed loudly at him.

"Please, Daisy, let me just—"

"Charm your way out of this one?"

Stewart scratched at his chin and I knew he wanted a smoke. He turned his head to me, then back to the road. Ignoring Des clearing his throat. Maybe I shouldn't have started that conversation when we had company and en route back to the flat, but I couldn't wait any longer. "You know the whole sex-in-public scandal from years ago. I accept responsibility for it, yet know it wasn't my greatest moment. I'm not playing the victim, but the press tore me apart. It's taken a lot to try and claw back a half-decent reputation. Anyway, the whole mistake prompted me to make a decision to stop shagging round."

I shook my head. Not that I especially wanted to picture Stewart in bed with anyone else, but I didn't believe him. "I've seen you with so many different women in the press," I countered.

"Publicity stunts," he shrugged, like it was the most normal thing in the world. "You know the deal with Ella. It's all fake."

"You can't have turned down every woman who crosses your path. You were such an outrageous flirt that night I met you."

"That's not all on me, Daisy." Stewart's hand reached

across the middle seat of the car, and squeezed against my thigh. "Sometimes, beautiful florists get my attention."

"Or sex workers? Are we in the same bracket? Is that what you look for in one; must like flowers, be sarcastic, not be impressed by apparent celebrity status?" My guard was raised, like Ackbar when he chases the solitary blackbird in the garden. I was poised for attack. Ready to eradicate Stewart from my life, leaving me alone to prowl in my own domain once more.

"No, fuck no. Sweetheart, let me explain. Instead of pointless one-night stands, I had a few dalliances with prostitutes."

"A few?"

"I didn't keep count, truth be told."

The city went by in a buzz of busyness and everyday life. Normal; people going to work, shopping, students loitering slowly to their lectures. Tourists snapping photos. Like I wasn't having a surreal conversation with my boyfriend about paying for sex.

My throat dried like soil surrounding the fern plants in the shop I always forgot to water. "Of course I wouldn't be enough."

"Daisy, Baby—you are enough. This was before you. It was easier, less complicated if sex was a transaction."

"And paying for sex is better than being with any and every woman because?"

"They won't sell their stories."

"Surely that's still a risk, though, especially in your mad world of celebrity?"

"I more than covered their fee."

Huh. I imagined he did. I wondered what the going rate was. Where he first met them, if they went to his flat.

If everyone knew. Shit, did everyone on the team think I was a prostitute? Has Des driven him to meet them?

"Do you still see them?"

"No, I don't do it anymore, Daisy. I wouldn't do that to you."

"When did you last see them? Use them? I'm not well versed in the correct terminology here."

If this were a plant or anything related to horticulture, I'd be fine. But sex workers, well, it was a field I never thought I'd have to sow.

"Last year, December. Pat threw a party at a hotel. I had another stupid argument with my brother. I got drunk. The usual."

"Your usual, maybe."

The silence echoed around the car as we parked, and Des climbed out to take a well timed call. Stewart closed his eyes and his head dropped towards his chest.

I couldn't say I was angry with him or even disappointed, just confused. In all honesty, what more did I expect from a bona fide pop star? Plus, I knew all about his sexual rendezvous before. Hell, who didn't? Now that I considered it, Ella was the only woman he'd been reportedly with since the whole sex-in-public incident. Aside from the 'mysterious blonde,' i.e., me, who has not yet been identified by the press and fans. Though I suspected the Cardinal fans were getting closer, nothing gets past teenagers.

I placed my hands on his jaw and tilted his head up, making his eyes meet mine.

"Did you think I was a prostitute on sight?"

I knew I shouldn't judge these women, but I was pretty

certain my floral dresses and boots were not the usual attire. Vivian in *Pretty Woman* sure as hell wouldn't raid my wardrobe.

Stewart looked aghast and shook his head. "No. Daisy, that's not how it works. It was a conscious choice on my part and the women. They're not bad people, and hopefully you know I'm not a bad person. I'm not ashamed of what I did, but I wanted more. I want more than that now, Sweetheart. There was just something about you, a florist called Daisy."

"You mean I didn't fall for your charms?"

He laughed, the sound bouncing off the seats of the car. His dark brown fringe danced against his eyelashes. "You totally did. Don't try and deny it. But you were so reluctant about it."

I placed my palms against his face and pulled him gently to look at me. I frowned at him a little and sighed. "You don't do it anymore? The whole paying sex workers and shit? Or—I mean, if that's what you want, I can't tell you what to do, I—"

The words tumbled over one another as they tried to arrange themselves into coherent sentences. I bit my lip to stop the muddled questions. I couldn't change the past, his past, but I was pretty certain I couldn't, wouldn't cope with him still sleeping around, a paid transaction or not.

"No, Daisy. I swear it. I don't ever want or need anyone but you," Stewart implored, his eyes never leaving mine, his whole body turned towards me, his hands holding my shoulders.

"I believe you, Stewart." I shrugged and smiled, and kissed his pouting lips.

What more could I say? Did I have any right to judge

Stewart on previous actions that didn't include or involve me? I already knew he'd slept around a lot before we met. Did it really matter if he paid for it or not? Maybe I was ridiculously naive, but I did believe him. Still do. I stroked at his beard and placed my forehead against his. He snuffled as my hair tickled his nose. Cute.

"Just you, just me, Daisy." Stewart smiled shyly.

I nodded. Repeated the phrase back to him as a sigh of contentment came from deep within my soul. It broke through the protective walls around my heart, and, if it were visible, would take on the shape of love hearts as it escaped my mouth. Ugh, I disgusted myself. Almost.

We moved forward from it. The past is, after all, something neither of us can change.

"You're such an enigma. Is it not exhausting keeping everything inside?" Izzie says, bringing me back to the present, picking up her phone again, bored of not being the centre of attention. She'll mention Sophia soon and bring the focus back to her. My shoulders slump at the thought. She's still grieving; I shouldn't be too harsh on her.

"I struggle to let people in, Iz. You know this."

"But I'm your best friend. You should tell me everything. It's part and parcel of being female friends. We share and overshare."

Now I'm her best friend, but in everyday life I'm usually referred to as the 'oldest' or 'childhood' friend. Despite me always referring to Izzie as my best friend, it's not always an equally balanced relationship. I tend to ignore it most of the time. She's usually around; that's enough.

"I know more about Rob's sex life than yours," she continues.

"Everyone knows about Rob's sex life. He has no filter." I smile and finish my drink, but make no move to depart towards the bar. I've got an early start tomorrow, heading up to Edinburgh to spend the weekend with Stewart, Eddie and Ash.

"I'm like a butterfly. I want everyone to enjoy me! You're more like a snail, Daisy," Rob says seriously as Izzie snorts into her wine glass, draining the last few dregs.

"Thanks, Babe..."

Rob places a hand on my shoulder. "Hard exterior shell, keeps anything and anyone out. Protecting yourself from harm,"

"And fun," Izzie sneers, which I ignore.

"But crack through the shell and..."

"I'm a slug?" I ask, not liking one bit how this metaphor is panning out. "Prime prey for all predators. Ugly and slimy," I continue. The Killers changes to heavy drum and bass from the speakers, fitting as it matches my headache.

"No, no ..."

"Snail shells are pretty, Babe," Izzie says patronisingly.

I place my hands on my hips and my mouth drops open. I remember how I felt up at the wee cottage; fitting in with the Cardinal unit almost instantly, like interwoven alyssum flowers. With Izzie, I'm a nettle in amongst striking foxgloves. I glance at her, recalling how poisonous foxgloves are.

"I'm alright to look at but have a shit personality?"

"I didn't say that," Izzie mumbles. "You have a nice personality, if a bit boring."

"Alright, Iz. Don't take it too far. Daisy's gorgeous."

Izzie rolls her eyes. I'm not a slug, but I'm nowhere

near Izzie's gothic beauty of a black swallowtail butterfly. Impressive, beautiful and even secretes a scent like pineapple. Rob, I would say, is more like a queen bee. Wants everyone to do the hard work while he preens and takes charge. Like a busy bee, though, he flits from man to man, party to party, making everyone smile and welcomed. Dazzled by his bright stripes.

"When do I ever take things too far?"

"All the time. You're mean to Daisy." Rob flicks his fringe from his hydrangea blue eyes.

"She knows I'm kidding."

Rob and I ignore her and exchange a fleeting glance.

Izzie half glances at me before returning to her phone. "Babe, you're always so serious. It's boring. Lighten up."

Rob places a hand on my shoulder. "What does the boyfriend think of you?"

"Well, I'd like to hope he at least likes me." I ignore a snort from Izzie. At this rate I'm going to flip the table and yell at her that I'm shagging Stewart from Cardinal, and he does find me attractive and not at all boring, especially in bed, so she can stick that on the fangirl bonfire and light it with a fucking match. Fuck the Force, I need to go to bed. Lack of a routine and even less sleep but with still the same number of hours at work is catching up with me. Why did I agree to get the early train tomorrow too? I have to catch a bus to Penrith at half seven.

"He must have broken through your spiral shell. It's good that you're letting someone in."

"Either that or he's damn good in bed. Or perhaps you are," Izzie adds.

She is on form tonight. I usually laugh along when I'm the butt of jokes. But there's only so much one person can take. Perhaps she views me as lower than a slug; wild parsnip fronds on which her butterfly eggs are laid, caterpillars grow, chrysalis formed in striking stripes, before she's done with me and I'm nothing more than a stepping stone so she can flutter into the sunlight. Leaving me in the shade, nothing more than a common weed.

"Actually, we have so much in common. It's scary at times." I smile tightly.

"Is he a geek like you?"

"If you mean does he appreciate the cinematic genius that is Star Wars, then yes, he does." I pick up my glass, remember it's empty, then slam it onto the table. Half of me wishes it would break so I could press a sharp edge into my leg to relieve some tension. "I'm going home."

"Daisy, don't," Rob pleads.

"Why not? So I can sit here and have you two pull apart my looks, personality and relationship? No, thank you."

"Babe, come on. We're sorry, aren't we, Izzie?"

"I don't really think we need to apologise. She's overreacting, taking things too seriously."

"Night, guys," I say with an air of defeat as I push my chair out and weave out of the pub.

I slam my bedroom door closed and push my bookcase behind it. I want to be left alone. Rob might tumble into my room later, drunk and giggling or apologetic and tearful. I can't bear to deal with either.

I lie on my bed, prop the phone on my pillow and video call Stewart. He takes an age to answer, and I wonder if he's actually on stage or in interviews. I check the diary, nope. He's scheduled to be in the studio, so perhaps he's doing his vocals.

He answers with a blinding smile and sunglasses on. "A florist called Daisy! Hi Baby!"

"Why are you wearing sunglasses inside at half ten at night? You look like a twat."

He pulls the shades off and ruffles his dark hair. "Sometimes you can just say hello. You don't have to jump straight to an insult."

"Hey you," I smile, sorting out my fringe after a glance at myself on the screen. "How's things?"

"Good, just laying down the brass, which really gives the album a lift." He smiles.

Most of the time, I have no idea what Stewart is on about in terms of productions and music, yet his smile and passion for it are infectious.

"How are you, Sweetheart?"

"Izzie and Rob are being bitches. Or maybe I'm just exhausted and taking it the wrong way." I rub my forehead. Then clench my fists, revelling in the pain my nails cause on my palms.

"Aww, Sweetheart, I'm sorry. What did they say?"

I shrug, wanting to dismiss my own feelings and validation, as always. It's easier to squash them down. "I'm boring, too serious, no fun..."

He laughs a little. "Do they even know you?"

"Not as well as you, obviously. Maybe they're right."

"They're not."

"Izzie's more fun. Prettier," I say with a pout. A cloud of anxiety covering my brain.

"She has far superior taste in music than you, that's for sure." He chuckles. I ignore his attempt at humour, not even saying he's in a boyband like I usually do.

“Izzie’s probably better suited to you. Always on hand to give you an ego boost as well as your record sales.”

“Nah, she’s not my type.” He shakes his head, then pushes Patrick out of the screen, telling him to fuck off and go record his vocals.

“She is, though, isn’t she? Naomi was a goth.” I shrug, referring to Stewart’s ex before the sex in public scandal broke them up.

“Naomi dressed like it was always Halloween. She wasn’t a goth like Izzie.”

“Compared them much?” I sneer. Fuck. He can’t win. Clearly I’m in dire need of a long sleep.

“You’re my type, Daisy. I only want you, Sweetheart.”

“Who would you have picked? If Izzie had been with me at the afterparty?”

“What after—” Stewart blinks, the moving shadows and lights dancing across his frowning face as he walks down a long corridor lined with shiny gold discs. “For real, Daisy? You’re asking me if I would’ve shagged your best pal?”

“Brett wanted to date Iz over me. I was second choice,” I state, as if it’s a justification. Butterfly over a snail. Surely it’s not a close competition.

“You are so enough, more than I could ever want. More than I deserve.”

My heart skips a beat at Stewart’s words. As does every other part of me.

“Every single fucking time, Daisy. It’s you.”

“You have to say that, though, we're in a relationship.”

A smile covers his face. “Have you finally admitted we’re in a serious relationship?”

“Only because I’m sick of you asking me about it.”

"Wee menace. Actually, Sweetheart, I choose to be honest with you because we're in a relationship. And because—"

Stewart pauses, licks his lips and his eyelid flickers. I sigh. Wish he was here so I could scratch at his beard, see him preen like a kitten beneath my touch.

"Because?" I prompt.

"Because there's something about you, about us." He smiles, and I believe him. I smile properly for the first time tonight. "Now I suggest you go and sleep off this day, leave it all behind."

I yawn. "I will, sorry."

"You don't need to apologise."

"I'll see you tomorrow, yeah?"

"Yep. Twelve at The Dome. Do you need Des to pick you up, Baby?"

I laugh a little. "No thanks. I am capable of making my way from the station to the hotel."

"It's not a hotel, we're staying somewhere else. It's a bar and restaurant."

"Why are we not staying at your flat?"

He scrubs a hand over his heavy beard. "Because Pat's got a date, and trust me, you want to be as far away from his bedroom as possible when he has a man over."

I feel the weight of the night lifting from my shoulders at the sound of his laugh.

"Go get yourself some sleep, Sweetheart. I can't wait to see you."

"I will. Can't wait to see you either."

"You know, Izzie has one huge flaw," Stewart continues.

Just one. Shit. It's the fan and stalker thing, isn't it? I know he'd never date a fan. If it wasn't for that fact, then—

"She's not you."

17

I'm late. Very late. I flick my wrist over to look at my watch, the Spring sun glints off the glass. I falter, seeing I'm ninety minutes late. Stewart, Eddie and Ash have surely already eaten lunch.

I run up the stone steps leading to the imposing building. The pillars on the outside wider than oak trees in the park back home. My heels clack on the tiled floor, my suitcase clattering behind me. The tiles are so smooth and polished they could be slabs of ice.

Approaching the desk, I look through the open doors and gasp at the bar. Standing tall and proud are the biggest floral arrangements I've ever seen. The flowers in hues of pinks, purples and blues; and the chandelier that is so magnetising I feel it could hold Jedi powers, are hard to tear my eyes away from.

"Madam, I'll place your suitcase behind the desk here while you attend your luncheon," the suited and booted man informs me with a slight bow.

"I can take it up with me; it's fine," I say dismissively, not really looking at him, still focused on the blooms.

"No, we insist, madam. You don't want it to get in the way," the man says, more emphasis on each word as the sentence flows from his lips.

Oh. He means my blue and neon pink leopard print suitcase will ruin the ambiance of the Georgian tea room, where my "superstar" boyfriend and bandmate are waiting for me. Right. Fine.

I smile tightly, slamming down the handle and leaving it behind the biggest desk I've ever seen. My embarrassment hidden by anger. Who takes a suitcase to afternoon tea anyway? I am an idiot.

The plush carpet of the stairs welcomes my steps, almost caressing my shoes into the deep pile. I can't take my eyes off the shining chandelier that hangs like a collection of icicles from the ceiling. It reminds me of The Glass Menagerie studied at school. Crystal shapes glisten in highly polished rainbow hues. The stairs wrap around it like presents surrounding a Christmas tree.

Well, this is a step or hundred away from soup and a sandwich at the dairy farm on the outskirts of Cockermouth, isn't it?

Ash waves at me manically. Stewart and Eddie turn around. It's strange to see the two of them (and Ash) missing a member. Patrick is on a date, apparently shrouded in secrecy, yet knowing how much they all talk, I imagine he'll be sharing details as readily as Rob does with all his sexual conquests.

The three of them are tucked into a corner, almost hidden behind a pillar topped with a marble bust. Eddie wearing a trilby hat hiding his neon orange hair looks almost smart. Ash's brown hair is twisted up into a seemingly effortless chignon. My blonde waves rest against a floral dress; were I edgy enough, I would give off 90s grunge vibes. After the delayed train and the power walk from the station, I certainly have the dishevelled look of a woman who gives zero fucks. Yet teamed with my heeled stiletto boots and cardigan Nan knitted, I am nowhere near looking like Courtney Love. Great. Hardly the look that blends in with the fellow afternoon tea diners. Shit. I should have taken my cardigan off. Possibly bought a blazer en route.

Stewart smiles and stands up, and I forget about looking out of place. My heart jumps, and my insides shiver wonderfully. Fuck he's beautiful. His strong set shoulders and neck, the pale skin that stretches from his scruff of a beard. Smells like lavender, tastes like excitement and happiness, and strangely, marshmallows. I don't know why. I'd quite like to wrap my thighs around it and—*oh, would I?* That's new and highly inappropriate. And weird. Now I have a thing about necks. What does this man do to me?

He bumps at the table, then tries to right a silver pot of sugar cubes. A waiter glides in like a magician and clears the mess of sparkling sugar granules. Stewart wraps his arms around me as I reach the table.

"A florist called Daisy! Missed you, Sweetheart."

"Hey you. How many times? Just Daisy is fine, or are you hinting I should refer to you as Stewart from Cardinal on greeting?"

"Nope." He kisses me far too deeply and open-mouthed than I ever would have let Brett do in public. But then, Stewart Burns is in a different league to my ex.

"Alright, pal. Don't give the game away," Eddie says, his eyes rolling.

"No one cares," Ash counters as I step round the table and give them both a hug.

"The fans will care."

"I doubt your fans' pocket money can stretch to eating here," I reply, sitting down.

Stewart winks a delphinium blue eye at me. "Wee menace."

"So sorry I was late. I got lost getting out of the station; there's like twenty platforms and several exits."

"Did you walk from the station?" he asks, the three of them looking at me like I announced I arrived on a spaceship.

"Yes. Not all of us get driven around by Des, you know."

Ash laughs loudly. "Eddie claimed he was starving, sorry he couldn't wait Hen. Here, have a coffee. Love that dress." Ash starts her usual high-pitched yet friendly barrage of questions and comments.

Stewart shuffles his chair close to mine, placing his arm around my shoulders.

A waitress appears and places two stands of food in miniature in front of Stewart and me.

"Have you not eaten?" I ask, noting how Eddie has almost nothing left on his tiered stand.

"Stew insisted he wait for you, Daisy," Eddie says as he pours more champagne for him and Ash.

I place a hand on Stewart's thigh. "You didn't have to. It was my fault for being late."

"Charmer like Stewart, course he did."

Stewart's phone rings. People at the tables near to us scowl at the tinkling tune. He shrugs an award-winning grin at them and apologises. Of course, they melt under his smile. Charmer.

"Is that Jed?" Eddie asks through a mouthful of sandwich. He's eaten two from Ash's plate and a scone since I've arrived.

"Nah, just Ella."

I shake my head and fiddle with my limp waves on my shoulders.

"Call you a lot, does she?" I say with a sneer I can't quite disguise. Envy is not an attractive attribute.

"Jealous?" he asks with a smile that is usually charming, but my envy contorts it to being a smug smirk. Of course I'm jealous. Ella Egan is a model; stunningly beautiful, and pretending to date my boyfriend. I've poured over photos of Ella, she's petite with endless legs. Thighs as wide as her knees. Mind you, she probably hasn't eaten a carb since hitting puberty. She's gorgeous. Like a real life Disney princess, I expect woodland animals sing when she first wakes up.

"Yes," I answer honestly.

The directness and lack of following sarcastic comment shocks him. The smile slides from his face and he looks confused.

"Baby, I've told you, she's just a friend."

"You'd be jealous if I was pretending to date Ronan Keating," I counter.

"The difference is that I do not want to sleep with or date Ella, whereas you, Daisy—"

"Every woman wants to sleep with Ronan Keating," Ash cuts in. We nod at each other in understanding.

Stewart's phone rings again but he silences it almost instantly.

"Ella's at the event tonight at the gallery," he says casually, fiddling with the collar on his oversized shirt.

I take a drink of coffee, then the synapses in my head join, realising what his statement means. My hands shake, placing the cup down on the saucer.

"So you've got to attend an event with Ella, your fake girlfriend when your actual girlfriend is visiting?" I ask.

He blushes almost as bright as the raspberry on his cake. "I told you I had to quickly pop into a gallery tonight."

"For work."

"This is work."

Anxiety and anger creep into my veins. I try to breathe deeply to quell it. Instead, I drain the glass of wine. It doesn't help.

"You didn't tell me you'd be with a supermodel."

"It's still just work; a few photos then I'll be free for the rest of the weekend. You will have my full attention, Baby."

"Once you've given your attention to Ella?" I sneer.

"It's not real, Daisy."

"You're just friends with her?" I've already asked this countless times. But I can't help it; the whole fake relationship thing is a world away from my small town life. And the press, even fans, are convinced Stewart and Ella are dating for real. They must put on a powerfully persuasive show.

"Yep."

"Ella's desperate to get you into bed, though," Eddie says, trying to balance a spoon behind his ear, nestled in his bright orange hair, after being asked to remove his hat.

"Who isn't?" Stewart asks with a wink.

"Don't be a dick," I roll my eyes.

"I don't see Ella like that, never have." Stewart shakes his head at me and tops up his coffee cup, then mine.

I don't miss the flicker of his eyelid. He glances across the table at Eddie before looking back at me. My teeth push together as I hold his eye contact. He shuffles on his seat and rubs a hand over his beard.

"Once, years ago, I slept with her."

Honestly, I'm not surprised; even Rob would struggle to turn her down. And the last time he went near a vagina was twenty-six years ago when he was born. But I wish I'd known prior to today. Hours before my boyfriend is doing a publicity stunt with Ella and her perfect endless legs.

"Ella's pissed she won't get as many column inches when you two go public. Hence her trying to get her claws into Stew before it's too late," Ash clarifies, trying to diffuse the situation, before pouring everyone another coffee from a shiny silver pot.

The mere thought of people—strangers—reporting and reading about me fills me with dread. Sometimes it gathers in my lungs and I struggle to breathe, yet a few cuts into my skin with a blade eases the anxiety.

"It is too late," Stewart replies, holding my hand. "Just you, just me."

I half listen to their quiet chatter overlapping, but mainly stare at the panelled ceiling or out of the window. I look past the slate grey and mustard curtains, made from so much material I feel they could cover the entirety of Cumbria. The street below is an eclectic mix of buildings, new and old—classic old buildings ornately decorated, history spilling from the stonework, nestled amongst glass-fronted shops, all neon signs and radiating success and temptation. People bustle by and mingle on the wide pavements. Trees, and patches of green, I noticed on the way from the station seem to pop up often, despite being in the middle of a capital city. Though it doesn't quite cancel out the masses of cars and buses, or indeed the noise they cause.

Stewart places a hand on my thigh. "You ok, Sweetheart? You're quiet."

"I'm sorry." I send them all a genuine smile. "I can't stop looking out of the window. Edinburgh is so pretty. It doesn't feel like a city, does it?"

"You not been before?" Ash asks.

"In January, but my exploration was cut short by my attendance at a gig," I say with a playful roll of my eyes as I stroke a palm on Stewart's leg, who, of course, calls me a menace.

"We can go to the castle later if you like?" Stewart offers, spreading jam on the last of his scone.

Ash waves her hand dismissively at him. "Don't waste time at the castle. We can go shopping—"

"Yep, Ash, Harvey Nicks is the cultural highlight of Scotland's capital."

"Go to the castle, Stew. I'll take one for the team and go shopping," Eddie says, leaning over for the last of Stewart's cakes.

"Shall we meet you back here in the bar? Grab a drink then head to the gallery?" Stewart asks as we both stand up and he helps me into my jacket.

"Do we all have to go?" Ash asks, mumbling that she has no interest in art galleries or museums.

"Nah, I'll be a half-hour; photos, wee interview then free."

"We'll wait at the bar," Eddie decides for us all. I must admit I'm conflicted about it. I'm relieved I don't have to face Ella in all her perfect glory, yet desperately want to see her in the flesh. Even if it will spark off a spiral of self-loathing and comparisons I'll never get over. Ash seems to be able to read my mind.

"Trust me, Hen, Ella's like a pretty butterfly but has an acid tongue like a wasps sting."

"Ash, that was quite poetic for you," Eddie nods at her, impressed.

"Heard Stew and Pat say it millions of times."

"She's pretty, is she?" I ask, wondering how he's going to charm his way out of that.

"I said she masquerades herself as a dainty butterfly but is more akin to a wasp, actually. I'll let you know when we're done, Eddie. I've gotta head back to the flat and pick my stuff up, drop our bags off at the hotel," Stewart replies with a nod and a ruffle of his dark hair.

"We'll see youse two later, after you've taken full advantage of that hotel room, no doubt," Eddie says with an eyebrow raise, closely followed by a sharp nudge in the ribs from Ash, which makes his ears burn red again. He places his hat over his neon orange hair. I laugh quietly. I like how honest they are with each other; it shows their closeness.

"Due to that comment, which I would have expected from Pat, not you, you're paying."

"The fuck?"

"I'll get drinks tonight." Stewart picks up his jacket and slides his arms in.

Eddie laughs. "You'll regret that, pal."

Stewart fastens his denim jacket that smells of soothing lavender and scrolls on his phone to book both a taxi and tickets for the castle.

"After shopping with Ash, you'll be too tired to try and fleece me for expensive whisky."

***

Hours later, after a visit to Stewart's flat and then a wander around Edinburgh castle, I'm back at The Dome. As I'm applying my lip gloss, hitching the hem of the dress down as low as it will go, I notice Stewart's phone is still in my bag. I clutch it in my hand and feel my heart melt, seeing I'm his background. The romantic sap.

Squeezing through a newly assembled throng of people in the grand foyer of the bar, I open the doors and stop, as if the cool spring air has frozen me in ice.

The breaths seep out of me in shallow pants. Panic and anxiety flood through my veins, gaining speed and more traction until it spirals in my head and body, replacing all vital organs with gaping holes of redundancy. My eyes glaze over with insecure tears.

I'm not into the whole glamorous world of celebrity, unless it's Beyonce and Jay-Z; but even I would stop dead in the newsagents to look at photos of Stewart and Ella hand in hand, as will everyone who sees them gracing the front of magazines, newspapers and gossip sites.

The lights shine off her dress, not a hair out of place. Beauty that can never be achieved with just makeup, the epitome of figure goals. Ella is flawless. Stewart, of course, looks ruggedly attractive, scruffy in a sexy kind of way. Dark hair too long to be tamed, beard too heavy for him ever be branded as clean cut. Their smiles match, heads and bodies angled towards one another. Talk about couple goals. Were it real. Yet it does look so real. I almost believe it myself.

Ash tugs on my arm and pulls me away from the flashing cameras and steps of The Dome.

“Come on; you need a drink.” She loops her arm into mine, and I reluctantly turn my head from watching Stewart and Ella pretending to be a happy couple.

“He needs his phone,” I say pathetically, my eyes leaking with fat salty tears.

Ash plucks it from my shaking hands and taps a man in a red t-shirt on the shoulder, a headpiece looped around his head. “Harry, give this to Stew. Cheers, pal,” Ash pulls me into a hug, her deep brown hair tickling my face. “It’s all fake, Daisy. Stewart’s crazy about you. Don’t forget it.”

I observe his posture and know how Stewart holds himself; right now he looks stilted, taut, not relaxed at all. It is fake. I need to try and remember that.

18

"Why aren't you with Ella, Stewart?" I ask with a sneer as we sit in the back of the taxi. Flashing lights of passing cars dance in my head like we're still in the club we've just left.

Ash and I ordered every cocktail on the menu. The alcohol made me forget about seeing Ella Egan draped all over my boyfriend. I may be a little drunk. More than a little drunk. I wonder what Ella is like when she's drunk. Snippy and bitchy, or giggly and funny. I hope the former, yet that's probably wishful thinking. But— "She is beautiful."

Stewart flexes his fingers then wraps his hands around my wrists, gently. "How many times do I have to tell you this, Daisy? I don't want to be with Ella. I want to be with you."

"You make a gorgeous couple."

Absolute couple goals; were it real. I had to keep prompting Ash to remind me it was all fake. In the end she turned my phone off and tucked it away from the temptation of scrolling Cardinal update sites. The images of them, palms pressed together, his arm looped around her tiny waist, her hand on his chest; they're tattooed onto my eyelids.

"Maybe you owe it to her to date her for real. She'd let you buy her a catwalk or whatever. I won't let you buy me a florists."

Stewart ignores me for what feels like hours before sighing loudly.

"I offered to buy you a florists because chasing your dreams is fucking hard. We all need help sometimes."

"Hey, do you play rugby?" I ask, suddenly changing the subject.

"Like I have time for sports, Sweetheart." He laughs. The lights from outside making his eyelashes cast shadows on his cheeks.

"Have you played it?" I draw flowers in the condensation of the taxi windows with my fingertip.

"Not since school."

"Rugby players are my usual type. You've seen Brett. Maybe we should end this now—"

"The fuck, Daisy?" He snaps at me; tension clouds the back of the taxi.

"I'll go find a rugby player, they're my usual type, you know? Not pretty boys in designer jeans. And you can go be with Ella. Driver! To Murrayfield!" I shout, banging the plastic partition.

Stewart leans forwards, speaks in hushed tones to the driver then leans back.

"So this is about Ella, not us?" he asks, shoulders relaxing a little as he scrubs a hand over his beard.

"It's about me not being good enough."

Stewart places his fingers on my lips. I bite at them a little bit. "Menace. You're drunk and talking shit, Daisy. But, just in case you remember any of this the morn; you are loved, wanted, needed. If you want my help in any way, you've got it."

My head feels heavy, and I rest against Stewart's shoulder. See the cigarette box poking from his pocket and pull it out. I rip off the lid and tear it into confetti-like pieces. My gaze drifts to my handbag, where my floristry tools are wrapped in a canvas holder. I long to feel the cool blade against my skin.

"Do you want to help everyone? Is it your mission in life? To be a hero?" I ask, closing my eyes to stop picturing the silver of my floristry knife dotted in bright red smears of blood.

"Is your mission in life to be as stubbornly independent as possible?"

"People will expect you to buy me a shop, a whole ready-made business," I say, fearing I may be slurring a little. Attractive.

"Right," he sighs and mumbles about me drinking way too much. "Because you always do what people tell you to do."

"The fans and shit, they'll be all, 'Why do you need anything else, Daisy? Why have a shop to run when you're dating Stewart from Cardinal?' Should you be enough for me? Do you replace my goals?"

"No, that's not you, Sweetheart. You long to be your own boss. You talk about it all the time."

Some people don't understand the desire to have a business of my own. But the day I open my own florists, with '*Daisy Gordon—proprietor*' as the byline, I'll know I've made it, that I'm good enough.

"I don't want you to buy me a florists. Then I'd be tied to you forever," I spit out.

"Really nice words, Daisy. I'll treasure them for the

rest of my days," Stewart mutters, loud enough for the sarcasm to be obvious. He removes his hand from mine and crosses his arms.

I should apologise.

I don't.

"Who helped you achieve your dreams?" I ask, minutes, seconds, maybe hours later. Time seems to jump in my mind. All I know is we're back at the hotel and the spiral black and white tiled stairs up to our room are endless, but Stewart didn't think the motion of the lift would help in any way.

"My talent spoke for itself," he laughs, more than a hint of bravado in his tone.

"Twat."

"Pat, mainly," he replies seriously, opening the hotel bedroom door.

I stagger towards the sofa and flop down as he hands me a glass of water. It churns in my stomach. He throws his jacket over a chair and ruffles his already messy hair.

"Things were shit at home when I was a teen, worse than I made it out to be. It came to a head one night in a massive row. I went to Pat's house after my parents kicked me out."

"Did they really kick you out just because you didn't want to be a baker?"

He nods, eyelid flickering as he peels open a packet of fruit pastilles.

"It was a culmination of things, but, yep. I didn't think I had any other option but to call it quits. I had a black bag full of my meagre belongings and a guitar in my hand.

Told Pat he could have them. Couldn't see what else to do except jump off the bridge."

"Stewart—" I start as he sits on the small sofa with me. The sweets lie forgotten on the table. He places a palm on my thigh and traces his fingers along my tattoos. It's like on some level he knows about my secret of self-harming.

"What happened?" I ask, my head pounding, nausea rising in my stomach.

"Pat was waiting for me at the bridge. I still don't know how he knew my plan."

"Fate? Is that why you believe in it?" I really am drunk if I'm choosing fate over a coincidence or rational explanation.

"Maybe. Pat said, 'Mum's made up the spare room; it's yours. Get in, I need to copy your homework, you nerd.'"

A smile tugs at his lips fleetingly. I laugh, then realise I'm crying and wipe my cheeks. I shuffle over, sit on his knees and place my chin on his shoulder. His hands smooth up and down my back, the sequins on my dress rattling under his palms. The touch is heavier, more pronounced than it was against Ella earlier.

"Which bridge?" I ask.

"Near my flat. I'll take you there. It'll replace a bad memory with a good one,"

"You're such a sap," I chide playfully with a kiss on his cheeks. "Do Eddie and Ash know? Does Ella know?" I ask, pulling back, smoothing his fringe from his face.

"Eddie and Ash do. And the team, as I had therapy when Cardinal got signed. Ella doesn't. Why would I have told her? We're not close. Pat, Eddie and Ash are my best friends, they've become my family. You're my girlfriend, and despite you saying the opposite all fucking night, I want and need you in my life."

"I'm so small town," I repeat for the millionth time today.

I tear a cardboard coaster on the table into the neatest circles and squares I can manage.

"You're perfect for me. I'm fucking crazy about you, Sweetheart."

"You have low standards," I mumble.

Things blur. I can't tell what's real, what I'm saying or not saying; can hear my voice but can't distinguish if I'm talking out loud or just thinking thoughts that jump like fleas.

"I think I love you." Surely I don't voice that out loud.

"When you know for certain, I'll say it back, Daisy."

I rub at my forehead, feel both hot and cold and not in a good way. "I do know something, Stewart Christopher Burns." I stand up and grip onto the walls to help me move across the room, the carpet as soft as candy floss beneath my bare toes.

"We're on full names are we now?" He chuckles. "What do you know then, Daisy Gordon?"

"I'm definitely going to throw up," I announce as I all but fall into the bathroom.

I feel his hand on my back, and the other scoops my hair out of the way as I throw up in the bath. Yes, the bath. Classy.

"I know that red wine makes you horny, and gin-based cocktails make you both honest and sick."

"It's a good thing to know," I say, I'm sure I say, as I hug my knees to my chest on the floor. The cold tiles feel soothing against my clammy skin.

I also know, as if I didn't already, that Stewart Burns is a literal angel. I think I tell him so. He helps me out of my clothes, into a shower and washes my hair. He wraps me in the fluffiest towel, followed by the softest of dressing gowns. He sits me up in bed and pokes at my exhausted skin until I drain at least two glasses of water.

"I'm so sorry." I feel my eyes scratching closed as I rest my head on his chest. His skin smells of lavender even though he's been in the shower.

Stewart talks to me once I feel better, not a tactical chunder, but at least I'm sober now.

His lilting accent repeats information about investment plans and loans, but my mind is not clear enough to comprehend, or if I've imagined the whole one-sided conversation.

"Dreams are heavy. They can't always be shouldered alone. I am fortunate enough to be able to help you with a florists; the offer is there."

Offered he has, a few weeks ago. At first I thought he was joking about buying me a florists, and laughed right in his face. Then when realising he was serious, we had a huge fight that spiralled in several directions like a gardener's battle against ditch-weed. He hasn't mentioned it since. Until I brought it up earlier. I still don't know exactly why I did. I rest my head against his shoulder, feeling a little calmer. Though that may be because I've shredded the cardboard coaster to nothing but multicoloured dust.

"But if you help with a florists, it becomes yours too, not just mine. I need it to be just for me, done by me. If someone helps me, I'll feel I've failed," I admit, my eyes closing then jerking open. My head and body can't decide to fight off the alcohol with sleep or wakefulness.

"Baby, that's a fuck ton of pressure to put on your wee shoulders. It could be an investment."

As if that makes it better, being handed a blank cheque, rendering my hard work and own dreams useless. It would be like I'd made it off the back of someone else; him. I'd feel I'd owe Stewart more than just the repayments. Every shag or blowjob would feel like a reduction of the payment. And that's no way to be thinking of a relationship or investments.

A churn of anxiety raises its heavy head. Not being good enough to do it alone, it sneers at me, in time with my slightly panicked breaths. My nails push into my thighs.

Stewarts tell me I won't be a failure and would it be so bad if I had help. The city lights shining through the windows make me feel like I'm in a fairground. Maybe the last cocktail or three was a mistake.

I feel Stewart's hands on top of mine. "You're going to hurt yourself, Baby," he says as I awkwardly pull my hands away. I focus on the crescent shapes left on my thighs by my nails. I scoff. That was the point.

"Can you get me a hair thing, please?" I ask, changing the subject.

Stewart's voice floats across the room as he searches through my handbag. "You really shouldn't have taken these out with you, Sweetheart, even if they aren't your first murder weapon of choice," he smiles, lifting the wrapped floristry scissors and knife from my bag, and places them in my suitcase.

That's what you get for running late for the bus this morning, bringing floristry tools into a different country.

"Tell me about it. After seeing Ella and you, I had an urge to slice my leg completely off, never mind stopping at making cuts in my skin." My hand comically covers my mouth.

"Daisy? What are you saying? What?—" he gasps out in a mixture of question and statement.

Shit. My eyes fly open and I sit up, hoping I dreamt or imagined my confession. Stewart's ocean blue eyes are wide and full of concern, with a hint of shock. Well, I'm not drunk anymore.

If my stomach wasn't already empty, I'd throw up instantly. This is why I am usually the designated driver; my mouth starts running away with me before my brain engages after one too many drinks. At uni it resulted in arguments and fall outs, the odd smashing of glasses, not revelations about self-harming.

"Daisy?" Stewart says, approaching me.

Knowing he's watching but needing a distraction, I tear a sheet off the headed notepaper from the table. The paper makes a zipping sound as I pull it into strips. The noise settles my pounding heart a little, like ice-cold milk after a curry. Tearing paper, my therapeutic origami. Though sometimes it takes longer to clean up flakes of paper than it does cuts and blood.

"What are you saying?"

"I self-harm."

That's a sure-fire way to send him running for the fells. Stewart blinks at me. Here I go again, not being enough for someone by just being me.

"The tattoo on my thigh covers my self-harming scars," I say, swallowing thickly.

Stewart crouches down in front of me, his palm instantly going to my thigh, scarred with inks and healed yet raised cuts. "You mentioned self-harm the night we met."

"I thought I'd got away with that."

He pulls his hair before gently stroking my cheeks. "You still do it?"

"Occasionally."

Stewart looks horrified and bewildered. Clearly, he's never felt the need for self-harm and is struggling to grasp why I would intentionally hurt myself.

"It helps me. I feel grounded, in control, enough, when I do it."

"Does it not hurt, though?" His fingers don't follow the shape of the petals and stems, as they usually do, but of the raised scars that, until close inspection, remain buried beneath the colourful inked blooms.

"The focus is on the release, not pain."

"When did you start?"

"You know my fucked-up parents' story; mum left and I don't know who my dad is. I guess it's an expression, an extension of that abandonment. Small-town life was something I hated as a teen. I begged Nan and my mum to let me go to Spain."

I had an image of it being non-stop summer parties. Mum and I would be best friends, my big brother's friends would fancy me, and I'd have the freedom I could only long for in Cockermouth.

"Turned out mum didn't want me invading her sun-filled life with teenage drama. A rejection from a parent, you don't get over it."

"Daisy, I'm so sorry, Baby."

"The cuts are a release, something I can always control. They're a physical response to internal shit in my head." The slices in my pale skin with a razor blade have always been hidden from the world. Even now I know how long my skirts and dresses should be to hide the scars, or fresh wounds, depending on the state of my head.

"It eased off once I started flower arranging. I could manipulate the flowers, and it gave me a focus, a goal. When I was at uni, I got the scars covered over in colourful flowers. It matched the job I wanted to have and hid my biggest secret. Win-win."

"Thank you for telling me, Sweetheart."

"No one else knows. Not my Nan, Rob, Izzie, anyone. You can't tell anyone."

"I won't. Just you, just me." Stewart smiles. He kisses my forehead, his fringe dancing over his eyes, the shadow of his eyelashes lingering on his cheeks. He flicks off flakes of paper from my lap. "Is this a form of self-harm, Sweetheart?" he asks quietly.

"It's a coping mechanism. I can usually silence the thoughts of cutting with distraction. I fight against it more often than not, but that itch will always linger. Sometimes life and my head run away from me, and I turn to it."

Stewart grimaces, his face contorted in pain as if I've just dragged a knife across his own thigh. "The self-harm, that's why you like to stick to a plan."

"I like being in control."

"And don't like being told what to do, well, most of the time." He winks, and I laugh at him, hit him feebly, playfully on his chest. "It's shit that your mum didn't want you with her, Daisy."

I shrug, play it down. Dismiss it. I'd rather be kept awake by over-sharing and feeling sick than thoughts of mum, of me not being good enough.

"Thank fuck you didn't go." He throws an arm around my shoulder and laces our hands together. "Cardinal don't have a huge fanbase in Spain. It might have taken years longer for us to meet if you'd been living over there."

The stale alcohol, toxins still on my breath, in my bloodstream and the fact that he's so unapologetically romantic make me cry.

"What's wrong, Sweetheart?" he asks in a panic.

"You're just so romantic!"

Stewart exhales a laugh in relief that my tears don't mean anything more in-depth. "It's a curse, I know. I mean, I've got nothing on Cathy and Heathcliff, though, have I? *'I cannot live without my life! I cannot live without my soul!'*"

"Ugh, Stewart Christopher Burns, I hate you and your knowledge of Bronte."

"Funny, you said the exact opposite a few hours ago, Daisy Gordon."

Stewart and I climb into bed. He kisses the top of my head and squishes me close to him before we both shuffle down. He pulls the duvet to cover us and then reaches to turn off the lamp. The darkness makes my head and stomach feel physically a bit smoother.

"Daisy, my life is so unpredictable, my schedule is crazy, it's always full of unknowns."

"Don't I know it? Tonight you had a date with your fake girlfriend."

"I'm sorry. I should have told you about Ella."

Images of the two of them hand in hand flash across my closed eyelids. Even though she didn't see me, I imagine Ella flashing me a fake and smug grin. Raking her emerald eyes down my body before laughing at me, sneering at Stewart about his choice in a real girlfriend. Seeing her from a distance was bad enough; if I ever meet her face to face, I might melt into a puddle of anxiety, shimmering green with envy. She'll walk through me, my insecurity splashing at her crystal-embellished Jimmy Choo shoes. I shudder, then push my nails into my palms and wait for my heart rate to slow down.

"That she'd be at the event or that you'd shagged her?" I ask with more sharpness in my tone than I intended.

"Both."

"Will you sleep with her again? Do you want to?" I blurt out before stopping the words from escaping. My fingers trail across his chest, his ribs, making patterns. Noticing they're love hearts, I stop and place my hand flat against his skin.

"No," Stewart answers instantly, like a reflex. "I won't, Daisy."

"Just you and just me?" I ask in a whisper, hating how I need this constant reassurance. The image of my mother jumps into my head, fleetingly, as was her presence in my life.

"Yep. Always, Sweetheart." He kisses the top of my head. "I can't guarantee you a plan or set in stone schedules and timings. My life won't help with your need for control."

"I know. But I pick you."

"Are you sure? I couldn't bear it if I was the cause of you hurting yourself."

"I'm sure. I'll be ok, I promise." I place a kiss against his heart. I close my eyes and feel so relaxed. I could stay here with him forever.

"Why haven't you told Rob and Izzie about me yet?" he asks, fingers making patterns on my arms.

A siren blares past the hotel, drifting up from the city streets. I wait until it's faded out before replying. My shoulders tense, the relaxing feeling being chased away. I suddenly feel hot and peel off the crisp duvet.

"She—" never really listens to me, always wants to flip the conversation back to herself. Or Cardinal. And she probably wouldn't believe I was dating Stewart. But kill me on the off chance it might be true. She wouldn't even hear me out. My happiness wouldn't count for anything. It would be eradicated in honour of the girl code. A code that I don't even understand and certainly haven't followed. And in my alcohol-misted brain, I find I don't care about it or Izzie as much as I thought.

"She's got a new boyfriend, so I haven't seen her much," I reply instead.

"We could double date. You should sort that out."

I yawn and slot my bare legs over his. "Shh. Sing me to sleep with that pretty voice of yours."

He chuckles quietly, his fingers dancing up my arms. "You must still be very drunk if you're asking that, Sweetheart."

"Enjoy it while you can, Petal. I'm never drinking that much ever again."

19

How do I answer the phone to my secret boyfriend who I haven't seen for weeks due to his scheduling, and seemingly every couple in town wanting extravagant floral displays at their weddings? Should I answer with a questioning hello, even though I know it's him? Casual? Desperate? Swooning? Declaring instantly that I've missed him? Berate him for not calling sooner, even though the time difference between Cockermouth and LA has been a nightmare and not his fault? And the fact he lost his phone for a day and a half, which had him in a mild panic and he used Patrick's phone all day.

"Daisy, answer your phone!" Izzie's laughter echoes around the pub, where we're having an early lunch. Cutlery and the clinking of glasses overlap with chatter and the muffled commentary of the horse racing crackling through the TV speakers.

Should I just ignore it? Let him leave a message, or call back again later? I chuckle a little. He's the type who will ring straight back as soon as he hears the voicemail message kick in. No one ignores Stewart Burns. I feel my eyes roll, him and that damned ego that he likes to pretend is far more inflated than it actually is.

He hangs up before I can answer, and instantly a message and pouting selfie comes through.

'Found myself in Cockermouth and can't find my girlfriend. Can you send her my way?'

'Where are you?'

'The florists. Miss, you Baby.'

Of course, the girl code dictates that I should tell him no. I'm with my best friend. I am busy. Stewart and his demands should wait. Izzie and Stewart battle it out in my head and heart. Friend versus soulmate. I can never decide who should win.

My fingers tap out a reply before I can mull it over too much.

'Give me five minutes. I'll meet you there.'

"What's the matter with you?" Izzie asks, her green eyes narrowing.

"What?"

"You look stressed. And scared."

I exhale and start pulling apart the cardboard coaster. "Can I tell you something?"

She nods before looking at her phone and scrolling. I watch her, lips pouting then smiling as she taps on photos and comments on the screen. I love Izzie, but she never gives me her full attention.

"I've been doing some reading."

"Ugh, you always are. Can you not watch the film instead?"

I ignore her. "I've been reading about grief."

She laughs hollowly, her eyes flitting to mine for a second before her phone beeps again, drawing her back in. "Why?"

"Just to try and help you."

"I'm fine," she says, crossing her arms and looking somewhere behind my head.

"When we lose someone, we want to replace that loss. We search for something to fill the void they've left. Maybe it's something different, new, or it could be something that reminds us of that person."

"Right."

"Like, their favourite band," I add on, my cheeks matching the band name.

"Sophia's favourite band was Cardinal."

"Exactly!" I say with far too much enthusiasm. "They were never your favourite band, Iz. You listen to heavy metal, songs filled with rage,"

"I also listen to Cardinal. They're my favourite band, now."

"You are allowed to take a step away from Cardinal. It's ok to admit you like them to keep your sister's memory going. If it's not you, that's ok. Stewart isn't your type. Cardinal are about as far away from the other music you listen to as Star Wars is from Bridget Jones. What I'm saying is, you listen to them because of Sophia. You've become fixated on Cardinal and Sophia's favourite member as a way to remember her."

"I love that band."

"You must admit, they're not your usual genre."

Izzie folds her arms across her chest after flicking her raven locks over her shoulder. Even in the dingy light of the pub, it glistens like spilled diesel.

"When I lost my sister, Cardinal helped me through it. Their songs eased my pain a little. When I go and see them, and Stewart smiles, I think of Sophia, how happy she'd be to see him."

"So, technically, you don't feel as much for Stewart as you infer. Right?"

I despise myself for having a fizz of joy in my bones as she shrugs in response. Maybe she will be ok with me dating Stewart.

"When your mum rejected you for the second time, when she flat out refused to have you in Spain, what pulled you through that?"

Self-harm. Time. A lot of tears and wild nights out drinking myself into oblivion in the local park. But I know what she's getting at here.

"I started flower arranging."

"Did it save your life?"

I never wanted to end my life; I've never been suicidal. I was sad, angry, hurt, lost even. But to say flowers saved me is a slight misrepresentation.

"I'm not sure I'd go that far," I say cautiously.

"Stewart Burns saved my life."

Did he, though? I was with Izzie a lot after Sophia died. She was devastated, knee-deep in grief, but she never spoke about ending her life, and she was very extroverted in her grief.

"Are you still at your bereavement counselling? Have you spoken to them about separating yourself from Sophia's interests?" I ask, half changing the subject before she starts telling me outlines to her more recent fan fiction.

Izzie slaps her palms down on the table before folding them with finality across her chest. "I'm not talking about this anymore."

My phone rings, offering a welcomed conversation break.

"Why have you got a photo of Stewart from Cardinal on your phone?" Izzie snatches the phone from the table.

Shit. Shit. Maybe not quite welcomed then...

I grab at the phone. My cheeks blazing like the fire in the far corner of the room.

"Here's the thing." My mouth opens and closes uselessly like a broken padlock before a following sentence escapes my brain. "I'm going to be working with Cardinal."

Izzie leans across the table, stretches her arm towards mine, and grips onto my hand, trying to squeeze information from me.

"They want a florist to adorn their venues and studio spaces with flowers to match and inspire their creative mindset. It's all the rage in America."

This is the biggest, most absurd lie I have ever spouted off; and I once told Rob a bottle of vodka tasted strange because it was organic when actually I drank it while he was on holiday and replaced it with water.

"A band florist? For Cardinal?"

"Why else would someone from their team be calling me, Iz?"

Clever. Throwing it back to her. My heart pounds. Thuds. Harder than ever. If she asks me outright if I'm dating Stewart, I'll have to tell her. Though she's more likely to assume I'm dating Patrick before even considering Stewart would give me a second or first glance.

She narrows her eyes. "But it's not just anyone calling you. It's Stewart Burns, the love of my life."

"No, that's just a photo to remind me it's someone from the Cardinal team. I put it on so I'd think of... you." I hate myself.

"So, do you get free tickets with this job?" Izzie asks,

hope colouring her tone.

"I—"

"Forget the tickets. Will you set me up with Stewart?"

My eyes close after noticing a stack of colourful magazines on the bar. "Is he not seeing Ella Egan?"

"Lucky cow. If you see her, you have to get rid of her for me. At least give her a slap or two on the face," she laughs, but the green of her eyes have hardened to an Indian fig colour as opposed to the usual fern. I half expect her skin to sprout spines and yellow flowers.

The phone vibrates in my hand. I ignore it for as long as I can before swiping at the messages appearing from Stewart like popcorn jumping from a pan.

I throw Izzie a watery smile as I stand up. "Iz, I have to go to work."

I pick up my red coat from the chair. I hate lying to her, especially right to her face. In my defence, I'm doing this for her. To protect her feelings, just until she's ready to—I sigh. Ready to accept I'm dating the man she's had a celebrity crush on for years. The frontman from her favourite band. Will she ever get to that point? Grief isn't linear. Will there ever be a right time?

Clearly today is not that day. Our conversation fell flat, she seemed to be arguing against me even though I could see her taking in my words. Maybe I should just call it all off with Stewart now, march up to him and tell him I can't do it, for my sake and Izzie's. That my best friend needs me more than I deserve to be happy. Or should I spin Izzie to face me and tell her that I'm dating a man she thinks she has a claim over?

"Are you meeting Stewart from Cardinal?" she asks with hope in her eyes.

“What exactly would he be doing in Cockermouth?”

“Me. Hopefully.”

My teeth push together and I use all my willpower to swallow down a scream. “There’s been a disaster with the delphiniums at the florists. Look, Iz—” I slide my arms into the coat and try not to look too lost for words.

“I’ve got a therapy call tonight at five, then meeting some girls from work. You can come if you want?” she asks, fingers back to scrolling through her phone.

Something jars in my head; she probably wants me to drive her into town and back home.

“Why are you doing your lippie?” Izzie asks.

“Dry lips,” I blurt out, wondering whether I have time to dive into Boots and put their full range of makeup testers to good use. I don’t, and I won’t. What am I, eleven and on the way to the weekly disco with electric blue eyeshadow?

“I’m gonna finish my drink and call Tori. I’ll see you later, yeah? Come round about six. You can drive me into town.”

“Maybe I’ve got a date tonight,” I say defiantly.

Izzie snorts, picking up her phone. “See you at six, Babe.”

I’m already making an excuse to not meet her later. Thank fuck Rob is away on a work conference; Stewart and I can make full use of the empty house.

***

“Fuck!” Stewart groans, extending the vowel sound. I look up from the sofa, where, while he was packing up his stuff

I quickly plaited my wet hair. There wasn't time to dry it after I jumped through the quickest shower ever. Neither Jane nor the customers would appreciate the scent of frantic last-minute sex nestled amongst the floral fragrances of the shop. He's zipping up his beloved guitar case and looping wires into his laptop bag in the hallway, a frown on his face and lips pushed together in a pout.

I flick through a textbook from college, about to make some notes quickly, in writing I'd never be able to decipher, when Stewart stands in front of me, sending the lampshade spinning as he hits it with his head. I glance at the clock; ten minutes before I have to set off on the short walk down the hill back to the florists.

"I don't want to go," he whines like a small child wanting to stay at the park for longer. His hand scrubs through his hair, leaving it haphazardly sticking up, down his face and scratching across his beard.

I stand up after checking I've got my floral scissors and secateurs in my handbag.

He watches me, his eyelid twitching.

"Yes?" I enquire, know he's thinking about something.

"Have you cut yourself with your knife? Or anything?"

My eyes widen; that was straight to the point, not wrapped in his usual lyrical prose. "Why do you ask?"

"I worry about you. But I didn't know how to ask in a less direct way."

"Surely you would have noticed, seeing as we've spent the last forty-eight hours mostly naked," I half laugh, trying to double bluff him again.

He sighs heavily and tugs at his hair. "Am I meant to pretend you're not lying right now?"

I move my hands behind my back and squeeze my nails

into my palms, trying to keep my face relaxed. His oceanic eyes seem to be staring into my soul. My cheeks flame and my heart drops to the pit of my stomach.

He scrubs at the back of his neck, scrunches his eyes closed then sighs. "Do you think I haven't noticed the scabs on your thigh?"

I fiddle with my earrings, fringe, tights, anything to avoid his eyes. "Sorry. I find it hard to admit."

"You can tell me, Daisy."

"I know."

"Why did you do it?"

"It helps me cope when I feel life is running away from me."

His shoulders slump. "You mean me and my life?"

"No. I mean my plans. Life can take detours and I'm not good at dealing with them. I am happy, so happy, to be with you, Stewart. But the lack of control fucks with my head. I can control the cuts."

He grimaces before shaking it off with a lick of his lips. He holds my hands, thumbs tracing across the veins of my wrists. "Please, Daisy, don't do it again. Promise me?"

"It's not that easy," I snap at his naivety, rubbing my forehead.

"I know, Baby, but–"

"Do you?" I resent how I snap again, pushing him away before he can try and help in any way. He scoffs. I recognise the flash of frustration and anger clouding his eyes.

"Yep, actually, I do. I'm trying to." He unzips his laptop bag and pulls out two books on self-harm. "See? I want to help you, Daisy. You don't have to deal with this alone,"

My shoulders drop as he shoves the books back in his

bag. I place a palm on his back, and he turns to face me.

"I'm sorry. It's easier to be alone sometimes. I'll try not to push you away. I appreciate the help and concern." I place a finger on his lips before throwing my arms around his neck, looking into his eyes that remind me of—"Brunnera macrophylla."

Shit. My eyes widen.

"'*Brunnera*' what?" he asks, smiling, the bright blue of his eyes back and sparkling.

"It's Latin." An embarrassed blush stains the entirety of my skin. "Far too prestigious for you, Stewart. Some of us graduated from university instead of pissing around writing tunes."

"You're such a wee menace. Are you flinging insults at me in a different language now?"

I laugh a little, covering my mouth with my palm. "It's a flower."

He looks around the living room, pristine as Rob dusts almost daily. "What made you say it? Are they invisible flowers?"

"They remind me of your eyes."

Great, my brain decided to go straight for honesty.

"Are you paying me a compliment, Daisy?"

"Maybe I am."

"And all when you're sober. Careful, Sweetheart, you'll admit you love me next."

"I'll stick with the pet name for now, my little Brunnera."

I shake my head. Ugh, we're now one of those couples. "Can I come up and stay with you? Not today, obviously," I ask. I'd like to spend time in his flat and not have to worry about keeping him away from my best friends. To enjoy some time together without the illusive girl code and guilt of being happy hanging over my head.

A smile dances on his face as he nods animatedly. "Message me some dates and we can sort that out. Des can come get you if need be."

"I'd like that. To stay at yours, not necessarily Des picking me up."

We both laugh softly, quietly. Like there's an unspoken rule that we can't be too joyous when we're saying goodbye.

Stewart sighs, holding my hands in his. The blue of his eyes reflects the snaking loss I know I'm going to feel the second he leaves. Dull. Faded. Paling into insignificance.

I extract myself and thread my arms through my red peacoat. If I'm late to the florists again, Jane is going to start docking my wages.

"I have to go." I sigh.

He ignores me and kisses my neck. "Come over for the gig we're playing next week."

"Stop it. I need to go!" Swatting his arm and pulling his lips away from my skin, holding onto the collar of his denim jacket. He isn't perturbed, sliding his hands to my waist. I remove them and scoop up my handbag. I usher him towards the door, pick up his laptop bag and loop it over his shoulder.

"Come over to the gig next week. I can pick you up the night before."

"You mean Des can pick me up. You and your boyband lifestyle."

"I'm not in a boyband, you total wee menace. Cardinal are an indie band; we're not even mainstream signed. Therefore we have the freedom to explore with our sound more. We have a balance of the standard pop accessibility that coincides with a level of freedom, combined with sensitive, emotive lyrics masked by rock riffs and tribal beats. Actually."

I try my hardest not to laugh at him, the way he knows I'm joking, yet can't leave it.

"I'm very sorry if I offended you," I shout from the kitchen, dashing to check the back door is locked, that last-minute panic dancing in my head.

"No, you're not. And I meant I'll drive down from the studio Friday lunchtime for you."

"You can drive?" I open the door, practically pushing him outside. He trips over the paving slabs, as always. "I assumed you couldn't."

"My car is one of my favourite things in the world."

"I may regret this, but what type of car is it?"

"Do you mean that, or do you mean what colour is she?"

"Don't be a dick."

"Bentley Continental. Royal Ebony."

"Black?"

"Royal Ebony. She's beautiful." He looks almost wistful.

"Why do you always get picked up?"

I'd get driven around if I had the option; knowing I didn't have to fork out a small fortune for the pleasure, or indeed listen to a taxi driver's life history when all I would want to do is stare out of the window, pretending to be in a music video. Stewart probably sleeps on drives, especially as he spends half the nights awake.

"Because I've usually got work to catch up on before I get back. I know I'm talented, but I can't drive and read or type at the same time."

"Work?"

"Believe it or not, Daisy, my job is more than writing and singing songs. Pat and Eddie usually pick up my share when I'm with you, so I get caught up before I return to the madness." His hands smooth up and down my back.

When did it get so hard to say goodbye? It crept up on me like the dark autumn nights. Without realising it, I'm sat with all the lights on at four o'clock. Longing for Stewart to keep me company. If only I had longer to say goodbye. Or longer together in the first place.

"What is it again, the wee flower?"

"Brunnera."

"You're cute, giving me a pet name at last."

"I can revert to my usual of twat or dick if the romantic side of me is freaking you out?"

"Nah. It's about time you stepped up to my romantic plate. Ring me after work."

"Are you not in the studio?"

"I'll take a break," he shrugs and laces our fingers together. Stewart always has an answer. For pretty much anything. I pull my hands from his, reluctantly.

"I hate work."

"No, you don't. You hate saying goodbye to your incredibly handsome and talented boyfriend."

"I do. If you see him will you tell him that, please?"

He laughs, pulling me towards him. He kisses me, or maybe I kiss him. At this point in our relationship it doesn't matter anymore. The realisation of it being an actual relationship, definitely more than sneaking around for sex and cigarettes, doesn't scare me like I'd expect. I'm not planning a wedding or anything remotely on that level, but fuck the Force; Stewart Burns makes me happy. He really does make me feel like I'm enough. Almost.

I push him away and start walking down the hill, turning to look at him.

"Don't look at me in that way."

He's like an adorable rescue puppy. The ones they always show on adverts. Adorable ones with perfect glossy coats to lure us in with; before we know it, we've come home with three dogs of varying degrees of ugliness, medical issues, patchy fur and missing limbs.

Stewart opens the car door but still doesn't clamber in.

"Go before I cry."

"Are you actually falling in love with me, Daisy Gordon?"

"Absolutely not," I state, busying myself with fishing a lighter from my handbag, increasing the distance. "You know I have a weakness for pretty things; flowers, eyes—"

"Good thighs. Ring me later, Baby," he calls from the car.

A mammoth sigh escapes me as my shoulders drop. I put a cigarette between my lips, maybe the nicotine will replace the feeling of, what?—loss? The absence of Stewart? The sting of having to carry that feeling around, not being able to cry to Rob or Izzie how I miss him, that I can't tell anyone how I feel.

The lorries roar up the hill at a far higher speed than required, shaking the ground beneath my feet. Or at least it feels it. I dash down the hill at speed, not allowing myself to turn around or check my phone. Stewart will have messaged already. Needy, but wonderful.

The blue sky is steadily being covered by a blanket of

grey clouds. Great, it's going to rain now, like some microcosm macrocosm shit. The trees sway in the ever-increasing wind, the shadows stretching.

20

"What is this?" I ask, registering the blaring horn coming from Stewart's infamous car.

Once I discovered he could drive, I kept picturing him behind the wheel of a ridiculous and impractical sports car, but this is almost normal. Not normal, it's not a standard car, even with my limited knowledge, I know that. The black colour of it looks like it's made from onyx. It exudes wealth and luxury.

"My car. She's a beaut, yep?" Stewart leans out of the window as I rest against my front gate.

Not to play up to the generic female stereotype, but it's a black car with wheels as big as a tractor. To be fair to him, it does reek of extravagance and quality. A far cry from my old-style red Yaris.

It's quite nice as cars go. Stylish. Clearly expensive, and not just because it's polished to hell and back. No need for a mirror with this thing around.

"What's with the lights?" I ask as I climb in. Little lights changing colour like a rainbow dance subtly around the interior. It reminds me of a jazzy fish tank.

"Mood lighting."

"What is it, a disco or a car?"

"Sweetheart, this is a Bentley Continental GT Speed. She is the best and most beautiful thing I have ever seen in my life." He leans over and kisses me briefly. "Aside from you."

"What a charmer. I'm in the same league as a car."

"Not just any car, Daisy."

I confess, the seats are softer than butter. Though why anyone needs a heated steering wheel or, indeed, mood lighting escapes me. My own car's heating barely works, being noisy and flitting between blasting ice cold and stuffy hot air towards my feet.

We pull up outside the exclusive boutique hotel nestled into the Cumbrian fells, and Stewart swerves the car into the carpark surrounded by trees.

"What's with the colour scheme?" I ask. The seats remind me of Iris chrysographes and the popular but unimaginative red roses. Though I doubt the leather will be named after flowers.

"Beluga and Cricket Ball; classic black and red. It's cool."

"Like the Dark Side?" I laugh, referring to Star Wars as the two of us often do. "Are you actually working for the emperor?"

His face shows a flicker of hurt before he shrugs. "According to my family, I am indeed the epitome of the dark side."

"How dare you want to be happy, Stewart."

"No time for happiness when there's morning rolls to bake. Wait until you meet them; you'll see what I mean."

I put a hand on his thigh as he turns off the engine. He starts talking about the Bang & Olufsen sound system and a diamond knurling something. Whatever that is. Part of me is surprised it can't just park itself.

"You're just saying nonsense to me." Though with that soft lilting accent, I could listen to him all night.

"I love this car."

"I can tell. It's very... nice."

"Nice?" he asks, his tone incredulous.

"Pretty, then."

"Pretty? Pretty?" Stewart spits, sounding insulted. "Daisy, she is quite possibly my favourite thing I own. If it was a choice between her or my guitar, I would have to think twice."

He really does love this car. I know how much he adores his guitar.

"You know it will stand out like a cow in a sheep pen if you park it outside my house."

"No, she will stand out due to her aesthetic of beauty and sophistication. She is a contemporary dynamic machine with striking majesty."

It's a pretty car. But it's a black car, that's all. Though these seats are very nice. Hm.

"Can I make a suggestion of shagging in it?"

Stewart's delphinium blue eyes widen in shock. "Absolutely not. She'd never forgive me. You know this stitching is—"

"Whatever." I shrug. Try not to laugh at him. Now I've put the idea in his head I know he's mulling it over, at least internally.

"There's not that much room, actually," he muses, scratching over his beard as he turns to face the back seats.

I smile, knew he wouldn't just let it go.

"Never tried?" I bite my tongue to refrain from asking about Ella, even though I know they only slept together once years ago.

"Fuck no."

"Not public enough for you? Hardly outside a prestigious London party, and I'm neither married nor an actress..."

"Daisy..."

"What? Might as well laugh about it."

"You're the first girl who's been in this car. Aside from Ash, but she doesn't count."

"I am extremely honoured," I say sincerely, placing a palm over my heart.

He looks towards the back seats again. Stewart has a bank balance and a job I can't begin to imagine, but he's still a man beneath it all. Horny as hell. If this was an early morning drive I'd have already given him a blowjob.

"Thinking about sex in the back seats?"

"Not when there's a hotel bed waiting for us upstairs."

I nod at him, pout and scratch at his scalp, knowing he'll shiver under the touch.

"Tell me about your beautiful car then. I'm desperate to hear more."

His hand runs across the red seat next to my arm. "This is hand cross-stitched detailing on the leather, you know?"

"That right?" I comment, undoing the seatbelt, unlacing my boots and kicking them off. He glances at my hands then bare feet, but carries on.

"The leather is sourced from—"

"Hard to clean. Is that what you're worried about?"

I unclip my hair, ruffle it loose, and feel exactly how it looks in films, all glamorous and sexy. The highlights might be extortionate, but the colour is so pretty, I can almost convince myself and the bank balance it's justifiable.

"Sourced from where?"

"It's hand-picked from Northern Europe and—" His gaze lingers on my mouth as I reapply my lip gloss.

"Riveting. You'll be telling me about the wood next," I comment, purposefully fiddling with the hem of my dress, showing just a flash of the colourful tattoo on my thigh. "Is it hard?"

Stewart nods, his eyes dancing across me. I try not to laugh at him. He's so cute and so sexy, but so predictable.

"No, it's walnut. Open pore crown cut."

I trail my hand up to his dark hair and trace the shape of his ear with my nails. Once I go for his ears we both know that it's a lost battle. We're so shagging in his beloved car. Thank the Force for tinted windows.

"Walnut, you say?"

"Yes, walnut." He shivers, his eyelashes dancing down to his cheeks. "It can only be found in North America."

My hands move from his hair, scratching at his neck, fingers dancing beneath the collar of his top.

"I know what you're doing, Daisy."

"Good, I've been pretty obvious so far." I ghost my hand up his thigh.

"It won't work. We are not tainting the perfection of my car."

"Uh huh." I hitch up my dress, full thigh tattoo on show. "What were you saying? Something about that hard wood?"

"It's also known as—as—" He stutters as I slide my knickers, black like his car, down my legs and off the end of my feet.

"Yes?"

I pick up the knickers from the carpets or mats. I'm

pretty sure he's already talked about them, how they match with the seat colours, which he picked himself. I don't even think I've seen a car with different coloured mats than standard black. My footwells are littered with leaves and rubbish. Not La Perla lingerie.

"And the—shape of the—" He clears his throat and swallows loudly.

I drop my underwear onto his lap and pat his delicious thighs. "Do carry on, Stewart. I'm enthralled. Aching for more," I manage to say, somehow, gracefully climbing over the centre console and into the back seats. "Anything else?" I ask, wriggling into the seats. It was pointless paying for a bed with seats this soft and comfortable.

"The wheels—"

"The wheels, do they turn, Baby?" I know the pet name will totally work in my favour.

"They're forged ten, ten—"

Why is he insisting on carrying on with the Bentley based chat? Still, his persistence is to be admired. Maybe he deserves a gold star for that too.

"Ten wheels?" I ask, sarcasm in my tone.

He shakes his head, his fringe dancing across his eyes as he looks at me in the rearview mirror. "No, Daisy. Ten spokes and the—"

I lean forward and catch his ear lobe between my teeth. Stewart moans.

"Carbon ceramic brakes with, oh for fucks sake," he says loudly, a smile on his face, as he clambers in the back to join me. Silencing my laughs with kisses and the removal of his jeans.

He's right, there's not much room. But I do love a challenge. His beloved car will, I'm sure, forgive us. After all, we leave her with extremely satisfied smiles.

***

Stewart and I are wrapped in nothing but sheets in a king-size bed at the luxurious Inn on the Fell. It's a hotel we frequent when meeting up in Cumbria. I love him being at mine, but keeping quiet and Rob out of my room is a constant challenge. Here Stewart and I can relax and spend all day in bed without getting up to feed the cat, or sneak across the landing to the bathroom, or downstairs for a coffee whenever Rob leaves.

The rain eases to gentle taps against the window. The clouds move steadily across the sky, a hint of clear blue colour breaks through.

Stewart's phone beeps and he frowns while scrolling through it before sighing loudly and standing up. He pulls the curtains closed with more force than necessary and shakes his head at me.

"You haven't told Izzie, have you?"

We keep having this same argument. Over and over, but he doesn't understand.

"I just couldn't—"

"You couldn't tell her we're dating but could lie to her face about being Cardinal's official florist?"

Shit. How does he know this?

"She messaged me just the now. 'I hear my best friend Daisy is working with you? Adorning venues and dressing rooms with blooms to match the Cardinal mindset and creativity.'" Stewart puts on a high-pitched voice that sounds neither Northern, or anything like Izzie. "'Maybe that means I'll be seeing more of you? Wouldn't that be nice?' Then she invited me out and made it abundantly clear she expects to spend the night in my bed."

Oh fuck.

"Have you told Rob?" he continues before I can even attempt a half-hearted excuse or explanation, sitting on the edge of the bed. I watch him turn his phone off and drop it into his bag. He turns to face me, his eyes darken from summer skies to storm clouds over Bell Bay on Cumbrae. I shake my head as Stewart sighs, tilting his head to the ceiling. I want to trail a fingertip down his neck, so I do. He grips at my wrist to stop me. I guess I won't be able to distract him from our familiar argument with sexual favours this time.

"You promised me, Daisy. If this was the other way round, and I hadn't told Pat about you, you'd be fucking furious with me," he states, climbing into bed.

"Does this mean you're not furious with me?"

"I most definitely am."

"I'm sorry," I say quietly, my fingers sliding through his hair. His eyes close, and shoulders relax a little.

"Why won't you tell her?"

"Because—"

"Is it the stalker thing?"

"She's not a stalker," I insist.

He leans out of the bed and rifles through his bag before passing me a wedge of folded pieces of paper adorned with purple skulls. The colour drains from my features as I recognise it.

"What is this?" I'm almost too scared to find out.

"This, Sweetheart, is one of many letters from Izzie. Your best friend. My stalker."

No. I shake my head. Can't, won't believe him. He gently pushes my fringe from my eyes and I blink at him. Of course I believe him; with the evidence in front of me or not. He's never lied to me for any purpose. He takes the letter from me before I can unfold it and skim over Izzie's curly scrawl.

"I won't read it to you, Daisy. No doubt it will be the same as the previous ones. They are getting more descriptive, she holds me in very high esteem. She's a stalker. Mild, but she is becoming more intense. I assume that's Tori's influence, seeing as you insist Izzie's a nice person."

Hanging around after or before a gig to catch a glimpse or have a selfie with a band member is one thing. Writing him love letters like a forlorn teen and then depicting him as a hero in her works of fiction doesn't exactly scream standard fan.

"She is a nice person," I defend, "though not to me. She's always nice about you."

"If you're worried about the stalker thing, it's an issue that can be dealt with."

"It's not that–"

"Next weekend, invite Rob and his man out with us for the full weekend. We'll all come back here. I'll pay for the food, drinks, room, all that shit. Then I can tell him if you don't. I can almost excuse you not telling Izzie, with her being a stalker, but it fucking hurts you haven't told Rob about me, about us."

"I'm sorry, Stewart. This isn't a reflection on us."

"It feels it." He pouts.

"It's not. You know how I feel about you."

"Do I?"

"I'd be lost without you," I play with his hair more, dance my fingers down his neck, relieved to see him smiling, though I know he's more hurt than angry. Guilt grips like a fist around my heart that I haven't told my two best friends about the man I'm dating, who makes me stupidly happy, and the hurt I'm inflicting on Stewart by not being honest with my friends.

I sit up and shuffle, thighs either side of his; his cold hands stroke down my jaw and neck as we kiss. Our lips slide together slowly, tongues not dancing but caressing. Like always, my hands go to his hair, his to my waist and hips.

"Tell me a secret," Stewart hushes into my skin while kissing at my neck, collar bones and shoulders.

"What are we doing here, reenacting our first night together?" I whisper, so used to keeping quiet in my bedroom or on the tour bus.

"Baby, I remember every detail of that night,"

"Wrote it in your diary, did you?"

"Stained on my heart like a tattoo, Sweetheart."

"You don't like tattoos."

He tickles me and I squeal, rolling off him and settling down in the duck down pillows.

"I like yours a lot. But I'd never have one myself. Why mess with perfection?"

"Twat."

"Come on, indulge me. We usually only exchange the filthiest of words in bed. I fancy a wee change."

Right. Secrets. I steal a glass from each night out I have, just for shits and giggles, but who doesn't? I actually quite fancy Edward Scissorhands, but am aware that physically, it would be an unmitigated disaster. Nah, that one is too weird to voice.

"I miss you. When you're not here. When we're not together. I miss you so fucking much."

"You do?" he asks, kissing at my tattoos. He pays extra

attention to the flowers on my thighs, hiding my scars. I love him for it, even though I'd never say so.

"I really do," I admit, only part reluctant. "It's like half of me is missing. You take a part of me away with you."

"Tell me a secret," I whisper as his hands smooth back up my thighs.

Stewart shakes his head smiling as he lays back down, our noses almost touching, hands intertwined. "You know all of mine."

"Indulge me," I repeat his own words, tracing the shell of his ear with my tongue.

He sighs out shakily, "I'm falling in love with you, Daisy."

My hands smooth over his back, bringing him towards me. Always wanting him closer. Our hearts aligned. I drown in his eyes over and over, like being pulled beneath the waves of the brightest blues.

"I mean it, Baby. I'm falling in love with you."

The tenderness of his tone and softness in his eyes makes my stomach and heart swirl like whirlpools, revelling in the intensity of it. Of him. Part of me fears I may blurt out I love him back.

"You make me feel like—" I stop myself. My throat tingles and I might cry; from being completely overcome with emotions and feelings I can't, or don't want to label.

"Like what?" he asks, nudging at my nose with his.

"You make me feel like I might be enough," I confess quietly, opening my eyes and allowing some of the defensive walls to drop. My eyes fill but no tears fall, I do have an ounce of decorum left about me. Just.

His lips part as he blinks rapidly. Eyes are so vivid and bright, like flax flowers.

"You are so enough, Baby. I can't believe that you weren't enough for anyone in any capacity. You're everything to me. Everything, Sweetheart."

I feel dizzy with it, all these emotions and feelings I can't deny in my head and heart. He repeats almost constantly how I'm enough for him, more than enough.

"Look at you being all romantic," he says with a smirk once I can't take the praise anymore and call him a twat. I extract myself from the bed and his hands, and walk over to the window after wrapping myself in a silken blanket. I open the curtains to let the evening sun shine into the room. It dances over his skin, picking up on the raindrops still clinging to the windowpane.

I glance at him before looking across the lake and fells sweeping up towards the clouds.

"Not romantic, honest," I counter.

He runs a hand through his hair, head on the pillow, he licks his lips and rubs a hand across his beard. "*Whatever our souls are made of—*"

Amusement dances on my features as I see his cheeks blushing. The sun streams through the window, bathing the room in warm stripes of yellow and a gentle melody of singing birds.

"Quoting Bronte is going to make up for my lack of poetic declarations, is it?"

He shrugs, his eyelid flickering as I climb back into the bed next to him. Stewart rests his head against my shoulder, palms smoothing across my ribs, down to the curves of my stomach, which I hate and he seems to love. Having only been surrounded by models for the best part of a decade, he's probably forgotten that concave stomachs aren't evident on all women. Especially not florists who like eating pizza and crisps as many nights as she can afford to.

"Worth a shot, Sweetheart. *Whatever our souls are made of—*"

"*His and mine are the same.*" I trail the back of my nails across the silver chain low on his chest, placing my palm flat over his heart, feeling it beat in time with my own.

21

"Daisy, a wee word?" Hipster Harry asks as I pick up my handbag, about to go and find Ash.

I sit on the leather sofa pushed against a wall in the studio, dotted with cardinal red cushions. I try to ignore the anxiety stacking up in my head and lungs. A private word with Harry, head of the Cardinal team, is never a good thing.

"I'm going to be straight with you. Stewart cannot have a girlfriend who is suicidal."

I laugh nervously as I look around the makeshift studio in a hotel suite. Walls lined with mattresses, the floor dotted with laptops, headphones and wires like the world's largest, most complex spider's web. Speakers on various makeshift surfaces of tables, chairs, stacks of books and boxes of wine. A drum kit is set up beneath the window, and several guitars and cases prop themselves against the soundproofing mattresses. Three microphones stand in the middle of the room.

"I'm not suicidal. Where has this come from?"

Harry ignores me. Perhaps I'm meant to sit and listen, follow orders and rules like a puppet. "The team aren't happy with your self-harming. We're worried about the effect it could have on the image of Cardinal."

The colour drains from my skin. "How exactly do you and the team know about my personal issues?" I ask, hands and voice shaking.

Harry shrugs a bony shoulder and keeps his eyes focused on his clipboard. "Oz, my colleague, overheard you and Stewart discussing it. If this gets out into the press we could have a nightmare on our hands. We need to handle this strategically."

"How inconsiderate of me to not have Cardinal at the forefront of my mind at all times."

"The fact is, Daisy, the band should be at the forefront. It has to come first."

"Cardinal weren't even a band when I started self-harming," I snap out.

Harry looks at my bare arms, as subtle as a train wreck.

"I cut on my thighs, for your information. Shall I call you next time I pick up a blade? Do you need photographic evidence for your clipboard?"

"It's not a great image for Cardinal, for Stewart's girlfriend to be suicidal."

I sigh loudly, looking towards the ceiling. I notice a long cobweb swaying from the lights. Harry won't be happy about that if he spots it. He claims dust interferes with the vocal chords or something. Thank the Force he can't see my bedroom. A layer of fluffy grey dust tops all frames and furniture.

"I am not suicidal! Self-harm is a coping mechanism. Perhaps you should read up on it."

I almost add on that Stewart has several books on the subject and often quotes them to me over the phone. He wants, longs to help and understand. Most of the time I push him away, and it ends up in arguments as far away from self-harm as sunflowers are from cacti.

"The team feel you should sort yourself out before you and Stewart go public. It's that or you break up," Harry states seriously as if discussing meal choices. Chicken or fish? Self-harm or break up?

"Sort myself out?" I repeat, the wobble on my voice evident, all bravado lost.

"Of course, there is another option."

I shuffle to the edge of the sofa, lean forward.

"You two go public, scars and all. Cardinal do a few campaigns and charity events. Possibly a single to raise money and awareness for self-harmers. Photoshoot with you and Stew. You, Daisy, do an honest and open letter to the fans who feel the same as you, who self-harm in times of trouble and all that. It will really endear you and Cardinal with the fans. It could be great publicity and a marketing strategy."

I desperately want to argue with Hipster Harry, at least tell him he can fuck off, yet not sure I trust myself to speak without sobbing or screaming.

"Something to think about," Harry pushes himself off the sofa and leaves me alone in the room full of everything Cardinal needs to produce a new album.

My eyes, more glazed over with tears than I'd like to admit, skim the surfaces. Of course there wouldn't be a spare razor blade or knife lying around within reach.

I run my nail up my leg, from my thigh to my hip. The stripe turning white under the pressure and then raising into a pink line. It stings a little. Not enough to make me feel release, or more in control. I repeat the action again.

Again, again. Pull the skin taut, press into the same line until bloodspots bloom under the top layer in uneven blemishes of purple and red. I exhale, yet the weight pushing down on my shoulders remains.

Cardinal's album playing quietly provides me with an inescapable narrative. I'm dating the frontman, and we can't keep our relationship, or indeed our personal lives locked away from the fans and press forever.

The night surrounds us as Stewart and I stand in the carpark after the mixing is done for the day, waiting for Des to drop off the car so Stewart can take us back across the country to Cockermouth. I look up to the sky, hardly any stars on show, and no sign of the light of the moon. Just darkness and the floating noises of city life.

"So, the hipsters tell me we have to split up, all because I take a blade to my skin."

"The fuck?" Stewart exclaims, dropping his lit cigarette from his lips.

"Harry told me I have to sort myself out, his words not mine. We break up or go public and tell the world about my self-harming. And top that off with Cardinal releasing a single for a self-harm support charity."

"The fuck? Harry said that?" he repeats, looking furious and shocked; taking his phone from his pocket and frantically messaging, I assume Harry. "I'll meet with him tomorrow night and sort this shit out."

My lips wobble. I wipe at the tears on my cheeks. Hating myself for getting so attached to Stewart, for my own issues being the reason behind the impending break-up. He pulls me to him, my head against his chest, hands stroking through my hair and down my back.

"Baby, I swear, that's not what they talked about to me."

My defences raise, walls that start to fall in close proximity to Stewart begin to stack up against him. I fold my arms. "You should have talked to me first!"

"I was going to but didn't feel the midst of recording our new album was an appropriate setting. There's fucking microphones everywhere. Harry had some misconceptions about self-harm in general. He questioned the severity of your injuries and the seriousness of our relationship."

"What did you say?"

"I said that everyone has issues to fight with, and there's different coping strategies. Also told him we're in this for the long haul. I'm sorry about Harry; he can be a bit blunt. Generally, the team are really good. They are here to help you. They want to help you."

"It'll be shit for the image of your band unless we play it how Harry suggested," I say with a sigh, the defeat and acceptance swimming in my brain.

"Daisy, being with you, looking after you and keeping you happy and safe is more important than my career."

I scoff a little. Liar, but what a lovely lie. In one way I know he means it. "You can't put your career above me, Stewart. I won't let you."

"I won't let the team tell us what to do. But we can't sneak around forever,"

"I have to tell my best friends we're dating and instantly stop self-harming before we go public. That's what you and your team mean, isn't it?"

Stewart shakes his head before tilting it in that adorable puppy-like way. "I'd like you to tell Rob and Izzie, as it's unfair on everyone to keep our relationship quiet. No one will know about your self-harm, Sweetheart. I will endeavour to keep it out of the press." He kisses my forehead, and the action makes me feel safe and heard.

"I'll tell Rob and Izzie when I get home. I promise."

"Can I quote Anne Bronte the now?"

"Anne not Emily? Makes a change."

"*He who dares not grasp the thorn, should never crave the rose.* We're in this together, Daisy. Just you, just me."

"Fuck, I'm stuck with you, aren't I?" I say with a smile and sigh of relief, the silver moonlight breaking through the clouds.

"Yep. I'm afraid the fates have aligned, and we'll be together for the rest of our days."

I chuckle, place a kiss on his lips, and try to ignore the independent woman inside of me screaming at me to run away to open my own business years before I'm ready. As long as I'm alone, it will all be ok. Or that's what I always made myself believe...

22

"And where are you off to, all dressed up and with a suitcase?" Rob asks with an exaggerated pout as I slide my arms into my red coat. He's leaning against the hall wall, flicking his orange fringe. I would ask why he's suited and booted, especially as it's his day off, but I have more pressing matters to deal with. "Off to see the married man?"

"I've got a date and overnight stay with my unmarried boyfriend. Wanna join me?"

Rob raises an eyebrow and cackles. "Babe, I love you, but your distinct lack of cock and balls puts me off."

"I know it's short notice, but I'd really love it if you and Zach would come meet him." I rub at my forehead, knowing I should have invited Rob and Zach to join Stewart and me earlier, yet I've chickened out each time I've attempted to broach the subject. I've spent the entire week building it up, my mouth opening, words on the tip of my tongue, before running off into my room or excusing myself for a smoke.

"The married man?" Rob repeats.

I roll my eyes. Rob and Izzie deduced that the only explanation for my sneaking off, secrecy, and late-night phone calls in hushed tones was that my boyfriend has a wife sharing his bed.

"He's not married. I'm heading to the Inn on the Fell now to meet him. We'd love for you to join us. There's a room for you both if you fancy? Obviously separate from ours. We can pick Zach up en route. Actually, I wanted to tell you something—"

I also still haven't told Rob about my self-harm, past or present. There never seemed to be a right time. Over tea—'This knife reminds me, I cut my skin when I'm overwhelmed?' At bedtime—'Goodnight, by the way, I self-harm. Ok, sweet dreams?' Straight after work—'Work was tough today, was tempted to slice at my skin with my floristry knife to relieve some tension?'

Rob spins on his black Chelsea boots as Zach pokes his head around the door. Oh, he's here already, also dressed top to toe in a smart suit. My confession sits heavy and silent in my throat.

"Told you," Rob pouts. Zach hands his boyfriend a crisp twenty-pound note.

"I overheard you on the phone last week saying you'd invite us both tonight. I've been waiting all week," Rob sends me a wink and holds Zach's hand, two suitcases by his polished shoes. "Come on then, don't want to be late, do we?"

"Why didn't you say anything?" I ask, blushing.

Rob shrugs and straightens his tie. "Because it was your invite to make. I won't tell you what else I overheard, Babe. But in future if you're going to have phone sex, make sure your door is closed. That's the second if not third time your dulcet tones have drifted from your room into mine."

Fuck.

*

I've avoided all questions fired at me from Rob and Zach for the entire drive down twisty roads heading deeper into the Lake District.

"Tell us one thing. What's he like?" Rob pleads and throws a polo at my face. "Come on, Daisy, one thing about him before we meet him. And don't say he wears scuffed DM shoes because I already know that."

"Fine. He's—"

Do not say nice.

He's obsessed with his car. Messy. Such a good listener but can also chat for hours. A closed book, apparently, but seems to tell me everything. A total wind-up merchant. Sings constantly, all the fucking time. Arrogant, but that hides his insecurities. Caring, desperate to be helpful. Has a hero complex, not that he'll admit it. Sarcastic, witty. Fucking hilarious. Clumsy. Almost embarrassingly romantic. A world-class dreamer. The best friend to Eddie and Patrick and Ash. Anxiety-ridden, especially at night. A total bookworm. Horny, constantly, particularly first thing in the morning. Yeah, he is a bit geeky and goofy. A little bit of an attention whore, if I'm honest. Passionate. A perfectionist. Kind, so kind. Loving.

Fucking hell, he's pretty perfect.

"He's funny," I reply eventually. "Makes me laugh."

"You could do with a bit of light relief in that carefully planned life of yours, Babe."

"So you keep saying."

"Is he good to you? Treats you right?" Rob asks seriously.

"Yes," I answer instantly. Rob squeezes at my shoulder. My eyes flit to his; he nods then smiles.

"Can I guess what he looks like?" he asks, clapping his

hands. “Shoulders as wide as scaffold planks, great thighs, a smattering of tattoos on his arms, slightly crooked nose, battered ears. Can be found in either the pub with a pint or running around a rugby pitch,”

Zach laughs. “You say it with such confidence, Rob,”

“Daisy only dates rugby players, the whole rough and ready men. The Six Nations is like her porn,” Rob cackles turning round to face Zach.

“Rob!” I berate with a blush, but he’s not lying. Until Stewart, I did have a type. All my exes are rugby players, with no designer hats or skin-tight jeans in sight. And I couldn’t call any of them pretty like I do Stewart. “He’s not my usual type actually,”

“How long have you been together?” Zach asks.

“I met him at a party in January. It was a weird connection thing,”

Rob flicks his fringe as he turns to face me. “Hold on, you’ve been dating this guy since January?” he asks, the time scale throwing him off the only party he knows I went to while he was attempting to hook up with Stewart’s bandmate.

“February, actually.”

“I thought it was a casual thing. You haven’t dated anyone else bar Brett for years, and not even that was consistently serious,”

“It’s serious ok? Truth be told, I think I’d be lost without him.”

“Daisy, we don’t keep secrets. We’ve never kept secrets. I haven’t kept anything from you in nearly ten years.”

Folding his arms, Rob pouts and pushes out his lips so far I can see despite concentrating on the road ahead. He sighs dramatically.

Guilt makes the ghosts of scars on my thigh tingle. He's right; we don't usually have secrets, and certainly none of this scale. Rob told me that he'd slept with his tutor at uni to pass a module, and that he once stole a 10p lolly when he was six and felt guilty for weeks afterwards. We know everything about each other. He knows more about me than Izzie. Mainly because he listens more and doesn't always want to flip the conversation back round to himself like Izzie does.

"What does he do then? Play rugby?" Zach enquires.

"He's in a band."

Rob laughs hollowly. "A band? Is he fifteen and still chasing the pop idol dream?"

"They're independently signed, tour smaller venues and stuff. Quite big on the festival scene, actually."

"He must be doing alright if he's meeting us here," Rob comments as we turn up the country lane to the Inn nestled into the fell side. "He'd better be paying. I can't stretch to a meal here, let alone a room."

"Don't worry about it," I say dismissively.

"Will we have heard of the band?" Zach asks.

Ok, here goes. I wish I wasn't driving, so I could at least allow my nerves to rip a piece of paper into shreds. The blood rushes in my ears, taking over the engine noise of the car and the wheels crunching over the gravel.

"Before I tell you, you both need to promise to not tell Izzie."

"Izzie? Why?" Rob turns to face Zach, and they both swap shrugs. "Is he that dude from Cardinal she's obsessed with?"

"I love Cardinal! Their latest album is fantastic!" Zach gushes.

I stop the engine and look around the car park, Stewart's beloved Bentley shining like onyx beneath the early summer sun. Unfastening my seatbelt I stare straight into Rob's pale blue eyes.

"Yes."

A slow smile breaks out on Rob's round face before he bursts out into high-pitched laughter. Zach joins in too, but I feel that's through awkwardness, not humour.

"You expect me to believe that you're dating Stewart from Cardinal? What is this, a belated April Fool's joke?"

A sting of hurt flares that Rob doesn't believe me. Maybe he doesn't think I'm good enough to be dating Stewart. Maybe he's right.

"You won't tell Izzie?" I repeat.

Rob's laughter quietens, but his face still looks amused. "If Stewart from Cardinal is actually waiting for us then yes, I promise, we'll keep it quiet from Izzie."

I look into the rearview mirror at Zach. "Can you give us a minute, Zach please?"

He nods and says he'll meet us at Reception with the bags.

I face Rob, sigh then smile shakily. I will my hands to remain still in my lap and resist the urge to push my nails into my palm.

"You're my best friend, right?" I ask. Rob nods. We both smile. We're in lots of ways closer than Izzie and I. More on the same wavelength, share the same humour and taste in TV shows. Neither of us is self-absorbed, self-centred, draining... Fuck. Why do I seem to have more negatives to say about my apparent best friend than positives?

"Finally, you're admitting it," he says dramatically. "I'm better in all ways than Izzie. And you know I'm nicer than her, especially to you."

"Yes but—"

"She's your oldest friend, not your best friend. You feel bound to her because you grew up together."

"But I can't just abandon her, especially not now."

Though would she even notice? She'd definitely notice my boyfriend.

"I get the guilt. I feel it too. We both decided to phase her out years ago,"

"Cut her out, you said. I wasn't quite as harsh."

"That's because, Daisy, you're a much better person than I am. Admit it, if Sophia hadn't died you and Izzie would have drifted apart."

I make a non-committal noise. I know he's right. Rob and I had decided to create distance with Izzie a few years ago. She wasn't bringing anything positive to either of our lives. It wasn't a balanced friendship and still isn't. Then Sophia died in the car crash, and Izzie leant on me. I knew Sophia, had grown up with the family. I could share memories and stories, and I felt a loss too.

"She only clung to us because she was jealous you had me when we moved back. We were always her backup plans, her second choice; then she relied on us after Sophia died."

"Rob, she's grieving. She still needs us."

"Babe, you never get over a death. You learn to survive, cope, move on. Izzie will be mourning her sister forever. Put yourself first, whether you're dating Stewart or not," Rob cackles. His sentiments hidden by humour.

"Izzie aside, I've always been honest with you, yes?"

"Yes."

"There's two secrets I've been keeping; one, I'm dating

Stewart Burns from Cardinal. Have been since February. Honestly, it's fun sneaking around. Both of us wanted to see how things played out before telling anyone, and indeed the press and his fans finding out. I'm sorry I kept it from you."

"Babe? I'm actually starting to think—" Rob shakes his head, flicks nervously at his neon orange fringe that reminds me of Eddie's natural colour.

"Two," I continue, distracting myself with reapplying my lip gloss. Ignoring my shaky fingers.

"Are you actually Beyonce in disguise or something equally as ridiculous?"

"I self-harmed as a teen. Sometimes I still do it now. My thigh is covered in scars, hidden beneath my tattoo."

Rob gasps, his hands flying dramatically to his open mouth. "I vaguely remember seeing scars on your leg back at uni, before the tattoo. I didn't make a link at all."

"I've been trying to tell you for weeks."

"About your apparent secret superstar boyfriend or your self-harm?"

"Both."

"Daisy, Babe, you hurt yourself? On purpose?"

"Yes. I promise, when we get home, we'll have a proper heart-to-heart about it. It's not a cry for help or a failed suicide attempt, ok? It's how I cope with life. Some people run, meditate, eat; I arrange flowers or take a razor blade to my legs."

Rob hisses air through his clenched teeth. "Daisy—" He places a hand on the top of my arm and squeezes tightly.

"I'm ok. I promise. There. That's all my secrets. Let's go meet Stewart." I squeeze Rob's shoulder and climb out of the car.

Rob leans against the car, shaking his head in bemusement. "Daisy, this is a fuck ton of information."

"I know. I'm sorry to spring it all on you, Babe. But there we have it." I shrug and point to Stewart's Bentley. "And I had sex in that car. Ok, I'm done. No more secrets."

Holding my hands up in surrender, I walk up the path towards the front of the Inn. My steps lighter.

After leaving our bags at the front desk, we push open the doors to the lounge. Smooth jazz music plays quietly, and the scent of flowers drifts in through the open windows from the walled gardens.

Stewart, nose in a book, is tucked into the far corner of the lounge.

"Fuck me," says Rob, gripping at my arm.

"No, thank you, you're not my type," I reply.

"Neither is he," Rob fires back, shock replaced with an eyebrow raise and pout. "Izzie will kill you without a moment's thought."

"Let me tell her so you don't get pulled into it," I say, rubbing at my forehead.

"Screwed him outside a party yet?" Rob smiles slowly, mischief glinting like his eyebrow ring in his narrowed pale blue eyes.

"He's not like that," I state, leaving Rob and Zach stood motionless in the doorway.

I totter over in my heeled boots, clacking like a Stormtrooper, weaving amongst the comfy leather chairs. I bet Stewart tripped over the opulent rugs spread on the wooden floor.

"Hey, you," I nudge Stewart's leg with my foot. He

looks up, dropping the book into his lap.

"A florist called Daisy," Stewart looks past me, stands up and holds out his hand to Rob. "You must be Rob? Great to meet you. I'm—"

"Stewart, yeah, I think I might know, mate," he replies shaking his hand, eyes wide and fixated on Stewart's face, before tracking up and down the height of him.

"I'm Zach, Rob's boyfriend. I'm such a huge fan," Zach gushes and pulls Stewart into a hug before either of them can stop it. Rob looks mortified, mumbling that he's almost as bad as Izzie.

"Pleasure to meet you, Zach. Sit down, both of you. I'll get us some drinks."

As he judges everyone on their footwear (this is the man who once broke up with someone purely because he wore Nike Airs), Rob focuses on Stewart's shoes.

"Great shoes, mate. They'd make some fetching plant pots, right, Daisy?"

I raise my middle finger at him as he and Zach sit down and discuss the wine menu, both taking sneaking glances at Stewart. Rob closes the menu with a dramatic snap, eyes fixated on Stewart. Eyebrows raised, pout at the ready.

"I'm going to get this out of the way. Let's see if your stories match up. Shagged her outside a party yet?" he asks, as subtle as the colour of his fringe.

Stewart shakes his head, eyes looking a little guarded, as they always do when the sex scandal is mentioned. "Come on, Rob. You know Daisy's better than that."

I push my nails into my palm to stop me from blurting out how that statement isn't strictly true. Blowjob on a deserted beach is fine, various sexual endeavours backstage or while Des is driving us, to be expected and encouraged, sex in a tiny cramped closet and in the back of the Bentley almost acceptable.

"What about you then? You're always reported to be jumping from one bed to another. Still shag anyone who takes your fancy, married or not?" Rob daringly raises his eyebrows.

"Rob!" I snap. Stewart chuckles. Rob shrugs. Zach watches the two of them, wide-eyed and opened-mouthed.

Stewart looks at me, his features softening as I smile in apology. "I'm not like that anymore. Daisy makes me a better person."

Rob fiddles with his eyebrow ring, then points a finger at me. "You two are actually dating? And it's serious?"

"Yes," Stewart and I reply in unison.

"Daisy Gordon, You have some explaining to do."

Don't I know it? At least this will be more straightforward than explaining the last few months to Izzie.

***

Stewart stands up to go for a smoke and Zach heads to the bar to order more wine.

"Well?" I ask Rob, leaning back in the chair. It annoys me how Stewart would smirk if he heard me. He knows me so well, I long for the approval of my best friends. I shake Izzie from my head. Right now, Rob's opinion matters.

We watch Stewart strolling by the windows, taking photos of the fells swooping down to the open lake nestled in the valley; and, of course, the usual filtered selfies, most of which he sends to me straight away. Poser.

My eyes follow Stewart and I smile. My heart seems to jump, and I realise whatever Rob says, I'll stay with Stewart. I want approval, yet I don't need it. My happiness and feelings are more valid and important than the opinions of others. Fuck, maybe I'm dealing with some trauma from childhood at last.

Rob flicks his fringe and fiddles with his glinting eyebrow ring. "I like him. He's a charmer, and a flirt, lives a life I'm pretty jealous of too, but I like him. He's good for you. I've never seen you smile so much, Babe, I mean that."

My cheeks ache with another smile, but it's a pain I'd never complain about.

"It's obvious he is head over heels in love with you. Do you love him?"

My lips twitch, and words dance around my mind, my heart. Battling against one another like the broken bottle on the beach; will the tides wash it away, or will it remain lodged in the sand?

"I think so."

"You're really well matched too. He's a dreamer, a romantic; you're a realist, pessimistic and very practical. And your humour is so in sync, it's almost scary. Clearly, you're both on fire in bed too. The sexual tension between you is distracting."

I pretend to be highly invested in my hair. "We're pretty compatible, I guess."

"And I shall endeavour to hear about that another time," Rob replies with a wink and a chink of our almost empty glasses.

23

I carry the teapot to the table set outside of the residential home where Nan's waiting for me. There's a few families and old couples sat around the tables. The wind blows the tablecloth gently, the sun shining down, and with an extra blanket over her shoulders and knees, it's nice enough for Nan and me to have a high tea outside.

"Haven't you got a spring in your step, Poppet?" Nan asks as I skip around the small table to retrieve the cups and saucers. Sending smiles to the other residents and families as I go, like a demonic carousel horse.

"The sky is the brightest of blues, and the sun is shining on us. I'm having cake and tea with you. It's just a wonderful day." My arms are thrown wide as I look up at the clouds. Dammit, maybe some of Stewart's exaggeration is rubbing off on me. I slice a scone in half for Nan and spread it thickly with butter and jam.

She hums, her dark eyes narrowed. "I haven't seen him for a while. How is Stewart?"

"He's good but busy. Sends his love, of course."

"Is he up in Edinburgh, writing his songs?"

"Yeah. Travelling a bit at the minute so we haven't managed to meet up."

I haven't told Nan the extent of Stewart's career, just that he makes music and travels for it. She seemed content with that but did brand him as a bit of a dreamer.

"We're going to Sorento at the weekend. I can't wait!"

"Do you two do the whole phone sex thing?"

"Nan!"

"Come off it, girl. I've been around the block. I know the look of a woman who is getting a damn good seeing to." Her lined face as straight and honest as ever. "So unless you're seeing someone else too—"

"I am not, thank you." I fold my arms, ignoring the blushing on my cheeks.

"'*The sun is shining?*' What's that about?" she comments, shaking her head, a mischievous grin on her coral-lined lips.

"It is!" I laugh, my hands lifting towards the cloudless sky.

"Yes, and you can tell now that you're not holed up in bed, can you?"

"Nan!" I repeat, conscious of her embarrassing, well, me, not herself.

She won't care. If Nan doesn't vocalise her thoughts, her face usually shows it. She's been in countless 'disagreements' in the home with other residents. 'Life's too short to stuff a mushroom' is her motto, which correlates to always being honest. Brutally so.

"I like Stewart, Daisy. And not just because he sends us cakes from his family's bakery every week." Nan smiles over her teacup.

I chuckle and take a bite of cake, revelling in the fact that the sun is indeed beaming down on us. The golden circles of Nan's rings glint like treasure.

"Stewart's good for you. He's polite, kind, handsome, and I haven't seen you this happy in years, Poppet. Your eyes are sparkling, your cheeks must be aching from all the extra smiling, and I bet your inner thighs are getting a good workout."

"Nan! For goodness sake!" I hiss and throw an apologetic smile at the family at the table within earshot. "He's a good egg."

"But?" Nan slurps her tea noisily and unapologetically. The wind ruffling her permed curls the colour of fudge.

"No buts as such." I pour more tea for Nan from the white teapot. "He works a lot, a ridiculous amount. The distance is tough enough without his crazy schedule."

"Move in with him."

"That's not part of my plan."

"Plans change, especially when love is thrown into the pot."

Yes, that's what I'm apprehensive of. Life, plans and routines have a habit of spiralling or veering off into different directions now I'm with Stewart.

The distance between us is obviously, at times, a challenge, but it's the snatched moments that are the hardest to deal with. It feels like we've just been reunited, and he has to go for an interview or flight. Or he's on the phone for hours, tapping away at his laptop, singing and muttering about production and layers of guitars.

"What's the name of the band he sings with?" Nan asks once I've shaken my head at several pouting selfies Stewart has sent.

"Cardinal. Why?"

Nan is an avid listener of Classic FM, the sudden interest in popular music is out of character.

"I could have sworn I saw a picture of him in the paper this week. He looked miserable," she continues, picking up her crossword puzzle. "I thought no, that can't be my Daisy's Stewart, because he's always full of smiles."

Photographers like to get snaps of Stewart looking sad, drunk, angry or in an unflattering light. Scandals sell more than happiness, apparently. His whole world is madness. I'll never understand or like it.

"He was with a blonde stick of a woman who could do with gorging herself on Stewart's mothers' cakes, let me tell you."

Ella Egan, of course. The girlfriend of Stewart from Cardinal, as far as the press are aware. I swallow down the unnecessary jealously Ella evokes, with her perfect hair and face that could have been sculpted from marble. I sigh out loudly and replace the second scone back on the plate. My hands go to my pockets, and I start shredding a tissue to dust.

"Again, I thought no, Daisy wouldn't stand for that."

"It's not real, Nan—"

"Then I got Frank to go on the Google thing to hunt Stewart down. I said to him, 'hit up this young man, and I'll give you a game of chess.'"

I push my lips together, finding it amusing that she's getting her words muddled, yet can understand her perfectly.

"And what did you find?" I ask with a heavy weight of dread in my stomach.

Nan places the book and golden biro on her knees. "What did I not find might be a better question, my girl?"

Shit. The first result will have been Stewart and the married actress shagging outside the hotel years ago. He'll never escape from that, even when we get married. I gulp down the coffee in my mouth and almost choke. When *we* get married? Fuck the Force. Where did *that* thought appear from?

"The answer is you." She holds my gaze, leaning forward for her dainty china cup and matching saucer. "There's no mention of you."

Not strictly true. After our weekend at the Inn on the Fell with Rob and Zach, there were reports of Stewart dating each one of us. It was soon made explicit by the Cardinal team that I was the band florist, and nothing has been reported on me since. I'm relieved. Izzie took a little more persuading. I had to spin a lie that I'd been stood up, and Stewart, coincidentally in the area, sat down for a brief moment to talk flowers and creativity. She believed it. Me. My thigh ended up with four new cuts as a result, which fleetingly cancelled out my guilt.

"I know. That was our decision."

"Dating in secret, Daisy, it can only end in disaster."

"It makes sense to us. We didn't want to be thrust into the pages of newspapers at the start of a relationship."

"And now? You two have been together a good few months, Poppet. How long is this secrecy going to last?"

I sigh and watch fluffy clouds appear and drift overhead, changing shape, extending and stretching like slow-motion yoga poses. Like time Stewart and I have together in between his manic schedule and my work and college, there's a limit to how long we can date in secret.

"I still need to tell Izzie," I admit.

"You haven't told your best friend? What on earth does she think is going on with you? You haven't been this happy for years; she must suspect it's down to decent sex."

"Honestly? Izzie thinks I'm seeing a married man."

"As if you would, how could she think that of you?"

It makes more sense to Izzie, the reason for my sudden packing and leaving, the secrecy. The last person in the world she'd put me with is Stewart Burns. Even if I told her, she'd think it was a sick joke. And Rob had agreed with her at first. I think he secretly still enjoys encouraging that train of thought.

"I'm a bit scared, Nan," I confess. Scrubbing a hand over my face and fiddling with my fringe. A bit, well that's an understatement.

"Scared? About telling Izzie?"

"Yes, but I like Stewart. I mean really like him. I love him." A smile twitches my lips, wanting to backtrack, yet knowing it's pointless. Aside from myself, and that was a struggle, I haven't told anyone how I feel about Stewart. It is a huge thing to reveal out loud. "I think I love him."

"It is allowed, Daisy."

"I know but–"

"Drop that guard of yours. Don't keep pushing people away."

"It is dropping." Slowly. Stewart's doing well, already making it through any and all defences I throw down like landmines, but he hasn't yet made it safely across the battlefield.

"Not everyone you let in will leave you or let you down. I'm still here."

"Nan, you will survive any and all apocalypses."

She squeezes my hand, the paper-thin skin feeling familiar, leaving behind a scent of rose and talcum powder. I have an urge to go back in time and spend every waking moment with her. Not begrudging her old-fashioned ways, curfews and making me do any and all jobs around the house. It's times like this when I'm so overwhelmed with love for her. I can't believe at sixteen I longed to be living in Spain.

"If Stewart makes you this happy, keep him. I don't mean lock him in your bedroom, though who would blame you if you did? Handsome chap he is. But don't push him away because you're scared to show your feelings. Izzie will be desperate to meet the man who's managed to bring you out of your rigid lifestyle."

I doubt that. I press my nails into my thighs.

"Give her a call and tell her about Stewart. Izzie will be happy for you,"

"She won't. She thinks she loves him," I admit, my cheeks blushing in embarrassment for Izzie being stuck in the mindset of a fifteen-year-old, more than how my choice in boyfriend is sort of breaking the holy girl code.

"Come again?" Nan asks, the cup halfway to her mouth.

"Because he's in her favourite band. They were Sophia's favourite band too. Izzie feels connected to them, to Stewart and even Sophia through their music."

I remove my nails from my thigh, yet know as soon as I get home, I'm digging out a razor blade from the bottom drawer in the bathroom.

"I see. That doesn't give her a claim to him, Daisy."

I know. Maybe on some hidden level, maybe Izzie knows it too. But still, I shouldn't have even given Stewart a second glance back in January, except to pass on Izzie's number to him or room key and ask him to give her a medicinal shag to cure her migraine. Yet here I am, months later, in love and dating the man she believes she's meant to be with. Yes, she exists in this fantasy world, but have I broken the girl code, the grounding of female friendship? Or is it an exception? And do soulmates—and I do believe Stewart is mine—go above best friends?

24

My back is aching, my arms protesting after the first day at work after a blissful weekend in sunny Sorento. Makes a change from my thighs. After four days off, I'd almost forgotten the physical side of being a florist. Lugging silver buckets of water and crates of flowers back and forth all day.

The scent of sweet roasted garlic and tomatoes, and homegrown herbs fill the whole of the house, drifting up the stairs, no doubt. My stomach rumbles. Good job I've lived off nothing but alcohol and the minimalist amount of antipasti all weekend.

"Aren't you the romantic, whisking her away for her birthday?" I hear Rob comment to Stewart, who stayed over, letting 'Eddie and Patrick do the press shit for a change.'

Shit. I didn't tell Stewart it was my birthday while we were away. I knew he'd be all extravagant and exaggerated. Usually I try to bypass the day as best I can.

"It was Daisy's birthday?"

I picture Rob's round cheeks stained red in embarrassment. Despite their first meeting not exactly running smoothly at first, the two of them have become friendly, finding common ground in winding me up about being short, and bonding over copious amounts of wine and sending one another insulting memes.

"When was it?"

"Saturday. Don't take it personal. It's just her way. She hates being the centre of attention."

Stewart, who lives most of his life beneath a spotlight, won't understand this. He embraces being on stage and holds the attention of everyone all the time. Pushing open the kitchen door, I see Rob, wearing a floral apron, stirring a pan of bubbling pasta.

"Hey, Sweetheart," Stewart smiles, pulling me into a hug and peppering kisses all over my face. I beam at him, pretending to be annoyed at his affections. I feel my exhaustion and hangover dissipate.

"I missed you," he says, picking me up and spinning me round, kicking my feet into the bin.

I swat his arm playfully. "You saw me at lunch."

"Coffee, Babe?" Rob asks.

"I'll make it," I say as Stewart puts me down.

"I am the worst boyfriend in the entire world," he hooks his chin over my shoulder, hands around my waist.

"I know, but why?"

"Wee menace. Why didn't you tell me it was your birthday?"

I shrug, step away from him and fill the kettle. "It's just another day. I never bother with it."

"Speaking of," Rob hands me an envelope. I open it and see a cartoon Beyonce on the card. I lean and kiss at his cheek.

"Thank you, Babe."

Rob flicks at his rainbow-coloured fringe. "I will, of

course, treat you to the traditional pizza and bottle of vanilla vodka."

Stewart watches then leans against the kitchen counter, his feet crossed at the ankles. I try not to think about him bending me over it a few weeks ago.

"Really? Card, pizza and vodka? That's how you celebrate birthdays down here?"

Rob shrugs. "The only time I've known Daisy celebrate was her twenty-first at uni. We went to Ibiza for a week and got so drunk we slept through her actual birthday. Woke up with foam drying on our skin, glow sticks around our arms, and hands still clutching empty cocktail glasses. Personally, I have at least three parties and want to be lavished in gifts."

I feel their eyes on me as I make three coffees, counting the grains to delay me looking at Stewart.

"Why don't you celebrate it, Sweetheart?"

I sigh, rub at my forehead, and stare at the knife block. "My mum stopped sending cards or presents when I was ten. I lost all interest after that."

Stewart reaches for my hands, "Daisy, I'm so sorry."

I shrug, dismiss it. Place the oat milk next to the brewing coffees.

"Can I at least buy you a wee belated present? I feel fucking awful," he pleads, his blue eyes as mesmerising as the sea we spent most of the weekend in.

"No, being in Italy with you was perfect."

"Next year I am going to spoil you rotten."

"Please don't," I shake my head and stir the water in the mugs.

"I can't promise, it's in my nature."

We all turn to look into the hall as the doorbell rings.

"Shit!" Rob whispers and drops the salt pot, the granules dusting the table like frost. "It's Izzie dropping round your card and shit. I said she could stay for tea too."

My eyes widen, and my heart starts pounding like I've run a marathon.

Stewart chuckles. "Should I be prepared for a full-blown Cardinal fan freak out?"

"More like witnessing your girlfriend's murder, mate,"

"Why?"

Rob points a stubby finger between us. "Izzie doesn't know about you two,"

My eyes go towards Stewart. He looks both furious and full of hurt. He shakes his head slowly, his eyes darkening.

"You still haven't told her?"

I flinch beneath his gaze and find I can't speak.

"You said you'd told her," he seethes.

"I couldn't."

"You didn't."

The doorbell rings again.

"Ok, so how are we playing this?" Rob asks, unfastening his apron.

Stewart rubs a palm over his beard. "Obviously, you're going to have to tell her."

"I can't!"

Rob puts his hands on his hips and pouts his lips. "Come on, Babe, Izzie can't keep pretending to live in Sophia's shoes. Stewart isn't even her type. She likes guys dressed in leather with souls as black as her hair. Not some pretty boy who sings about the fucking ocean. No offence mate. Izzie thinks she likes him because Sophia did. It's keeping Sophia's dream alive, not her own."

"Rob, she loves that band," I exhale, eyes flitting to Stewart's.

"She loves Cardinal because her sister did, because Tori took her under her stalker wings when she needed a distraction."

"Wait, what am I missing here?" Stewart asks.

"Izzie can't see you. She can't find out like this," I rush out, feeling myself start to sweat, ignoring Stewart's question.

"What are you going to do, hide me in the pantry?"

I open the door to the walk-in cupboard. "Yes! Get in!"

"I am not hiding in a fucking cupboard, Daisy. Just tell Izzie about you and me."

"I need to go let her in. I'll stall her for as long as possible while you two sort out your domestic," Rob says and pulls the kitchen door closed behind him.

Stewart pulls at his hair as he steps over Ackbar, who mewls at him to give him love and attention. We both ignore the fat cat, Stewart almost tripping over the black fluffy mass.

"Please, Brunnera," I beg, my hands pushed together in a prayer.

"This is so fucking stupid," Stewart sighs as he sits on the floor in the pantry, his legs crossed like he's been sent there as a naughty child.

"I'll make it up to you."

"You'd better. I want the best blow job of my life." He smirks.

"Absolutely," I nod, pushing the cupboard door closed.

He opens it a crack. "And, you're telling Izzie. Now."

"About the blow job?"

"Don't be so sarcastic, you wee menace." He squeezes his fingers around my wrists. "You are telling Izzie about us, right the fuck now."

I nod. I won't but whatever.

"I hate you a wee bit for this, Sweetheart."

I bend down and kiss his lips, but he doesn't respond. I step out of the pantry.

"Trust me. I hate myself for this too."

"Over dating me, or keeping our relationship a secret from your best pal?"

The answer becomes stuck in my throat, like the last stubborn thorn on a rose stem.

"That's reassuring," he says before slamming the door closed.

Izzie and Rob's chatter gets louder, and the tomato sauce spills over the side of the pan. I feel I may faint; I slump onto a stool before I collapse. Rob and Izzie appear in the kitchen. I assume I look as nervous as Rob does. The headache bangs right between my eyes.

"Hey Iz!" I smile as naturally as I can.

"How was the convention? Wow, good weather down south?" Izzie asks as we hug. I hope she can't hear my heart pounding.

"Actually, I've been in Italy."

"Lucky you. A flower show in Italy. The furthest I go with work is a boardroom in Leeds."

"I went with my boyfriend."

Izzie blinks, her false lashes as black as coal. "Are you actually in a serious relationship with someone other than Brett?"

"Yes."

"This is the Cardinal guy, right?"

Rob spits out his coffee. We both turn to face him. "You know?"

"Yeah. Daisy told me she was seeing someone on their team, but it was complicated." She shakes her head before squeezing her hand around my arm. "Is he married? We won't judge you for it, Babe,"

"He's not married. And did I actually say that?" I enquire, my eyes on Ackbar, who is scratching at the pantry door.

"Lucky cow, landing a job with Cardinal then dating someone who knows them." Izzie's phone beeps. Pulling it from her checked jeans, she smiles. "It's Alex. I know you invited me for some tea, but can I be a bitch and go to his after a coffee?"

"Why does that make you a bitch?" Rob asks.

"The whole girl code. Chicks before dicks and stuff but—"

I stand up, beam at her. "It's no problem. You should go. Relationships require effort. Go, have the best of times and—"

"Why are you being weird?" Izzie asks suspiciously, her fern green eyes narrowing.

I ruffle my fringe. Lean a palm against the pantry door and nudge Ackbar away with my bare foot. "I'm not."

"Yes you are. I was expecting a full-on Beyonce-inspired speech about being independent and not needing a man,"

"It's her boyfriend," Rob comments, stirring the pasta into the tomato sauce. "Someone has actually broken through her hard-as-nails exterior."

Izzie laughs as she pulls an envelope and wrapped box from her bag. She places them on the table. "That can't be right. You're a cynic, Daisy. Career-minded, focused. You won't be swayed by a man. Not even Brett could hold your attention, and he was your ideal man."

I blush. Hope that Stewart can't hear this, but realistically, I know he can.

"Izzie, I'm really happy," I admit.

"Cute. So can I tell you my news before I shoot off? It's about affairs of the heart."

She flicks her raven locks, which glisten beneath the strip lights. My stomach twists with how dismissive she is towards me. Rob nudges me sharply in the ribs.

"Actually, Iz, I need to tell you this. It's about Stewart."

Her head snaps to mine. "So's my news!"

"What?" I ask as Rob hands me the cutlery.

"My beloved Stewart from Cardinal, the man who saved my life, has a girlfriend."

I drop the knives and forks with a metallic clatter. Ackbar mewls and goes scurrying off as fast as his stumpy legs can carry him.

"When you've been working with them, have you met her? Who is she? How long have they been together? More importantly, how can I get rid of her?" Her questions fire at me like machine gun bullets.

"Izzie, you shouldn't say things like that."

She ignores me. "I thought he was dating Ella, but it's someone else. Some blonde bitch. He's just been on holiday with her. She's in all his posts, subtly."

Suddenly, it's imperative that the cutlery is lined up exactly on the table, which holds my full attention.

"You want Stewart to be happy, Iz, right? As a fan, you know?" I feel my cheeks starting to blush. I gulp and resist the temptation to grab a bottle of vodka from the shelf and down it.

"I'd rather he was taking me to bed than some random slag."

I try not to flinch. I pass her the coffee meant for Stewart as she sits down.

"What is with this?" she asks, pulling a face after taking a sip. "This milk is rank."

"It's oat milk."

"Why have you got oat milk?"

"It's better for the environment and such."

She looks at me like I've told her today is Christmas. "You take your coffee black."

"Iz, Babe, you know Stewart didn't actually save your life or anything, right?" Rob asks, sitting down next to her at the table. "The music Cardinal makes helped you navigate a really tough time ..."

She shrugs, "What's the difference?"

"You don't know, Stewart," I pitch in.

"I know everything about him."

Rob and I exchange a quick glance before my eyes dart to the closed pantry door.

"As a fan, maybe. But you don't know him as a person away from Cardinal. He's a separate entity to the band," I say cautiously.

"So you're both ganging up on me? And you wonder why I never want to spend time with you anymore. You seem to be on another planet, Daisy. You used to be there for me, all the time. Now you're always busy."

Living my own life. Following my heart, putting myself first.

"We just want to help you gain some perspective, Babe," Rob adds on, a hand on her shoulder, which she flicks off like he's an annoying fly.

Her phone rings and her face lights up. "I'm going to Alex's, and I'm taking this back," Izzie says, snatching the unopened birthday present from the table. She pours the coffee down the sink. The house seems to rattle with the slamming of the front door.

Rob places two bowls of pasta on the table, then flicks his fringe. He pouts and shakes his head.

"She's such a drama queen."

"Maybe we went too far."

"Daisy, nothing we said was out of order. She stormed off because she knows it's the truth. If this was the other way round, she'd have made you cry unnecessarily several times."

I sigh. As much as it hurts me to admit, Izzie is cruel to me more than anyone. Maybe because she knows I almost owe it to her for looking out for me after mum left.

"She's grieving."

"That doesn't mean she has to be a shite friend to you."

I know he's right. I'm so confused. My loyalty seems to be crumbling in front of me. My hands cover my face. Part of me hates myself. What sort of woman am I, putting a man before a friend?

Rob pulls my hands away. He looks to the closed pantry door, then lowers his voice to barely above a whisper. He flicks the colourful fringe from his eyes. "Stewart's good for you, good to you. This could be the thing Izzie needs to snap out of her Cardinal obsession."

"She's not obsessed."

"It's not a healthy interest, Daisy. She's pushing thirty. Izzie needs some perspective. And really, she's horrible to you at times."

"She's always been there for me."

It's true, well, Izzie's family were welcoming to Nan and me after mum left. I went to theirs after school half the week, playdates most weekends with Izzie and Sophia. Once our foray into the goth scene made me realise I did not belong there, yet Izzie had found her niche, we drifted apart as teens. Away from school, where she ignored me as I had no common interests with her clique; we spent several evenings together at her house. Had sleepovers most weekends, where she talked about her plans to change the world using her individuality and freedom of speech and spells she was learning. I wasn't always her first choice. I knew that. And now, as adults, Izzie usually calls the shots as to where we go or what we do. I'd never dream of asking her to attend a flower show; it's not her thing at all. A Cardinal gig was my idea of hell too, yet she bought me a ticket for Christmas. My shoulders drop. Maybe Izzie's not as good a friend as I hold her to be. Sometimes, I feel like the gazania daisy to her hollyhock. Izzie thriving in the full sun, blocking out the light so my own petals close up and shrivel until she steps away. I blush, I'd never voice those thoughts out loud. Plus, I'm kind of used to it after decades of friendship. Though, should friendship be a more balanced seesaw, not leaving one of us stuck on the ground while the other flies high and free?

"That's just her way. The three of us are horrible to one another."

"There's always an edge to Izzie."

"She's been through a lot," I counter. "I admit, she's become more snippy and brusque since losing Sophia, but..."

"We've been through a lot too. I was shunned from my family for being gay, you were abandoned by your mum and self-harm because of it. We haven't let that make us cruel."

"Her sister died, Rob."

Rob raises his palms. "It's not a competition. We all have battles we're fighting. I've got your back, you've got mine. Always. Don't forget that Stewart's on your side too. Is Izzie on your side?"

I hesitate. Of course she is. Yet the words become lodged in my throat, like the potent scent of hyacinths.

"The fact you didn't answer instantly speaks volumes. You know we would've cut her out if Sophia hadn't died,"

I drag my nails up my thighs. Rob picks up the third bowl of pasta and mug of coffee. He knocks on the pantry door before opening it.

"Grubs up, Stewart, mate. I'm going to eat in the living room. Give you two some space," he says as he leaves the kitchen. The pantry door creaks open further.

I wait, but Stewart doesn't step out of the cupboard. I push my nails into my palms then walk towards the open door. He looks furious as he lifts his head. His eyes are darker and cold, fists clenched, knuckles white. I shuffle under his gaze. I know he's both disappointed and annoyed at me.

"Why haven't you told her?" he barks at me.

"I couldn't find the right words."

"Just going for the fucking jugular, 'I'm dating Stewart from Cardinal,' would be better than saying fuck all right now. You met her last week and went out for lunch, for fucks sake. And today was the perfect opportunity."

"You didn't see her face—"

"No, because you locked me in a fucking cupboard,"

"Technically you weren't locked in, Baby," I say, using a pet name to try and soothe him as I sit down in front of him. My hands smooth down his chest. He realises I'm about to try and distract him with sexual favours and frowns at me, his hands around my wrists.

"This isn't fair on any of us, Daisy."

"I'm sorry," I say as he stands up and knocks into the shelves. The jars of pasta and grains rattle. A scrunched-up ball of plastic bags floats to the floor.

"So you keep saying," he sighs; an air of defeat clouds the enclosed space. His phone rings. He glances at the screen but doesn't answer it. "I was going to approach this with caution, but I don't see why I should. The team wants us to go public in three weeks."

"What?" I ask in a scared tone. I scramble to my feet, the jars wobble, two falling to the floor, sending glass and pasta twirls skidding across the floor.

"Countdown is on, Daisy. Three weeks to tell Izzie or she'll find out from the press."

"Go public in three weeks?"

"It's that or we break up," Stewart stalks away, and the back door slams.

I step towards the kitchen, broken glass crunches beneath my feet. The clear shards mixed with dried pasta glint tauntingly at me. I hold a piece in my palm.

How Izzie reacts to the revelation I'm dating her celebrity crush, or how the public and press and thousands of Cardinal fans are going to think of me, is something I cannot control. I shudder; the thought of being so publicly scrutinised makes me feel sick to my stomach.

I keep trying to convince myself Izzie will be fine. She is, after all, dating Alex and seems happy with him. Yet my head is heavy like a hammer about to smash into an anvil.

Alex wasn't the thing that pulled her through the dark clouds of grief. He isn't the man who makes her feel connected to Sophia. Who gave her a reason to plough through those long lonely early days of losing her big sister. That man is my boyfriend.

I am the worst friend in the world.

The glass, as clear as ice and just as deadly as a frozen lake in the depths of winter, I can control. I can have complete manipulation over cutting my skin, and it would be a brief yet welcomed escape from reality.

25

Stewart doesn't sleep well. Sometimes he lays awake for hours at a time. And when he does sleep, the smallest of noises can jolt him awake.

Still, I can't fight it; the need for release, control.

I shuffle away, extract myself from beneath his arm around my waist. Opening my bedroom door, I pause as the hinges squeak. I turn with bated breath to look at him. Expect him to sit up and ask where I'm going. He doesn't. He snuffles, rolls over, fringe covering his eyes.

My heart aches in the best way. I love him. But not enough to stop cutting my skin to shreds over his crazy life.

I step over Ackbar, snoozing on the landing, and tiptoe down the stairs. Avoiding the second to last step as it always creaks. Creeping through the hall and kitchen takes twice as long in the dark. But the lights would alert Stewart easily as to my whereabouts. I don't have to worry about Rob; he once slept through an earthquake.

I open the back door painstakingly slowly, every sound feels amplified in the darkness. I sit on the back step, the stars starting to fade into the lightening sky. Despite it being a little after three am, the songbirds have started chirping quietly. Streaks of morning appear above me, pushing the darkness away.

I unfold my canvas roll and exhale in relief, already feeling calmer at the sight of my yellow-handled floristry knife. I hold the plastic handle, the weight so familiar to me; for work and self-harm. The blade bites into my flesh as I drag it across my thigh in a straight line. I hiss at the first shock of pain, yet it's replaced with calm and relief as the blood appears from the cut. The cool air on my skin is soothing. Goosebumps raise, but a feeling of relaxation and control brings warmth to me. I repeat the action three more times, leaving four fresh cuts on my thigh with no tattoo or scars to hide behind. With each cut I feel more powerful, well equipped to face the next days, weeks and months of the unknown.

I realise too late that I haven't brought a damp flannel or towel to clean myself up with. Shit. I pull my oversized hoodie off and press the sleeve onto the four bleeding slices.

"Daisy?" Stewart asks as the kitchen light flickers on. I place the knife and canvas into a plant pot and hope he doesn't notice. I bend forward, fold my arms across my thighs and try to look both comfortable and nonchalant.

Stewart will hate me for self-harming. We'll argue, shout and scream about it, then he'll soften, possibly cry and beg me not to do it, to get help. I'll refuse.

"What are you doing, Sweetheart?" He sits next to me, rubbing at his sleepy features.

"I wanted some fresh air."

He places a hand around my shoulders, then nuzzles at my neck. "I'm sorry,"

"You don't owe me an apology, Brunnera. I'm in the wrong. But you have a foul temper," I reply with a playful shake of my head before kissing his cheek.

"So do you, Baby," Stewart places a hand on my thigh and traces the old scars beneath my tattoo. The new ones still hidden from him. "The unknown is daunting, isn't it?"

My eyes glaze over as I nod. I'm so small town, I struggle with the train station at Edinburgh. In three weeks, my life and my relationship is going to be invaded by the public. And although I know it will be hell, I have no idea how Izzie is going to react.

We spent the rest of the evening sidestepping the topic of Izzie, as Stewart and Hipster Harry emailed me rules and timelines, plans and advice about our relationship and going public. It's terrifying.

"It doesn't matter if I'm physically here or not; we're in this together. Just you, just me." Stewart places his hands on my jaw, tilts my head towards his and we kiss. My fears dissolving under his touch. We rest our foreheads together.

"Promise me you'll tell Izzie?" he pleads.

"I will."

"It makes me feel like shit you haven't told her. Like you're ashamed of me, of us."

"Well, you are in a boyband," I go for sarcasm, one of our long-running jokes. But it falls flat. "I'm not ashamed of you at all, Stewart, I promise."

He pulls away, hands in his hair. "Then why haven't you told her?"

Ok. Here goes. I inhale then exhale deeply. Three times. He takes it to be a hesitation, a refusal to speak.

"Come on, Sweetheart, what's the deal with Izzie? I've ignored it for months, but I know there's more to it. What was Rob talking about earlier? Who's Sophia? Is this all about the girl code? The whole Beyonce shit?" He scratches at his beard, turns his head to face me, his coffee-coloured fringe dangling to almost his cheeks.

"It's more complicated than that. Izzie's big sister, Sophia, loved Cardinal. Izzie went with her to a few shows and stuff. It was Sophia who was a fan first. She died in a car crash a few years ago. Afterwards, Iz latched on to Cardinal. It's all a connection to Sophia. You are a direct line, a link to her sister, and she gets caught up in it."

Izzie's interest in Cardinal and the whole boyband thing jars with the rest of her image. Izzie listens to metal music, lives in boots with studs on the toes, only wears black or purple, watches horror movies; all those gothic stereotypes. She just loves Cardinal too.

"Yes, maybe Izzie is more of a stalker than I care to admit, but she feels the link to Sophia that you and your band provide, which gives her justification for that. Izzie feels she loves you."

"Well, fuck."

"It's tangled with her grief and she can't separate it. I know it's not real, but," I hold my head in my hands. Stewart pulls me close and rests his head on mine, "I am the worst person, the worst friend in the world."

My nails scratch at my tattooed thigh like a bad but well established habit, yet he places his hands on top of mine.

"Don't hurt yourself, Sweetheart."

"I am the worst person. I know I am."

"No, Daisy. You're the best person, and your pal should be happy for you. I wish you'd told me sooner. You should've told me."

"It was just easier to pretend I could keep you both separate."

Stewart dances his fingers through my fringe. "Will Izzie not want you to be happy?"

"Not if this is the cost," I reply, threading my fingers with his.

"Then what sort of friend is she?"

I struggle to answer. Whichever way I look at things, it always reflects badly on me. Izzie is my best friend, and I'm in love with the one man who she feels helped her survive her darkest depths of grief. I'll always be the enemy, the villain. The aphid on her prize rose. Destroying the beautiful thing she holds dear for my own benefit.

"Maybe start to distance yourself from Izzie."

"Because we're dating?" I ask.

"Yes, and also because she's a stalker. But Sweetheart, she seems to be a terrible friend to you. You've said how you always feel drained or belittled after seeing her."

"She's grieving."

"Izzie wasn't always full of snipes and cutting comments?"

He's heard her on the phone with me. Knows how she takes jokes too far and how hurtful and personal her words towards me can be.

"She's always been that way, if I'm honest."

"Then why are you still friends with her?"

"Because she's still always there. She's consistent. Perhaps not pleasant or even enjoyable company, but, like

Brett, Izzie was always there. I don't like change, Stewart. I don't like to let others into my life in case they let me down and leave. Izzie may be cruel, but at least I know where I stand with her. Like my mother's absence, I can deal with the consistency."

"I appreciate your reasons for being so fiercely independent and stubborn, but, Baby, you're carrying so much on your wee shoulders. A problem shared is a problem cut in two and all. Catherine feels better after telling Nelly how she feels about Heathcliff."

"Trust you to bring it back to your favourite love story," I laugh quietly, rolling my eyes.

Stewart kisses my cheeks, then peppers my whole face with exaggerated kisses. I protest weakly as he pulls me onto his lap, my thighs either side of his. He holds my face in his hands, smooths his fingertips on my cheeks, then down my neck, shoulders, and arms.

"Seriously, Daisy. I'm here for you. Any time. You can talk to me about anything. About your stalker pal, flowers, Wuthering Heights, or your—"

He stops, and his hands freeze on my thighs. I tilt my head at him. His face morphs from happiness with a hint of mischief to shock, confusion, then horror and a touch of anger.

"Stewart? You ok?" I ask nervously.

His raised palm has smears of blood lining his skin. He looks from his palm to my thigh.

Fuck. The cuts on my skin, the forgotten hoodie now abandoned on the ground, and the hidden tools in the plant pot; all come hurtling at me like unexpected pelts of raindrops on bare skin.

Ever so slowly, Stewart raises his face to look at mine.

He exhales loudly and looks towards the sky streaked with blacks and paler blues.

"Did it make you feel any better, the cutting?" he asks after a pause.

"A little," I confess. I can't deny it. I've been caught red-handed. Literally.

"Do you want to do it now? Shall I grab a knife for you? Or have you brought your own outside with you and tried to hide it from me?"

We do this when it comes to discussing my self-harm; either scream and shout in which Stewart gets angry (or frustrated and confused as he calls it), or he's calm and borderline patronising. Either response is fuelled by care and love, I know, yet I'm never sure which reaction I prefer.

"No."

"No to both?"

I feel my skin blanch with shame, and my eyes flit towards the plant pot before I can stop them. He leans over and sighs as he sees the tools wrapped in the canvas material.

"You don't understand," I blurt out, shuffling off his legs.

"No, I don't. Because you don't talk to me. I want to help you, Daisy. I hate the lies, the selfish side, the fucking manipulation that goes alongside your self-harm."

"Ironic, isn't it? That you want to help everyone when you can't fix things with your own family."

He stands up, clenches his fists, and bangs the side of his palms against the wall. He turns round and kicks at a bin, an empty water bottle skitters along the floor. The sound echoes around the dark yard. I grimace. I should apologise for my words. Yet the dominant side of me squashes down the apology and I carry on with my destructive words.

"The quick fix for that is to return to the kitchen and bake bread every day with your family, but you're too busy writing your pissing tunes." I hate myself.

Stewart turns to face the wall, the breath heaving out of him. I wouldn't be surprised if he punched a hole in the bricks.

"Stewart, I'm sorry."

"It's fucking true, isn't it?" he says with an air of defeat.

I go to him, wrap my arms around him, pleased on all levels when he hugs me back and bends down to rest his head on my shoulder. "I'm sorry."

He turns his head and kisses my neck. "You know exactly how to push my buttons, Sweetheart. Clever wee thing, aren't you?"

"With my low shots?"

"You totally derailed the conversation."

"I'm sorry."

"Sorry enough to get help?"

"Back to this are we?" I sigh loudly, go to walk away, yet he holds my wrists gently.

"Sweetheart, you clearly do not have control over your self-harm."

"I will deal with it my own way." I step away, stalking into the kitchen. I sit on the stool, ignoring Ackbar mewling at me.

"All on your fucking own, that's what you want isn't it?" Stewart sneers as he closes the back door. He places the wrapped scissors and knife on my knees. I ignore them and him. He's pacing round the room like a caged lion, frustrated yet trapped.

"Go on then," Stewart says standing in front of me, his arms crossed. "Show me what I'm missing."

I stare at him finally. "Don't be a dick."

"My involvement in your life has made you return to self-harm, you might as well do it in front of me."

I stand up, the tools falling to the floor, unwrapping themselves. The blade sneers at me beneath the strip lights. I push him in anger, my palms flat against his chest. He stumbles backwards before trying to grab at my hands. I jerk them away.

"You're such a fucking dick."

"Daisy—"

"I hate you right now," I hiss out as I stalk upstairs.

I climb into my bed. Stewart's scent of lavender, nicotine and herby mint shampoo clinging to my bedding calms my senses.

This is exactly why I didn't tell anyone about my self-harm. Why I don't let people get too close, it becomes their issue. It's now on Stewart's mind, bringing drama and conflict to the two of us.

The door squeaks open. I pick up the rattling of his bracelets, picture him scratching at his neck.

"I was out of order. I shouldn't have done that, or said those things. I'm sorry, Daisy."

I sniffle, push my teeth together, feel my lips quivering, yet I try to refrain from crying.

He sits on the edge of the bed, fingers threading through my hair. "I'm so sorry. It destroys me that you hurt yourself, especially as it's down to me and my crazy life."

I could blame it all on him. It's true, I haven't felt so out of control of aspects of my life since I was a teen. Yet I've never allowed myself to stray from a plan before. It's me, my brain slipping back into old habits. I sigh out, feel myself relaxing beneath his touch. He kisses my forehead.

"I don't know how to handle this. I've tried being nice and you still do it. I thought losing my temper and shouting would snap you out of it."

"It's not that easy," my voice cracks. Sometimes I feel like I'll never do it again, other times I feel like I never want to stop it.

"I get that. I'm so sorry, Daisy. So, so sorry."

"I'm sorry I'm such a fuck up."

"You're not a fuck up," he half chuckles as he pulls me up. I fold into his embrace. "Any and all issues you may have are mine too. We've got this, Sweetheart. But I am begging you to seek help for your self-harm. You cannot keep doing this."

I nod at him. Make a half-hearted promise to myself that I'll try harder to only use the blade for work. Know that I won't stick to it.

"I don't deserve you," I say, tears rolling down my cheeks.

"You deserve so much more, but fate decided we should be together."

I sniffle, chuckle a little as I rest my head on his shoulder.

"And who are we to go against the powers of fate and destiny? We are mere mortals, pawns in their bigger plan," he says dramatically.

"Looks like you're stuck with me, then." I smile.

He pulls me closer, places kisses all over my face and

neck, calling me a wee menace as I squeal and call him all the names I can think of.

"You're so enough, Sweetheart. For me or anyone," Stewart says once I've run out of insults to playfully throw at him. I almost believe him. "Not that I'll let anyone have you."

"All yours am I?"

He smirks, lifting me with him, to wrap my legs around him, his mind drifting from self-harm to sex. "Yep. You know it. Come on, I'll show you."

I shake my head. "I want a shower first. I need to clean up my leg."

Stewart kisses my neck. "Shower sounds perfect, Baby."

26

Someone, a nameless face in a Cardinal t-shirt—subtly never comes into play with this band—leads me down the longest hotel corridor to the photo studio. Thank the Force Stewart is there waiting and I don't have to do this alone.

As soon as the door was opened for me, I froze in a state of shock. I thought backstage at a gig was busy. People of various sizes and shapes, all wearing bright red t-shirts, so I know whose orders to follow, though I bet there was a hierarchy within it, buzz around like worker bees. It is a hive of activity, which doesn't help in calming my nerves. I wonder who I have to ask for a bottle of vodka.

I wait to be guided into place as if I'm a statue in a museum, or rather a lump of clay ready to be sculpted. People talk over me, at me, but don't wait for a response or reply. I am under strict orders from Hipster Harry to follow all rules, to only speak when spoken to and to listen to any and all advice from the team.

A tape measure is slung around my hips, when I feel the weight of hands I know on my shoulders followed by the familiar scent of lavender.

"Give us a minute guys, thanks," Stewart says as they scatter at his words. Thank fuck. I am so overwhelmed and they've barely gotten started. I exhale and feel my shoulders drop in relief at Stewart's presence. I spin around and manage a wobbly smile as I snake my hands up around his neck. He smiles before kissing me, taking with him most of my lipstick.

"How do you do this?"

Not even a hello.

He rolls his eyes as he squeezes my waist gently. No doubt that measurement will be taken too.

"How do you get used to collecting fresh flowers at four am?"

"Well played," I say as I run my fingers through his hair.

"Want to compare careers more or can I kiss you again?"

"Hm. Tough choice."

"Menace." Stewart kisses me, deeply, probably way too passionately for the middle of the bustling room, but I don't care. Forget the whole official couple's photo shoot, I'll just stay here forever, wrapped in his arms, lips joined, tongues dancing.

"Fuck, I've missed you," he says quietly as our foreheads push together.

"Missed you too, a little bit, I guess." I nestle my head into his chest and whine. "Do we have to do this?"

"Yep," Stewart replies on a sigh, his hands smoothing down my hair. "We cannot sneak around forever, Daisy. This way, the team are in control. We get to call the shots on when our relationship is made public. Trust me, it'll be far easier this way."

Already I know I'm going to miss the days when I lied to my best friends' faces and had to sneak Stewart in and out of my bedroom.

Red-clothed people hold up and dismiss various dresses and shirts as they observe Stewart and me as if we are blank canvases. Huh, maybe we are.

“I wouldn’t blame you if it was too much. Everyone wants a simpler life,” Stewart says, once we are both dolled up in layers of makeup and designer threads.

“Seriously, how do you do it?” I repeat. I am pleased this photoshoot announcing to the world about our relationship is the first and last press stunt I have to do.

“Roll with it, shrug it off. Focus on important things. Like you, Daisy,” So smooth. But I know he means it. Hopeless romantic that he is. I smile, my heart feeling warm despite the almost freezing cold air conditioning. “I appreciate that my life is complicated.”

I run my fingers through his silky dark hair. “Maybe I like complicated.”

“Just maybe, yep, that’s reassuring.”

“I’m here aren’t I?”

“You’re not very forthcoming with your emotions, Daisy.”

A suited man weaves past us both, talking into a dictaphone as he goes. Stewart pats him on the back as he passes. “Though you are incredibly specific in bed,” he whispers in that accent which lingers in my brain, taking up way too much space, more than I will ever admit. I blush a little.

Being open and honest about feeling isn’t one of my strong points. “Can I play the traumatic childhood card? Abandonment issues?”

“You could just tell me how you feel,” he says with a shrug, and his eyes imploring into mine like he’s a lost kitten.

"Stewart, if I didn't want this, you; then I wouldn't be here." I stretch up to kiss him. Can almost see the makeup artists cringing as I leave a smear of lipstick on him. "Just you, just me, remember Brunnera?"

***

It feels like it's been an age since I last saw Stewart. Really it's only been ten days. Not including those few hours spent being primed and posed for the official photoshoot. But that was so exhausting and out of my comfort zone, that I felt nothing but relief once the cameras had stopped clicking.

Work has been crazy, and while the busyness has kept me from missing him too much, it's made the days so long, the same floristry shit but different days. It's the first time that I've not been satisfied with my own company and small town life. Even Rob's presence has irritated me, and it's usually only Izzie whose comments and company jar in my head when I'm tired.

Stewart's touring, and in rehearsals or ready to go on stage when I finish at work so there's been lots of missed calls, and phone calls at stupid o clock in the mornings.

"Ok, I confess," I begrudgingly admit to Stewart after the show.

He's all sweaty and hyped up, bouncing on the balls of his feet, still energised from being on stage. T-shirt sticking to his broad chest, the only time he wears a fitted top is on stage, hair messed up and a hint of black eyeliner around his sky blue eyes.

The stretch of time between our last meeting dissolves like squishy marshmallows in a steaming hot chocolate. Dissipating until it's merely a distant memory, making way for new magical ones. I feel like he's the only person in the world, the one sole light against a pitch black night. This is love, isn't it?

"The whole being on stage thing is pretty hot."

"Sorry, Daisy, I think I misheard you."

"You heard me. Even if you're in a boyband."

"Fucking menace. Cardinal are not a boyband."

"Hot boyband," I counter, smoothing a palm down his chest.

There must be something magnetising about the rock star thing. If he'd walked over to me sweaty and straight from the gym, I'd direct him to the shower. Alone.

"Am I as hot as Ronan Keating yet?"

"Stewart, don't talk such nonsense."

"You'll be a fully-fledged fan in no time, Sweetheart."

"Maybe I'll start wearing a Cardinal t-shirt to bed."

He kisses me, pushes me against the table. I jump up onto it. Pull him closer with my feet, and kiss him with such fervour I'm instantly frustrated that we're not in private. His hands glide up my thighs and push into my hips. He only ever pushes my dresses up, runs his palm over my tattooed thigh when we're not in sight of others. I could be cold and dismissive, say it's a coincidence or him thinking of the impact my self-harm could have on his band. But I know it's for my benefit, so my scars and secrets remain hidden.

I tug at his hair, he moans deliciously into my mouth.

I'm vaguely aware of people, crew, the team, even Patrick and Eddie entering the room. Ash's voice chatting to

Eddie, or anyone who will listen, drifts into my ears. Everyone is busy and bustling. Excitable chatter overlapping and instructions given out. Boxes and suitcases being filled, merchandise being carefully packed away. The pop and fizz of bottles opening, drinks pouring, the rustle of crisp packets and sweets.

But all I really care about is Stewart and his mouth on mine, his hands on my thighs, my nails scraping at his ears and down across his beard, which makes him bring me as close to him as is possible.

"Fucking hell, Stew. Get a room," Eddie chides, and Stewart smiles against my lips.

Stewart clears his throat as he pulls away and kisses me gently on the forehead.

"While I would like nothing more than to bend you over this table, Daisy—" he says as I interlock my fingers around his neck, his eyes sparkling with mischief.

"Losing my privacy via social media, I can maybe cope with..."

Maybe. I've had various media training meetings from various people in suits or Cardinal red tops. I should say this, shouldn't say that. Try not to smoke in public, don't say anything that could be construed as offensive, plug Cardinal's album whenever possible. I think I'll just stay quiet and hope for the best.

Neither Stewart or myself feel the public announcement of our relationship, all set for three days' time, will be a huge shock to the fans or press. There's been talk for months online and from Izzie, about Stewart's blonde girlfriend, but my identity has, thus far, remained a secret. By the start of next week though, our relationship will be out there. The photos, a short statement, and accompanying brief interview with Stewart is to be released on Sunday night. All set for the Monday morning papers. Stewart and I officially together, plastered in print for the world to know about. I'm terrified. Yet I'm almost ready for it. I know, with Stewart by my side, I'll be ok.

"... sex in front of your bandmates, both of them and the entire team, is something I cannot and will not cope with," I continue.

"Pat still hasn't forgiven me for the kitchen bunker incident." Stewart laughs.

"Which time?"

We kiss again, gently, tongues slowly moving like the last few ripples on the lake after rain.

"Do you wanna get out of here?"

I nod. Probably far too quickly to ever be casual. Ugh, who cares? I'm way past playing it cool with Stewart.

"Fancy a drive back to yours?"

I frown at him playfully. "Any excuse to drive the Bentley. It's like two hours away."

"I know, but I've got two days off, before you head up to mine for the dreaded pap walk prep. I'm sick of hotels, and I love your bed, Baby."

"You mean you love me in it."

"Daisy, I love you anywhere."

Shit, did he just—

The room blurs out of focus behind him. My eyes widen then I feel the stuttering of my eyelashes, like they can't settle on being wide or want to block it out by closing. My lips drop open.

Stewart's expression mirrors mine.

I blink. No, no, he didn't just say that. He didn't mean it that way, did he?

We've both skirted around the illusive L word.

It scares me that there's been times when I've nearly said it. Once I do release it into the open, that's it. It's not a phrase or feeling I can take back. It can't be wound back in, like when I drop a roll of ribbon at work. No matter how tightly I tried to tie it back up, we'd both know it was said. It would be out there forever. And forever is a fucking long time.

"I love you, Daisy. I'm so in love with you," Stewart whispers, his flax blue eyes close as he chuckles softly, his gentle accent making me melt, like ice cream on hot days.

I gulp, ignore as best I can, the swoop of nerves and excitement in my stomach, how it twists like he's just pushed his thumbs into my hips. Maybe I am a romantic just as much as he is.

I don't know what to say. Words, all words ever to exist have dried up like a covered over well. My throat burns with scratchy dryness. Not even a sarcastic comment about him setting the scene with rose petals and candlelight flows from my locked voice box. My brain has turned to mush like over-watered gerbera stems.

I avoid his gaze. Moving my arms from around him, to rub at my forehead nervously. I look towards my lap, the floor, anywhere, but those delphinium blue eyes that I do want to get lost in, even if it's hard to admit.

"Stew, give Harry a call," Patrick says.

Stewart doesn't look at Patrick, his focus still entirely on me. His features stricken, like he's frozen in time. I should say something. Say anything. Tell him how I feel. I remain silent.

Patrick appears in my eye line, dark curls pushed under a baseball cap, a towel around his neck.

He stands behind Stewart, a palm on his shoulder. "Stew? Harry says can you call him? Your phone's off."

"I didn't charge it," he snaps, then scrubs a hand over his face.

Patrick holds his hands in surrender. "Don't shoot the messenger,"

"Sorry, pal."

"Call Harry, he said it was urgent."

"Pat, I've just told Daisy I'm ridiculously in love with her, I don't give a shit about Harry or the press the now."

Patrick slaps him on the back before sauntering away. "About fucking time."

Stewart's cheeks show a light dusting of pink as he faces me, licking his lips then grimacing.

"Sorry, Sweetheart, I should've planned it better—"

I shake my head, my words quiet. "No, no, you can't plan something like that,"

"You would, it's probably outlined in your five-year life plan."

I roll my eyes and smile a little.

"Sorry, Daisy, I caught you off guard. Fuck, I caught myself off guard a wee bit."

"You mean it though?" I long for this reassurance, despite those three words terrifying me like horror films watched on Halloween at teenage sleepovers.

"Of course, Sweetheart. I love you."

I exhale and feel the urge to cry, even though I'm elated. I place my hands either side of his cheeks. He tilts his head like a confused puppy, his hands over my wrists.

"Please Brunnera, don't ask me to say it back. Despite how I feel about you, I'm not ready to say it out loud—"

"No pressure, Daisy. Although I do recall in Edinburgh

you saying something similar," he smirks.

"That totally doesn't count. I couldn't have told you my name that night," I reply, referring to the night I got horrendously drunk while out with him, Eddie and Ash. The hangover lasted days.

"We should've expected me to say it first of course."

"You and your poet's heart."

"Compared to you and your heart of stone."

"I do not have a heart of stone!" I laugh and ruffle his hair, not even minding that it's sweaty and messy. "If I did, you would be reducing it to rubble."

He frowns, ignores Patrick repeatedly asking if we're going to mine or the hotel. "Are you ok with that?"

I rub at my forehead. "I don't like the lack of control that goes with love, to be honest."

That vulnerability runs alongside love, like the shoreline to the waters; there can't be one without the other. I'm not scared of being with Stewart, as such. It's the whole admitting to needing someone else. Him. That I want him, with me. Not just physically, but that I always want to be able to call him mine. To know while he may be on stage or writing songs in Edinburgh, and I'm arranging flowers in Cumbria; that we have each other.

He licks at his lips, pushes our foreheads together.

"How much don't you like it, Sweetheart?" Concern colouring his tone.

"I'm not about to carve chunks from my skin because we're in a relationship."

Stewart winces, which he always does when I'm so blunt about my self-harm, past or present.

"I have to take care of you, Daisy."

"I can take care of myself," I state, stubbornness raising its head, as always.

"Let me in, Daisy."

"Stewart, you're in."

"Can I ask you to move to Edinburgh yet?" he asks with a wink and smirk.

"You can ask, but I'll refuse. Some of us have college courses to finish, jobs to uphold. We don't all have it as easy as you; flitting off to write songs."

"Fucking wee menace."

"Hello? Earth to Stew and Daisy?" Patrick says loudly, his hands on Stewart's shoulders.

Stewart blinks again, those sky blue eyes finally leaving mine as he shoves Patrick away playfully, and I jump down from the table.

"We're going to Daisy's, I'll be back in two days, pal."

"Inseparable, aren't you? Call Harry when you get there."

"Aye I will. Hey, Daisy?"

"Yes?"

"I love you."

I turn to face him. My legs shake, though I'm standing still, I feel I might fall over. Just collapse. My heart thuds against my chest, the butterflies dancing in spirals inside of me. I have a sudden, stupid urge to cry. I bite my lip, which is hard to do when I'm smiling the widest smile ever to have covered my face in the entire twenty-seven years of existence. I blink up at Stewart, getting lost in his sea blue eyes. Again.

"I know."

I am absolutely in love with this man. I kiss him again, slowly, tenderly. I lay my hands against his chest, imploring with him that I love him. I just can't say it. The high walls around my heart need longer to fall, though they are weakening and crumbling with each day. Stewart can't reach the depths of my heart and soul just yet, more bricks need to be destroyed. But I hope he gets there. If he doesn't, then no one else will.

27

I'm en route back up to my bedroom with two cups of coffee when the doorbell rings. I hear Izzie shouting my name from outside. I put one mug down and open the door.

"Hey, Iz."

Her lip snarls, reminding me of a fox. The cruel grey ones from *The Animals Of Farthing Wood.* The ones that gave me nightmares as a child for being so vicious and callous.

"Is he here?" she grits out. Her hands grip around a newspaper. I expected her to buy every paper on Monday morning, drawing evil faces on my image, ripping my picture out from the pages, or maybe set fire to them as a sign of my apparent deception. But today? It's two days too early for the official statement and photographs of Stewart and I to be immortalized in print.

"Who?" I ask, hoping she means Rob. A sinking weight within me knows she doesn't.

"You know who." Fire flashes in her eyes as she slams the newspaper down at my bare feet. I notice the headline. 'Stewart from Cardinal's mystery girlfriend revealed' and accompanying grainy image of Stewart and me, hand in hand, kissing in front of his flat. Shit. She really will fucking kill me.

I try to hold Izzie's gaze, yet my eyes flit towards the stairs for a split second. She notices and pushes past me in a blur of black.

With shaking hands I put the other coffee down, knocking it into the first, the hot liquid spilling onto my Stormtrooper lamp.

"Stewart Burns!" she barks out, snarling at me once she reaches the landing.

"It's not what it looks like!" I shout out as I chase her, the steps have never seemed so steep, so mountainous.

Izzie bursts through my bedroom door with such force, she could have easily ripped the hinges out.

"It looks like you're shagging Stewart from Cardinal!" Izzie screams.

Then yes, it is what it looks like.

My mind swirls, like I've drunk a bottle of vodka on an empty stomach. I wish I had.

Izzie's eyes slide towards me. I'm familiar with the phrase 'if looks could kill' but didn't realise just how close I could come to fearing for my life from one stare. I feel I've been stabbed with millions of rose thorns. The prickle of unease, the constant lies and the impact of being found out making goosebumps rise on my skin.

Shit. I should have told her. I should have told her months ago. Not tried to hide from it and leave the revelation of my relationship status until two days before the official announcement in the press.

"Dating," Stewart says casually and confidently, putting down a book he's been reading, as I pick up the pillows from the floor and throw them onto the bed. "We're dating, actually. Morning, Izzie. Sorry, I said that in the wrong order, let me start again." He shuffles up, props a pillow behind his head and sweeps his fringe from his eyes. "Hi Izzie, good morning. How are you? By the way, I'm dating your best friend. I'm guessing Daisy still hasn't told you. Shall we have a chat about it the now, then?"

I ignore him, not even Stewart's charm or blatant honesty can help me now. For a split second I hate him. But it passes instantly. Like the sneak peek of a dolphin in the waves. Not even sure it was there in the first place, or just an overactive imagination.

"You're dating Stewart Burns from Cardinal? You?" Izzie spits out. Her widened eyes regard me with a look of hatred.

I feel about as small and selfishly ugly as a squashed mushroom. Izzie, though ranting and raving, distress etched on her face, looks beautiful. I'm struck with a ridiculous sense of comparison. Izzie, dressed head to toe in black, skin-tight dark jeans and an oversized leather coat that whips her ankles like a cape, atop her checked jumper and, of course, studded boots. Makeup perfect, eyes lined like a cat and lips a daring shade of purple.

In contrast, masses of my bleached blonde hair pile on top of my head. Knots looking like I've been hung up on a washing line in a tornado, when actually the blame lays wholly with Stewart's fingers and my lack of leave-in conditioner. My makeup-free face and short grey PJs make me look like a female version of Darth Sidious to her stunning Princess Leia. She may as well be wearing a gold bikini.

"Iz, I can explain—"

Her eyes linger on the bruise caused by Stewart's mouth blooming on my neck.

"You don't need to. It's pretty damn clear what you've been doing with—" She pauses, her eyes scanning my face, then his. "Him," she swallows. As if now saying Stewart's name, in full or with his band tagged on the end is too much for her to bear.

I finally look towards Stewart. Fuck the Force, this couldn't be worse. He's naked beneath the floral duvet tucked under his arms. Even if he wasn't, the unmistakable scent of sex hangs in the air.

His half-unpacked suitcase on the floor, discarded clothes from yesterday, beloved guitar on my desk; more wires than I ever thought one man would need spilling like cooked spaghetti from his other bag litter the room. My bra dangles like forgotten tinsel from the door of my wardrobe. I think I might cry, I turn away from him. Though looking at my devastated best friend isn't any better.

"Izzie, I'm so sorry—"

"How could you do this to me?" she barks, and her fists clench.

"Iz—" I try to cut in, yet feel I should let her have her full say.

"Tori kept seeing you at the gigs. I told her you had that floristry job with Cardinal, which was obviously a lie. And I'm so stupid for believing it! But then why wouldn't I trust my best friend, Daisy?"

I rub at my forehead, want desperately to cry into my hands. Again, now I'm her best friend, when she's hurt and angry with me. The label itches like poison ivy. "I didn't know how to tell you," I whisper, know it sounds pathetic.

"So you let me find out from a newspaper?"

I glance at Stewart. His eyebrows jump beneath his fringe and he scoops his phone from the floor and starts scrolling through the no doubt endless missed calls. That must have been what Harry was wanting to talk to him about yesterday. The one night he doesn't turn his phone on...

I push my nails into my palms, then remember the cuts on my thigh. Izzie is screaming at me, both valid points (I'm a liar, Stewart and Cardinal are special to her) and things straight from a fan-fiction (she's connected to him in a way I never will be, they're destined to be). Luckily for me, she hasn't noticed the cuts on my leg. Too focused on the man in my bed. Or perhaps herself.

"I was going to tell you,"

"When? Because apparently you two have been together for most of the year,"

"Today. I was going to tell you over lunch today. I swear it." My eyes dart quickly towards Stewart. He'll resent me for this. I skirted around the issue for these past few weeks. Maybe let Stewart believe I'd already told Izzie. I hate myself that I didn't get around to it. I knew the closer it got to the press release, there would be more chance of Izzie finding out about Stewart and I. Yet I never expected an early leak of the story, or paparazzi photos being printed that I had no idea even existed.

Izzie exhales loudly, sharply. She pushes past me and out onto the landing. She leans her hands on the banister.

"How could you do this to me?"

"I'm sorry Iz, I am, but—"

Izzie folds her arms. "Got an excuse ready have you?"

"This is more than a celebrity crush—"

"Are you actually belittling my feelings just because you're shagging him?"

"I love him," I say quickly. It may have danced out of my throat at the speed of lightning, but I mean it. I feel like Ariel in *The Little Mermaid*. If only I could transform and swim away into the depths of the ocean.

"I love him," I say, slower, measured.

The silence echoes around the whole house. The breath pants out of me, eyelashes blinking as if working on double time.

Izzie looks like a waxwork. Frozen to the spot. Eyes wider than natural, pinned open in shock, like a bad taxidermy in a dodgy pub.

Stewart appears, leaning against the doorframe, hair messed up, jeans on, yet bare-chested.

Izzie gasps at seeing him, before turning away from us both.

"Daisy—" he says quietly. I know he's been desperate for me to admit how I feel, despite only saying those three words last night himself. He stretches to hold my hand yet I step away. I don't want to rub Izzie's face in our relationship, yet I also don't want to push him away; though that would be easier.

"Put on a fucking t-shirt, you twat," I hiss at him, but round it off with a smile.

Izzie's bitter laugh smashes the silence fully. "You love him? Stewart from Cardinal?"

I shake my head and hold her gaze. "No, Izzie, I'm in love with Stewart Burns; the person, not the onstage image."

"Is there a difference?"

"Yes. I don't give a fuck that he's on stage every night, that he sings rhyming couplets to make Shakespeare envious. I don't care about any of that. I love him for who he is, standing on stage or not. You think you love him but it's not real. None of it is real, Iz. It's escapism for you and you've lost sight of reality." The anger bursts out from me, although it's on the tip of my tongue to apologise.

"And you think you can love him without liking his band do you?"

"Yes, because I do," I implore, the hysteria having reached its peak, settles on my shoulders like a weight.

"I think we all need to calm down, maybe start over." Stewart returns to the conversation, now fully dressed.

"I think I need to wake up from this nightmare," Izzie mumbles, looking towards the ceiling.

"This is the reality, Izzie," Stewart says with a helpless shrug.

"Izzie, I should have told you. I'm so sorry," I say quietly. The anger retreats, replaced instantly with guilt. "This is on me. I should have told you. I wanted to tell you before it became public knowledge but—"

"Sometimes stories get leaked earlier, Izzie. Daisy and I were meant to go public on Monday. I'm absolutely positive she was going to tell you today."

Izzie has tears threatening to spill over her black-rimmed eyes. She looks from me to Stewart. He throws her an awkward smile. I'm half surprised he doesn't wink at her. Of course, he still looks beautiful, despite his eyes looking worried yet alert, he keeps glancing at his phone, unsure which to pay full attention to. Why is he so good, so lucid in the mornings?

"How long have you been seeing him? Since that date with Rob? Or are the papers right? Is it longer than that?" Izzie asks, ignoring his presence.

I run a hand through my hair, my fingers snagging over a knot the size of a tennis ball, using it to stall for time. I do know, of course. But I also know admitting it to Izzie will make her feel more betrayed. I hate myself for not telling Izzie sooner. And now it's out there for everyone to read about. Two days earlier than the Cardinal team planned. Before I could tell Izzie.

"We got together after the Cardinal gig up in Edinburgh at the start of the year," Stewart offers, as the silence bounces off the walls.

"What?" Izzie's features settle, anger sliding off her face. Replaced with shock and hurt. She almost collapses, her body dropping to sit on the top step, her limbs limp. My hand reaches to touch her, to console her, before thinking better of it.

"What?" Izzie repeats quietly, like she can't believe it.

"I believe you had a migraine and missed the gig," Stewart says casually, his fingers tapping manically on his phone.

I look at him and he grimaces, mouths an apology at me. Clearly he answered without thinking. Distracted by sorting this press shit out.

Izzie's fury returns, she jumps up from the stairs, stepping towards me, her face contorted in pain. "The gig in January? You've been lying to me since then?"

I feel my lips start to wobble. My nails push into my palms. I wish they'd break the skin, drip blood out from my clenched fists in an act of control and release.

"Have you been shagging him since January, Daisy?"

I'm too guilty, ashamed almost, to look at her, let alone respond. She pushes me, I stumble backwards. Stewart stands in front of me and holds his palms up to Izzie.

"Izzie," he warns, and she exhales towards the ceiling. "We met in January and have been dating since February. Daisy and I are—"

"How did you even meet?" Izzie asks, side-stepping

Stewart and ignoring him completely, as if she's just discovered I saw the Millennium Falcon fly overhead, and not a pop star she's met countless times. The press report must be light on any details if she didn't know. The official release was full of flowing romantic words of the two of us having met across a crowded bar. It was true, but doused in Stewart's usual lyrical prose to play up to the fans who apparently would revel in a love story.

"At the hotel we were all staying at in Edinburgh. In the bar," I admit.

"Afterparty," Stewart amends.

I ignore him. Do details really matter? Will she care who gave who the first drink? Who kissed who first?

"I swear, I didn't know the band would be there. I barely knew what he looked like before the gig, you know that," I implore.

"She didn't. I am better looking in real life though."

"Stewart! Shut the fuck up!" I shout before I burst out laughing with nerves and fuck knows what other emotions. A trip down memory lane in front of Izzie at this point will not help anything.

"And what? It was love at first sight?" Izzie places her hands on her hips, like a teacher telling off a wayward pupil.

I find it hard to answer. My heart stamps like it's trying to break free from my chest. Rose thorns puncturing through my skin.

Izzie's green eyes slide towards Stewart. He smiles, tight mouthed. Please do not let any romantic prose fall from his lips. This is not the time.

"I think what's important to remember here, is that you and Daisy are best pals. She cares about you, and would never hurt you intentionally. She's not like that, is she? We're both really sorry you had to find out this way, that wasn't what either of us wanted."

He looks at me fleetingly and I don't miss the set of his jaw.

I don't know if I'm grateful for his attempts or if I wish he'd just shut up and leave me and Izzie to fight it out. Not literally fight it out, that would be stupid. I think about Izzie and Tori's fictitious stories online; the ones where the narrative takes a violent angle and they dispose of Ella and Ash, and any other woman standing in their way of Stewart and Eddie, using all forms of violence and torture. Were there a vat of boiling oil here, I know she'd push me in.

"I'm sorry, Iz," I repeat.

"I can't do this." Izzie tugs at her lower lip, before turning to stomp back down the stairs. "I just can't understand it. How could you do this to me, Daisy?"

"I didn't plan this," I call then follow her.

"You didn't mean to lie to me for months on end, it just happened? The lies just kept falling from your mouth did they?"

"Izzie, please don't go. Let's talk about this—"

She spins, pulling open the front door, her green eyes sheen yet they're angry. "I hate you for this. Fucking hate you. Don't ever speak to me again."

The slap to my cheek isn't unexpected. I ignore the sting of it, the burning of my skin. It's my turn to be frozen to the spot.

28

Stewart's phone buzzes. He claps his hands a few times, Ackbar jumps and runs off the sofa.

"Ok, we're good to go."

"Are we?"

"It's a wee walk down your garden path to the car, Sweetheart. Des is right outside the gate, engine running, ready to go."

Great. Blocking up the entire road down the steep hill. The neighbours will moan about that, accosting me in Sainsbury's then via the local papers' complaints page just for good measure.

The door pounds.

"Give me your keys, B will lock up and bring our bags."

This is happening. We have to face those reporters loitering in the garden wanting to report on our relationship.

"Can I make a last-minute plea to stay here?"

"Locked up forever? No, Daisy. It doesn't work like that. They want a photo."

"They had the official photo earlier, and are getting a full paparazzi walk tomorrow." It transpires that unofficial leaking of stories is a million times worse than a scheduled statement. Stewart's phone hasn't stopping ringing, all the official photo shoot and accompanying interviews have been largely ignored in favor of 'exclusives' and rumours about the two of us. Online, Stewart and I are married with children, and a cover for his relationship with Ella or Patrick, or I'm possibly his long-lost sister, depending which sites I read.

Stewart lets the burly security man known only as B in the door. He slams it closed behind his back. He's enormous, proof that Sasquatch could exist with a frame that size.

"But they need it now, to sell instantly, they want one before the pap walk."

I leave him tapping on his phone while I double check the back door is locked. When I return, he holds my jaw in his hands, licks his lips then kisses me. His tongue slow and gentle against my own. I feel myself relaxing, focusing only on this, on him and not on the madness outside.

"Stew, we need to go," B announces in a deep, gruff voice.

Stewart kisses the end of my nose. "Remember; keep hold of my hand, don't say anything—"

"Follow you into the car. Don't smile, don't frown. I know, I know." How many times are these rules going to be repeated?

"Des says the car's open." B steps aside, hand on the door handle.

"Cheers, pal. It's those two bags and my guitar please." Stewart smiles then hands me a pair of sunglasses.

"Expecting sun, are you?"

"The photos can't be used if the cameras show up in the reflections."

Clever. He places mirrored shades over his blue eyes.

He turns and kisses my forehead.

B opens the door and Stewart strides out, for once not tripping over the loose paving slab. I follow, my hand holding onto his, like it's the end of the rope that if I let go of I'll plummet to the depths of the burning pit of fiery hell. The noise increases instantly, and I try to not frown, to keep breathing.

Focusing on Stewart's back, his denim jacket with the red tag on the hem, I count my breaths, struggling to get past five. It's mayhem, way worse than I expected; there's so many people here. Light bulbs of cameras flash constantly, the incessant clicking. Men, they're all men I note, step in front of Stewart, who swerves round them without halting. He's undeterred, used to this level of close proximity invasion into his crazy life. He continues on regardless of the journalists trying to stop him, to interrogate and provoke him.

The paved garden path must have been extended overnight, it's never taken me this long to reach the squeaky metal gate. I blink, eyelashes batting like a hovering Kestrel at the roadside. My heart rate increases with each second, each flash of a camera. I've never heard my name shouted so much, married next to Stewart's. Both accompanied by compliments and insults (we make the most beautiful of couples, I'm naturally gorgeous, Stewart sleeps with anything that moves, it'll be over in a week, I'm a poor Ella Egan imitation), attempting to evoke a response from either of us.

Stewart pulls the car door open and lets go of my hand. I glance back at the house, see B shutting the gate. Stewart folds himself with practised ease into the car and slides across the leather seats. B appears behind me asking if I'm ok before opening the boot. I smile shakily at him and nod. Then blink several times as my mouth falls open and I peel off the sunglasses.

In amongst the madness and mayhem, I spot my best friend.

Hair as black as burned trees, eyes lined in kohl like ash, her height pulled up tight, seemingly like she's touching the clouds on her platforms, her face as stony and unmoving as a carved image of a Greek goddess.

Stewart hasn't seen Izzie. He expects me to be right next to him on the leather seats in seconds. We've been over this countless times; follow Stewart, get into the car. Ignore the cameras, the journalists and reporters. Don't think. Just toe the line and follow the rules.

But she's my best friend. My oldest friend at least. I push past, weave back through the commotion of cameras and shouts, which are getting louder with each passing second.

"Iz—"

"Alex persuaded me to come and hear you out. But yet here you are, already loving being the centre of attention."

"I'm not loving it."

She must know this. I was the one at school who always claimed to feel sick whenever there was an assembly or performance; making a miraculous recovery as soon as the audience had dissipated.

"You fucking should be. I would be. You don't even like Cardinal!"

"No, I don't," I admit with a shrug.

"You disgust me," she sneers, leaning against the garden wall. The lush green hedge providing her with an aesthetic background Stewart would be impressed with. I hear Stewart calling over the clamour of journalists honing in on me and Izzie.

Izzie leans forward, her tone low. "You must be damn good in bed if he's stuck around."

"It's more than that. I love him, Izzie. We love each other."

The waiting journalists hush, part of me realises this will be recorded, videoed, commented on for however long myself and Stewart and Cardinal are relevant for. The Cardinal team are going to kill me for this. Yet Izzie's my best friend. She came to see me, that must mean she doesn't hate me. A thought creeps into my brain, like ivy. Izzie may be my apparent best friend, but she is horrible to me at times, always has been since we hit teens. I'm always her seconds choice, I'm the constant butt of her jokes and she goes out of her way to make snide comments about my life. Even now, I know I've hurt her, yet she refuses to even consider my feelings and motives for a microsecond.

"How could you do this to me? I was the one who was there for you after your mum left."

The tears spill from me instantly. I try to fight them, to swallow down the pain from my past that still stings but I can't. The journalists shout, asking where my family live, probing questions about my childhood history.

"Don't you dare cry about this," she hisses like a viper.

I wipe my cheeks. But I'm allowed to cry too, when my emotions make me, surely?

Izzie's pacing, unsettled. Each time she approaches, I fear she may slap me on the cheek. Again. Right in front of the press, that would go viral. It would increase Cardinal's record sales for sure. Maybe they'd thank me. Perhaps I'd welcome another slap from her. Would it eradicate a slither of guilt? I swallow a chunk in my throat. Is my guilt, like Izzie's love for Stewart, actually misplaced?

I've fallen in love. I've done nothing wrong, aside from lying to Izzie for months. But the lies don't cancel out my feeling for Stewart. I barely believed in soulmates until I met him. He's shown me they exist.

The press surround us both. B shouts at them to let him through. It's a choice between being on the receiving end of Izzie's harsh words, or trampled by a pack of journalists.

I stand up straight. "And I was there for you when you lost Sophia. We've been through so much together—"

"You don't deserve him, Daisy. You know he's special to me. You've ruined this for me. Ruined that band for me."

Well, this is one way for Izzie to find a new favourite band, with the frontman shagging her best mate and all, I guess it kind of ruins the listening experience.

"He's really special to me," I try to counter, but emotion distorts my voice.

Izzie shakes her head at me, she doesn't look sad anymore, just enraged. I don't know which is worse. "You're such a fucking bitch! Putting a man before your best friend!"

I almost laugh. So now I'm her best friend? Yet she usually refers to me as friend, childhood friend or oldest friend. I'm only the best friend when it plays in her favour. How has it taken me this long to realise our friendship is so unbalanced? Izzie was always a poor if present friend, I just excused her behaviour as grief.

I feel Stewart's arms around my shoulders, flit my gaze around wildly and see both B and Des pushing the reporters away.

"Izzie, we'll talk about this in private, another time," Stewart states.

She folds her arms, not looking at either of us. "What's wrong with now?"

Stewart exhales loudly, scrubbing a hand over his face. "Five minutes, inside." He stalks away and we follow him. The press yelling and clicking cameras from outside the garden gate.

Stewart paces the length of the hallway talking into his phone, while Izzie stares at a spot on the wall directly above my head.

"I hate you for this."

"Izzie, this is ridiculous," I say quietly, pushing my nails into my palms to quell my anger. Losing my temper won't help anyone. "Cardinal are still your favourite band, they're still special to you. If Stewart was dating anyone else it wouldn't be an issue,"

"Yet he's dating you."

"I love him. This isn't some celebrity crush. I know I've hurt you, but it was never my intention. I'm so sorry."

"Who would you pick? If I made you choose; our friendship, or dating Stewart, who would you pick?"

I swallow. Ignore the stabbing pain within my chest, focus on slotting my fingers together, not pushing my nails into my thighs.

"Would you break up with him if I asked you?"

"You're better than that, Izzie. You wouldn't ask Daisy to do that," Stewart says, lacing his fingers with mine as he appears by my side. His phone rings and beeps constantly, sounding like R2D2.

I'm glad he interrupted. Izzie would not have appreciated my answer. No matter how happy I am with Stewart.

"What about you?" Izzie tries and fails to hold Stewart's gaze. "Who would you pick—Daisy or Patrick?"

"It's not a choice. Pat's my best mate. Daisy's my girlfriend. There's space in my life for both of them. Pat wouldn't ask me to choose, nor would Daisy."

"Fuck I hate you," she sneers at me.

Stewart sits on the bottom step, shakes his head. "Izzie, why aren't you cross at me? Daisy and I are in this together."

"Because the blame lies with her. It's the girl code."

Stewart pulls his hair and stands up. "For fucks sake. This is ridiculous! This isn't about some made up feminist document!"

"Isn't it?" Izzie asks before she opens the front door. She points at me, finally looking me in the eyes. "You know he saved my life. If it wasn't for him and Cardinal, I wouldn't be alive right now. Although that would make things easier on you, wouldn't it?"

"Izzie, please," I start to plead.

"I can't bear to look at you. Either of you." She slams the front door.

I lift my eyes to Stewart who doesn't look at me.

"Get in the fucking car," he mumbles before stalking away. I follow behind him like a sheep trailing after the collie dog.

29

The car door slams and we zoom off into the road, shouts drowned out by the engine and the incessant ringing of Stewart's phone, and two phones from the front of the car, I assume belonging to B and Des.

B turns round and passes me my house keys. I squeeze my palm around them. Feel I may have pushed the key through my skin, buried it between my veins and bones.

Stewart sighs loudly, I see from the corner of my eyes his fingers flying over his phone screen.

I rub a palm across my forehead and turn to look at him. His bearded jaw set, his eyes staring wide, at the seat in front of him, the colour of them almost as dark as Anchusa Loddon Royalist, an unforgiving deep navy blue.

"This is more than your pal being upset, Daisy. This is my career. There's a reason for those pissing rules that we'd been over countless times. Not just so the team can keep a tabs on the press reports, but to keep us safe. You and me." He pulls at his hair. "I know they're just guys with cameras and dictaphones, but Daisy, they are ruthless. You could've got hurt, physically hurt. They stop at nothing to get an exclusive."

He mumbles about me being a wee slip of a thing, that

they wouldn't have thought twice about pushing, pulling, touching me to cause more drama, under his breath.

"She's my best friend." I start to cry again and his fingers twitch, like he wants to touch me, to console me, yet knows he should be mad at me for longer. He stretches out a hand, places it on top of my hands and caresses my fingers.

"Is she? She's a terrible friend to you, even before this performance. She's your oldest friend, Rob is your best friend, as we all know." Stewart's phone rings again, he removes his hand from mine, and like a koala to a tree I want to hold on to him forever, while the bushfires rage beneath us.

"If you'd told her—"

"You cannot possibly make me feel worse about this right now," I snap at him, once my tears have stopped.

"My life is shitting crazy, but this is on you, Daisy."

"How delightful that you can sleep soundly tonight, having had zero part in this. First time it's not your actions being ripped apart in the press, what a novelty."

"You fucking promised me you'd tell her!" His words bounce around the car.

I expected this to happen, an argument about Izzie. We've fought about it often enough, before she found out I am in fact dating her celebrity crush, and apparent saver of her life.

"I was going to tell her, today. I swear, I was."

"Talk about leaving it until the last fucking minute, Daisy."

"The news about us wasn't meant to break in the press until Sunday night. I had time."

Stewart pouts, taps a rhythm out between his fingertips and thumb and scrolls through his phone. I reach out, put a hand on his arm. He shucks me off. I squeeze at his hand, slot my fingers through his, before his phone rings and he pulls away.

"It's a choice. Your choice Daisy. Your friend, or me."

"You," I reply without hesitation. "Every time, Stewart."

The car is silent, Stewart ignores his phone for at least an hour. Both of us stare out of the windows, leaving the small town behind and heading towards the motorway via lots of passing green fields and tractors. I look at his profile in the reflection, can't bear to look at myself.

I turn to face him as the car steadily moves along the motorway. Stewart picks up his ringing phone, the latest press reports flash up before he can shelter me from them.

'What you need to know about Stewart from Cardinal.' 'Chicks before dicks, is there an exception?' 'The girl code; it's not one for breaking.'

I sigh. I know I'll need to fix this. Fuck, am I going to have to hold a press conference or something? Read an open letter of apology to Izzie and the entire female population for breaking the girl code? I'll do whatever I have to, to sort this out, for Stewart and I.

Stewart's hand runs up my thigh. A stinging sensation itches beneath the weight of his palm. I hiss. Stewart pushes my dress up, showing a fresh scrape etched into my pale thigh, done earlier with my floristry knife when he was in the shower.

Mother doesn't want you— self-harm. Feel out of control— self-harm. Lie to your best friend and have a public argument— self-harm. Become half of a 'celebrity couple'— self-harm.

"Why do you keep doing this to yourself? I don't understand," his blue eyes flashing darker in anger.

My cheeks blush, my heart pounds and I feel the cold sweat of shame and regret prickle my skin.

I pull the material down quickly, swipe the tears from my cheeks.

Stewart's features soften. The colour of his eyes appearing more calm and welcoming, not the harsh storm clouds they were. He leans over towards me, repeats the action of pushing up my dress and shakes his head.

"Why do you keep doing this?" he repeats calmly.

I sob, tears of guilt line my cheeks. Before him, my self-harm didn't include anyone else, it was my own. Now it drags Stewart into my messed up head too. Stewart stretches his arm out, places a hand on my thigh. I lock my fingers with his. His fingertips push into the gaps between my knuckles.

"Tell me what to do, Daisy. Do you want me to shout at you? Beg you not to do it? What do you need; to talk, reassurance? How can I help you?"

I don't need your help, I almost say. But evidently, I do.

"Will you speak to someone? The team are really good—"

"No. I can't speak to anyone. Not yet. I just need to feel like I can control something in my life. It's a replacement for the need to cut," I confess, not wanting to talk to anyone about it, on the Cardinal team or a professional.

He nods, wipes the tears from my cheeks falling like autumn showers. "Leave it with me," he mumbles, fingers tapping away on his phone.

"It's not your issue to solve."

"It is. Just you, just me. I love you, Daisy."

I blink at Stewart, feel a smile pushing up my cheeks, despite a nervous flutter of my heart. I'm stunned at how often he says 'I love you,' as if it's practically weightless like delicate peony petals, despite the power those words carry. Each time he says it, I can see in his eyes he means it. But still, for me, the three words are more like a terracotta pot, laden down with soil, plants and pressure. I want to, but I can't find it within myself to say them.

"I'm sorry, about the argument with Izzie," I repeat as we pull up in front of Stewart's flat hours later. I'm relieved there's no sign of fans or journalists waiting for us. Just darkness staining the sky. Chatter and noise from bars and pubs drift towards the quiet cobbled street, like moths fluttering looking for light; it's a welcomed normal sound after the shouts and screams from the press back home.

"My circle of friends, of people I love is small. I'm scared to lose someone else from it."

"Izzie adds nothing positive to your life, Daisy," Stewart says bluntly, yet I know he's not trying to hurt me on purpose. "Yes, she was there for you in the past, but that doesn't mean you're tied into a negative friendship forever. People change, move on. Your circle doesn't get smaller, it changes shape."

"Mine's currently Nan, Cardinal, Ash and Rob shaped."

"That's no bad thing." He leans down and kisses my forehead as he holds a hand out and pulls me gently from the car. "Don't stress about the Izzie thing. It'll get sorted, the team are on it,"

"I keep bringing all this shit to your life—"

"Yep, because I've brought nothing but ease and positivity to yours, right, Sweetheart?" He smiles a wonky grin that always makes me feel relaxed and safe.

My forehead rests against his back as he finds his keys. "Maybe we're well matched, both causing carnage."

Stewart open the door, we both step in, as B places our bags in the hall. They shake hands and B departs silently.

"We are well matched. Not sure carnage is accurate, but we'll get through whatever awaits us, together."

"Hand in hand, quoting Bronte and all that, right?" I laugh a little, knowing he's ridiculously romantic.

"If that's what you want, Daisy." His eyelid flickers as his face becomes serious. "I'm sorry that I came between you and Izzie. I can't and won't feel bad for falling in love with you. But for you, Sweetheart, I'm sorry you had to lose her friendship."

"I think I'm starting to see she wasn't the best of friends to me."

"You deserve a best pal who is happy for you. Like Rob."

Maybe one day Izzie will forgive me, it'll work out. Right now, that seems impossible. But time is a great healer. So they say. Though do I really want her back in my life?

I stretch up on my tiptoes and kiss him, my hands sneak up to his neck, and he scoops me up. My legs around his waist.

"I want you. I also want a quiet life, but—"

"I don't do a quiet life. I may have to ask you to choose." He frowns, I play with his hair and the frown is replaced with a smile and a contented moan.

"You, Stewart Christopher Burns. Every mad crazy thing in your life, is now a part of mine. And that's ok."

He licks his lips, eyes lingering on my thighs. "Is it really ok? Seeing the cuts you did fuck knows when—"

I place a finger on his lips. "I'll be ok. I need a distraction an—"

"Element of control, I know. I may have something waiting for you upstairs."

"Will it be you tied up in bed and at my total mercy?" I whisper into his ear before licking the shell of it. I always turn to the distraction of sex when faced with serious conversations with Stewart. It allows me to keep part of myself safe and held back. I sigh, wish I could totally let my guard down, especially around him.

"No, but if that's what you want, Baby, I need zero persuasion," he replies kissing my neck before his teeth scrape over my pulse point.

Stewart puts me down and we walk up the curved stairs together.

"It's not going to be easy is it? The whole press scrutiny?" I state the obvious.

It can't be, especially not as I've just had a public argument on friendships versus boyfriends. I've made it ten times worse for us both.

"Nope, I'm afraid not. But I'll be right with you, Daisy. Maybe not always physically next to you, but it's me and you in this together, yep?"

"Onto the next chapter?"

"Like part two of Wuthering Heights." He smiles referring to our favourite book.

I nudge his shoulder with my hand and smile up at him. "For the love of The Force, Stewart, please don't dig up my corpse, no matter how romantic you feel Heathcliff was."

"You don't want to be buried, you want to be cremated with your ashes scattered off the coast of Cumbrae."

I chuckle, we really do talk about any and everything with one another.

"Just to clarify, Daisy, you and I are not Catherine and Heathcliff. We're more like Han Solo and Princess Leia."

"But in reverse. Don't tar me with your romantically poetic brush. I'm practical, like Han. You can be the romantic one in a gold bikini."

Contrasting music and a commentary from a TV baking show, float around the open landing from various rooms. Stewart and Patrick's flat is never quiet. Patrick even sleeps with the radio on. Stewart places our bags outside his bedroom door and ruffles his hair.

"I'll let you tie me up, but I'm not wearing a bikini."

Patrick appears from the studio, a heavy drum beat drifting from the open door. I wave at him with a smile on my face. He shakes his head, his dark curls dancing. "I do not want to know what conversation I've walked in on." He saunters over and plants a kiss on my cheek. "Hi Hen, good to see you."

"The things I've heard coming from your room over the years, pal, nothing should shock you," Stewart says with a flick to his best friends' ear.

Patrick laughs and winks before pushing open the door of his bedroom, the sounds of a dance track floating out into the landing.

"By the way, the flowers arrived. I assume they're for you, Daisy."

"Flowers?" I ask looking from him to Stewart.

Stewart wouldn't buy me a bouquet of flowers, I'd be livid. It would be akin to me buying him a CD full of songs he hadn't written and claiming they were better than his own.

"Cheers, pal," he replies, squeezing Patrick's shoulder as we walk past, the lightest of pinks showing on his cheeks. "Arranging flowers gives you an element of control when you feel life is running away from you. So I ordered a shit ton of flowers, and floristry tools, ribbons and shit."

"You did?"

"Of course, Daisy. Anything for you." Stewart pulls me towards the kitchen, the scent of flowers invades my senses from the open kitchen door, bringing a sense of calm to my buzzing mind already. He threads our fingers together and smiles, eyes as honest and clear as the shallows of Bell Bay on Cumbrae.

"Florist away until you regain an aspect of control, Sweetheart. If you run out of flowers, I'll get more. If you ever need this distraction, I'll send them. Whatever the time, wherever I am. Please don't hurt yourself again, I can't bear it."

I love him, the very moment I see the piles of flowers covering the kitchen counter; as if I didn't before. I turn to face him, tears in my eyes, lips wobbling with unshed tears and love.

"Stewart Christopher Burns, you are the best person in the world." I turn towards him like he's the sun. My floral counterpart's outer white petals open beneath his warmth and love. Yet the yellow disc florets at my core remain closed, keeping the three words I want to say silenced. I place my hands on his handsome face. His cheeks push up in a smile under my palms. He smiles and I beam back.

"Really, truly. You are the best person in the world. The best person I've ever had in my life. You're my favourite person."

"Yep? More than Beyonce? Or Enid?"

I nod. "Yes. You are my favourite. The best part of my

life, I'd be lost without you."

He bought me flowers to arrange, and tools to use. Spools of ribbon and vases. He's perfect.

"I love you, Daisy," Stewart says quietly.

If I were named Lily, perhaps I'd be more forthcoming and open with my feelings. Bold and never shying away from light or emotions. Confident, with upward facing petals and intoxicating fragrance. But I'm named after a heliotropic weed.

I step closer to him, nod against his chest. Silently repeat the sentiment back to him. I hope Stewart knows I love him, despite the words remaining anchored in my heart.

30

I never thought I'd say this, but I miss the Bentley. I wish I was in it right now, with Stewart telling me off for pressing buttons, while I complain about the lack of sweets in the glove box, and moan playfully about the coloured lights in the footwell. I would even rather be in my battered red Yaris, with its icy heating, chip in the wing mirror and rubbish littered on the floor.

But, we're in an actual limo, which is more like a spaceship from Star Wars than a car, and we've pulled up in front of a red carpet. A red carpet which I have to walk down, lined by screaming fans, photographers and cameras.

"If you let go of my hand, for even a second, Stewart Christopher Burns, I cannot be held responsible for my actions, but I can assure you that Cardinal will need a new frontman."

He chuckles a little then kisses my forehead. "Daisy, the only reason I will let go of your hand is to put my arm around your waist."

"And don't leave me. Or I'll murder you."

"With a knitting needle, I know."

"I mean it. Don't let me go."

"Never, Sweetheart," he says with a smile. I know I've again, accidentally quoted a Cardinal song, but I can't find it in me to make a joke or correct myself using Beyonce lyrics.

"I can't do it, what if I faint, or—" Fuck, I'm going to fall arse over tits. Everyone will either laugh or sneer and I'll cry. Stewart will instantly leave me for Ella. My mind spirals, I need to slow it down. I gulp in air, but it doesn't reach my lungs. Stewart places his hands around my jaw, his fingertips stroking at my neck. I feel my shoulders relax as I look into his delphinium blue eyes. I even manage a wobbly smile.

"Baby, listen to me, you can do this. It's a walk along a red carpet. I've got a few wee questions to answer before we go inside and then we can watch a film, easy." He places a hand on the door handle.

"Wait, by wee questions do you mean interviews?" I ask, eyes wide, my fingers pressing hard into his arm.

"Don't worry, Daisy. Just smile and nod. I'll do the talking,"

"You mean you're happy to be the centre of attention? What a shock."

"Menace," he says smiling before kissing me. "Come on, we got this,"

The flashing cameras are almost blinding. The shouts of mainly Stewart's name are interposed with questions and screams from the fans. A woman with a clipboard instructs us to stand on an x stuck to the carpet and pose for the cameras. Stewart looks at me as we approach. I know I'm as out of place as a fluffy dandelion amongst delicate purple Aubrieta flowers. Even though I'm wearing a silk Ana Sui dress, in matching navy blue to Stewart's shirt, the small town essence of me must radiate. I feel out of my depth. Drowning.

"You look so beautiful," Stewart says into my ear, adorned with earrings he bought me.

"It's the makeup," I reply deadpan, focusing on his sparkling eyes, not the cameras or shouts of my name.

"Yep, you look a fucking mess without it," he laughs, which makes me laugh, and I forget about the setting I've been plunged into, on some level. I actually smile, a proper smile.

"Then why are you with me?"

"For your quick wit, Sweetheart,"

"I'm only with you for your thighs, so I guess we're even," I shrug as he leans down to kiss at my forehead.

His eyes dance with flashes from the cameras and that flirty arrogance which seems to radiate whenever he's in public. His hand snakes around my waist. "Ok, left to right, smiling into the cameras one at a time, then we'll move on."

I nod, place my hand over his and stand up a little straighter, those sea blue eyes of his always ground me, filling me with confidence and security.

***

Although the movie premiere went without a hitch, it did not lessen the press interest in mine and Stewart's relationship.

This week, according to magazines and online sites, I'm both fat and too skinny, happy and trapped in a miserable relationship. A cover for Ella. Actually in love with

Eddie. And of course, the antichrist for choosing a man over a female friend. It's exhausting. There's blogs about me. My clothes and style—as if I have style. There's fansites filled with affection for Stewart and I, which are sweet, but it all messes with my head.

Stewart writes, composes, produces songs based on inspiration. The entire track listing of Cardinal's new album are a terrifying echo of my life now I'm one half of a minor celebrity couple.

Pariah.

Not fitting into the glitz and glamour of Stewart's world, where Cardinal are always beneath a spotlight. Feeling like a misfit, aside from when I'm with Stewart or Ash and the band.

The constant intrusion from the press and fans. Wherever I am. On my way to yoga. Walking up to Nan's. Putting the bins out. At work. Buying tampons. It's endless.

I expect this kind of attention when I'm with Stewart, or we're out in Edinburgh, or Glasgow with Patrick, Eddie, and Ash on her student nights. Though the post and undergraduates are usually too drunk or so unimpressed by Cardinal that we blend in seamlessly into the background of cramped and dark student bars.

In Cockermouth; a town of less than 9,000 people, I would have said the arrival of Stewart would go by largely unnoticed. And no one would take notice of me, certainly not the press. Though maybe that's me being too naive. The only small town I've ever known, is starting to suffocate me. At least in Edinburgh I can weave amongst the countless other people and disappear. And on the Isle of Cumbrae, no one cares who anyone is. It's smaller than Cockermouth, but it doesn't feel cloying, as if the sea air, the waves surrounding the island give me freedom and a sense of space, without being restricting or making me feel trapped.

Negotiate With Me.

Being offered endless deals with glossy and trashy magazines. Harry and the Cardinal team filling my inbox with sponsorship offers, advertisement deals. From flower subscription services to stop smoking campaigns. I turn them all down. Stewart and I don't want any further attention or intrusion into our relationship. It's ours, no one else's.

You Break All My Rules.

The girl code. If it were a physical document, it would lie in tatters at my feet. Izzie is still refusing to speak to me. She and her Cardinal stalker friends write bitter, twisted things about me online, but I largely ignore them. She's entitled to a freedom of speech and expression.

Always A Choice.

I had a choice; Izzie or Stewart. I picked him, I picked me.

Izzie has a choice, to forgive me, to attempt to push through my betrayal. She's ignoring me. Refusing all offers of olive branches. She's even pushed Rob away, only agreeing to meet him if he promises not to mention me. Once he did, and she stormed out of the Italian restaurant before she'd even had a bite of garlic bread. If I had to choose again; I'd pick Stewart. Always.

Null and Void.

My life today is summed up in three minutes of verse, chorus verse.

"We need to talk about this, Daisy," Jane says, leaning against the counter in the back room of the florists.

I busy myself with arranging a bouquet in muted pinks of roses and carnations, with flashes of green rosemary and eucalyptus. Jane passes me the cellophane and brown paper to wrap the completed flowers.

"I'm sorry, Jane. I was sure the press interest would have eased by now. Stewart promised me the movie premiere would lessen the intrusion."

We've argued about it. Me shouting at Stewart, laying blame on him and his team. Him asking me what the other option is. To stick with it, with him. That the scrutiny won't be forever.

"It's a strain," Jane admits, wrapping her pink scarf around her neck.

"I know, I feel it too." I nod, selecting a deep green ribbon to complete the wrapping.

"It's impacting on my business. I'm losing money. Stock. Customers." She places a padded envelope on the table. "I don't want to do this, Daisy, but I can't keep you on."

"You're sacking me?" My heart sinks. I rub at my forehead. Fiddle with my earrings, anything so I don't push my nails or silver blade into my thighs. Or cry.

"I read in the papers you're planning to move to Edinburgh, anyway."

"I'm not."

I collapse on the chair, it creaks. I scratch at the cuts lining my skin, now always present and open on my thigh without the tattoo. My teeth grit, yet my shoulders relax a little with the release caused by the pain.

"You could, you're talented and experienced enough to open your own florists. It won't be long until you complete the college course."

"I don't want to go, Jane. I love working here."

"Are you a florist, or Stewart from Cardinal's girlfriend?" Jane asks with a shrug.

My limbs and soul feel heavy with a weight of emotion I can't place.

"Can I not be both?" My voice shakes, like tall gladioli trembling in the slightest breeze.

Why is it a choice? Why does something have to give? My eyes blink back tears. It wasn't a conscious choice to fall for Stewart and his ridiculous job. I didn't wish for this, for him, for any of it.

"I've paid you until the end of the month," Jane says standing up, pushing the envelope towards me on the table.

I trudge up the hill towards my house. Feel I'm carrying the weight of the world in my handbag. Dragging me along the seabed like a rusty anchor attached to a sunken shipwreck. Defeated. A failed voyage. Not only has my relationship ruined things with my best friend, but it's also now made me lose my job. I sigh, willing my tears to refrain from falling until I'm behind locked doors. I push open the squeaking garden gate, thankful a glamour model has slept with a married footballer. That seems to have taken precedence in the 'news' over Stewart from Cardinal's love life.

My legs are laden as I climbs the stairs, ignoring Ackbar rolling on the landing. A hot shower will make me feel better. Well, that and a blade to my thigh.

Running the shower, I turn it up high and unwrap the knife from the canvas material. Grip at the comforting weight of the yellow handle in my hands. I trail the blade up my thigh so it leaves a scrape but doesn't break the skin.

I strip off, step into the shower. My skin turning pink instantly with the heat. The blade breaks the skin, releasing anxieties from my mind. The droplets of hot water wash away the tears on my cheeks and blood trickling down my leg. My shoulders relax, I feel peaceful. Like I'm able to cope with life. Maybe. I stand under the water until my skin wrinkles and the heat makes me feel faint, but my head feels settled.

31

The sun keeps making a brief appearance over us as we sit on a wall outside the venue, a full carpark and the tour bus our view. It's neither the sprawling lakes of home, nor the sea at Cumbrae. But the company makes it bearable.

Stewart sighs then turns to face me, the last smoke ring dancing around his head like a halo. "Perhaps this isn't the greatest of times, seeing as you're anxious about Izzie arriving."

Izzie has largely refused to see or speak to me since the news of Stewart and I broke. She's never accepted tickets or invites to shows. There's no reason why tonight, five months later, will be any different. Yet I always hope. Perhaps to ease my own guilt that refuses to fade from my mind.

"But?" I ask, lighting another a cigarette.

"I've got a proposition for you, Sweetheart." He pulls a cardboard folder from his jacket and slides it towards me on the wall, then places his hands on top of it to stop me from opening it. Fuck the Force, if he's booked me another stall at a festival, I'll scream. Although it was lots of fun and hard work at the autumn festival last year, running my own flower stall, I felt I didn't deserve to be there. Like

I was an imposter, using his name to sell flower crowns.

"I want you to hear me out before you dive in feet and mouth first."

I open the folder, see a contract for a shop in my name. No, please don't say he–

"I knew you'd never accept it if I bought you a shop outright, but this isn't permanent. It's for a week, just to show you that you can and will do it."

My harsh exterior cracks. Looking at him, I know he hasn't done this to splash his cash, or as a publicity stunt. I check the date, it's for June when Cardinal are scheduled to be in the studio and shooting access all areas videos of their album making process, so he'll be nowhere near the shop, or indeed, Cumbria that week.

"You did this? For me?"

"Happy belated anniversary!"

"The bracelet, underwear and Coach bag didn't count did they?" I ask him sarcastically.

All I got him for last weekend, to celebrate a whole year since we got together, was myself wrapped in a bow and as much sex as he wanted. Not that he complained.

"This is extra."

"A florists pop up shop? In Carlisle?" I'm stunned, yet excitement fizzles in my brain.

"You can do this, Daisy. Shoot for the fucking moon!"

He's such a dreamer, and while I admire that quality, I am definitely a realist. "You smashed it at the festival, selling your flower crowns."

"Most people were drunk or high. Or just wanting a selfie with you."

He shakes his head, his fringe dancing as the wind picks up. He pulls his collar up on his jacket. "No they weren't. Don't play it down, Baby."

"A stall for a weekend is one thing, but a pop up shop. And the cost—"

"Don't worry about it. The shop, the flowers, stock, I'll sort it for you."

I feel panic rising a little. Like I can't keep afloat with all this help and support. Worry passes through the colour of his eyes. He climbs off the wall, almost falling over en route and stands in front of me.

"I can't. You can't—"

"You can. You need this, Daisy. I know Jane made you go part-time, so the press interest wasn't constant at her business. You've got time to do this."

If only he knew.

"My life isn't meant to be like this," I confess, thinking back to my detailed plotted and perfect career outlines on my desk. I might as well burn the damn things.

"Please, do the pop up shop. Use it as a way back onto your carefully crafted life plan. Life is fucking tough, Sweetheart. You don't become less of a person by asking for or accepting help."

"I didn't ask."

"You wouldn't have asked me anyway. You're too fucking stubborn." He smiles.

"Thank you, Brunnera. For this—" I say, hand on the folder as I stand up, the chill seeping through our clothes. "Thank you for being just so—you."

"You are welcome, Sweetheart. Promise me, after your pop up florists, put an offer in somewhere. Please, Daisy. For you. Shoot for the fucking moon," Stewart exclaims, spinning in a circle.

"I will," I promise, reaching up to kiss him.

"And if you could tell me where it is you'll be based, that would be great. I hear Scotland is in dire need of a good florists. Edinburgh especially,"

"You know an awful lot about florists, do you?"

He pouts and scratches a palm over his beard. "It has been documented I know my way around a florist..."

"You're such a dick."

The wind picks up, chasing rubbish across the carpark ground. I'm sure I hear a rumble of thunder in the distance. Both of us shiver; Stewart jumps a little on his feet, complaining about the cold. The clouds pull closer, bringing with them deeper grey skies and probably incoming rain.

***

I look at the clock. Izzie clearly isn't coming. She's missed Cardinal's soundcheck. I expected her to ignore me, or possibly slap me again, but I thought the access all areas pass, front row tickets and spa day tomorrow would have enticed her here. Rob said she sounded almost keen.

Stewart walks into the room and trips over a wire; he never stumbles on stage. He flops down on the sofa next to me.

"Hey Sweetheart. No Izzie?"

I shake my head. He kisses my forehead, then cheeks, then mouth. "I can't blame her, really."

"You can. I know I'm biased towards you, to us, but she's out of order being so petulant about this. You're allowed to put yourself first."

"I need to talk to you about something." I sigh loudly,

wish I could smoke inside. Exhaling, I build myself up for it. I swallow my pride, my own feelings. This is what I have to do. My eyes glaze over and my lip wobbles a little.

Stewart clasps my hands in his. “Sweetheart, you’re scaring me,”

“I’m sorry, I’m so sorry to do this–”

“Twelve,” Rob announces as he pushes the door open.

I’m relieved to see him, that must mean Izzie is in close proximity. At least she hasn’t brought Tori.

Rob points at Stewart. “There’s twelve pairs of Gucci boots in your dressing room, mate, yet you insist on wearing those scuffed Doc Martens.”

Stewart laughs hollowly and the two of them hug.

“Seriously, are you unhinged?” Rob laughs.

“He doesn’t have much sense if he’s dating her,” I hear Izzie snarl and I jump up. She looks flawless, black poker straight hair and a new dress that clings to her perfectly proportioned curves. Her eyeliner bold and lips purple.

Rob spins to face her. “What did we just talk about, Iz?”

Izzie rolls her green eyes. I hope her latest posts online about shoving a smashed bottle into my chest and ‘ripping out my heart like I deserve’ doesn’t become a real-life version of her fan-fiction. Though the hatred flashing in her eyes indicates it’s likely to be more than a fantasy. I shudder.

“It’s good to see you, Izzie.” I hug her, but her arms remain lodged at her sides.

“Pat!” Stewart shouts, leaning out into the corridor, “Take Izzie and Rob for five minutes for me.”

I turn to him and frown. Pat and Rob swap open-mouthed stares before they mirror one another with hair ruffles, blushing cheeks and awkward smiles.

"Do you wanna come with me? I mean, come this way, I mean—follow me," Patrick mumbles, hands deep in his pockets.

"Why?" I ask, gripping Stewart's arm, he looks nervous.

"We were in the middle of a conversation, Daisy," he prompts. Shit, yes, we were.

Stewart pulls me back to the sofa after shutting the door. He intertwines our fingers and sighs.

"I get it. You want to build bridges with Izzie, and she's finally here after months of refusing to spend any time with you. That's great, truly." He pauses.

I frown at him a little, but keep smiling. Is he going to give me a lecture on Izzie being an obsessive stalker? Again? Best to smile through it, arguing about it never gets us anywhere.

Stewart mumbles as he opens a packet of sweets about Izzie's presence easing my misplaced guilt. He may be right.

"Izzie's struggling with this, us, because of the grief thing, and you feel guilty. This whole girl code thing you two seem to view as the holy bible of life as a woman doesn't help anyone. But, Daisy, you're not a bad person. We're not the enemies here for falling in love with each other."

"No, wait—"

He continues, eyelid flickering. "This isn't some chicks vs dicks thing. It's more than that. This is me and you, Sweetheart. We're soulmates. I know we are. I'm going to fucking fight for our relationship. Even if that means going up against the illusive girl code, and making you choose me over Izzie." He stands up and paces around the room.

"Stewart Christopher Burns, you are the cutest." I follow, hold him still by his wrists and smile up at him. My heart flips wonderfully in my chest. "I want to be with you. I've chosen you, over Izzie, be that a good or bad thing. I very much appreciate your speech; but actually, I was trying to say something else."

"You were? I thought maybe you were going to back out of it because of Izzie?"

"No, Brunnera. Just you, just me, remember?" My fingers stretch up and I play with his messy hair, scratching at his scalp. I exhale loudly. "I lost my job."

"Fuck. When? Why?"

I could shout and scream at him. Flip it all onto him and his crazy celebrity life. I've managed to keep it from Stewart for months. I expected the press or fans to report on it, but they didn't. I've picked up extra shifts at the pub instead, and will finish my business course months earlier too. After weeks of ugly crying about not working in the florists, I can see the positives. Most of the time.

"The press interest was impacting too much. With me out of the shop, Jane can actually run her business."

"Sweetheart, I am so sorry."

"Don't worry about it, I have a pop up shop to aim for now," I say, my heart stuttering a few times for various reasons.

"Daisy, you should have told me, when did this happen? I knew something was going on."

"Don't push me on it, ok?"

"Your independent streak is infuriating at times."

"I'm behind with the fees at Nan's." I change the subject, my cheeks blazing. "Can I please borrow some money? Just as a loan."

"Absolutely."

"I'll pay you back as soon as I can," I hurriedly add on.

"I'll do a transfer for you, Daisy. It's not a problem. Have you got the details?"

I pull the letter from my pocket, folded and creased so much it has holes in it. My skin burns in embarrassed defeat, the independent woman in me is crushed.

"I need it today, please."

Stewart nods, pushes his fringe from his eyes as he skims the letter. He picks up his phone and taps away at the screen. "Done."

"Thank you, Stewart. I should be able to manage next month, but can I let you know? I hate this, absolutely hate this, but—"

His face shows a lopsided grin as he shakes his head. "Sweetheart, I paid for the full year."

"What?"

"It's not your worry anymore. Now concentrate on opening your own florists; after that pop up shop your incredibly handsome boyfriend sorted for you."

"Brunnera, you can't."

He pushes a ringed finger to my lips. "It's done, Baby."

"Thank you," I say before kissing him.

I squeal as he picks me up and spins me round, like he always does. Sometimes to wind me up, to knock me off my train of thought, or just because he can. I pretend I hate it, but really I love it. Miss it when he doesn't do it. Actually, I miss everything about him when we're not together.

"Move in with me." Stewart's mentioned this before, but I could never tell if he was serious or being his standard over fanciful and romantic self. "Please, Daisy?"

"Ask me again as soon as my course is done," I say honestly and kiss him as best I can while smiling widely.

"Shall we interrupt now, or wait for you to propose, Stew?" Patrick's voice jolts us both. I look past him stood in the open doorway, with Izzie scowling in the corridor.

I jump down and shuffle nervously towards her. She ignores me. Rob pulls me into a hug instead.

"Iz, good to see you again. Sorry about kicking you two out, we were in the middle of sorting something out. How have you been?" Stewart asks approaching her, weaving past me and ushering her into the room.

She scoffs slightly. "Do you care?"

Stewart places a hand on her shoulder. "Of course I care. You're my girlfriends' best pal, and you have excellent taste in music."

Izzie giggles a little, the frown slipping from her perfectly made up features.

"I'll go grab some drinks. I'll just be a wee tick." He turns and winks at me.

Izzie sits on the sofa, and I take the chair. Rob and Patrick are trying their hardest to have a conversation without making eye contact. Izzie sings quietly along to the songs playing over the speakers.

"Thanks for coming, Iz," I say.

"I'm not here for you."

"Izzie, be nice. Daisy's not the type to hurt you, or anyone on purpose," Rob chides, and he rolls his eyes at Patrick who smiles and blushes.

"You should've told me you were dating him." She turns to face me briefly.

"I know. I'm really sorry I didn't." I join her on the sofa. She doesn't look at me, but nor does she move away so I take that to be something. "But for once, for the first time since I can remember, I put myself and my feelings first."

"Some friend you are, only thinking of yourself. After all I've been through."

"Life isn't a competition of who has it harder or easiest. I fell in love, I followed my heart. There's nothing wrong with that. Yes, you got hurt in the process, which I never, ever intended to happen. And I am sorry for that. But I'm not sorry for finding someone who makes me happier than I've ever been."

"I'm here for the band, Daisy. To try and claw back a bit of joy in my life before you ruin Sophia's memory."

I glance around the room, security milling about, Rob and Patrick discussing shoes, Eddie on the phone. Stewart walking back in with glasses filled with vodka. Hipster Harry takes photos, setting it up so Izzie and I are in the background. He'll angle it so we look like we're the best of friends again. Izzie steps away to take selfies with the band. I quell the urge to roll my eyes, instead I clench my fists and push my nails into my palms.

Rob places his hands on my shoulders, his round cheeks pushed up in a smile. "Proud of you."

"What for?"

"For standing up to Izzie. For putting yourself first. You deserve to be happy."

"Does she not too, though?" I ask.

"She is happy. She's got a great job, a house, friends a plenty, stalkers and not, she's in love with Alex. She's happy. Izzie's holding onto a grudge because she's jealous. Her jealousy, like her apparent feelings for Stewart, are misplaced."

I nod. I know he's right. And I'm happy with my choice

(if one argues there is indeed a choice in choosing love and soulmates), with picking myself and Stewart over my friendship with Izzie. But still, the guilt clings to my veins, burns through my mind like toxic Wolfsbane.

Harry ushers everyone towards the door. “Come on you three, let’s get you the best seats in the house.”

“I’ll wait here,” I say.

“Are you not coming to watch the gig?” Harry asks me with a frown.

I shake my head. “I’ve got some work to do.”

“Daisy doesn’t like Cardinal,” Stewart states, kissing my forehead.

“She just loves you, right Stew?” Patrick says with a nudge to Stewart’s ribs.

“I love her too.”

Izzie blinks at him then me. I will myself to hold eye contact and not flinch, while also not looking too smug. I feel I fail, on both counts.

32

I hear the door open and call out that I'll be there in a minute. I finish pouring water down the sink, then jump as a copper bucket falls to the floor—water and stems spreading like spilled milk, no doubt. I pick up a towel and rush out into the front of the pop up shop that's been my own for a week and a half, an acceptance of an apology on my tongue.

I gasp, the towel falls to the floor as I see Izzie. Arms folded across her chest, hair glistening like a waterfall of diesel, heavy makeup perfect. Dressed in black like a shadow. I'd almost forgotten how beautiful yet intimidating she is.

"Iz," I whisper.

Tori, Livia, a few other women whose faces I recognise stride though the door, treading on the flowers. As if I've been slotted into floristry foam, I freeze as Izzie swipes her hands across a table; vases, buckets and flowers clatter to the floor.

My entire body flinches as I watch Izzie raise a platformed metal-toed boot before stamping on the flowers on the tiles. I swallow loudly, then straighten my back. I will not shout, I will keep calm, controlled. The last thing Stewart or I need or want is another argument between apparent warring best friends in the papers.

"You're pissed at me Iz, I get it," I state as she knocks another vase to the floor, the glass smashing. I am determined I won't rise to her anger. I begin sweeping it up, eyeing up the bigger shards, picturing them cutting through the skin on my thigh.

"Beyond pissed. I hate you."

I expected Izzie's anger at myself and Stewart to be short-lived, like a firework display. Full of explosive words which would sizzle out once the aggression had been voiced. I thought her violent outlet of my torture and occasional demise, through the medium of fan fiction, was enough for her. Clearly not as she's taking it out on my flowers.

"This is my job though, my income. If you want to argue with me, cause a scene; then we'll be at Ash's cousin's wedding next month. It'll be crawling with press as Eddie's best man. You can have your moment then."

"But that means there will be security there," Tori says innocently, flicking her gingery hair. Fuck, she saw right through that.

"And Stewart," Izzie adds. His name from her mouth, almost a snarl, sends fear and nerves zipping up my spine.

"More people to stop us."

"To stop what? Your vicious tongues?" I ask, trying to not think the worst, and ignoring the cardinal red flags waving frantically at me.

Izzie pushes me backwards by the shoulder. Not hard, but with enough force to shock. The brush and dustpan full of glass clatters to the floor. Shit. Is she going to slap me again? My heart pounds. I must look terrified, my eyes wide and breath heaving. Still, I don't respond though I want to. There will be nothing for her to throw back at me. She'd love that, to tell everyone how 'Stewart from Cardinal's bitch of a girlfriend' hit her.

"Come on, Iz. You're better than this," I try to reason.

"Better than what? Lying to your best friend for months? Breaking her heart?" Tori spits, pulling flowers from buckets and snapping the stems. The dripping water stains her jeans like tears. Wickedly I wish the stems she's snapping were alstroemeria, the irritant sap burning and causing blisters on her skin. Where's karma when you need it?

"Going against the girl code?" one of the other stalkers asks. I recognise her face from her filtered profile picture online. They really rounded up the troops.

This is ridiculous. I want to laugh at the hilarity of it. I understand the girl code, but I'm also aware after wasting too much time worrying about it that true love, happiness and soulmates are more important than a document which doesn't actually exist. I lost Izzie because of Stewart, yet I found someone who always makes my heart and soul happy. Who loves me for who I am, not as a second choice of a night in or someone to drive her home after too many vodkas.

"You love Alex, Izzie," I address her directly, try to get through to her.

Fleetingly, I wonder if I can subtly get to my phone, but know it will make things worse.

The unease builds in my gut. I'm alone with a group of unhinged, unbalanced obsessed fans of my boyfriend's band. Even Stewart and Nan, with their positive outlooks on life, would struggle to find a rainbow amongst these brewing storm clouds. Why has the street outside suddenly emptied? Where are the late afternoon shoppers, concerned members of the public walking by to come in and help me diffuse this situation?

"You're not fifteen and convinced you're in love with someone in a band," I continue.

"Stewart's rightfully hers. He should be with Iz, like Eddie should be with me and not that bitch. If I ever see her again I will break her legs. Then her neck." Tori shrugs.

No wonder Ash has a restraining order against Tori. I honestly didn't think people had this kind of mindset about band members once they passed puberty. Izzie was never this invested in Boyzone when we were six, and I didn't realise she'd take her tangled up grief with Cardinal this far.

"No one belongs to anyone. They're people, not possessions," I say, but it sounds wistful and childish.

"You knew, know, how I feel about Stewart," Izzie hisses.

"But Iz, let's be honest here. Stewart doesn't feel that way about you. He loves me, and I love him."

I turn away from them all. I'll distance myself, remain aloof, unbothered. They'll get bored when I don't respond. Bullies thrive off attention. "Does Alex know you're here?"

I begin to sort out the remaining flowers into bunches and stacking empty buckets. I spin around, a bunch of yellow germini in my hand as another glass vase and two fish bowls smash on the tiled floor. The five of them and Izzie transform from women into vultures; tearing life from the flowers as they see fit. Flower heads in summer colours, petals, leaves stripped and crushed between their claws.

"We shouldn't be doing this," Izzie says, her hands in a prayer position.

The others, including myself, look at her with wild eyes. I relax a little. I can write this off as peer pressure, a moment of madness. Anger spiralling out of control. Grief clouding clarity.

I'm about to thank them, even do the British thing and apologise, when Izzie's flat palm slaps my cheek. Stinging instantly, like nettle prickles bubbling beneath the skins surface. Izzie slaps my cheek again. My eyes water from it. Twice on one cheek, blooming like bright red tulips.

"Fuck!" I exclaim, my palm against my burning cheek.

Livia throws a fist straight into my mouth. My hand moves to my lip, the yellow flowers scatter on my shoes. Blood stains my fingertips.

My eyes blink, flit from one thing to another. The narrowed eyes of the girls, women, crazed stalkers of Stewart's band; bared teeth like rabid wolves. I panic that they might kill me. The falling vases, buckets, flowers from the display units. The flicks of their perfect hair, even in that moment I'm jealous of Izzie's dark locks.

They push, pull at me until my back hits the wall and I become their personal punching bag, slaps and fists all over my face. My arms twist, bruises will show themselves tomorrow. Tori kicks out. It knocks my knees and I fall under myself, sliding to the floor. Izzie kicks me in the ribs before I curl myself up like a closed peony. Part of me is now tempted to grab Izzie's ankle and pull her to the floor. Fight back and rip at her perfect glossy hair. But I shouldn't. Know I won't. Pushing aside how Stewart and the team and press will react; there are six of them, and they'd be relentless. Probably wouldn't stop if I try to take them on.

All of them kick at my ribs, my back, my face before I hide my features behind my palms. They hiss insults at me; Izzie's are the most personal, and even if they weren't, they hurt the most. I'm spat at, on. They leave with lingering snide comments as they cackle, and crunch over broken glass and battered flowers.

Automatically, without thinking, imploring with myself to focus on the tasks and not pain, ignoring the tears on my cheeks, the dried blood sticking to my lip, I clean the space as best I can.

The glass tinkles and jingles as it's swept into the bin. The specks of shards sparkling like minute crystals. I right the pots, vases and buckets. Salvage the stems, water them. Throw out the ruined ones, stems snapped, petals torn and bruised like my skin. I can't even save the petals for dried confetti; they're stained with impressions from clacking red nails, or imprints from shoes.

I wipe at my cheeks, feel the tenderness of bruises already blooming, and look at my ruined shop. All the flowers are tainted by the whole day. I'll never be able to look at them without thinking of Izzie and her stalker friends. The bright colours mocking me with their beauty, the muted pastel shades changing in my vision from gentle colours to insipid and washed out. I throw them all into black bags. Stems, thorns, leaves and flower heads stretch the plastic in differing angles. The petals feel cold, tacky. Fake. The scent cloys in my nostrils and throat. Momentarily, I hate them. I don't know if I'll ever want to touch a flower again by choice after today.

I cry. Although I hate Izzie for this; I'd let her break my bones, crack my skull, drain my blood, whatever. I'll heal, and maybe one day I'll see things from Izzie's point of view. Almost justify the pain she's inflicted on me. But if she's ruined my passion for flowers for me, I'll never, ever forgive her. What am I without flowers?

"I'm not cut out for this," I say into the phone, almost crying again, as my back pushes against the locked door.

Stewart chuckles a little. "Not cut out for what, a functioning relationship?"

He sounds exhausted. Without me adding to his already stacked shoulders.

"How can you even begin to call it a relationship when we get next to no time together and even less time alone?" I'm angry, upset, hurt and scared. I take it out on him.

"Baby–"

"Our entire relationship is dissected online and in print. It's fucking ridiculous."

"Daisy, that's just how my life is."

"I never wanted this," I snap.

"You, we, made a choice," he fires back instantly.

I sigh, rub at my forehead, see scratches on my palm, bruises on my arm. "I know, I'm sorry. It's been a long day."

"Busy at the shop? Rushed off your wee feet?" I hear a smile on his words. He's always positive, it infuriates me at times. Right now I just want to cry about everything.

"Izzie came by," I say, hoping my voice doesn't waver too much.

"Not to rebuild bridges I guess?" he asks before yawning then apologising.

I won't tell him, he's exhausted and stressed, the tapping on his laptop tells me he's still working. "Not quite. What's going on with you?"

"Don't change the subject, Sweetheart. Tell me what happened with Izzie?"

"They were all here."

"Who?"

"Izzie, Tori, Livia, all of them."

"The stalkers were at your shop? Fuck. I knew it was strange to not have any of them at the studio today." His lighter clicks followed by a long inhale. "What did they say?"

"Nothing I hadn't heard before."

"It's worse hearing insults directly, as opposed to reading it. I get that. Sweetheart, I'm so sorry they were cruel. Please, try not to let them get to you."

The playing of a piano in the background soothes me slightly. Music follows Stewart around. He doesn't do silence. Even in his anger he's loud.

"Can you come down? Please?" I ask, beg, so unlike me, unless we're having sex.

He chuckles quietly, awkwardly. I pick up the scratch of his beard against his palm and the rattle of his bracelets. "I can't, Daisy. We've got studio time the morn. We're on a time scale with the mixing—"

"Please? Just for a night—"

"Sweetheart, I've got work. I'm sorry. Let me check the diary."

I sniffle, feel the itching of tears in my throat and nose, a few escape from my eyes. I wipe my cheeks, my fingers shaking, smeared in black makeup and dried blood. My breathing is shaky, loud. Stewart inhales, like he's picked up something is wrong. It's wonderfully weird this soulmate connection I sometimes refuse to admit exists. It's like our thoughts, feelings are interlinked at times, and we just know when the other needs extra care.

"Has something happened? Are you hurt? Did they hurt you? Have you hurt yourself? Please, Daisy, tell me they didn't do anything."

It comes hurtling back to me, like I've been winded. Not that I'd forgotten, but I tried to push it away. Part of me wishes Izzie had stamped on my chest until my ribs cracked, puncturing my lungs so I couldn't breathe. Left me amongst the flowers to inhale the heady scent of mingling floral notes and never awoken.

My eyes linger on the silver blade of my florist knife, glinting at me. Just showing enough to be taunting and tempting. My thigh thrums, the itch of having control of something covers my skin.

"Daisy? Did they hurt you?"

"Yes," I squeak, before my sobs bounce off the walls and bags of rubbish.

"Where are you? Are you at home? Is Rob with you?" he asks. I hear Patrick shouting at him, before the front door of their flat slams.

"I'm at the shop," I say so quietly I wonder if he's heard me.

"Don't move, I'll be there in two hours. I'll call the police, get them to speak to us once I'm there. Don't touch anything."

Too fucking late, I think, the shop looking bare but mostly clean. Certainly no evidence. Apart from my battered skin and bones. No matter what Stewart and the team say, I do not want to press charges. Imagine the furor in the press about that. I'd never cope with it.

My arm stretches out to grip onto the yellow handle of my knife.

"Stay on the phone, Sweetheart."

I shake my head, although he can't see. I long to hang up and press the blade into my skin.

"Daisy, put the knife down."

I hold the knife tighter in defiance. Not even Stewart's voice can pull me out of this dark spiral.

"I'm right here. I'm on my way, Baby. Please don't hurt yourself."

I wish that was all it took for me to resist the need to cut. Stewart knows as well as I do that it's not enough. I inhale as silently as possible, watch the blade cut through the skin, the blood bloom, flowing to match my tears.

"Talk to me, please, Daisy."

I hang up. Stewart rings back, yet I turn my phone off. Block out everything but the release the blade gives me. Relief, control, floods my mind, fills the silence of the shop with a feeling of calm.

33

Ash jumps up from sitting on the bottom step as soon as Stewart pushes open the door to his flat.

"Fuck!" she shouts, her mouth and eyes wide, then pulls me into a hug. "Hen, I'm so sorry this has happened. How are you?"

I don't answer, just start crying into her shoulder. Stewart slams the front door so hard the entire building quakes. I feel him place a hand gently on my back in juxtaposition.

"Stewart, you ok?" Ash asks, as she throws an arm around my shoulder and walks me up the curved stairs.

"I'm fucking raging, Ash. If I ever see the fucking stalkers again, I swear I'll kill them."

"Stew, they're not worth it,"

"Look at her, Ash. Look what they've done to Daisy," he shouts. His temper won't change anything.

"They're not worth you going to prison for. Daisy needs you here."

Stewart's bracelets rattle as he messes with his hair. "Aye, you're right. Anyone from the team here?"

"Harry's dealing with shit from his place. Make sure you call him. Ed and Pat are upstairs. Come on; I'll run you a bath, Daisy. Then let's get you in some comfy PJs."

My eyes dance towards Stewart then away to stare at the window, the steeped roofs replacing the sloped mountains I see from home. He looks at me, almost weighing up my expression. I swallow and avoid his gaze, again.

"Give us a sec, Ash," Stewart says, placing a hand on my shoulder, halting me on the stairs. I love yet also hate how easily he can read me.

We head up to the first floor. His bedroom and living room doors open. Patrick and Eddie shout hello. I assume Ash has told them not to make a fuss.

Stewart pulls the living room door closed before returning to stand in front of me, leaning against the banister.

"You self-harmed, didn't you?"

I knew I wouldn't be able to hide it from Stewart. I hoped I'd get away with it for longer, though. My eyes fill with more tears. Blinking them away rapidly, I look at the buttons on his oversized shirt, which are misaligned. Shame colours my cheeks as I nod.

Stewart covers his eyes with his hands. The silver of his rings glistening like galena crystals. "Sweetheart. How bad is it?"

"Not as controlled as usual," I confess.

He stands, frozen. Staring at me, his lips parted slightly, his shoulders squared, spine rigid. He scrubs a hand across his beard and he inhales deeply before exhaling shakily.

I pick up my bag from my feet, loop it over my shoulder. I ignore the tears on his cheeks, though it pains me to do so.

"You didn't ask for this, for any of this. I'm bringing

shitty drama to your life. Me and my friend arguing over a man in a fucking band. Cutting my skin to make me feel like I have an ounce of control over my life. You don't need this, Stewart. I'm sorry. I'll just go."

I turn to walk towards the stairs. His hand grips round my arm, and I collapse into him. I ignore the throbbing pain from my ribs as they press against him. He pulls back, hands on my jaw, which aches. His thumbs trace over my tender skin, my split lips. My hands wrap around his wrists.

"Baby, I didn't ask for this, but I don't love you for only the good parts. I love you, all of you, Daisy. Your self-harm too." He looks totally helpless, his cornflower blue eyes glassy, and tears cling to his eyelashes. "I am so sorry. It's my crazy life that has made you do this. I could turn myself inside out with the pain I feel because of this, Sweetheart."

"Please don't blame yourself, Brunnera."

"Show me."

I shake my head. The weight of anxiety pushing out from my insides. I freeze like I'm carved from ice. I hold my breath as he pushes my dress up, before crouching down in front of me.

Fingers trailing down my thigh, the tender skin jumps beneath the swirls of his fingerprints. His forehead rests against my legs, breath on my skin. He cries quietly before standing up and holding me close. I reach up to wipe the tears from his face. Kiss him, because I can, because it's a distraction. Because it's normal.

"Ash!" Stewart calls. "Come here a wee tick."

"Shall I run that bath, Hen?" Ash assumes. She gently taps my shoulder.

I shake my head, know however childish, clingy and

downright impractical it is, but I want to stay as close to Stewart as possible for, well, right now, the rest of my days.

Stewart slides the bag down my arm. He inhales then exhales loudly. “Take Daisy’s bag. Take out her floristry shit, scissors and knives. They’re wrapped in a cloth with sunflowers on, and hide them. Don’t tell us where they are.”

I cry despite my cheeks blazing in embarrassment.

“Why?” I picture her fiddling with her conker coloured hair, plaiting it using one hand, like she does often.

The silence between us is weighted. The opening theme of a film plays in the living room, and the ever-present plucking of guitars starts up. The normality of music and sound in the flat makes me feel like things will be ok. Stewart shuffles on his feet, his arms still wrapped around me. I sigh out and pull myself away from him, turn to face Ash, my shoulders slumped, head heavy, physically and mentally.

“Hi, I’m Daisy, and I self-harm.”

“Shit.” Ash falters then shakes herself and takes my bag from Stewart’s outstretched hand. “I mean yes, I’ll do that. But first, we’re going to get a flannel for your face, ok? You’ll feel better.”

Stewart steers me towards the bathroom and without missing a moment, Ash takes my hand and pulls me gently away from him. “I need to take some calls, Ash is right here. Ed and Pat are here. You’re safe, Sweetheart. I’ll be right back,” he says, kissing at my cheeks before leaving Ash and me.

After cleaning my face, with me perched on the edge of the bath like a child, Ash talking in soothing tones and plaiting my hair with her fingers that shook, she hands me a set of ironed short PJs that I left here ages ago. I look at them and sob out.

"Do you cut on your legs, Hen?" Ash asks and I nod. She takes off her leggings silently and slides the PJ shorts up her legs. She hands me her leopard print leggings with a smile. I think I love her for it.

"Let's clean you up and then we won't talk about it once we step out of the bathroom. Unless you want to." She squeezes my hand. "I'm always here, Hen. We're pals, right?"

I nod, avoid her eyes, even though they're always so warm and welcoming. I pull my dress over my head, put the PJ top on and then can't bear to look at the slices in my skin. I close my eyes, feel her wiping at the few smears of dried blood, then rubbing lotion on them.

"Yes, I hope. You probably think I'm boring and—"

"Not at all. I think you're great. You're funny, kind, and quick-witted. We should meet up, just us two. You're genuine, it's nice to have someone else who is, aside from the four of us. The hipsters are fucking annoying. And Ella or whoever else is clinging on to Stew, they're fake, and not my type of friends."

"Izzie always thought I was boring. She always changes the subject if I start talking. She makes me feel out of place, worthless. I can handle it most of the time when I'm sober, but after a few drinks I want to tell her to fuck off and let me just be, me."

Ash squeezes my hands. "Izzie seems to be a shite friend, even before today."

"You're a better one."

"I don't feel that's saying much."

"I mean you're a good person, a good friend. Izzie's always been a self-centred bitch." Funny how a physical attack can bruise your skin yet make you see clearer.

Ash shrugs, plaits my hair. "Sounds like you should have cut her out long ago. Friends are meant to bring you joy, happiness, they're meant to love you for being unapologetically you."

I reach out to hug her. I always feel comfortable with Ash, have done since the minute we sat down and started talking. She listens, she believes in me and values my conversation and opinions.

"The self-harm is a control thing, I know, almost embedded in you, but don't let those stalking bitches get into your head, Hen. It's not your fault you and Stew fell in love. They're jealous, empty souls. Don't let them steal your happiness. You deserve it."

"Do they not deserve to be happy? Does Izzie not—"

"No, not after this," Ash replies with such finality I believe it.

We walk into the living room, past Stewart's closed bedroom door, where his voice goes from shouting to hushed urgent words. Ash leads me to the chair that sits below the huge Star Wars print on the wall. Eddie and Patrick jump up and hug me, which makes me cry again, but in a warm, safe way. Ash dismisses them and instead brings Eddie's attention to her bare legs and starts talking about getting a tattoo.

"Coffee?" Patrick asks, he flicks on the radio, muting the TV as he fills a mug with hot liquid from one of the several coffee pots he and Stewart own.

I nod, even though it's heading towards midnight, and they don't own decaf.

Neither of them mentions the attack or asks how I am. Which I'm grateful for.

Eddie pours a packet of sweets into a bowl, the sound reminding me of wearing all of Nan's jangling necklaces at once when playing dress up.

Patrick hands me a coffee and rubs gently on my arm. "Are you pressing charges against the stalkers?"

I shake my head and turn to look out of the window. The wooden blinds splicing the view. "No. I don't want it dragged out. And the band don't need it. I just want to forget about it. The police have taken statements and stuff, but I've told them I don't want to press charges, and it'll be an insurance job I guess."

Not that I care about the money side of things at this moment in time. I never want to see that pop up shop again in my life.

Stewart comes back into the living room, holding out his arms and I step into the embrace.

"I feel fucking awful. I'm so sorry this happened, Daisy. I feel so guilty. I know I'm a dramatic sod, but I feel like I could die from it."

My heart constricts at his honesty, at how much I love him and he loves me.

"It's not your fault," everyone echoes in similar sentiments.

"It fucking is. This is because of my life, my fucking band." He covers his face with his hands. "I wasn't there."

They would've got to me somehow. We all know it. Stewart's just choosing not to think about it.

"I don't lay the blame with you, for any of it."

Stewart exhales, the Star Wars bracelets clanging against one another as his wipes the tears from his face. This hurts more than the slaps to my cheek and kicks to my ribs, more than the cuts on my thigh. "You should. You so should."

"I don't, and I'm stubborn as fuck so, best deal with it." I smile. Ignoring how my lip seems to pull and crack with the movement.

"We're getting restraining orders on the stalkers. All of us. You and Ash included, Daisy. The band will release a statement, just in case this gets out before we say anything. We don't want it to look like we're scared or hiding from them," Eddie says as Stewart and I sit down, as close to each other as possible.

Patrick nods in agreement. "We pride ourselves on our gigs being a safe, welcoming space. If we didn't say something, it goes against that. There won't be specific details; someone close to the band was a victim of a hate attack, and we're banning those involved from any of our future gigs."

"And as shallow as it is, Sweetheart, you are not leaving this house until you're healed. The press won't have any photos of what happened. I'm not having it following you like ghostly footsteps," Stewart says, his hand squeezing at my arm gently.

"Ok. I can go with that," I nod.

He sighs, in relief. Probably thought I would put up more of a fight. "How are you feeling?"

"Sore, but ok. I really want a hot bath and forget about it all."

"I'll run you one the now," Stewart says, standing up.

*

"Rob's on his way," Patrick says, cheeks blushing. "I texted him, and he wants to see you,"

"He didn't have to come up," I sob out tears of happiness. And realisation. Izzie would never drop everything and come to my aide. Even before I fell in love with Stewart.

"He's your best pal, he wants to check how you are," Stewart counters, smoothing my hair down. I know if things were different, Izzie wouldn't drive three hours up the motorway to see me.

"He suggested you two go away," Patrick adds before tapping out a rhythm on the coffee table. Ash jokes about where exactly Rob will be sleeping, yet Patrick ignores her.

"You've all suddenly got time off have you?" I half laugh, the movement making my ribs ache. Though I do wish we could just run away and hide out from the world.

"You should do it. Escape for a wee while."

"We can't just flit off," Stewart says with a head shake.

"Pal, look at the state of things. Press interest following the statement will be rife."

"He's right, Stew," Ash adds.

"Maybe a break will be good for us all. Could we actually have time to look at wedding venues?" Eddie asks turning to Ash. She squeals and claps her hands. Her excitement is contagious. I smile at them both.

"Should we? Can we?" Stewart scratches at his beard and flicks through his diary which is always within arms reach.

"Let's just push the promo for *This Won't Change* back a few weeks. If we all stand together the team will have to listen. We can easily convince Harry," Eddie says. Patrick agrees, stating how he fancies taking up baking.

Stewart nods, his eyes twinkling. “Ok, let’s do it.” He picks me up and twirls me round, and I ignore the pain in my ribs. “Let’s go away, escape the madness, Baby.”

“Where are youse going to go? Some five star exotic location?” Patrick asks.

“You could go back to Sorento?” Eddie suggests.

“Nah. Maybe somewhere closer to home,” Stewart replies smiling.

I think of Cumbrae, imagine the two of us making memories together on our treasured island. Standing in the sea with him as the sun sets, water lapping at our bare ankles, Stewart keeping me grounded. Happy. Safe. My eyes close as I will myself to believe it. I long to ask, demand we go to the Scottish island we’ve both loved for years as individuals. I’d go to Jupiter right now if it meant we could escape reality.

“Where?” I ask hope in my tone, fingers playing with his long fringe.

“Only our favourite place in the world, Sweetheart.”

34

'Going on holiday with the love of my fucking life!'

A familiar pair of blue eyes, captured looking up from under his long dark fringe, fills the screen of my phone. A smile tugs at my mouth, excitement filling my veins. Cardinal's planned, or unplanned, break wasn't granted by management as quickly as everyone hoped. But perhaps it's worked out for the better. It's the middle of August, and all festivals are done and dusted, so Stewart and I can have two whole weeks together, uninterrupted.

My feet dangle over the seal coloured rocks. Toes making patterns in the warm pale sand dotted with seaweed, stones and pearled shells. A book is open on my lap, but my eyes focus more on the sea than the text.

I lift my eyes towards the sun, then look around when I see him. Wearing a faded red shirt that billows in the gentle breeze. It sparks a memory of the trip to Sorento that seems a lifetime away. Sunglasses perched on his head, nestled in his chocolate brown hair like a secret. Denim shorts cling temptingly to his thighs, leading to bare feet, flip flops swinging carelessly in his hand. The sun highlighting the silver rings on his fingers, bracelets on his wrists and the chain slung low across his chest.

"A florist called Daisy!" Stewart calls.

The pounding of my heart like a bass drum doesn't surprise me as I hear his voice. Stewart's head is tilted to the side, his fingers twiddling at the silver chain hanging low on his chest. Like I'm in an overly predictable romcom, I scramble off the rocks, abandoning the book, and run to him, flip flops slapping against the ground.

"Hey you."

Stewart picks me up, spins me around in circles like he always does. My flip flops fly off like wayward frisbees, but I don't care. Let a dog chew them, swallow them, shit them out, even if they did cost over twenty quid from FatFace.

I can't begin to hide the smile as I push my face into his neck. He smells of lavender, spices, and leather from the car. Nor can I fight against the rhythm my heart is beating.

"Happy to see me?" he asks.

"Nah, not really," I reply, scrunching my nose and shaking my head.

He laughs, loud, unapologetic, wholesome. His pupils dance from my eyes to every feature of my face. "Two weeks of bliss with you, Daisy."

"Dreams come true, huh?"

"Let's hope so, Sweetheart."

Surrounded by what I'm pretty sure is the entirety of the deli and bottles of water and vodka, Stewart and I lay staring at the clouds. Only one passing shower had us diving to the car. And yes, he did have a minor panic attack at the sight of sand in the beloved Bentley's footwells. No, my laughter didn't help.

My head rests on his thighs, our fingers intertwined, bodies stretched out on a floor of faded towels, forming a t-shape. I follow a swooping gull across the pale sky as I nestle my feet into the almost white sand. I love the feeling of the grains burying into the crevices of my skin.

"Your hair's different," Stewart states.

"So's yours," I reply flicking at his fringe, which is still long, but the rest of it has been cut shorter.

He rolls his blue eyes beneath a frown. "The stylist thought I was Eddie, and started to give me his haircut."

I laugh. "Managed to save the fringe though?"

"Just in time, it was a close call let me tell you. These curls though, did you get them done earlier? Ash curled your hair a few times."

"No, I only arrived last night. It's the sea air and the water. Makes it curly. It always does this. They'll drop as soon as I get home." I pick up my long hair, still adorned in expensive highlights, it's certainly more defined than my usual wavy mess.

"I feel like I haven't seen you smile for weeks, Daisy," Stewart says, ripping a chunk of bread to eat.

"We haven't seen each other in weeks."

"We video call every day."

"It's not the same."

"I've seen press reports online."

I scoff, steal the bread from him. "That's definitely not the same. Wait, you read those?"

"Yep. The team thinks you did a stellar job following the—"

Attack from my ex best friend and the stalkers of my boyfriend's band. My cheek and ribs sting in memory of it. I sit up and watch the waves. Breathe shakily, the memories swirl in my head, and I try my best to shake them out.

I hold Stewart's hand to bring me back to reality. He soothes his other hand down my back. Places kisses at the top of my spine.

"You're ok now, Sweetheart," he whispers into my skin.

I exhale. "You mean when I actually followed the rules it worked out ok?"

"The press were desperate to know what happened, I know they tried everything. But you stayed so silent, so poised. Even Ash told them to fuck off."

In truth I liked to pretend none of it had happened, and the questions they asked were just their usual fictitious rumours.

"Why do you read about me? Not bored of Bronte are you?"

"I like to know which journalists to be nice to, and which to be a dick to. Depending on how they report on my girlfriend."

They all say the same; I'm miserable, a loner. Too fat. Too thin. Too plain. Too fake with my out of a bottle blonde hair. Not as pretty as Ella. Too small town for a pop star. Inconsequential. The perfect match to Stewart. One in a long line of girlfriends Stewart has dotted around. I can't keep up with what they report, so try my best to ignore it.

"I don't know why you think the press hate you, they don't. The fans love you, there's cute wee blogs about you."

"Your fans have no taste. They also love you," I reply seriously and flick at his fringe again.

He shakes his head, a smile on his features. "Such a wee menace."

*

"I wonder if a florist would work on the island?" I murmur, not looking for a response, just musing. Toying with the idea in my head. Stewart sits up, threading his fingers through my hair. It's so knotted already, and I'll probably wash out half the beach in the shower later, but it doesn't matter. "I don't think it would. What with the ferry and such. Deliveries for the fresh flowers would be too complex. And I imagine the turnaround or demand wouldn't be great."

"Buy a place on the mainland then," Stewart says, exhaling smoke rings, which he keeps trying and failing to teach me to do.

"I can't."

"Why not?"

"I can't afford to–"

"I can buy–"

"Don't you dare finish that sentence, Stewart," I warn, sitting up, the damp sand sticking to my bare feet.

He rolls his eyes. "You and your independent woman Beyonce shit."

"I'm not having you buy me a florists." The pop up shop was enough. More than enough.

"Fine, buy it yourself," he says, pulling me onto his lap, his hands on my thighs, my arms loop around his neck, and I kiss his forehead.

"I fully intend to."

"What time scale are you on with, Daisy? Is this the one day dream? Or the next step?"

"Both, maybe. I don't know. I'm never happier than when I'm here."

"You're actually smiling."

"Ah that's all down to my handsome boyfriend."

He smirks then licks his lips. With more pressure, subconsciously or not, his palms smooth over the skin on my thighs.

"I'm ok," I assure him. The splices on my bare thigh are nowhere near as prominent as the ones beneath my tattoos were. They'll fade.

"It's my job to worry about you, Daisy." Stewart's eyes linger on my thigh. "They're not healing that great, Sweetheart."

"I picked the scabs when they itched; it was accidental."

He nods, I try my hardest to exhale quietly, so he doesn't pick up on my relief. "And the truth?"

Shit. I wonder if I can get away with not answering. His hands go to my jaw, our eyes meet. Nope, I can't not tell him.

"I scratch them, just with my nails. It's not a cut." I swallow, lift my face to the sky, his fingers slide down my neck.

"See what I've done to you?" He closes his eyes. "Look what my life does to you."

"No, Brunnera, this is on me," I implore with him, shaking my head.

"You've done that how many times? The scratching?"

"Most days," I admit with burning cheeks and a pounding heart. It shows more of an effect when done beneath the hot water of the shower. They look angrier, more pronounced. It makes me feel better.

Stewart's hands cover his face and he pulls on his hair. "Baby, you're breaking my heart. I don't know whether I feel angry at you, at myself, or just fucking devastated."

"I haven't done it for a week," I say, like that makes up

for it. But if I'm honest that's only because I knew he'd be livid with me if he saw them so angry and vivid.

"Daisy—" He scrubs a hand over his beard. I can tell from the blues in his eyes that he's tempted to argue about it. He does have a foul temper; always short-lived, though. I know he won't start anything in public, for his benefit more than mine. "Do you want to talk to someone? You should talk to someone. You've got a direct number for the team. I feel you should."

I shake my head. "I won't do it anymore. It's stopped. I promise." I place my hands around his face. "I promise, Stewart. That's it now, ok? Please believe me."

"It's not something you can just stop. We both know it's more complicated than that. If I find out you've done it again, I'm sending you straight for therapy, counselling, and help of any and all kinds available. Non-optional. I mean it." His eyes are the same colour as the bay behind me, yet topped with a frown.

"And I mean it when I say I won't do it anymore."

"I can't have this happening, Baby, to you or me. I love you so fucking much."

I kiss him before continuing the conversation, back on our original tack. Both of us seem relieved to nudge the topic of my self-harm to the back of our minds. Though his hands stay on my thighs.

"I can't open a florists back at home, I'd be stepping on Jane's toes."

The goal was always to have my own florists; the location never mattered. Thc drcam was always to be up here, but I never let myself believe it. But now, I can't settle on anywhere because my heart isn't there. That carefully carved life plan is certainly not being followed as I intended.

"Will you move up to Edinburgh? Please, Sweetheart? We can get our own place." Stewart asks.

I stand up, then sit back down next to him, and look out to the sea, the boats bobbing gently in the distance, the gulls diving overhead against the creamy clouds. Then I look closer, at the purple floating blobs of the jellyfish on the sea's sapphire surface, at our legs stretched out. Toes buried in the pale sand. Salt water splashes, drying in white spots on his tanned legs.

"I can buy us somewhere. That's not me being all macho and quashing your independence. That's me being practical and realistic. I can afford to get us a place so we can live together. You can't as you're saving for a shop and business. I want us to live together, Daisy."

"Leaving Nan, it would be such a wrench."

My heart almost stops with the thought, then a quick look towards Stewart, and I feel it beat in time again. Those blue eyes I probably fell in love with on sight over a year and a half ago, that wonky smile that makes me weak at the knees.

"But?" He smiles, eyes wide and hopeful like the bay in front of us, before his happiness drops a fraction, and his expression becomes more reserved. Sometimes I think he's picked up my reluctance and caution of the world.

"You're worth it. Let's do it. Let's live together. Once we get back, I'll speak to Rob, but I can't leave him in the lurch. He'll have to find a new housemate. That mortgage is a killer."

Stewart throws his arms around me, pulls me close to him and kisses my head repeatedly. I complain, but the smile shows I'm pretending to hate his affection.

"Fuck that. I'll pay your share until he finds a housemate."

"You're such a dick," I laugh.

"But a dick with a very healthy bank account. I cannot wait to live with you, Baby. I promise, we'll visit Enid at least once a month. I'll have a clause put in the contract when we re-sign with the label next year." He winks, and I can't stop smiling at him.

"You're a good egg, Stewart."

I kiss him to distract my heart and mind from spiralling out of control too much. I'm not going against my plan; I'm taking a detour. Really though, the plan is already shot to hell. But being in Edinburgh I'll be closer to this coast, my dream location for a shop. Maybe dreams do come true.

"I wish we could live here, actually," I admit, looking back over the bay.

"Is there a reason we can't?" he asks, pulling his sunglasses from his hair. His gaze slides past me. "Hold that thought, Daisy," he smiles before kissing my cheek and then standing up, replacing his mirrored sunglasses.

I turn and see a small circle of girls with braces and bikinis, their skinny pre-teen bodies bouncing on their feet at the sight of Stewart from Cardinal. They giggle in apology for talking to him on holiday, but they seem so excited, I know he won't mind.

I grip his hand and look at him in a slight state of panic. He bends back down and leans his palms on my thighs. I love how he knows what I mean. The fans observe every detail, store them away and analyse them. I'm aware the scratches on my thigh, like Stewart says, are angry and inflamed. They're noticeable if you're looking at every inch of me. Who better to recognise self-harm scars than teenagers? Shit.

Stewart wordlessly peels off his already unbuttoned shirt and lays it over my legs with a kiss against my temples. I bite back a smile as I observe the teens swooning.

"Daisy's always cold. Does she not know this is the height of Scottish summer?" he laughs as he approaches the group. They all giggle in response and a few wave at me.

Stewart greets the fans with careful hugs and smiles; he signs scraps of paper in their shaking hands, clutching at their phones as if their lives depend on it. They all gather around him and pose for several selfies. He has endless patience with his fans, and I admire him for that, yet I know he'll make a playful comment later about never having any peace. The girls coo over him as he says goodbye, and they wave at me, all with giggles of 'bye Daisy' making me feel accepted into the little clan.

"To be fair, I would live here," Stewart continues as he sits back on the sand.

"Do you not need to stay in Edinburgh?"

"There's such a thing as vehicles, you know, Sweetheart? You can travel from place to place. Look, there's a fine example of one." He points to the Bentley.

"Fuck off."

I place a hand on his thigh. And only make one sarcastic comment when he takes photos of the two of us and then edits the hell out of them. He posts the photo; sunglasses on, smiling, laying on the colourful towels found in the holiday home, the sea and bobbing boats in the background behind us.

"Do you want to live here, on Cumbrae?" Stewart asks.

"Yes." I nod. I have done ever since I first visited the island over ten years ago.

"But?" He smiles and hands me a cup of coffee that's still hot, despite having bought it hours ago from the deli.

"But I'd want, need my shop on the mainland first, or I'd just sit and watch the waves all day. And while that would be an idyllic way to spend my days, it's not productive to my career."

Stewart throws an arm around my shoulder and pulls me close, so my head rests against him. He smells of salt and lavender, and coffee.

"Life would be easier if you accepted help, Sweetheart."

I know what he means: life would be easier if I let him buy me a florists. After the stall at the festival last year, and the pop up shop, I know he expects me to relent and let him hand me a blank cheque. We've stopped arguing about it, instead agreeing to disagree. Though I have promised to break up with him if he ever buys me a shop outright.

"I want this. I need this business to be my own, my own achievement." I don't want to be defined purely by my relationship status, celebrity boyfriend or not. I need to prove it to myself that I'm good enough and capable of doing this alone.

"I'm sorry, Daisy, that your mum has made you feel you're never good enough. That she made you believe you can only rely on yourself."

My hand goes to the charm around my neck as I stare out at the sea. Not even looking at the waves, as the glassy film clouds my vision. "That's not your apology to make."

"You are enough, Baby. It's her failing, not yours."

"I feel like I don't know who I am anymore."

"You're a florist called Daisy."

I laugh a little, brittle like dried poppy stalks. “I’m not, though. I haven’t even touched a flower since June.”

I miss it. The silky petals, the different stems and leaves. The mingling scents and myriad of colours. I’ve lost my confidence with it; my memories and passion for flower arranging have been chased, scattered and blown away in the wind like the seeds usually protected inside poppy heads.

“You’ll get there, Sweetheart. You can do it. Shoot for the fucking moon,” Stewart implores me to believe him. And I do a little more each time he encourages me. I place a kiss on his lips and smile.

I wipe a stray tear from my cheek then nod, a smile on my face. “I’m finally moving to Edinburgh. You’d best get flat hunting, Brunnera.” I kiss him again, changing the subject. No point dwelling on my mother or failings in following a plan any more than necessary.

“You’d better start packing as soon as you get back to Cumbria, Sweetheart. I’m not hanging around. I tell you what,” Stewart continues in between deliciously slow kisses, which almost make me drag him away from the beach and back to bed. “When you buy a florists on the mainland, I’ll buy us a house here.”

I blink at him in disbelief, yet a smile covers my face. It rivals that of his fans that have just left and are updating their accounts with selfies.

“You sort out your floristry business, so it's all yours and all that independent woman shit—”

“Beyonce will be so proud of you,” I say as he props himself backwards, taking me with him. I run my fingers through his hair.

“And I’ll get us a house. Now, which one do you want?”

He lies back on the sand and points to the enormous beachfront houses that overlook the sweeping crescent beach of Kames Bay.

"Going to pay for it in diamonds, are you?"

"Yep, although I also smelt my own gold now, you know?"

"Is that what you want, Stewart? Me and you living here?" I ask, scooting off him and laying down, the length of our bodies touching.

He shakes his head fondly, places an arm around my shoulder, and pulls my head onto his chest. "For fucks sake, Daisy. I've always wanted a life with you. You keep pushing me away."

35

"We should totally get a tandem!" Stewart enthuses as the two of us stand hand in hand in the bike shop overlooking the seafront.

The weather forecast isn't great for today, but after days of lazing on the beaches and splashing in the sea, both of us fancy a change. We decide to join the masses and cycle the eleven miles around the island.

"You know the saying goes that if you ride a tandem as a couple, it propels you towards where your relationship is heading." The man from the shop smiles politely at us.

I nod sagely before my eyes pull towards Stewart. As our eyes meet, neither of us can stop the laughter that bursts from our mouths and bounces around the cramped shop.

"Is this your way of breaking up with me, Stewart? Because frankly, I'd prefer you do it now, so I don't have to cycle around the island," I say dramatically, clutching at both the Rebel Alliance Star Wars charm and the new Brunnera charm necklace Stewart gave me for my birthday yesterday.

"Actually, I hope you've packed a white dress, Sweetheart." He winks.

"I'd rather break up. I do not need a white dress or a husband to feel validated as a woman, or indeed to find my place within the social constraints that I should apparently adhere to. Beyonce has taught you nothing."

Stewart blinks and looks taken aback. Shit. I kiss him, yet he responds minimally. Maybe even he has limits of accepting my levels of sarcasm.

"Shall I give you guys two bikes?" the man asks, shuffling on his feet.

That doesn't bode well. Though he's not a fortune teller, why should we take any notice of this silly myth? It's clearly just superstitious nonsense.

"You'd rather break up?" Stewart asks, his blue eyes looking like a dejected puppy.

I smile at the man apologetically, then hold Stewart's fingers in mine. Rubbing my fingertips across the soft skin of the back of his hands.

"No, of course not, Baby. You know I don't want to break up. You know how I feel."

He sighs, his shoulders sloping in, what—defeat? It may not have been enough. But it's so hard for me to set those three words free.

"Can I grab a selfie, by the way?" the man asks, still lingering close to us, with no sign of one or two bikes. Stewart nods, though his smile is forced, he slots his sunglasses over his eyes.

"Shall I take it for you?" I ask. I'm usually the photographer.

"You step in too, Pet. It's not every day a celebrity couple comes to my shop."

I grimace before I can stop myself.

After selfies and autographs, the man wheels out two bikes, and neither of us have the inclination to correct him.

The clouds darken in the skies as Stewart and I pass the ferry terminal on the two separate bikes, and continue round to the top of the island. The rain falls without warning, no tiny specks of water developing from a shower to a storm. It pelts down in sheets. Relentless, unabating. Fucking freezing, the marrow of my bones feels like ice.

Stewart and I stop by the stone monument, not that there's any shelter, merely two wooden benches and the exposed corner of the island.

"Why won't you say it?" Stewart shouts as we stand, bikes abandoned next to the obelisk monument overlooking the choppy sea, the waves like endless shoals of navy blue seal backs. The wind and rain swirling from all directions, sticking my sea-salted curls to my wet face.

"Say what?" I ask him, shivering like a dock leaf from the rain and a sinking feeling heading towards my toes.

"The final line in *Return of the Jedi*. The opening lyric of Cardinal's debut single. Cathy's speech in Wuthering Heights. What the fuck do you think I mean, Daisy?"

I shrug, avoiding Stewart's blue eyes that echo the colour of the crashing waves. I know; of course I do. There have been times I've been close to letting the illusive 'I love you' escape, but I've managed to silence the urge. Usually I've avoided it by instigating sex. Low shot, but neither of us complained. Yet the public place, the rain, and the fact that he's still annoyed at himself for the whole shagging on the rocks thing just a few nights ago down at Kames

Bay, even though we got away with it, doesn't play in my favour for a repeat of that.

"Really? You want this conversation now? In the pissing rain?" My heart pounds more than when the cameras were trained on us when we went public, more than when I met his parents and had an argument with them, more than when Izzie and the Cardinal stalkers attacked me. More than each time the phone rings from the care home and it's not the usual time Nan calls for a chat. More than each time Stewart looks at me, and I can see that he loves me exactly as I am. Despite being a bit of a fuck up.

"No, Daisy, I wanted this conversation months ago, but you keep resisting it."

"I don't see why it matters so much. You already know."

I rub at my forehead, hold my palms to the sky, catch raindrops on my skin. Is it appropriate if I quote Star Wars again? Point out that Han didn't tell Leia he loved her when she said it first? No, that would sink to the sea bed like the heaviest rock in existence. Stewart won't appreciate being compared to a princess right now either, I imagine.

He shakes his head and furrows his brows. His jaw set, spine pulled taut, shoulders squared. "How do you know that? You've never asked."

"Because that ego of yours believes everyone is in love with you," I snap out.

Stewart opens a bottle of water. I know he doesn't want or need it. It's just something to keep his hands busy, a distraction from his girlfriend being such a fucking coward.

"Just for once, can you not be so fucking sarcastic—"

"Me, sarcastic?"

He scowls, looking both hurt and bitterly disappointed. He throws the bottle, largely untouched, into the bin with more aggression than required. It bounces down the inside with several clatters that seem to echo around the sky.

"I know it's ridiculously dramatic, Daisy, but you're my whole world. I've never felt this way, ever," Stewart says into the salty sky, the rain rolling down his face, dripping off his hair that's almost black with the unabating falling water, curling at the ends. "I want you, fuck, I want you, Daisy. Any way and every way imaginable; on rocks, in my bed, in your bed, against hotel doors and every wall I see, wherever. But I also want to wake up with you each morning, to see you every day for the rest of my life. I want to fall asleep with you, knowing that you'll be there when I wake up, no matter what time of night it is. I want to share every moment with you, big or small, good and bad. Even when I'm in a foul mood, or you're snippy, giving me shit for my Star Wars stuff—"

"I mean, you do wear Star Wars boxers." I have to lighten the tone or I'll cry. However, I have a feeling humour won't lift the mood. The tightness in my chest feels like I'm drowning, struggling to breathe.

Stewart scoffs out a small smile but ignores my comment.

I'm hit with an anxious, abject fear that he might actually propose. It's cancelled out by the heavy dread of heading towards a break-up. Fuck, how have I messed this up by not saying anything? Well, that's my answer.

"And you say I'm intolerable." He shakes his head and holds my hands in his.

I sigh in relief at the contact. He can't end things, and

he won't be leading up to it. My heart thuds, surely I won't let him.

"There will never, ever be anyone else for me but you, Daisy. I promise it to you here and now, with the sea and this fucking freezing rain as my witness. It's you or nothing."

I know that I love him, know that he loves me. It's like finding the buoy in the wider expanse of the ocean. Stewart is the anchor to my rope. He won't let me drown. But still. I'm so scared. Scared to say how I really feel, there's no going back once it's been said. There's nothing left of me after I reveal my true feelings. Totally exposed and defenceless. Maybe I will drown if I'm the one to let go of the rope and feel the burn as it slices through my hands.

"You said it in front of Izzie. You've told your Nan. Why won't you say it to me? Why won't you tell me you love me?" He laughs bitterly. Shakes his head; at me or himself is unclear. "And now it's like I'm emotionally blackmailing you into saying how you feel."

"If you already know, why does it matter?"

I know it's stupid. I know exactly what to say. He needs to hear me say it. I love Stewart. Of course I do. I am so in love with him. I guess on some level I've always loved him. But I don't want to. I don't want to be so wholly dependent on someone, on anyone. It's not a shattered desire about realising I won't ever be the next Beyonce. Though in an ideal world, I too would be a glamorous millionaire businesswoman, with skin as blemish free as satin, but make bouquets, not records.

"Maybe it's me. Maybe I've had enough of this," Stewart says, his hands pulling on his hair in frustration.

I shake my head. "You don't mean that."

"Don't I? What are you, a mind reader now? Like I'm supposed to be with you. I'm just meant to know how you feel. Why should it be my job to carve away at your layers of sarcasm and distance to try and discover what you really mean?"

"I just—"

"I shouldn't have to tease it out of you, Daisy. It shouldn't be this difficult for you to say."

"Stewart—"

"You have zero desire to embrace my life."

"Your life is fucking crazy," I snap back, our anger rising like the waves. "Why does anyone need to know what I'm wearing? Or if we're still dating? Why does it matter? Why does everyone feel they need to know? That they have a right to invade our relationship?"

"It's part and parcel of my life. You knew this! If you spoke to the press, gave them something, smiled a wee bit—"

"I'm sorry that having my everyday life interrupted for the sake of gossip doesn't make me beam from ear to ear, Stewart. We aren't all egotistical like you."

"You make it out to be such a fucking trauma."

"It is a fucking trauma! I didn't choose this!"

"You chose me once." He sighs.

"And I still do. I struggle massively with the intrusion, that's all," I say, my tone more measured, careful. Trying to pull us away from an argument.

"But you don't even try!"

"I'm not arguing about this again," I state, folding my arms.

He scoffs. "Something else you refuse to discuss."

"Stewart, you know how I feel about you. I'd be lost—"

"Lost without me, yep. You've said that before."

"It's true. Stewart, you're my favourite person, the best person in the world."

"Daisy, that's not enough anymore." He holds my gaze.

I say nothing. My heart still guarded. Protected by stubborn thorns like spikes on the holly leaves. The glossy bright berries screaming for attention, yet the barrier of leaves keep them safe and unblemished. I will the leaves to fall like needles on a Christmas tree. I sigh in defeat, my spiked leaves unmoving.

"But, I—"

"I'm heading back." He stands his bike up off the grass that's transforming into puddles flecked with green strands.

My voice doesn't carry far on the wind as I shout after him, but I doubt he'd turn to face me anyway. I watch him cycle towards the town and the holiday home. I want to scream, to cry, perhaps to even laugh it all off.

Instead, I climb on the bike, push myself off, and cycle the other way around the island. It's an avoidance technique, I know, delaying the inevitable. Whatever that may be. It gives me time and space to admit to what I want. To try to make sense of it, that after nearly thirty years, it is ok to want someone. To want to share everything with that special someone. Even the realisation that there is a special someone out there, that he does exist for me. And he loves me, all of me exactly as I am. Flaws and all. Just like Mark Darcey says to Bridget Jones. Just like Beyonce sings about. My special someone is Stewart.

The cool wind and rain kiss my cheeks and tingle on my white knuckles. I pedal and pedal, freewheel down the slopes, swerve around slower cyclists with tandems and chubby toddlers in trailers. I smile at the walkers and watch the sea change colour as the tide sweeps in and out. I slow as I enter the small town. The sun beams down on the big houses I dream about, the grassy banks and palm trees, and everyone strolling enjoying the warmth. In the typical Scottish weather, the rain has blown over and been replaced with glorious sunshine. No traces of puddles left, just the summer sun beaming down in soft yellow lines like a postcard.

I step over his laptop bag and suitcase as I walk down the long hall of the holiday home, the ever-present scent of lavender in the air, along with coffee and the linger of lemon-topped pancakes from breakfast.

Stewart is placing his guitar back in the case. A quick glance to the living room shows that his notebooks, wires, books, headphones, and all his usual mess have gone from the coffee table.

"What are you doing?" I ask with a nervous chuckle as I hang up my coat. It slides off the hook and lands on the floor with a wet thud.

Stewart doesn't respond.

"Stewart?" I gulp. He's never silent. Even in his anger, he's loud.

"Brunnera?"

Nothing.

"Stewart, Baby?"

"My parents are heading back to Edinburgh today. I'm going with them." He shrugs, avoiding my gaze.

My heart hammers. "But we've got another week here?"

"I want to go home."

"You want to spend a week with your parents? Out of choice? You'll have the week from hell, that's even if they let you in the house." I can only grasp at straws that he's joking.

Please let him be joking.

"Beats being here with you," he sneers as he slams the guitar case closed and pushes past me. I follow after him, and place a hand on his back. He ignores me.

"Don't do this, please."

"Is this not what you want, Daisy?"

"No, of course not–"

"I can't do this. I can't be the only one invested in us."

"You're not! You know how I feel!" I shout, well aware I'm heading toward hysterical.

"I really don't, though." He shakes his head. His eyes looking more dull than ever. As if the colour is muted from my own silence.

"You know me better than I know myself!"

The delivery of it makes it sound angry and resentful. It has always terrified me; love. The whole vulnerability of it. I've never had that role model, the inspiration of happy, functional couples in my life. I know it's a cliche with a glacé cherry on top, to blame my childhood. But if the cake needs a finishing touch...

"I knew this would happen. Of course I'm not enough for you." Defeat colours my tone. It always comes back to this.

Stewart spins around. "You are enough, Daisy. I just need to know how you feel. It's selfish, but I need to hear you say it."

"You know–"

"You said you'd rather break up than anything else. You'd rather break up and stay where we are than push forward and have a future. How do you think that makes me feel?"

"That's not what I meant. We're about to move in together. Doesn't that show you how I feel about us? Stop being so dramatic. It's not like you're about to propose or—"

Shit. His skin pales and he completely avoids me. His eyelid twitches with nerves. Oh fuck, please don't tell me he was thinking about asking me to marry him. And I fucked it all up before he could.

"Stewart—" I rub my forehead and stretch out to touch him. "Were you?"

"It doesn't matter, does it? You can't or won't tell me you love me."

Stewart is a romantic. He wears his heart on his sleeve as brazen and bold as the Star Wars bracelets looped around his wrists. Of course he's going to need more than a sassy comeback and sex.

"I love you! There! Are you fucking happy now? Is that what you want me to say?" It jumps from my mouth way too quickly, harshly, like sparks from a blazing poker.

"I want you to mean it. I want you to want to say it."

"I told you I'd push you away, and you promised me you'd be here."

"You've pushed me too far. I'm exhausted from it. I can't carry on like this." He shakes his head, scrubs at the back of his neck, his eyes glassy with unshed tears.

"Stewart, you don't mean that."

I try to soothe him, placate him or perhaps more myself. I touch his chest, his cheek. Love the feel of his scruff of a beard beneath my palm. He sighs, eyes closing as if he's relaxing under the touch.

I kiss him. It's gentle, loving. It soon turns more passionate, aggressive almost. Stewart pushes his body into mine. My back hits the low bookcase, the vase toppling over, smashing like glass confetti, we both ignore it. My feet instinctively raise onto their toes. My hands pull at his hair at the nape of his neck. His hands grip at my wrists, slide down my arms, over my ribs to my waist. Suddenly, he takes a step backwards, the breath panting out of him as my chest heaves like I've just run a marathon.

I miss the contact instantly. I look at him from beneath my too-long fringe. Smile a little and I reach out to link my fingers to his, he slides a hand up to his hair instead.

Stewart wipes his lips with his thumb, the Star Wars bracelets and wooden beads catching my eyes like the familiar bright peek of a rainbow in dark rain clouds. He blinks at me; a scowl etched on his features.

"I love you," I repeat, my voice cracking pathetically. It sounds empty, hollow, fake. I don't believe the words myself even though it's the truth.

"Fuck you, Daisy," Stewart snarls as he turns and stalks away without a backward glance. The echo of the front door slamming indicates he's had the final say.

Turns out we didn't need the tandem after all.

36

Another standard day; laying in bed, inhaling the lavender plant like oxygen, resting my head on one of Stewart's shirts. Lots of tears. Lots of anger. Lots of cigarettes. Ackbar picks up on the atmosphere of darkness radiating from my crushed heart. Instead of laying down, comforting me as a loyal pet should, he blinks from a distance and largely ignores me. Clearly pissed off Stewart isn't here to lavish him with attention, crumbs of toast and cups of oat milk. He's even taken to sleeping in Rob's room. Traitor.

My phone buzzes against the desk. I turn it over without looking at it, so I don't have to see the constant unknown numbers flashing across the screen. It won't be the person I want it to be. The phone vibrates still, so I shove it too aggressively into the chest of drawers. Let it buzz itself flat, it can make friends with my rampant rabbit.

The doorbell rings, sounding like a trapped wasp in a jar. Rob is working from home in the dining room, and Nan is at the care home. It's the press. There's no one else it can be. I know from the persistent ringing of the bell, the shouts of my name drifting up to the window, that it's a reporter or several. I am not going to make the mistake that Julia Roberts' character in *Notting Hill* does. I will not be answering the door, eating toast and standing in Hugh Grant's shirt for the world to see.

I know what they want. A glimpse, a photo, sighting of me. So they, the fans and anyone else who reads about relationships of people they've never met can play compare and despair. Which one of us has come out on top from the break up. There's always someone who flourishes and thrives from heartbreak.

Stewart left it a week after the break up, then it was like nothing had happened. Straight back to work, back in the studio. Posting selfies or arty shots of microphones with witty captions. The career and image comes first. What more did I expect?

The first photos and sightings of him post break up made me throw up until I thought I'd turn myself inside out. Cardinal's team are clever. Stewart was in identical clothes to those he had on at the afterparty where we first met. Like piano keys, black jeans stretched tight across his thighs and that white oversized shirt practically unbuttoned to the navel. The battered denim jacket that's nearly always his first choice; with pockets full of cigarettes and fruit pastille wrappers. The same jacket he's thrown around my shoulders countless times. The one I borrowed and left a smudge of foundation on the collar, and he complained for three full days while I washed and dried it. The one like all his clothes, his skin, hair, smells of lavender. The hint of bracelets looped around his pale wrists, sticking out from the cuffs. Eyes so blue I'd claim they were edited had the pictures been posted on his square filled grid. Stewart looked fucking gorgeous. Management wouldn't let him look anything but, would they?

He was the clear winner, even with no photos of me

for anyone to compare with. It was always going to be Stewart coming out on top. Beautiful and magnetizing, basking in the sun, like Diphylleia grayi. The delicate petals that beneath raindrops turn to an iridescent pearl. Skeleton flowers they're called. I'm like crumbling, decaying bones of death. Rotting into obscurity.

***

The bedroom door pushes open. I spin my head like it's attached to the door by elastic. My heart soars then drops at the realisation I want it to be Stewart, but won't be. Rob stands in his silken PJ top that he insists is a shirt and jeans, hair tips a bright purple, tentatively steps towards me and places a cup on my cluttered desk.

"Brought you a coffee, Babe."

"Thanks."

He perches on the edge of my bed, clears his throat. "Do you want me to call Ash to come and see you?"

I scoff, stare at the light fitting, until it blurs out of focus and all I can see are memories, alternate versions of my life playing out above me. Ash is one of Stewart's closest friends. I am surely the enemy. The one at fault.

"No," I state. I do, but I know my place. I caused the break up, therefore I lose my friends and life I made through Stewart.

"Izzie?"

"Izzie?" I echo with a frown.

"She was your best friend and—"

"Before or after I lied to her for months, and then she physically and verbally assaulted me for falling in love?" I snap.

Rob shrugs. "Maybe this can reconnect you both."

I sit up. "I don't want to reconnect with Izzie. She's probably celebrating that I'm heartbroken. Or hitch hiking her way to Edinburgh to try and shag—" My mind and mouth falter over Stewart's name. I swallow thickly. Attempt to clear my throat before lighting another cigarette. Rob doesn't have the balls to berate me for smoking inside anymore, and since we found a photographer hiding out in the shed, I have no desire to smoke outside. I inhale deeply, but the nicotine has no calming effect.

"She called."

"Izzie called?" I ask. I haven't heard from her at all since June. Not that either of us tried to reach out. Not everything broken can be fixed. "What did she say?"

"She asked how you were. What happened."

"Don't tell her anything. I mean it, Rob."

Not only do I not want Izzie to hear the truth, or indeed find out anything about my life, the Cardinal team made me agree to a vow of silence, aside from one key phrase I was allowed to repeat regarding the termination of our relationship. '*Unfortunately relationships don't always work out. Stewart and I remain close friends.*'

If any more than that exact phrase appeared online, Hipster Harry threatened me with legal action. I'm too emotionally drained to work out if he's serious or bluffing.

'*Termination*' like it was a choice me and Stewart made together, willingly, after careful consideration. That it didn't snake up on us, sneaking from the shadows like a monster until we couldn't ignore it any longer or fight against it. Even armed with the three magic words of ammunition, it wasn't enough to slay the beast. I had the right arrows, but missed the target.

"Daisy, even if I want to, I can't tell her anything. You've said nothing about Stewart since you came home. I found out you two had split up from Patrick."

I look at him. He blushes slightly.

"He asked me if I knew why you and Stewart had split up."

Strange. Patrick must know. Stewart tells him everything.

"Apparently it's not just you staying silent. Even in a break up you're both freakishly aligned. Stewart hasn't said a word about you. Patrick found out from the team's statement."

My shoulders slump. Stewart rarely talks about his family, and never publicly. Perhaps I'll be another blacklisted topic. Why talk about something when he can ignore it?

"Come on Babe. It's been three weeks. Tell me what happened. I can't believe that Stewart would do anything to hurt you this bad."

I sniffle. "He didn't."

"Then what?—"

"I just couldn't do it. I wanted to, but I couldn't be—"

"Couldn't what?"

"I wasn't enough," I say flatly, with a sigh that makes my shoulders slump.

"You are enough. I know Stewart loves you, I know you love him. You two are meant to be. It's obvious how much you love each other."

"He doesn't know."

"Then tell him."

"He won't believe me," I admit, returning my gaze to

the lampshade again, ignoring the tears dripping down my neck. "I didn't tell Stewart how I felt."

I flick the lighter but it doesn't catch on the cigarette. How many have I had today? I shake the packet, one left.

"But he knew," Rob counters.

That's what I had always claimed. Yet when it came down to it, Stewart needed me to say it.

"It wasn't enough, Rob. Even when he asked me, I couldn't tell him. Then I shouted it at him. Fucking shouted, like I was telling him off for not putting the wash on or something. Snapped it out in anger, and it was so hollow. Meaningless. I meant it but it didn't sound like I did. I might as well of just stayed silent."

"What did Stewart say?"

"He left. Left the house, the fucking island. Said he'd rather spend the rest of his time off with his parents."

Rob looks blankly at me. Of course, he doesn't know about the whole Stewart being kicked out at seventeen and almost throwing himself off the bridge because of family tensions.

"His parents don't even let him in the house. He and his dad can't stand the sight of one another. Last time he lived at home he was suicidal. And he'd rather have spent a week with them than stay with me." I burst into tears, wailing sobs that ricochet not only around my room but my lungs, veins, and the depths of my being.

"I chased Stewart down the drive of the holiday home, watched the car disappear from sight then rang him constantly. The phone wedged between my shoulder and ear. I knew my battered Yaris would never catch up with him and the Bentley. I raced down the curved roads to the ferry terminal, breaking every speed limit and overtaking cyclists with wild abandon. Only to see the ferry departing. What I wouldn't have given to have seen it parked there shining in all its Royal Ebony glory with its twenty-two-inch wheels and fucking hand cross-stitched leather seats. Three hours later, once he was back home, at his flat no doubt, he messaged me and told me it was over. He said he couldn't do it anymore."

A week later, I threw my phone, smashing the screen as a notification pinged up. At least he had the decency until I, too, was home for the news to break.

A stupid perfect photo of the beach Stewart had taken with me only days earlier. '*Returning from holiday with happy memories but mainly heartbreak tied to my soul. Both inspiration for songs.*'

I waited for Patrick, Eddie and Ash to comment, to call me out and slag me off. But they didn't. I turned off all comments on my social media, after the hate from the fans flooded in, demanding to know what had happened. Blaming me for breaking Stewart's heart. I deserved it, but couldn't bear to carry the weight of their words.

"Shit. You spoken to him since?" Rob asks as he starts brushing my hair for me. The brush will probably snap in two taken in to account the size of the knots.

Now I've started talking, I can't stop the flow and ebb of words, like the tides. "Once, the same day," I sob, unsure whether he can decipher my high-pitched noises masquerading as words. "Both of us flitted from tears to anger. He said I couldn't cope with what his world is like, that he fucked up too much of my life. I shouldn't have to deal with the shit that follows him. I just kept saying I loved him, that I didn't care, I'd pick him every time. But he felt it was too late. He thought I was saying it because he'd forced it out of me. I got angrier and angrier, cross at myself more than him. I said he only thought of himself, his band, that everyone else in the world loves him, did it matter how I showed it? Evidently, it did. He said I was always holding back, and he couldn't do it anymore, that he wouldn't carry us both."

"Daisy, you should call him again. Talk things through."

I shake my head. "It's too late."

"How do you know?"

"Stewart needed me to say how I felt, to be so totally open with him, to let him into me, my whole self, and I couldn't do it. I couldn't tell him I loved him. And then he didn't believe me. He's right, it was too little too late."

Rob exhales loudly. "Patrick said something that will probably make more sense to you."

I sniffle, surprised at myself that I can still produce tears.

Rob scrolls through his phone, I notice he and Patrick have been swapping pouting selfies. I turn away before the photos become explicit, or envy creeps through my veins.

He reads from his screen, "Tell Daisy to face the press; if she looks a million dollars, great; if she looks like shite, even better. The press wants that elusive first sighting of her. As soon as they get it, they're contractually obliged to leave her be. Fuck knows how he's done it, but Stew's done a deal with the devil to give Daisy her life back."

Stewart knows how much I despise the press, the intrusion into my life and our relationship. Even after a break up, he's still protecting me, considering me, and my life.

37

Come on Daisy, get your Queen Bey crown on, I say to myself after the scalding hot shower. I pull out the dress and boots I wore to the Cardinal gig and afterparty when I met Stewart. The dress, black with a ditsy print of coloured flowers, lay crumpled and creased on the plush carpet of his hotel suite all night. I find my sunglasses from my still unpacked suitcase. Smear a coral lipstick on and sigh. Hope I can hold myself together under the scrutiny awaiting me outside the front gate.

"Want me to come with you?" Rob asks as he lays on the sofa wrapped beneath a blanket, curled up next to Zach. He doesn't mean it. He won't move, even if I accepted his offer, which he knows I won't. Why would anyone, when they're enveloped in love, relaxation and comfort?

I shake my head. "It's fine."

"Where are you going?"

"Nan's."

"Driving?"

I shake my head. "Not sure the car will start first time. Hardly the impression I wish to present to the masses."

"Whose is the new Yaris parked outside?" asks Zach.

Rob elbows him in the ribs. I inhale sharply. Dismiss it with a shake of my head, ignore the pounding of my heart.

It's mine. Technically. Legally. Paperwork and keys, as promised by Stewart, on my birthday; all ready and waiting for me when I returned from holiday. I've ignored the gleaming red car entirely. Even refused to move it or accept ownership when the neighbours enquired about it.

Rob stands up, pulls me into the hall.

"Babe, I don't mean to add to your burden, but I'd be a shit friend if I didn't ask."

"Ask what?" I say, inspecting my face in the mirror. My skin is layered with tinted moisturiser, foundation, anything to make me look less like a zombie.

"About your self-harm."

"I promised Stewart on holiday that I've stopped. I will strive to stick to that."

Rob's eyes meet mine in the mirror as I reapply my lipstick. "Even though you've split up?"

My teeth push together, causing pain to zip through my jaw. "Yes."

He pulls me into a hug, and doesn't even complain or cough dramatically at the smell of smoke clinging to my hair. "I'm here for you, always, Daisy. But is a promise enough?"

"I'm going to start therapy. I'll call the doctor and a helpline as soon as I get back."

Rob holds me by the shoulders, smiles and nods. "I'll call while you're out. Get you an appointment. I'm proud of you."

I swallow. I can imagine Stewart having the same look on his face; pride and relief. My fingers catch a stray tear.

"I'm fine," I repeat, my standard response these days.

"I just need to deal with the photographers and then get back to normal."

Whatever that is.

"You can stay at mine if you like?" Zach offers from the living room. "Just until the madness eases a bit."

"Might be a good idea, Babe. Get rid of the press from the garden," Rob agrees.

Zach nods. I scoff at them. They just want to have loud uninterrupted sex without me in permanent residence. I'm too wrapped up in myself, longing to wallow in my heartbreak, that I ignore Rob's pleading eyes.

"I will not be chased from my own home by a bunch of failed journalists," I snap, shoving the glasses over my eyes and pulling open the front door.

***

"Girl, you look bloody awful."

I can always rely on Nan to be honest. Even with the September sun extending my Scottish holiday tan, a lot of tinted moisturiser and concealer to hide my puffy eyes, and an appetite that has refused to return, I know I look exhausted. And that's probably the most flattering word.

"Can you not just phone Stewart and ask him back out?"

"No, Nan. It doesn't work like that."

He wouldn't listen. More heartbreakingly, he wouldn't believe me.

Nan piles my plate high with cakes. I take a tiny bite of one but taste nothing.

"Nan, these aren't the cakes I brought," I say with a

little frown. I know a Mr Kipling angel slice, and this is certainly not one.

Nan places a hand on my shoulder. "They're from the bakers."

"Which bakers?"

Nan avoids my eyes for a second. Then she looks me square in the face. "Stewart sends us cakes each week."

"Still?" I ask, struggling to keep the cake from reappearing from my mouth in vomit form.

"Yes. He has done since he first came to visit and I offered him a lemon slice. I couldn't shut him up about lemon oil, zest and flour and whatnot. He claimed his mum made the best cakes—"

"She does," I reply with a small smile.

Nan lifts the rest of her cake towards me. "I know that."

"Don't expect it to carry on for much longer," I snide and cross my arms.

Nan regards me with another hard stare. "Whatever happened, girl, that young man is not malicious. Stewart's not going to deny us old dears excitement in cake form just because you two have had a falling out."

I sniffle, but I will not cry. What would be the point?

I look around the residents' lounge. Wrinkled and wonderful characters stooped over chess boards, a rowdy debate over the crossword, and families enjoying the time together. I bet all of them have experienced heartbreak, whether it be their fault or not. They're still here, ploughing on. It won't kill me. It'll just destroy me, crushing me into specks of dust, flakes of nothingness, until it starts to build up into a mound, a form of something I used to be.

"Have you heard from Izzie?"

"She wrote me a letter, said she was sorry to hear Stewart and I had split up."

I've barely seen Izzie since the attack at the pop up shop. She apologised and regretted her role in the attack in her letter. It was hard to believe her, though I wanted to. I don't think I could ever trust her now. She's restarting bereavement counselling, which I was pleased to hear, for her sake. Rob, who has minimal contact with Izzie, says she's moved in with Alex in the village on the outskirts of town. Tori and the other stalkers remained vocally vicious online following the attack and their restraining orders, yet Izzie's online presence diminished. I hope she steps away from Tori and the other stalkers, and the Cardinal world. In the end, it did her no good.

"That was nice of her." Nan smiles.

"I can't forgive her, I told her so. Yet I also don't wish her any ill will. I hope she's happy. " We'll never be friends again; she still feels I betrayed her and the memory of Sophia, and I can't forgive her for the attack. And not counting the attack, it was never an equally balanced friendship. She was happy to keep me in the gravel and dirt while she basked in the cloudless blue skies of being high on the see-saw.

"Has Rob been looking after you?"

"Of course."

"What's your plan then?" Nan asks, as I replace the cake on the plate, largely untouched. I'll take them home and feed Rob and Ackbar. They'll both appreciate it.

"About Stewart?" I ask, and my voice only breaks once over his name.

"Clearly you're going to do nothing about that. I'll ask again once your stubbornness has worn down a bit."

I roll my eyes, look at the fiery colours of the gardens outside. The pink hues of dahlias, rich oranges and reds of Mexican sunflowers, and crocosmia reminding me of Eddie's hair, fluttering cleome petals that look like butterfly wings. I ignore the lavender, and the last few summer blue blooms dotting the gardens.

"I got my old job back with Jane," I reply, ignoring the sinking weight plummeting my heart to my toes. I slide my hands beneath my legs. Push my nails into the skin of my thighs. Then as quickly as I started, I stop. Remembering how I promised Stewart I wouldn't self-harm again. I pick up a magazine, fold a page into tiny squares instead.

Confusion flickers over her face fleetingly. "I figured a move to Edinburgh would be on hold, but you're not going to buy your own florists either?"

I shake my head. "No."

"Why not?" she asks, thickly spreading bright red jam across a scone. I'm reminded of Stewart doing the same thing at The Dome.

I shrug, avoid her eyes and look at the trees out of the windows. Note how the leaves are already falling to the ground in hues of yellows, oranges and browns. "I don't see the point."

"Daisy—"

"Jane says I can go back, which is more than I deserve after the hassle I caused her. It's a no brainer, Nan. I get to do the job I love and not have the responsibility of a probable failed business."

"Daisy, having your own florists was your dream."

I shake my head. "Do you know how many businesses close within three years of opening? Nearly sixty percent."

"That means forty survive. Life is full of risks, Poppet.

You can't remain in a safety net for the rest of your days. It will become a prison, not just a protective barrier."

I scoff into the bone china cup half empty with milky tea.

Whatever.

38

I wake up every morning after a night of unrest, dragging myself out of bed to open up with Jane. Even when I'm not on the rota, or getting paid for it.

I stay late every night, locking up and faffing on way too much with things that don't need doing until Rob phones and tells me to actually return home.

The petals, stems, even the stagnant water and prickly thorns make me feel safe. Useful at least. The scent of the flowers, perfumed fragrances almost, almost drown out my thoughts.

The trees on the walk to work shed their leaves, the mornings and evenings seeping longer into the daylight hours, bringing with them frost and a bitter chill that burn my cheeks and fingers.

I see Brett, my ex. Well, not the most recent one now, push open the door.

"Morning." He smiles stepping into the florists, the bell jangling above his head.

"Brett," I sigh out with an air of defeat.

"Brought you a coffee."

"Thanks." I take it from him and sigh deeply.

"One sugar, splash of milk right?"

No, but it doesn't matter. I take a small sip of the hot liquid.

"Fancy a drink tonight, Daisy?" Brett asks, his hands pulling at his blonde spiral hair.

I trail a finger along the pearl-shaped flowers of the blue delphiniums, which will forever make me think of Stewart's eyes and the huge floral display he posed in front of at the afterparty.

"Sure." I shrug at him. Why change the habit of a lifetime.

"Grand. We can go through to the hotel, they've got a soul night on if you fancy driving?"

"My car's—" finally given up the ghost and is currently being crushed into a cube of once metallic red steel. Fuck it. I've got a brand new car with my name on it waiting to be driven.

"Six o'clock ok?" I ask instead.

Brett nods and places a kiss on my cheek. I hope I don't visibly cringe too much.

It's a car. Just a car. Four wheels, engine, red paint. A car. It's not like it's a Bentley, it's a Yaris. The same as my old car, but new. Bigger. Sparklier, better.

The cardinal bird-shaped air freshener swings tauntingly at me.

A few months ago I would have laughed, made a comment about Stewart being arrogant and egotistical enough to buy, or perhaps have someone design an air freshener to reference his band. The post-it note stuck to it in Stewart's messy block capital scrawl glares at me like Ackbar when I make tuna pasta for Rob.

'Nowhere near as beautiful as my Bentley, but still... happy birthday, my florist called Daisy! Drive safe, always! Love you.'

For a full seven minutes I stare at it, then rip it off—hating it and everything in the entire world as the elastic snags around the mirror and sends the cardboard bird dancing in front of me.

I breathe deeply as I gently unhook the offending item with my shaking hands. I open the glove box to hide it away.

Two small square presents fall out, wrapped in brown paper and tied with purple bows. The same handwriting dives into my eyes.

'Happy birthday again, Sweetheart!'

My heart feels like it's been stabbed with cactus spines. I can practically feel the air deflating from my lungs. My fingers shake so violently I can barely make out the shape of them.

Well, fuck, I have to open them, don't I?

Earrings; daisies, white jewelled petals and yellow stone centres glint at me. Almost winking, sneering under the evening light. Of course he'd buy me daisy-shaped earrings. He always said he loved my name.

I pick up the other present. It surely can't get any worse.

It's a key. I recognise it instantly. Attached to a Star Wars keyring; a key to Stewart and Patrick's flat.

'Insert wholly romantic comment here about you holding the key to my heart. Always, always welcome to stay at mine, Pat says it's cool too. Stay as often as you can, my favourite thing is waking up next to you. Love you.'

I throw the presents into the footwell and start the car.

I'm now over half an hour late to collect Brett. My phone keeps flashing silently with his name.

Fuck this. Just fuck it all.

***

I tap on the bedroom door, hear Nan inside, I poke my head around the door and throw her a wobbly smile.

"Daisy!" She smiles, looking over the top of magazine. She's propped up in bed; paisley printed PJs and a knitted shawl around her shoulders.

"This is a nice surprise."

"I needed to see you," I say with a sniffle, walking into her room.

Pictures in golden frames line the chest of drawers, her rug still on the floor by her bed despite me and everyone berating her for it. The photo from last Christmas of me and Stewart sits by her bedside lamp.

She pats the bed and I sit down, feeling I might deflate into the mattress. "Is this about Stewart?"

"It is and it isn't. I miss him so much. We had all these plans; getting a place in Edinburgh, me working up there, then buying a shop in Largs and us moving to Cumbrae. Not all at once, obviously interspersed with his job, tours, albums, festivals, flower shows, holidays, whatever."

I'm rambling, I know it.

"Did he break your heart, Poppet?"

"No, I broke it all by myself. And now, I don't know what to do. Should I carry on? Move? Stay? Buy a shop? Forget about it? I don't know who I am. And not just because I'm single, it's not about that; it's..." I sigh. My mind feels so cluttered. Maybe I'm just talking nonsense. "I don't know what I want."

"You do know what you want, girl. That's why your heart is aching."

"I wanted more than that. I never wanted to rely on anyone, least not a man. I was fine by myself."

Like a daisy, I was happy just being me, trampled over and dismissed by others while trying to carve my way through the lawns of life. Yet Stewart arrived into my life, and became the sun. I embraced the heliotropism of my floral namesake, and followed the movement of the bright sun, so I could grow tall and flourish with his support.

"I want him, I love him, but I messed it all up," I admit, my voice creaking with emotion as salty tears drip down my pale cheeks.

Nan lets me cry, clearly I needed it. I feel I won't ever stop. Eventually my sobs turn into sniffles and I catch my breath again. She pulls her handbag onto her stretched out legs.

"Do you remember when you first came back from Cumbrae? And you told me you wanted to live there? You couldn't stop talking about the beaches and the waves."

I nod. It may now hold the memory of where me and Stewart broke up, but I still adore that island. It was a wrench to leave it.

Nan flicks the clasp on her patchwork beige leather handbag, the same one she's had for as long as I can remember, the strap worn out and wrapped in duct tape. All the other ones I bought her from Next for various Christmases, still in the gift bags in her wardrobe.

She delves her bony hand into the depths of the bag.

The scent of talc invades my senses. She holds out an envelope towards me.

"Take it."

I open the envelope. A cheque. To me, signed in her cursive handwriting. A mammoth amount. An amount that usually only comes in the form of huge fake cheques for lottery winners to pose with. Where the fuck has she got this money from? Has she robbed a bank on her weekly trip into town?

"I've been keeping you in the dark, Daisy," Nan says, a shrug on her bony shoulders. "Gramps left a lump of money for your mother. But obviously, I didn't want her to have it after she left us. When I moved in here I had to declare all my finances, as you know, so I sent your mother my savings, for safe keeping, a loan. I needed, wanted you to have it when you were ready. It's taken me longer to get it back from her, believe me."

I'm cross with her, of course I am. The last few years have been a struggle to scrape together enough money each month. Even with her help towards my house. Until Stewart stepped in with his bulging bank account and kindness. I can't bear to ask what's happened with the fees for the rest of this year. Though after seeing the zeros on this cheque in my trembling hands, I could and should pay him back.

"I want you to take it. Buy a house on the island. Go open that florists."

The tears drip from my lashes like the leaking drainpipe outside the kitchen. I shake my head.

"I can't leave you."

"Yes, you bloody well can."

"Nan—"

"You were going to up sticks and move to Scotland anyway. It's not up for discussion, Daisy Gordon. Get on that internet right now and buy a house."

She holds her arms out, and I fold into her, gently, knowing her bones are frail. She smoothes a palm up and down my back. I feel like a child again.

"Actually, this is a two-pronged attack."

"What do you mean, Nan?" I ask with a frown. I pull away, frown at her as I kneel at the side of her bed.

"I want you to be happy, and I know that island will make you happy, even if your heart is broken. You need a boost to get yourself back into gear," she pats my hand. "And two, it's to get you out of the way."

"You want me out of the way?" I ask as my voice cracks.

Nan shakes her head, I see her eyes roll through my unshed tears. "Not in the way your pessimistic mind has taken you on, girl. Your mum is moving back."

"To Cockermouth?" I ask, though where else would it be?

"Yes. In the New Year. She's decided after twenty-one years that the Spanish sun isn't to her liking."

"She's split up with Wayne hasn't she?"

I jump up and fiddle with the already perfectly drawn closed curtains. Anything to distract me momentarily from the enormity of this revelation. I almost collapse, when I realise I'm holding my phone and scrolling through to text or call Stewart about this. Fuck. I slide the phone back in my pocket. Ignoring the constant flashes of Brett's name.

Nan nods. "That may have been a deciding factor."

"Fuck!" I snap out then grimace. "Sorry, Nan."

"I'll allow you the swear. I should be encouraging you to build bridges with her, Poppet. But I know your mum being here will make you miserable and angry. You're already about as much fun as a corpse—"

"Thanks."

"I can't forgive your mother for the way she treated you. But at the same time, she's my only child. Life's short, things won't be peachy, yet if Amanda's in the vicinity, I want to see her. Get to know her, maybe understand her."

"I'll get in your way."

"In a sense, yes. You and your mother have your own issues, that's between you two. Perhaps after over twenty years apart, Amanda and I can give a relationship a try."

"I won't ever begrudge you that, Nan."

"You're my favourite person, you know that Daisy? If it ever comes to it; I'll pick you. Over any and everyone."

I cry, sit on her bed and feel her bony hands on my arms.

"Wipe those tears, girl. Go and get yourself a house, a shop and a new start on the island. If you can't get Stewart back, then at least try to make the rest of your heart happy."

"But your fees?" I ask. Never allowing myself to stray from the practicalities too far.

We don't mention his financial help, yet we both know it's been a bigger struggle than ever for me to pay the fees these last few months since, I assume, Stewart stopped paying them. I never checked directly, just borrowed money on cards and delved into my overdraft and savings as soon as we split up to cover the costs again. No one from the care home told me it had already been paid, not that I expected him to carry on regardless.

"Ah, I'll be alright." She smiles dismissively with a wave of her hand before smoothing down the pages of her magazine then picking it up before holding it beneath her nose.

“How many more cheques have you got in that handbag, Nan?”

“That’s classified information. The less you know about it, the better.”

39

The radio in the kitchen crackles as Rob turns up the volume on a Beyonce song. We dance around like loons, like nothing else matters for three minutes. I love weekends like this, when Rob comes to visit me at Cumbrae. He complains about the sand scuffing his boots, but we spend the days and nights laughing. His visits always lift my heart.

It worked out well. Rob bought my half of the house and apparently had intended to rent out my room. But I have a sneaking suspicion Zach moved in before I even crossed the border. I made an offer on a flat in Millport and bought a shop on the mainland, which I opened in February. Just in time for Valentine's Day.

The song from the radio fades out, followed by a stream of adverts and inane chatter from the hosts.

"Welcome back guys. A lot has been going on for you since we last spoke. You're about to sign another record deal, getting ready to kick off another tour, and had a heartbreak too, right Stewart?"

"Shit." Rob gasps as I realise the radio presenter is in fact talking to my ex.

I haven't heard Stewart's voice since we broke up. Well, I've heard Cardinal, snippets of songs, videos playing at the hairdressers, familiar songs on the car radio, but I haven't heard Stewart talk. Not since he stalked out of the holiday home, laptop bag slung over his left shoulder, the taste of my mouth still on his lips. I block out the phone call we had later that day. It's still too painful.

I've seen endless images of him, whether I wanted to or not, his social media presence is hard to ignore. There's been countless tiled photos. He left it a week after the break up, then it was like nothing had happened. If there was to be a winner from the break up, Stewart had it in the bag. Gold medal slung around his neck, spraying the world with champagne, stood centre stage in the spotlight.

"We heard your ex-girlfriend has moved to Scotland, Stewart. The fans are desperate to know if a reunion is on the cards for you both? Yourself and Daisy did make a lovely couple."

Stewart pauses slightly and breathes a tad heavier than normal. I don't know if anyone else would pick up on it. But he's stalling. I bet he's rubbing the back of his neck. I strain my ears, desperate to hear the scratch of his beard against his palm.

Rob reaches out to hold my hand, both of us staring at the radio as if it's the TV.

"I mean, Scotland's a big place," Stewart says flatly before clearing his throat. I know he's fiddling with the rings on his fingers. "We're just so busy with the album, y'know? And the tour in the new year..." His words filter out; he doesn't finish them. He doesn't need to. It's not a serious dismissal. It's not direct. But I feel it clinging to my lungs like the cold.

"Are you two still in touch? Is Daisy still a florist? It was evident from your previous album that you were inspired to write lyrics about flowers—"

I jump, hear the dull thump echo down the radio. I know he's just slammed his diary down too forcefully on desk.

"Forgot he had a temper on him," Rob comments with a wry smile. His eyebrows hiding beneath his neon yellow fringe, which matches his painted nails.

"Our new album is—" Patrick starts, yet Stewart cuts him off.

"It's unfair that you're talking about her like this, it's fucking unfair that her life is still being hounded by the press. She hasn't asked for this."

I look at Rob, my own wide eyes reflected in his.

"Sorry, listeners, for the language then. Apologies, guys, we meant no harm."

"Eddie, have you and Ash set a date for the wedding yet? And Stewart, Patrick; is there anyone on the scene for you, romantically?" the other host asks.

"For fuck's sake," Stewart replies, void of emotion.

The team will be furious with him. I can picture Hipster Harry's knuckles white against his ever-present clipboard.

"It's much more important to talk about this than our music isn't it? Shall we go through all our past sexual conquests while we're here? Any particular incident you'd like to discuss?"

"Stew—" I hear Patrick across the speakers.

My eyes are pinned wide, my mouth dropped open. I feel I might have stopped breathing.

The host lets out a nervous chuckle. "Clearly Stewart, there's still emotions running high in regards to your ex. Why did you split up with Daisy?"

"I swear, mention her fucking name once more, and I'll—"

"Stew!" Eddie shouts.

"Fuck this." Stewart sounds almost as livid as he did the day we broke up.

I have a burning desire to call him. I blink rapidly, like my eyelashes are hummingbird wings.

A slam of a door punctuates the silence from the speakers. It jolts me back to reality. I have no right to phone Stewart, of course I don't. None at all.

"Can we tell you about the tour next year? We're buzzing to get back on the road," Eddie says, drowning Stewart's bad mood with forced excitement.

I exhale. He sounded almost the same, but tired, exhausted is probably more accurate.

Fuck the Force, I miss him.

Me and Stewart, it should have worked. I may be a florist from a tiny town, now living in an even smaller town, even further away from the life Stewart lives, but we're meant to be. My heart constricts. Look at Han Solo and Leia; a lowly smuggler and Princess in love and that still worked, overall. It wasn't perfect, but who has that, who even wants that?

Stewart and I, we're soulmates. I know we are.

I fucked this up. This is all my own undoing, my heart and soul aches for him.

I stand up, the stool legs scraping on the tiles. I take my mug to the sink, still full with coffee the colour of Stewart's hair. I pour it away, watch it swirl down the plug hole. Disappearing. If only it was that easy to forget him.

"I'm going for a walk," I state.

"I'll come with you." Rob pulls his coat from the back

of the door, and squeezes my hand as we walk away from the flat. The radio still bumbling in the background.

We both pretend I haven't got tears rolling down my cheeks, taking my foundation with them as the salty sea air whips at our skin.

I'm waiting for Rob on the sand at Kames Bay. He's, as usual, gone to buy a bag of chips. I don't choose to sit on the rocks, yet in my head I can see or hear the memory of Stewart tapping out a rhythm with his feet, remembering his hands on my skin, his voice drifting in the sea air, his footprints in the almost white biscuit crumb sand.

The waves dance at my bare toes. Arms shivering, hair whipping in the wind, the salt sticking to my tears and skin. Looking out over the crashing waves, watching the clouds carrying the rain across the sea and away from the island.

Sometimes that emptiness, regret washes over me as if I'm the famous Crocodile Rock on Newtown Beach. Suddenly hit with waves, covering me from top to bottom, drenching my mind with memories that I can mostly keep at bay when I'm busy. Nostalgia, times together, moments shared crawl into my head, clambering over me like the tourists posing for photos on the crocodile's uneven back.

Before I realise what I'm doing, I open Stewart's social media. I frown, rub at my forehead. I close the app, even turn off my phone and turn it back on. There must be a mistake.

"What the fuck?" Talking to an inanimate object, yeah, that's going to put me in good stead with the locals. My eyebrows pull down, mouth dropping open. No, this can't be right. He wouldn't. I even resort to being a teenager in the middle of Cumbria with no signal; stretching on tiptoes, holding my phone towards the sky like I'm trying to attract a hawk with a dead mouse. Nothing changes. The screen still reads the same.

This account has been deleted.

There are no posts yet.

User inactive.

A huge part of Stewart's career is online, the majority of his fanbase are behind screens, craving a square slice of insight into Cardinal's frontman. Now I might as well be back in the 90s, finding out generic information in interviews that are months out of date in magazines. Actually, it's worse than discovering that Ronan Keating was in London three months ago wearing a leather jacket; now I have zero information. I crave information about Stewart; new photos of him and the band, even of wires and trees, anything. Some nights I'd even welcome a photo of him with Ella Egan or any other woman.

I scroll through the private photos I've memorised, and ones saved to my own account. The screenshots I keep in a secret folder in my phone. I love the natural photos that he'd never dream of showing the world. The ones where he's sleeping, or kissing my neck, with a smile on his lips, eyes crinkling in laughter, eating dairy free pizza or leaning back to catch fruit pastilles in his mouth. Even the time where he attempted cartwheels in the park, sunbathing on the sand, splashing from the shallows of the sea on holiday, singing on stage or laying in his flat, nose buried in a book.

That's the man I fell in love with. The one who battled through my sarcasm and walls of hidden emotions. Not the man who sings on stage most nights, spends hours doing interviews for teens to swoon over and analyse in their fan fictions.

My shoulders drop in defeat, realisation. But if Stewart didn't have that job, I wouldn't have met him. If the fates aligned and I'd bumped into him at a coffee shop, I probably would have given him a once over, maybe twice, snickered at him ordering an oat milk latte and forgotten about him.

He wouldn't have engaged me in conversation and asked about flowers. I wouldn't have discovered that we had so much in common. He wouldn't have thrown around romantic declarations the next day. I wouldn't have spent hours, days, weeks thinking about him. Hoping he'd arrive at the florists.

Maybe the only issue wasn't my refusal to confess my feelings. It was my reluctance to accept Stewart for all aspects of his life.

"Christ, that interview really pissed him off, huh?" Rob comments, appearing beside me with salty chips, his yellow fringe whipping in the wind.

"I need to see him. I need to tell him I love him," I reply, putting my phone away.

"Daisy, you haven't seen or spoken to him for nearly a year."

We edge closer to the tidelines. Beneath my toes, I twist and turn a smooth rock that was once part of a larger rust red brick, now dotted with fragments of colour, shells and holes worn in from years of rolling through the waves.

"I could call him. The worst he'll do is ignore me or hang up."

I take the stone in my hand. Pass it through my fingers,

the surface dotted with confetti of collisions and crashes from the water. White, grey and pink quartz specks catch the sunlight. I smooth my thumb along the once sharp, defined edge, now rounded, shaped by years of travelling and life passing by.

"If hearing him on the radio has made you realise you still love him, then I wish I'd let you hear his voice months ago, Babe."

"Should I just go to Edinburgh?" I ask.

"No, you, you can't—" Rob says around a mouthful of chips.

"Why can't I? Why shouldn't I?"

"Because this is you! Daisy Gordon, you live for a plan."

"Sometimes, you can't plan these things. Life's full of detours, right?"

I pass the stone from one palm to the other, then throw it with an overarching arc into the sea. Watch how the water welcomes it, splashes up to catch it then pulls it under. Lost once more from the ground, taken in by the waves, wrapped in seaweed and covered back in salt and minuscule morsels of oceanic life.

"What are you going to do?"

"Rob, I'm going to shoot for the fucking moon. What have I got to lose?"

40

It's a coincidence, perhaps Stewart would say fate, or would have at one time; that I bump into the couple living in the flat below Stewart and Patrick's, coming out of the shared front door. The birthday gift of the still unused key clutched in my hands, the green of Yoda swinging between my fingers, not needed.

I exhale shakily as I knock on the flat's front door. Smile briefly at the scratch in the painted wood where Stewart attempted to drag in an up-cycled coffee table he ordered on a whim one early morning after seeing it advertised online. Obviously he didn't check the dimensions of it, and one edge took out a scrape of paint and Stewart's patience, before also not fitting in his bedroom.

My legs are trembling, I even think my knees might be knocking together. I feel like a cartoon character all wibbly lines and nerves almost visible around me.

The door swings open to show Patrick, shirt untucked and half fastened, smart trousers and pointed black boots on his feet. His curls, some more defined than others, are firing off at all angles and he balances a laptop in his hand, a chewed pencil between his teeth.

"I'm not ready yet, pal," he states on a mumble, without looking at me, then turns back into the flat and starts walking up the sweeping stairs. "He's suited and booted—"

"Hi Patrick," I say—well, I have to say something. He clearly thinks I'm, I assume, Eddie.

Patrick's head whips round, the pencil falls from his mouth and clatters on the keyboard. I watch it roll down the last few steps and settle next to the skirting board.

"Fuck."

"Is this a bad time?" I ask, despite the answer being glaringly obvious. Is there ever a good time for the ex-girlfriend to show up? Unannounced?

He looks back into the flat, up the stairs, his pine green eyes looking panicked. I can hear the usual sounds of music from various rooms drifting out towards the front door and beyond.

Fuck the Force, I've missed the music and noise that surrounds their lives.

"Daisy, hi." He throws me a slight smile and pulls me into a sort of half hug. Patrick steps towards me and then ushers me further out into the hallway, the door pulled behind him. "Hen, I can't let you see him."

I match his sigh, yet I wasn't expecting a welcome party.

"Any other day I would, but we've got meetings with labels, and Stewart's already in a state. Eddie and I have practically bribed him to attend."

"Mainstream labels?" I ask. Patrick nods, he looks tired, not the usual carefree character he always is, was. "You seem thrilled."

He scoffs. "We're not. But our label is merging with a mainstream counterpart. It's a fucking nightmare. Wait, you don't care—"

"I really do, Patrick."

I squeeze my hand around the necklace charms against my chest.

"Cardinal can't sign to a mainstream label. That's not what you're about, even I know that."

He shrugs and closes his laptop. "There's not many other options."

"Can you not set up your own label?"

I remember Stewart talking about it a few times. Patrick flicks a few curls from his eyes.

"Christ, I'd forgotten how alike you and Stew are, Hen. That's what he said. But it would mean months of work away from the band. And—"

"Pat? What are you doing, pal?"

I'd know that voice anywhere. It rings in my ears, the inflection of his accent; every word he's ever said to me seems to bury itself into the shell of my ears, my brain, my veins.

My skin feels both hot and cold, sweat prickles beneath my arms as I freeze to the spot, rooted like a stubborn weed. Huh, fitting.

Patrick and I stare at each other.

The door swings open. Stewart's eyes, like blue hydrangea petals fix onto my face, my eyes, like the sea rolling over the damp darkened sand. My heart twists in my chest.

"Daisy."

"Hey you," I squeak awkwardly, even raise my hand a little. I always said that to him when answering calls or upon seeing him. Some habits are hard to drop.

I smile at Stewart yet he returns it with a wide-eyed stare. He blinks a few times, frowning, as if trying to vanish me away. He looks both the same yet different. His toes still pushed together in DM shoes, his eyes blue but definitely not as bright, like delphiniums that need water. He let his hair grow longer, his fringe dangling messily over his face.

I want to both flee in a panic, and remain here forever, never wanting his gaze to leave mine.

"Why are you here?" he asks.

"Why are you in a suit?"

The fuck? That's what I say after not seeing him for nearly ten months? I might as well have told him another murder weapon of choice.

Stewart runs a hand through his hair. The white shirt stretches across his frame. The deep brown suit that almost matches his hair is fitted snugly across every part of him. A contrast to his usual choice of oversized shirts, usually open to show a Star Wars t-shirt or just bare skin beneath. The long fringe and beard thickly lining his face and neck still give him that edge of not being too formal and smart. But the suit detracts from his usual scruffy look.

"Meetings. Must make a good first impression and shit." Stewart almost smiles, then looks away from me at Patrick, who is watching our exchange open-mouthed, the laptop gripped by knuckle-white fingers.

"I was telling Daisy we've got that meeting to get to—" Patrick starts, but Stewart holds a hand up towards him to cut him off.

I notice he's wearing even more wooden bracelets looped around his pale wrist, either side of his silver Star Wars ones. Smugly, I realise he's still wearing the one I bought him, and the string of yellow beads that we got in Sorrento to remind us of drinking copious amounts of Limoncello. Mine snapped off during the house move, and

I cried as the yellow beads scattered across the floor of the removal van.

"Why are you here? For— To—" he pauses, seems unsure of himself, scrubs a hand across his beard and frowns. "Did you—are you ok? Is Enid ok?"

My heart skips at the mention of Nan. Fuck, he's adorable. I nod. "She's fine, yeah. I was hoping I, we could maybe talk. But you're busy, I can—" I look backwards towards the front door of the converted house. "I can come back another—"

"We can talk," Stewart says quickly. I turn to face him, watch his throat as he swallows, his eyes trained on his fingers twisting at his rings. "I've got time."

"Pal, we've got that meeting—" Patrick cuts in.

"They'll wait." Stewart shrugs, his eyes meeting mine. My stomach definitely flips. That arrogance shouldn't be as attractive as it is.

Patrick spins on his heels and runs up the stairs into the flat. "The team will be on you like a shot if we're late. I'll go get ready. Good to see you, Daisy. I've missed you. We all have."

Stewart's cheeks show a light dusting of blushing like pink kiss freesia. Stepping aside, he lets me into the flat.

He places a palm on my lower back then retracts it and strides ahead of me up the stairs. His spine taut, unmoving. Like the closed book his friends claim he is.

I shut the flat door with a click.

A memory of Stewart picking me up, my legs and arms wrapped around him as he kicked the door shut, and him instantly unzipping my dress flitters fleetingly through my mind. I rub at my forehead to scrub it from my mind.

He turns as we reach the landing, but doesn't look at me.

"The kitchen's a mess, Pat's taken up baking." He rolls his eyes, yet I don't miss his fond smile. "You ok if we head up?"

"Sure," I reply. He didn't have to explain anything. I think I'd follow him anywhere.

My eyes pull to Stewart's room as I walk past. It looks how I remember from the brief glance, aside from the pile of books now scattered on the floor like fallen dominoes at the foot of his bed, not stacked towards the ceiling. The scent of lavender drifts from the open door.

Stewart is sat in the chair, which is usually Patrick's first choice. Leaning forwards, elbows on his knees, fingers twisting his rings. His hair, still the same colour as Hibiscus rosa-Sinensis in Black Jack. Rich and deep like his coffee before he adds in oat milk.

My heart stutters, like it's constricted by tendrils of gorse bushes. I wait for it to deflate fully, for me to collapse to my death right now. Ironic, as Stewart's the one who makes my heart whole.

"How are you? How's life?" he asks, as I sit down, not looking at me, staring at the polished wooden floor.

My eyes fill, maybe I wasn't ready to speak to him. For this. But fuck it, here I am.

"Quiet." There's never anyone singing, humming melodies or lyrics from new or old songs. No rhythmic tapping of spoons while the kettle boils, no straining my ears to hear car doors slamming followed by the familiar footsteps of Doc Marten shoes, his laughter encasing me like the salt blowing off the water.

"You?"

"I wish things were quiet," he says lighting a cigarette, his eyes glancing over me and away. Several times. My stomach fizzes beneath his gaze, however brief.

"You love the drama," I say with a smile he doesn't return. Stewart shrugs, non-committal, then exhales smoke rings, perfect as always. "All your social media accounts have been deleted. Are you ok? It's so unlike—"

"Couldn't be fucked with it anymore."

"But you love a selfie."

"Wanted a break from it." He shrugs again, then licks his lips. He looks at me, for a fraction longer than last time, I feel his eyes snag over my legs. I resist the temptation to cross and uncross my ankles. Stewart raises his eyes and meets mine. The breath gets stuck in my chest, like the reluctant last thorn on the rose stem.

"Your hair's nice, Sweet—Daisy. Looks good."

"Thanks," I say, and know my eyes are glassy, my nose twitching with tears at the compliment and the almost use of the pet-name he always called me. Far too often really, but I soon got used to it, and missed it when he didn't say it. "So's yours."

"Obviously." Stewart rolls his eyes playfully, a smile on his lips, before he frowns and rearranges his features. He looks from me to the light fitting hanging from the ceiling. "I liked your hair curly. Liked it all the time but—" he scoffs and neither of us mention the pink colouring on his cheeks, akin to tuberosa.

"It's the sea air," I say, though he must know. I'm not the type of woman to curl her hair each and every morning. Especially not when there's flower deliveries to get up at the crack of dawn for. Or the beach to walk across.

Stewart looks at me, hand rubbing over his beard. The noise jolting all my senses delightfully. "Heard you'd moved. Fucking press know everything. You live by the sea, yep?"

"Yeah."

"I'd hoped so. For you, I mean." He exhales those perfect rings of smoke, I watch them dissipate into the air. "You get a place on Cumbrae?"

"Yeah. Tantallon Castle wasn't for sale." I smile referring to the tiny castle I loved behind the wee cottage, causing him to laugh quietly and very briefly.

"So, Cardinal are signing with a major label then?"

He pulls a face, nose scrunching, eyebrows furrowed. Sighs loudly. "Looks like it."

"You don't want that, Stewart."

"Sometimes choices are taken out of our hands. Decisions made for us. We run out of options." He speaks in staccato. No signs of his flowing lyrics. Though maybe that's my presence.

"Do it yourselves. Set up your own label, you and Eddie always wanted to do it."

He smiles, not at me but somewhere over my left shoulder, he shakes his head as he puts out his smoke, only half finished with.

"It's a big time investment. Pat's not keen. It would mean months away from another Cardinal release, no touring and shit."

"Take a break from it. Eddie and Ash can set a date, or actually get married. You guys can take time to write and set up the label, come back under your own rules. If I can do it, you can do it."

"Set up a record label did you?" he asks, humour on his features, before he stomps it out with a lick of his lips and a frown.

"If I did I wouldn't sign boybands." I smile, long to stretch out and touch him, run my fingers through his hair, yet know I shouldn't. I slot my fingers together and squeeze them tightly. Too tightly. "I opened my own florists in February."

"Proud of you." He smiles then scoffs and returns his eyes to the ceiling. "Fuck, like I have a right to be proud."

I catch the tear on my fingers and wipe it away before he notices.

"You should do it, start your own label, Stewart. Shoot for the fucking moon."

A smile tugs his lips upwards, he glances at me briefly. His phone rings, he doesn't answer it but shakes his head at the screen.

"Fuck. I need to go. So what did—"

The doorbell rings followed by Eddie's voice chatting to someone. I hope in a selfish way that it's Ash. But I also know I'd cry on sight of seeing her.

"Come on, you two!" he calls, knocking on Patrick's door as he passes. "They're always late. Shit—"

His eyes widen as he turns the corner from the wide landing and sees me. He looks the same, that shock of bright orange hair and green eyes, all skin and bone limbs drowned in a suit that makes him look young and vulnerable.

"Hi Eddie," I say, smiling at the pen and what looks to be a steel metallic purple straw behind his ears.

"Stew, are you ready, Darling?" A female voice floats behind Eddie.

Stewart closes his eyes and sighs, his shoulders dropping. "Can you give me a minute, guys?"

"How are you, Daisy?" Eddie says, ignoring Stewart, walking over and hugging me, despite my body being pinned to the sofa.

"You have company," the voice says as she rounds the corner. It's Ella Egan. Who else would it be? "I don't think we've met."

"This is Daisy. She's—" Eddie looks from me to Stewart.

Stewart shakes his head a fraction as he looks at Eddie. The awkward silence descends on us, I push my teeth together and watch Stewart's feet tapping a rhythm.

"Oh. You're Daisy," Ella says, her perfectly arched eyebrows raising as she takes in my figure. "You're cute."

"Hi," I say, realising I'm gritting my teeth.

Her long fingers tap gently against Stewart's shoulder, then push his fringe back from his face. Her nail varnish gleaming like pearls. Stewart ignores her touch. But then he also ignores Eddie so it doesn't give much away. Ella smiles, though it doesn't reach her eyes or indeed make her look happy in the slightest. I mean, she's still beautiful. This woman probably radiates beauty when struck down with a sickness bug. She stands up straight, all elegant limbs like a graceful antelope running in front of an ombre sunset.

"I'll meet you in the car," Stewart declares to no one in particular.

Patrick enters the living room, scoops up his phone from the sofa, then turns around. "I hate to rush you, but be quick. Come on, Ed. Good to see you, Hen," he calls in my direction.

Eddie looks from me to Stewart, to Ella and Patrick's retreating suited back, then squeezes my shoulder.

Stewart and I seem to be suspended in time as we hear their feet disperse and the front door close, Patrick's chatter about the fishing game following them into the stairwell.

"She's just a pal," Stewart says, eyes trained on the blank TV screen mounted on the wall.

"So you always claimed."

Ella's dainty hand on his shoulder, fingers in his hair, plays on a loop across my eyelids. Her amused smile at seeing me. Eddie's response.

"Have you slept with her again?" The words fly from my mouth, like an abandoned plastic bag caught in a sudden gust of wind. I blush instantly. Hate how I asked, yet am desperate for an answer. Either way. "Fuck, sorry."

Stewart blinks at me, then leans back and smirks. The non-answer hanging in the air, as obvious as the framed Star Wars print behind his head.

"Maybe I've also reverted back to the hookers," Stewart says flatly with a hint of an eyebrow raise and a slight pout of his lips. He opens his mouth again, to extend on that, but in which way I'm unsure, yet his phone rings taking the words from him. His fingers fly over the screen, the overhead light catching on his silver rings like promises. "I really need to go, Daisy."

Here goes. I'll tell him I love him. "Of course, yes. I just, I had to tell you—"

He raises his head from his feet tapping a rhythm on the floor, looking every inch the puppy he reminded me of countless times. All wide eyes and expectations.

"I—" my eyes jump to a photo pinned to the noticeboard, even from here I can make out Eddie and Ash. Clearly on a double date with Stewart and Ella. All dressed up with wide smiles and crinkled eyes. I will myself to believe it's a publicity stunt, and doesn't mean anything more. There used to a similar photo of the four of us out in Edinburgh in its place. My shoulders slump. I'm still not the bold and open stargazer lily I wish I was; closing up like a common daisy at night, the truth stuck in my throat.

"I should pay you back for the fees for Nan's." I hate myself.

"No, you shouldn't," he replies instantly.

"I should, I–"

"I don't want your money."

"It was yours first."

He pulls at his hair, then keeps his fists clenched. "That's what you came to say?"

"No,"

"So, what was it?"

My mouth opens uselessly. Fucks sake, I have never hated myself more. My spine has surely dissolved. If we were on the ferry I would leap off the side and hope the metal crushed me to a million pieces as I drowned in the seawater. It would be welcomed.

"Silence, yep, what's new there?" Stewart's words are laced with bitterness as he strides towards the stairs. "I have to get going," he calls, an edge to his voice that wasn't there before. I can't blame him for it.

I push myself up and my heart stutters over the photo I was thinking of; Stewart and I with Ash and Eddie, propped up against a ceramic sculpture. The edges curling. My heart leaps into my throat, like a grasshopper on the island reeds. I half consider picking it up and shoving it into my bag.

"Daisy?" Stewart asks, his voice drifting from the stairs.

My heels echo around the stairwell. Stewart has a hand on the door handle as I reach him.

"Thank you, by the way. For the press stuff, for dealing

with it all, for me, after we…" I shuffle on my boots. I desperately try and catch his eye, but he purposefully ignores me. I know he's staring at the flashing lights of the burglar alarm behind my head. Stewart shrugs again.

"You didn't ask for it. It's part of my crazy life, not yours."

"I didn't deserve for you to be so nice."

He shakes his head, dismisses it, then frowns. His eyelid twitches as he looks at me then licks his lips. "We did a radio interview in December, I was horribly hungover and said some shit. Unprofessional. I—"

"Yeah, I heard it. I was worried about you. I would've called but—"

"Couldn't bring yourself to do it?" he asks with a slight sneer, then sighs and shakes his head slowly, raising his hand to rub at the back of his neck.

Stewart opens the door. I step out over the threshold but still can't make myself leave completely. His eyes look more like the waters lapping at Kames Bay than ever.

"I miss you," I say before I realise I've said it. My petals opening a little, more like a heliotrope in the sun, not quite a tall, assured lily.

His lips twitch as he meets my eyes, then distracts himself by opening a roll of fruit pastilles he pulls from his jacket pocket.

"Stew, we're really late," Eddie grimaces as he appears in the hallway.

I turn to look at Stewart, tearing the wrapper yet not eating the sweets. Can't resist the temptation, the need, to touch him. I place a hand on his arm. My eyes lose focus as a glassy sheen of tears covers them like rainwater filling indentations in a mud-covered track.

"Don't sign with them, Stewart," I implore.

He nods a few times, looking at my hand resting against him. He raises his head and looks at me the way he's done millions of times. The breath catches in my throat. I feel I might burst into hysterical tears. Or kiss him.

"Shoot for the fucking moon?" he asks, a slow smile on his lips.

"Shoot for the fucking moon." I nod and walk away, past Eddie, through the front door.

I ignore the huge shiny silver car, engine running, waiting for them, and manage to halt my tears and possibly my breaths until I round the corner, and dive into the nearest cafe and sob into a cup of coffee that matches Stewart's hair colour.

41

My hands slide stems of green, topped with creamy roses and snapdragons into the oasis. Dotted with pitto, ruscus and dianthus. The scent of flowers and herby fragrance of the foliage transports me to an alternate brain space. Of course, it always loops back to flax flowers, brunnera macrophylla, differing shades of blue hydrangeas and the scent of lavender.

The door to my florists opens, and I do a double take on the woman looking around. Endless legs in heels that I couldn't walk in if I was paid, leggings and an oversized hoodie dotted in a leopard print neon pattern. Her dark hair dancing at her shoulders.

"Nice place, Hen." She smiles, her round face looking genuine.

"Ash!" I run round the counter to envelop her in a hug before I can question whether I should or not. "So great to see you!"

I'd missed Ash, all of them actually, in their own ways. The little quirks. Even Patrick barging in on Stewart and me, and the tinny music from his fishing game. The way Eddie always had at least one thing behind his ear and a story to tell that went on far too long and was constantly eating. How Ash never stopped for breath and always had wine to share, found any excuse to go shopping. How they all blended seamlessly into a tight family unit, made up of quick quips and lots of love, respect and alcohol.

"Good to see you, Daisy. Make us a coffee then. I would rather have wine, but you are at work, so caffeine it is."

"What are you doing here? How did you find me?" I call through as I flick on the kettle.

I lean against the doorframe, and she's sat in the window seat, watching the tourists and locals walk by, ice creams in their hands despite the cool crispness of late spring still clinging to the air.

"There's not many florists called Daisy, you know? Stew mentioned you'd moved to Cumbrae, so it was a simple deduction that you'd have a shop in Largs or somewhere nearby. I am, after all, the clever one."

"Did he say much? After I went round?" I ask, yearning for information yet filled with weighted anticipation that seeing me was a trauma for Stewart. Thus he never wants to see me again; making my planned surprise second visit to see him next week pointless.

"Stewart doesn't say anything about anything anymore, to be honest. He's miserable. Has been miserable as fuck since you split," Ash says as I hand her the coffee. She smiles at the Star Wars image on the front.

I can't imagine him being quiet. Certainly not around his bandmates and Ash. All of them have a 'ready for a party' atmosphere following them. They could have the best night at the cinema, or in hotel rooms, or exclusive clubs, student parties, cottages they hired out, anywhere.

Ash taps her nails, painted a bright neon orange similar to Eddie's hair, against the side of the mug and muses a little with a frown.

"He said you'd moved to Cumbrae, assumed you were living the dream. He's pleased for you, happy even. We all are. He mentioned your hair was curly, which totally suits you, by the way. But fuck all else."

"Reverting back to his closed book tendencies..."

I pull a stool across and sit opposite Ash, watching the world behind her through the windows. "Did he tell you what happened? When we split, I mean?"

"I got the gist out of him after most of a bottle of vodka last Christmas."

"He was with you at Christmas?"

Ash laughs, throwing her head back. "His parents wouldn't have him. It was a fucking nightmare. Burnt the turkey, didn't I? Stew dropped the stuffing on my carpet, not the tiled kitchen floor, and the dog ate it. Eddie didn't turn the potatoes on. Patrick passed out by eleven am. We ordered pizza in the end and drank vodka all day. It was the only time Stew mentioned you. I don't think he remembered the next day."

"I know I messed up, Ash. Believe me, I know it."

"I can see both sides. Stewart needed to know how you felt, and you thought it was enough without saying it. I get it. It was obvious to everyone that you loved him. But for all his arrogance and overt confidence, he's insecure. Probably convinced himself he was imagining it all. You've both got issues, sadly both connected to your parents. Neither of you feels enough as you are. Stew just hides it better than you, and as you know, then doesn't sleep."

I blink at her. She's right. Ash has summed it up completely, like a five-line review of a film.

"Have you done a degree in psychology since I last saw

you?" I ask with a small laugh.

"Sometimes things are obvious to everyone but those so involved. It can be hard to get that perspective if you're so close to the issues. Pat shags around because he doesn't want to risk a heartbreak, but he'll tell you he just loves sex and hates commitment. Eddie always has something propped behind his ear, so people talk about that, not his hair, which he was horrendously bullied for at school. I keep doing degrees because I don't know what the fuck I want to do with my life. You and Stew hide your apparent inadequacies behind sarcasm and humour, or bravado and selfies."

Maybe she doesn't need a degree. I'm amazed by her accurate take on us all.

Ash watches the people walk by, then turns to face me again.

"I wanted to thank you, Daisy."

"Me? What for?" I ask with a frown.

"Eddie and I set a date," Ash says, smiling, her eyes crinkling closed.

"Congratulations!" I beam. "When? And where?"

"Dundas Castle, early next year,"

"A castle, Ash? Impressive!"

"Paid an extortionate amount for a Saturday, but Eddie's gotta spend that money on something. You'll do the flowers, right?"

"For real?"

She shrugs with that carefree manner that all of Cardinal seems to have. "Of course. Without you, we wouldn't have been able to set a date. It would still be an unknown, floating around in the diary."

"Sorry, I don't understand."

"Cardinal turned down the record deals. One after another." Ash nods, pride colouring her features. "They're starting their own label."

"That's so good. I'm thrilled for them, and you."

"Eddie and Stewart mulled it over for a while, as you know. But they dismissed it. Then you rock up, somehow shake some sense into Stew, and they decide to go for it."

"I don't think that's on me, Ash." I did tell Stewart to shoot for the moon and not sign with the major labels. But I doubt I was a driving force.

Ash slurps her coffee and raises her perfectly arched brows at me. "Ask me what the label's called."

I pout, trying to mull it over. Some musical reference, maybe linked to their first album or the name they had before they settled on Cardinal, but I can't recall it. I assume Cardinal Records would be too obvious. I shrug.

"Shoot For The Moon Records." Ash smiles.

My mouth drops open. "No fucking way."

"So anyway, what's the deal?" Ash asks after I've served two customers, and we're left alone again.

"With what?"

"Suddenly, a week and a half after you see Stewart, your best pal calls Pat for a hook up on the last night of the tour and manages to wangle an invite to the afterparty."

I had begged and pleaded with Rob to phone Patrick. To pretend to be interested in meeting up at the Cardinal afterparty, to give their failed one-night stand another shot, when actually I wanted the location to put a plan into place. Patrick had instantly forwarded the address, timings and even his room number to Rob within minutes. Always keen for a hook-up is that man. I guess some things don't ever change.

"What's really going on? Pat may be only thinking with his cock, but come on—"

I sigh out and rub at my forehead. "I went to tell Stewart that I love him. But I couldn't do it."

"Why not?"

"For one, I met Ella."

"She'd knock anyone off their stride. The height of that woman, so jealous. Ella's paid to be there, you know, it's a publicity thing."

"Has he slept with Ella again?"

Ash shrugs. "I doubt it. Come on, Hen. You know that man. If he's not paying for it, he doesn't sleep with anyone unless his romantic, fate-believing soul feels connected. And no, he hasn't reverted back to his old ways of contributing towards the sex trade, either."

Seeing Ella did knock me for six, whether she was there as a press stunt or not. I'm an anxious coward. The words wouldn't follow my heart. And once I thought about it, after I stopped crying, I realised Stewart's a showman. Extravagant. Likes a performance. Three little words won't cut it, especially not given how much time has passed.

"I need to go all out, really show him that I mean it, in a way that he'll totally relate to." I need to transform from weed to stargazer lily in deep striking pinks and tall stems.

"You're not going to sing him a song on stage, are you?"

"No, his thing is music. Mine is—"

"Flowers," Ash comments, looking skeptical; the exact expression Rob showed when I video called him about it. "The afterparty, and flowers, that's your grand plan?"

"Yeah…" I swallow. Expect her to tell me it's pointless, that I should just call Stewart and tell him instead of anything extravagant.

"Ok. What can we do to help?"

"We?"

"Me and Eddie, and Pat, of course. We all want to get you two back together. He's miserable without you, and we all miss you. Plus, you and Stew are meant to be."

"Can you make sure Stewart hears me out, please?"

"Hen, you could stand on stage and tell him to fuck off and he'd listen." Ash laughs.

"Can you get the press there too? I know it's the Cardinal afterparty so maybe for just like an hour, if that."

"You want the press at the afterparty? Daisy, you hate the press intrusion more than me."

My heart rate speeds up and skips a few beats as the anxiety settles inside of me.

Her features show a look of unease. "You can't control how this pans out, at the party or in the press, you know that, right?"

I see her eyes dance over my thighs. I nod and hitch up my dress to show her the pale skin and healed scars.

"I promised Stewart on holiday that I wouldn't self-harm again, for him and me. I've kept that promise, Ash. And started therapy for it."

Ash winks at me and reaches out to squeeze my hand. "So proud of you. Wait til Stew finds out; he's gonna be buzzing. Still, you detest the press."

"I do, but it's how Stewart's world works. I risk crashing and burning in front of him, and everyone, but I lost him before by saying nothing, so can this be any worse?"

"I hope those aren't famous last words."

I chuckle and drain my coffee. "Me too, Ash. Me too."

42

Part of me feels I'm signing my life away each time I think of or see the journalists gathering. Flashing their Press ID badges like they're in the FBI. But I'm hoping it will all help in convincing Stewart that I really do love him. The full, public, nowhere to hide declaration of trying to win Stewart back is going to be live streamed.

If I didn't have the flowers to arrange, and keep my hands busy, I'd be so overwhelmed, and drunk, that I'd never have made it to the final floral arrangement. Every now and then I do take a slug of vodka from the bar, yet I don't feel anyone can judge me for it. Rob insists it will help with the nerves.

Rob and I sit, backs against the bar, as I inhale the atmosphere. The mingling sweet scents of the flowers, the blues in varying shades, all mirroring Stewart's eyes depending on his mood or the lights, filtered or natural. Cornflowers, globe thistles, hydrangea by the bucketfuls, Oxford blues and forget me nots, love in the mist and irises, and of course, delphiniums.

"If this doesn't work, what are you going to do?" Rob asks honestly, flicking his red fringe from his eyes.

"Use the photos for my portfolio," I reply with a shrug.

"If I shoot for the moon and miss, I'll still land amongst the stars, Babe."

"I'm sorry, who are you and what have you done with my realist, practical friend? The one who shies away from romance, the limelight and positive outlooks?"

"You can't always follow a plan, I recall you saying." I smile.

Rob throws an arm around my shoulder. "Think it'll work? The flowers, the speech in front of the press, and the man himself?"

"I fucking hope so."

Des, my old friend, and his whiskey based coffee that is definitely more spirits than caffeine today, informs us that Cardinal are on their way from the arena, suited and booted ready for the afterparty. There will be no sign of a suit, and the closest to boots they get is Eddie's favourite Doc Martens, which he refuses to throw out even though the heel has been replaced several times and there's a hole in the left toe. Des raises his brows and throws me what can only be described as a fatherly smile. Encouraging, but not too over-emotional. Just enough to let me know I'm not alone, without being gushing. He had implored with me via Ash to be involved in tonight. He told me upon arrival that, "Stew's a right miserable fucker without you, Daisy. I'm sick of looking at his face, it's bringing on a depression within myself."

My nerves skyrocket instantly, as the enormity of the upcoming events and, indeed, vulnerability I'm about to show, not only to Stewart but to everyone else at the party and beyond, creep closer. Guests start to trickle in, and I see wide-eyed realisation as a few familiar faces see me here. Fuck only knows what Stewart told them had actually happened between us two. Though according to Ash, not much. Members of the team, still in their full-on hipster uniform, give me a double take before attempting to rearrange their features into what they think is neutral and friendly but is mostly startled and confused.

Rob kisses my cheek. “I’m off to meet Patrick.”

“Don’t sleep with him until later,” I warn, only half joking.

“Daisy, I’ve got a boyfriend. I won’t!” He places a hand on his chest. I scoff at him. We both know he’s saying it to largely convince himself.

I’m watching the glittered hibiscus flower floating in the glasses lined up at the bar when a cheer goes up around the room. Red, white and blue metallic paper explodes from the ceiling. Typical of them to make a dramatic entrance. The music increases in volume, and cameras flash in sparks as the lights dim. Suddenly images project onto the silken white strips of fabric gracing the walls. Cities, buses, crowds of people, drum kits, microphones, pianos and guitars flash in succession. A familiar pair of blue, so fucking blue eyes, captured looking up from under his longer dark fringe, covers the fabric. The breath, the blood stills under my skin as pictures and videos of Cardinal manifest themselves on the walls. This is it. I’ve come this far, like Nan would say; go for it. Feet and mouth first.

“To the end of the UK tour!” someone shouts to raucous applause.

Rob and Patrick return shortly afterwards, surely not long enough for a quick sex session, though Rob’s shirt is now untucked, and Patrick's cheeks are definitely flushed.

Patrick places a kiss on my cheek.

"Let's do this, Hen! See if we can get Stew to actually crack a smile again."

He saunters past and not so subtly traces his fingers down Rob's arm, followed by a cheeky wink.

Rob smiles at him, then turns to me, pale blue eyes wide, his cheeks blushing.

I don't have time to even consider running away as Patrick Wallace takes centre stage, standing on top of the highly polished bar. The bottles of alcohol shining behind him, glistening like stones in the sea, the floral arrangements at either end of the bar in hues of blue.

Patrick claps loudly, and instantly everyone hushes. Power of celebrity, I guess.

Dressed in jeans as tight as an extra layer of skin and the colour of ink, a mustard yellow oversized jumper and of all things, a baseball cap which hides most of his curls, and Doc Marten boots with colourful graffiti patterns painted on them; he looks as far away from the image I held of Cardinal eighteen months ago as possible. Except from the swagger of confidence that never quite disappears from the three of them, even after the spotlight has faded.

"Hey guys and gals. I just want to make a quick announcement on behalf of myself, Eddie and Stewart—the legendary indie band known to you all as Cardinal—"

"Pat? What are you doing?" I hear Stewart's voice, worried and hushed, float across the room. He'll know something is going on. I can't see him, but I imagine him twiddling his rings. Probably fiddling with the chain around his neck. His eyelid twitching with nerves.

Patrick continues. "Cardinal are thrilled to announce the launch of our own independent record label—Shoot For The Moon Records. Our subsequent releases will be through this label. While we thank HeadScan records for their support for the past seven years, we will not be signing to them or any other major label. We, as a band, are taking the next year off from touring to write and focus on making Shoot For The Moon Records a success. And of course, one of us is set to get married soon. Cardinal will be holding a press conference and launch party in three weeks' time, after our well-deserved holiday following the completion of this White, Blue And Cardinal Red tour. Please follow our socials to be the first to know further details." He raises his palms, and I notice the journalists scribbling furiously in their lined, wire-bound notebooks.

"No questions tonight, thanks. I know you lovely folks from the mags and rags only have twenty minutes with us here at this private afterparty. Aren't you lucky to be granted even that amount of time? I'd like to introduce you to a wee pal of mine. She's responsible for all our beautiful flowers on display here tonight. Come on, Hen," Patrick ushers me out of the crowds and away from my neat vodka into the view of everyone, including Stewart.

"Ladies and gents, a florist called Daisy!"

My tongue seems to swell in my mouth like a hobnob dunked into a mug of tea, and my throat has definitely closed up. But tonight, as if I'm about to walk through the smoke machine sliding doors of Stars In Their Eyes, I am not going to be silent. Patrick holds out his hand, and I clamber up onto the bar.

I have a flashback of dancing and nearly toppling into bottles of cheap spirits at a gay bar in Liverpool after downing a bottle of vodka with Rob in a taxi.

I smooth down my dress that Stewart bought me for my birthday last year and just go for it. I spent hours writing a speech that shakes in my hands like the last autumn leaf. Exhaling, I ready myself to address everyone in the room and beyond with wit, honesty, and a touch of uncharacteristic romance; a winding tale of how I lost the love of my life. My eyes skim over the words. I have a plan, and I'll stick to it. Why change the habit of a lifetime?

"Hi. I'm Daisy, a florist from, shockingly, A Florist Called Daisy based over in Largs."

I said to myself that I wouldn't look for him, but of course, I do. Those blue eyes, like the sea dancing over the innocent white sands of Kames Bay, pull me in, much like the tides. Stewart's eyes widen as he follows the direction of my voice. His eyes meet mine for a split second, his mouth dropping open, eyebrows dancing to his hairline, skin blanching. He returns his gaze to his hands, those silver rings, and the table where he's sat surrounded by bowls of fruit pastilles and glasses of wine.

"I actually wanted to call my business A New Hope florists. Obviously, named after the best Star Wars film, and no, that's not up for discussion. But you know, trademarking and copyright shit got in the way. *A New Hope* has to be the best Star Wars film, after all; it's where Han and Leia meet. And we all know those two are meant to be together, despite their differences and constant bantering," I say to the crowd, trying not to throw up at all the attention.

Stewart smiles, despite looking despondent and not at me.

I focus on Stewart. His head drops further as I struggle

to speak, despite the words being written and rehearsed. His shoulders slump and he twists his wine glass round to avoid looking in my direction. Even with the Star Wars reference, he's lost faith in me and us as a couple. Still, I haven't. Not yet. The written words blur and jump like aphids as I try to read them.

Des, Rob and Patrick nod at me encouragingly. I see Eddie has an arm around Stewart's shoulders. Ash looks like she might burst, I assume from excitement, yet everyone else just looks awkward, aside from the press, who are lapping this up with glee. Maybe they'd prefer it if it doesn't work; if the world crashes around me. That would definitely go viral.

"I want to thank the press for attending this party and for listening to a slightly manic woman who is hopelessly in love with her ex-boyfriend."

Stewart's face lifts up, his lips parted and framed by his chocolate-coloured beard, the feel of which I've missed every day. No shame. My legs, toes and even my bones are shaking. One of my hands reaches to clasp the two charm necklaces; as blue eyes meet brown, and despite putting myself out there in a room full of strangers, I feel calm, grounded. Safe.

I could follow my heart and address Stewart.

I should.

Fuck it; I will.

"Hey, you. In case you haven't realised, I'm here for you. For us," I say, staring straight at him. He nods his head in silent acknowledgment and holds my gaze. "Don't worry. I'm not here to murder you with a knitting needle."

He smiles fleetingly before his eyes dart around the room. B takes a step closer to the bar.

"I did have a speech and a plan, but I'm taking your lead and speaking from the heart," I add, ripping the paper to shreds. It sprinkles by my feet like snowflakes.

"Stewart Christopher Burns, I met you two and a half years ago. You transformed my life and melted my stone-cold heart. You made me a better person. Showed me I'm enough and that asking for help isn't a weakness. Because of you, I know what it feels like to love and be loved. You're my proof that soulmates exist."

I'm not a stargazer lily or open lotus flower. But right now, I'm like the flower I'm named after; white and yellow petals standing out against the green grass, embracing the warmth of the full sun, and stretching towards it. Proud to be me—if a little scared of the bright light.

Stewart scratches at his beard, his eyes so serious, I'm hit with a force of dread. Shit. He's going to turn me down, isn't he? The press will record the moment my heart breaks, and I'll become a meme. Still, I've come this far. If I'm going to go out with a bang, I may as well be on fire.

"Once, Stewart, you said I was scared. I was. I fought against love, being dependent and reliant on you for anything and everything. When actually, I didn't realise until it was too late that you're the best thing to ever happen to me. I always thought I needed a plan, a tick list to follow. A destination and end goal. I was focused on my goals and my dreams. Yet, unless I've got you to share my dreams with me, my heart will never be truly full and happy. I miss sharing in your hopes and dreams, too, not that I know the first thing about music. I regret not saying I love you sooner than I did. I regret not saying it to you every day. Because I did. I do. I should have told you how I felt every day, multiple times. My biggest regret in life is not doing so. So...” I clap my hands once, shrug and smile at him. What more can I say?

“I’m a florist called Daisy and I am absolutely, totally and utterly in love with Stewart Christopher Burns.”

43

The band's table whoop and cheer, followed by the other party guests, all with their Cardinal red lanyards looped round their necks, and the press clap and shout happily.

Stewart, the man I love, is smiling, one hand propped up under his chin. He shakes his head fondly, and I can see from here that his eyes are twinkling.

Thank fuck, I'm maybe not going to go down in history as the dismissed nutty ex-girlfriend. All heads turn towards him, but he doesn't pay them any attention. His eyes lock onto mine as he stands up and stalks towards me.

Of course he looks as delicious as ever, if not more so. That familiar denim jacket thrown over a white t-shirt and dark jeans paired with his burgundy shoes.

"Get off the bar, you fucking wee menace." Stewart laughs, putting his hands on my waist and lifting me down.

He twirls me round in circles and kisses me. Relief escapes from every inch of my skin as my hands circle his neck, the familiar scent of lavender dances to my senses, pushing up my cheeks into a smile.

I hear everyone clapping and cheering, but in all honesty, I could've made that up. A nuclear bomb could be going off, Beyonce could strut herself in and start shagging Ronan Keating, and I wouldn't have eyes for anyone but Stewart.

Stewart places me down and takes a small step backwards. I can't stop myself from smiling, already my cheeks ache, but I'll never complain about it.

That soft smile, fringe grazing eyelashes, face lined with his heavy beard, eyes so blue. His knuckles trail up and down my arm, leaving goosebumps in their wake, despite being covered by fabric.

Stewart nods his head to the corner of the bar and sends a look to the crowd, encouraging them to disperse and give us some space.

"Nice dress," he says, trailing a finger down the length of it. "Is this a special occasion or something?"

I smile, remember opening it on my birthday last year. He insisted I wear it to the beach. I refused, of course, as if I'd let a dress this pretty and expensive get covered in sand and salt water. I insisted I'd keep it for special occasions, away from beaches.

"That was quite the speech, a florist called Daisy." He scratches at the back of his neck as we both reach the slightly dimmed corner of the room.

"I couldn't let you have all the attention," I reply with a shrug. "We don't want to over-inflate that ego of yours."

Stewart laughs like he did that first night, throwing his head back, the length of his hair dancing with the movement.

Patrick runs up and kisses me on the cheek.

"He laughed, I heard him laugh!" He spins and pats

Stewart on the chest. "There's still something inside that broken, empty soul of yours, pal. Good work, Daisy!"

Stewart pushes him away playfully and shakes his head. "I've been hard work. Miserable as fuck."

"That makes two of us. I'm so sorry. I should've told you how I felt. Feel. I mean it, I love you, Stewart. So fucking much."

Stewart holds my hands in his. He shakes his head and then raises an eyebrow. "Is this what you wanted to say at the flat last month?"

"Yeah, I couldn't do it," I confess, my cheeks blushing.

"You couldn't tell me in my living room, but could tell me in a room full of people? And you say I like the attention."

"I had to make sure you'd believe me. To know I meant it."

Someone approaches and asks Stewart if he'd like a drink. Stewart turns to address them, "I'm a wee bit busy, pal. Can we catch up later?" He scratches at the back of his neck and faces me again. "It's a lot to take in, Daisy," Stewart says seriously, shaking his head.

A sigh escapes me, and my shoulders slump. Of course, it wouldn't have been that easy.

"I mean, after what can only be described as a public declaration of your love, it's hard for me to accept that you may actually be the more romantic one out of the two of us, Sweetheart."

A smile bursts from me, and a happy sigh of relief falls from my lips. I lace my fingers with Stewart's, and they fit as perfectly as the last piece of a jigsaw puzzle, just like I knew they would.

"Got something to show you," Stewart says, his eyelid twitching.

He pushes his bracelets, including the Star Wars one I gave him, farther up his arm. He turns his wrist towards me. Hidden beneath his bracelets that I noticed and loved from that first night is a tattoo of a flower, technically a weed. White petals, yellow centre. My lip wobbles, eyes sheen with tears. Stewart's eyes sparkle like summer sapphire waves lapping against the pale peach sand of Bell Bay. It's ok if I feel like I'm drowning. I know that he's going to save me. We can rescue each other from the seas of the unknown.

My fingers trace the shape of the flower, my name, permanently etched into his skin.

"The accolade for the most romantic one definitely resides with you, Brunnera," I say, slipping back into the pet name I occasionally used. "When did you get that done?"

"Week after getting home from Cumbrae," Stewart replies with a shrug and a very obvious avoidance of my eyes.

"We'd broken up."

"But I loved you. Knew that I'd love you forever, Daisy," Stewart replies, his cheeks blushing a little. "I don't suppose I can spend the next two weeks at yours, can I?" he asks, smiling. "You happen to have caught me when I'm just about to start my holiday."

"Not got a tropical escape abroad booked?"

"If I did, I'd cancel it for you. For us."

"You can stay, but only if you use that time wisely."

"Trust me, Daisy, I have many plans," he replies with a smirk that makes my insides shiver.

"Like buying us a house?" I ask, not quite ready to leave all practicalities behind.

He shrugs and winks. "Of course. What else?"

He traces his fingers up my arms, to cradle against my jaw. I splay my palms flat, feeling his heartbeat. I slide my hands up to loop around his neck. I step closer to him, feet between his.

Stewart leans his head towards mine, and those blue delphinium eyes are the only thing I can see.

"Don't let me go," I smile at him, using a Cardinal song to reflect how I feel.

"Sure you want to quote my own lyrics?" Stewart asks with an adorable tilt of his head. The blues of his eyes sparkling and looking so enticing.

"Positive."

"Even though I'm apparently in a boyband?"

"Yes."

"Not going to throw a line or two of Beyonce at me?"

I shake my head and smile so wide I should be worried I look like a clown, yet I don't care. "No. I love you more than I love Beyonce."

"Fucking hell, Daisy. That is a bold statement."

"So." I shrug. "Don't let me go?"

"Never, Sweetheart."

"If I tell you I love you again, you're going to do the Han Solo response just to spite me, aren't you?"

He pouts, his eyes full of mischief. "I might."

"I love you."

"I know." He smiles before kissing me again. Fuck, I've missed that mouth. "I love you, Daisy Gordon."

"I know." I smile. I place my hands over his beard and implore with him. "I love you, Stewart Christopher Burns from boyband Cardinal."

"You're such a wee menace."

"But I'm your wee menace."

"Yep." Stewart nods, his fringe dancing over his eyes like always.

"Just you, just me," we both say in sync, our voices aligned like our hearts and souls.

ACKNOWLEDGMENTS

I'm a well known introvert and grinch, who doesn't like people very much; but I couldn't have written A Florist Called Daisy without the following people. A huge thank you to you all...

To my Hubs and Beans. You three will always be my favourites and my best. I love you.

To the parents in my life; Mummy, and Mummy & Daddy-in-law. Thank you for always being there and for your constant love.

To family, friends, friends who have become family and writing buddies near and far. Including my critique groups and select few beta readers.

In recent years, I've found platonic soulmates and people who I'd be lost without. Along with my oldest and best friends, you guys keep me going. You know who you are. Culture and cocktails? Are we ready for a red wine? Or do you fancy a shot?

To all at Atmosphere Press, again. You've always got my best interests at heart, and have been a delight to work with. Special shout outs to Nick for his belief in me and my story, and Erin who was so invested in the manuscript, she brought a new life to it.

To the Isle of Cumbrae, people and places – my heart

not only belongs to words, but to you and your surrounding seas.

To the inspiration of Stewart. Sometimes fanfiction spirals. I have no regrets.

Once again, I leave you with the words I live by...I can and I will.

ABOUT ATMOSPHERE PRESS

Atmosphere Press is an independent, full-service publisher for excellent books in all genres and for all audiences. Learn more about what we do at atmospherepress.com.

We encourage you to check out some of Atmosphere's latest releases, which are available at Amazon.com and via order from your local bookstore:

Icarus Never Flew 'Round Here, by Matt Edwards
COMFREY, WYOMING: Maiden Voyage, by Daphne Birkmeyer
The Chimera Wolf, by P.A. Power
Umbilical, by Jane Kay
The Two-Blood Lion, by Nick Westfield
Shogun of the Heavens: The Fall of Immortals, by I.D.G. Curry
Hot Air Rising, by Matthew Taylor
30 Summers, by A.S. Randall
Delilah Recovered, by Amelia Estelle Dellos
A Prophecy in Ash, by Julie Zantopoulos
The Killer Half, by JB Blake
Ocean Lessons, by Karen Lethlean
Unrealized Fantasies, by Marilyn Whitehorse
The Mayari Chronicles: Initium, by Karen McClain
Squeeze Plays, by Jeffrey Marshall
JADA: Just Another Dead Animal, by James Morris
Hart Street and Main: Metamorphosis, by Tabitha Sprunger

ABOUT THE AUTHOR

Finding teaching to be more about paperwork then expanding the minds of young children, and refusing to pay extortionate child care costs, Elsie G Beya started chasing her dreams of being a writer.

Elsie has attended several writing workshops and courses in her home county of Cumbria. She runs a book club in Carlisle, and is a member of two writing critique groups. She also looks good in any and all hats.

Elsie loves writing, reading, shopping, biscuits, tea, gin, and boybands. Like Daisy, she would very much like to love by the sea on the Isle of Cumbrae.

Elsie can be found procrastinating and/or researching on social media.

Facebook @ElsieBeya

Instagram @elsiegbeya

www.elsiegbeya.com

Also By Elsie G Beya

Staged

Lightning Source UK Ltd.
Milton Keynes UK
UKHW012120020223
416402UK00009B/129

9 781639 886951